"All too believable and disturbing....
When you finish [it], the morning
headlines may well seem a lot
different, and probably a lot more scary."
—*NEW YORK TIMES BOOK REVIEW*

"A seamless and authoritative tale....Easterman
...paints a horrific and absorbing picture of
unconstrained religious fanaticism."
—*PUBLISHERS WEEKLY*

Praise for

NAME OF THE BEAST

"Few will rival Easterman's [novel] for sheer power and
believability. Highly recommended for all collections of
suspenseful fiction."
—*Library Journal*

● ● ●

"Easterman packs more excitement into this tale than
most thriller writers produce in five. . . . *Name of the
Beast* will only help to solidify Easterman's place as the
most imaginative thriller writer working today."
—*The Denver Post*

● ● ●

"An ideal page-turner. . . . Mines a rich vein for those
who revel in international paranoia or conspiracy
fantasies."
—*News-Sentinel* (Knoxville, TN)

● ● ●

"There's something for everybody."
—*New York Daily News*

● ● ●

"Easterman writes horror with such skill that it takes a
little while to realize that his antagonists are not of this
earth. . . . Filled with detail and drama."
—*Star-Banner* (Ocala, FL)

● ● ●

"Easterman connects the threads of his complex narrative with riveting suspense."
—*Publishers Weekly*

THE NINTH BUDDHA

"The reader's attention is held from the first page to the last."
—*Booklist*

●　　●　　●

"An inventive impressive thriller . . . captivating language."
—*The Washington Post Book World*

●　　●　　●

"Outstanding."
—*Kirkus Reviews*

By the same author

The Last Assassin
The Seventh Sanctuary
The Ninth Buddha
Brotherhood of the Tomb
Night of the Seventh Darkness

By the same author writing as Jonathan Aycliffe

Naomi's Room
Whispers in the Dark

Daniel Easterman

Name of the Beast

HarperPaperbacks
A Division of HarperCollins*Publishers*

HarperPaperbacks   *A Division of* HarperCollins*Publishers*
10 East 53rd Street, New York, N.Y. 10022

A hardcover edition of this book was published in 1992
by HarperCollins*Publishers*.

Cover photographs by Herman Estevez

First HarperPaperbacks printing: February 1994

Printed in the United States of America

10 9 8 7 6 5 4 3 2 1

For Beth, naturally . . .

ACKNOWLEDGMENTS

I want to thank everyone who helped me work my way through this one, with advice, suggestions, and information. My wife Beth gave me invaluable feedback in the form of comments, hugs, and helpless laughter whenever I got carried away. My editors in London and New York, Patricia Parkin and Karen Solem, brought a turgid first draft to life with the most wonderful clarity and tact. Jeffrey Simmons got me moving in the right direction.

Thanks too to Roderick Richards of Tracking Line, Dave Miller, Customer Services Manager for Intercity Northeast, Geoff Bowder, Paul Starkey, John Dore, and Jamie Robertson-McIsaac, all of whom contributed many of the nuts and bolts that went into the making of the finished product (but none of whom is responsible for what I have done with their information!).

". . . against all the gods of Egypt I will execute judgement"

PROLOGUE

The Egyptian Museum
Cairo
3 January 1999

A strange winter had settled on Egypt that year. Not the worst of winters, but bleak and long. The pyramids were shrouded in mist, a thing unheard of. In the tomb valleys, the chambers of long-dead kings were filled with rain. Feluccas lay still and silent on the Nile, their tillers fast in heavy mud. In black fields, barley was sown in silence beneath pale clouds of frosted breath, planted by women with tiny hands and children woken out of sleep in the chill hour before dawn. There was rain where there had never been rain, frost where no frost had ever been. There were spiders in the houses of innocent victims. There were cobwebs across the doors of suicides. It was as though wonders were at hand. Or torments.

In the mosques, preachers warned of the world's end. From his pulpit in Cairo, Sheikh Kishk prophesied the coming of Dajjal, the one-eyed Antichrist: his footsteps had been heard in a narrow place in the old city. In Alexandria, a butcher had slaughtered a calf with two heads. In Tanta, a Jewish woman with red hair had given birth to a monstrous child. Hailstones the size of pigeons' eggs had fallen in the desert near Wadi Natrun. In an empty doorway in Sayyida Zaynab, children with old hands and old faces played with the empty, eyeless head of a white goat.

. . .

The bandages came away like strips of rotten silk. Her scalpel moved carefully, precisely, almost joyfully, opening a layer at a time, each cut a little death. And the greater death quiet as a July evening, scented and unmoving on the high gridded table. Nip and cut, nip and cut. The strips of ancient bandage were gently pulled away, plotted, and measured. Each had a position against the metal rules that edged the table.

The point of the scalpel struck the first amulet. A'isha removed it slowly, and with a certain reverence. It was a bronze djed pillar, a symbol of power. Near it lay a wedjet eye of blue faience. Then a clump of amulets, without sequence: figures of Maat, Horus, and Re seated, three ordinary scarabs, a heart scarab made of nephrite and set in a gold frame, another djed pillar, two tyet girdles, a papyrus column.

By now she was sure the mummy had been disturbed and rewrapped. There was usually a sense of order to the amulets: the heart scarab on or near the corpse's heart, a wedjet eye over the seal covering the incision in the flank through which the viscera had been removed, djed pillars on the abdomen and chest. But these were jumbled and misplaced, a sure sign that, at some stage, the wrappings had been tampered with. It was not unusual: tomb robbers had been active in Egypt from the days of the Old Kingdom. It was rare to find a burial intact. Archaeologists thought themselves lucky to come upon the leavings of robbers or bodies hastily reinterred. She had thought herself lucky.

"Definitely re-wrapped," she said.

Professor Megdi nodded.

"Not another Tutankhamun, then?"

She smiled. "I doubt it."

He could see the museum from the window of the office if he bothered to look. Behind the museum, he could make out a stretch of river flashing in the sunlight and, further back, the 590-foot pillar of the Cairo Tower rising crazily above Gezirah Island. But he had not come to Cairo to visit museums, sail on rivers, or climb towers to see the view. He was a practical man. A man with no time to waste.

He took off his linen jacket and draped it over the back of a chair. On the floor stood an open wooden case. The man bent down and tore away a sheet of brown waxed paper from the top, then lifted out a heavy object wrapped in thick black plastic sheeting. He laid the object on the table and began to unwrap it.

They had known from the beginning that the tomb had been broken into. The original necropolis seals on the concealed entrance had been tampered with. A priest from the temple of Amun at Karnak had placed fresh seals over them. And those in turn had been broken. A'isha had expected to find little inside: a smashed coffin, some strips of rotten bandage, a leg or arm torn off and abandoned in a robber's haste. All about them the tombs had been hollow, desolate; the valley had smelled like an undertaker's yard. She had been impatient. Impatient and afraid.

As she wielded the scalpel, she remembered the final entry to the tomb, the grating sound as the stone slab moved reluctantly aside. There had been steep steps cut into the rock, and suddenly bright painted walls on either side, burning in the light of her lamp. The flame had wakened a sleeping world. She remembered the first faces, the gods pale and silent on her left. And a long corridor stretching down a slope towards a broken door.

He finished unwrapping the gun. It was the short version of the Walther MPK sub-machine gun, a German-manufactured heavy-duty weapon first introduced as far back as 1963 and still popular. He raised the gun gently, cradling it in his hands, feeling a light coating of oil on his fingers.

On the table in front of him lay four briefcases. Black, impersonal, identical, they had been stacked in a rectangular pile. He lifted the first case from the top and laid it on the table. It seemed very heavy. With long, practiced fingers he spun the case's combination lock. It sprung open to reveal a molded tray with shaped indentations in which samples of mining equipment had been laid, solid metal pieces carried out from England in the hope of opening a new market with the Egyptian State Mining Corporation.

Megdi watched impassively as she used tweezers to pick out fragments of dead insects and slip them into little plastic bags. A small beetle, *Necrobia rufipes,* had worked its way into the bandages. There were several puparia and larvae of other, unidentifiable predators: each was labeled, numbered, and put away for future microscopic analysis.

There was very little resin on the bandages. She could be grateful for that. Earlier researchers had been known to take a chainsaw to mummies whose coverings had solidified to rock-hard casings. Such procedures were not only inelegant, they were potentially risky, and, with so few mummies left to open, to be avoided where possible.

The museum had agreed to this unwrapping only with the greatest reluctance. Ever since the unwrapping of the royal mummies found at Dair al-Bahri and the Valley of the Kings, the trustees of the Egyptian Museum had refused permission to carry out further work on bodies in their possession. The last unwrapping carried out anywhere had been at the Bristol Museum in England in 1981, when the mummy of Horemkenesi, a minor priest of Rameses III, had been stripped to prevent further damage from alkali salts.

A'isha had argued her case along similar lines. They had found eight bodies in the tomb, none of them in good condition. Wrappings had been disturbed in a frenzied search for gold and jewels. One had been pulled apart almost entirely. At some point, damp had crept in and caused further deterioration. The present mummy, for whom they had no name, only a code-number, J3, had shown signs of rot. The bandages had clearly been disturbed, yet the remains inside had been shown by X-ray to be intact. The X-rays, improved by the use of an image-intensifier, had shown the skeleton of a man of about fifty-five, five feet ten in height, without fractures or signs of skeletal disease. An excellent specimen for investigation which would simply rot if left in a storeroom in the museum basement. The trustees had assented.

Although there had been no magazine in the gun, he took no chances. He moved the selector to its "D" setting to uncock the action. Next, holding the body of the gun in one hand, he pressed the locking spring that held the connecting pin. The pin came out gently, allowing the barrel and action to lift free of the grip unit.

She had found the tomb, not by chance, but by a careful sifting of clues, a tortuous pursuit of an uncertain pathway. There was a possibility—not great, but exciting nonetheless—that she had stumbled upon the remains of several pharaohs missing from the caches previously discovered. It had not been unusual for priests in later periods, finding royal tombs opened and their riches pilfered, to transfer the shriveled bodies of their kings and queens to more modest resting-places, safe at last from predators. The discovery alone might make her career.

She made another incision. Behind her, her assistant Butrus aimed his video camera at the table, recording each step in the investigation. In England in 1975, Dr. Rosalie David had unwrapped a mummy in full public gaze, before television cameras. That idea had been considered and rejected by the museum authorities: the government would not approve. Orthodox Muslim opinion had always been opposed to the dissection of corpses, and there were fears that, in the present climate, the public unwrapping and examination of a human being, however ancient, however decayed, might excite unnecessary outrage. The board of trustees could not forget that, in 1981, President Sadat had closed the museum's mummy room out of fear of Muslim displeasure. Not many months afterwards, he was dead, riddled by an assassin's bullets.

On the edge of one strip lay a long hieroglyphic inscription, a passage from the Book of the Dead: "He is established upon the pillars of Shu and joined to the raptures of Ra. He is the divider of the years, his mouth is hidden, his mouth is silent, the words he speaks are secrets, he fulfills eternity, he has everlasting life as the god Hetep."

In a little while, she thought, in just a little while she would look on his face. Alone of ancient peoples, the Egyptians had preserved their bodies for future generations to see. No-one would ever look on the face of Caesar or Constantine, but she had stood once in a quiet room, stone-cold and shivering, alone in the stillness of a dead evening, gazing on the features of Usima're'-setpenre', Rameses the Great. Alexander was dust, Saladin was dust, Napoleon was dust; but in a moment of sorrow she had seen the sleeping face of Tuthmosis the Third, the victor of Megiddo. Face to face, the living and the dead, the brittleness of bone and the liquidity of blood.

Carefully, he pulled the bolt unit out of the rear of the gun body, then dismantled the spring guide rod. Now he dismounted the barrel, holding the body of the gun firmly while he pressed the pawl inwards with one finger. Unscrewing the nut at the end of the barrel, he removed it from the action.

She took the first layer of bandages from the neck and head. He lay like a lover while she undressed him. His limbs received her caresses in silence. The patience of death.

"What do you want to be when you grow up?" her mother had asked her when she was nine. A strange question to put to an Egyptian girl. What could most girls in that world hope for? Marriage and a family. The stumbling caresses of men much older than themselves.

But A'isha's parents had been educated and progressive, eager exponents of Nasser's Pan-Arabism, beneficiaries of Sadat's policy of *iftitah*. She had answered her mother's question without thinking: *"Athariyya"*—"an archaeologist." A female archaeologist, to be linguistically precise.

Every year since she was four, she and her parents had picnicked at the Giza pyramids, on the spring festival of Shamm al-Nasim. She had eaten colored eggs and salted fish, and played alone in the shadow of Khufu's monument. She had looked up every few moments at the towering mass of stone, diminished, frightened by its implacable presence, yet eager to know what lay inside, what darknesses, what lights, what shadows. It was almost as if it stirred memories in her, bleak memories no child could possibly have.

On her ninth birthday, she had been taken for the first time to the Egyptian Museum, through the high, white-pillared portals into halls of wonder. Her mother had led her directly to the first floor, up the north-east staircase to the rooms where the treasures of Tutankhamun were kept. In a long room to the right of the stairs, a glass case held the young king's death mask. It was the most beautiful thing A'isha had ever seen. She had stood staring through the glass, unable to tear her gaze away. That face, that face, those gold-surrounded lips, those eyes of black obsidian. And her own face reflected in their depths.

She had walked for hours through high, enchanted rooms bright with the imprint of the past. Everywhere masks of gold, boxes of ivory, lamps of carved alabaster, vases of lapis-lazuli. And as she walked, her childhood seemed to fall away from her, and the dead weight of the pyramids was lifted from her little heart and turned to gossamer. The gold of centuries and the painted images of ancient gods had awakened in her something that would never sleep again.

She had become a surgeon now, using a scalpel to cut through time itself, to take it to the bone. She was at the last layer now, she was certain. The wrappings were loose, they came away at a touch. He would belong to her soon: it was like a seduction, he was her bride. She wanted to bend and kiss his covered lips, as though to resurrect him with a single breath. With great care she ran the scalpel from the left shoulder to the wrist. She would leave the face for last.

He lifted one of the equipment samples from the briefcase and laid it on the desk beside the disassembled gun. The sample broke cleanly into two exact halves. Inside, the metal had been molded into a shape that matched precisely the trigger group unit of the Walther. He slipped the trigger group into the recess, then replaced the top half of the sample. He did this with each of the metal pieces in turn, then took them across to a worktop on which welding equipment was waiting. Each of the pieces would have to be welded together, then filed until it looked as good as new.

At the other end, the whole procedure would be reversed. The magazines would be shipped separately. It was worth the trouble, he thought. Worth any amount of trouble.

As it passed the wrist, the scalpel blade scraped over metal, the band of a bracelet that had shown up on the X-ray. She caught a glimpse of gold beneath the narrow incision. The position of the bracelet was unusual and had already excited comment. It was not uncommon to find jewelry on mummies, both male and female; but it was rare to find pieces on the body itself, rather than outside, on top of the bandaging.

She laid down the scalpel and began to peel away the linen cloth like a thin rind. Her fingers moved quickly, methodically, as though long accustomed to their task. Deep down, very deep down, her mind began to register that something was wrong, that things were not as they should be. The bandages came away, loosening as she pulled on them. What lay beneath was not withered flesh but cloth, the dark cloth of a heavy sleeve. And the weave and the fabric were wrong, all wrong.

She felt her heart race, felt it slip and slide away from her. Her fingers became blunt and clumsy, heavy things that acted without her will. She watched as they pulled the rotten bandages apart, watched the dark cloth spill from the opening they made. She could feel Megdi's eyes on her, his puzzlement. But she herself had passed beyond puzzlement to something quite different, to fear, to denial, to disbelief.

The gold bracelet came into view, the gold bracelet on the arm of her dead prince, yellow against white bone. She lifted the arm gently and turned it a little to one side. The room began to spin, she could hear her heart pounding a long way away.

"A'isha," a voice was calling, "A'isha, are you all right?"

She smiled and frowned and shook her head. With one hand, she held herself steady against the table's edge. In the other, the dead wrist lay like sin, bleached and unexpungeable. She heard Butrus's sharp intake of breath as he saw what she had seen, the crash as he dropped the camera.

And in her hand, circling a wrist of bone, its fingers set at half past five, a Rolex watch caught the hot white light from the ceiling and threw it back again.

A strange winter had settled on Egypt that year.

PART I

"The second woe is past; and, behold, the third woe cometh quickly"

REVELATION 11:14

PART 1

1

London
3 September 1999

The call came through at 5.23 in the afternoon. It lasted exactly seven seconds and was not traced. There had been twenty-six calls that day already, all of them hoaxes, but this one cleared the decks. For one thing, the caller had used an up-to-date INLA code word, "Carryduff." For another, he had known the difference between British Transport Police and their Home Office counterparts, and he had possessed the number for the BTP control room. Anyway, there had already been two explosions at mainline stations that week. Nobody was in a mood to take chances.

The earlier bombs had gone off at Euston on Monday, killing three "bystanders" and badly injuring forty-two others; and at Paddington on Tuesday, maiming a police-woman who had been helping clear the main concourse. Wednesday and Thursday had seen scares throughout the capital and in several provincial stations from Newcastle to Portsmouth. British Rail were doing their best to keep the country moving. The ever-worsening state of the motor-ways coupled with heavy fog made it imperative that the rail network stay open. The hoax merchants were having a field day, but nobody else could see anything to laugh at.

There had been an oddity about the phone calls. The

warnings of bombs at Euston and Paddington had employed authentic code words known to Scotland Yard's anti-terrorist squad. But the code words in question had belonged to radically different organizations: the first to the PFLP, the People's Front for the Liberation of Palestine, the second to ASALA, an Armenian guerrilla group formed in Beirut in 1975. Neither had any obvious motives for planting bombs in public places in London. The INLA did.

By 5.28, the Station Master at King's Cross had been alerted to the possibility of a bomb or bombs in his station. Police officers were already on duty in and around the station, both Transport Police and six men on loan from the Met. Both they and the station staff had had plenty of practice that week in clearing the platforms, shops, and buffets of travelers, but it still took over four minutes to get the last civilian out of the station and onto the street.

It was the rush-hour on a Friday afternoon, and nobody was happy. There had already been enormous queues for the 1800 to Edinburgh, a train that carried the bulk of the commuters heading back to the North East and Scotland after a week's hard labor in the big city. They had wives and children waiting for them at home. Around the back, short-distance commuters to Cambridge and Ely had been even more disgruntled to be delayed for the third day running. It was the worst possible day, the worst possible time.

As the last passengers trudged wearily out into a gray drizzle, the first sirens could be heard racing along Euston Road past St Pancras. Traffic was backing up all along the Pentonville, Caledonian, and Grays Inn Roads. Lights flashing in the faces of lonely people standing in the rain, the emergency units began to arrive in a mixture of police cars and unmarked Sierras.

The first to arrive were members of the Anti-Terrorist and Bomb Squads, followed about fifteen minutes later by Special Branch and Home Office Explosives Experts. The military were still on their way. Grim-faced men in plain clothes stepped out into the drizzle. Senior police officers joined them in quick, huddled consultations.

The worst part was about to begin: the painstakingly slow, inch by inch scouring of the huge station while somewhere a clock ticked nearer and nearer the time of the next explosion. If there was a bomb at all.

King's Cross is no place to sit out a bomb scare. The few cafés and sandwich bars in its vicinity are down-market dives, some the haunts of pushers, pimps, and prostitutes. There are no shops to speak of, and none at all open at this time on a Friday night. None of the innumerable guest houses and cheap hotels that fill the side streets at the top end of Euston Road have facilities for so much as a cup of tea and a plate of biscuits.

But there was no way out, unless you wanted to walk out. The underground entrances had been closed within minutes of the warning. Buses and taxis were caught in an ever-lengthening jam in every direction. And what, after all, was the point of leaving? Almost everybody gathered in the streets outside the station was there for one thing: to get home for the weekend, a weekend that was growing shorter every minute.

Inside the station precincts, the bomb disposal team was waiting for the order to go. There were four ATOs—ammunition technical officers—complete with EOD protective suits, and sets of Allen probes, extension rods, mirrors, magnets, and lock viewers. They were neither patient nor impatient. If there was a bomb, they would deal with it. If it could be dealt with. For the moment, it didn't matter whose bomb it was or why it had been planted. All that mattered was whether it was there at all and, if so, how big and how ugly it was. Or how big they were. Plurality was the other possibility.

In accordance with a routine set down during the railway station bomb scares of early 1991, King's Cross had already been cleared of any obvious depositories for explosive devices: wastepaper bins, letter boxes, charity collection tubs. The left-luggage office had been closed for days. Trawling the concourse and platform was a matter of routine. The shops and cafeterias would present more difficulties. But they had to be sure. Above the huge display board announcing now-abandoned arrivals and departures, the hands of the clock moved forward remorselessly. The searchers moved in silence, to the sound of their own heartbeats.

Just who was responsible for the oversight would be the subject of half a dozen inconclusive inquiries. In the end, the buck would be passed so far down the line it would vanish from sight forever.

Along the edges of the pavements all around King's Cross, the local council had thoughtfully placed a wastepaper bin on every lamppost, in the interests of hygiene, civic pride, and as a minor but handy source of revenue from the advertisements they carried. There were twenty-seven wastepaper bins, each three feet deep and emptied every day.

Tonight, the bins were circled by crowds of miserable commuters. Men and women leaned against them, slipped their suitcases underneath them, rested their briefcases on top, knocked ash into them from the ends of their cigarettes without thinking. And the rain fell on them and on their contents gently, like a sort of sleep.

They exploded, not in unison, but at intervals of ten seconds, just time enough for panic to set in, not long enough for anyone to start running, if anyone had known where to run to. If there had been anywhere worth running to.

They heard the explosions in the station, one after another, crumping through the evening air until it seemed they would never, ever stop, like a nightmare detonating again and again without ever bringing the relief of waking. And then, at last, silence fell, a thick, creamy silence that smothered the streets. Moments later, they became aware of the screaming. The screaming that would never stop in any of their heads so long as they lived.

2

Tom Holly was late. He was one of those unfortunates who contrive never to be on time for anything, to whom Fate has allotted the role of last in line. At school, he had spent many sunny hours in the misery of detention, writing lines of apology for his late arrival at Assembly or PE. As an adult, he had been late for his own wedding, both his daughters' births, and his mother's funeral. In cinemas, theaters, and churches, he was certain to make a nuisance of himself fumbling for a seat in the dark while others tried to watch or stood to sing.

Today it did not matter. Today everybody was late, the whole city was running behind. The bombings at King's Cross had thrown the capital into pain and disarray. Every mainline railway station had been cleared and the nearby streets evacuated. The tube stations were being shut down rapidly, by strict rotation. Police cordons were cutting off major thoroughfares everywhere. There was not a taxi to be had anywhere, and anyone who had thought himself lucky to get one was feeling envious of the rainsoaked pedestrians outside as traffic backed up in street after street or jammed entirely at crucial intersections.

Tom had heard about the bombings just before leaving Vauxhall House. For a dreadful moment, he had thought they might all be kept back, in case the combings might turn out to be the work of a Middle Eastern group. But word was already being passed round that this had been an Irish job. Relief was everywhere in the department, tempered by mounting outrage and pity as the dimensions of the massacre became better known. Pausing only to ring Linda with a warning to stay at home, Holly had locked his office—he was the Head of Egypt Desk within British Secret Intelligence—and made his way out into the steady drizzle. It had then been 6.45 P.M.

Vauxhall House was situated just south of Lambeth, not far from the now-dilapidated Century House that had served as the headquarters for the SIS until only a few years earlier. The new building stared out across the Thames onto the Tate Gallery and the roofs of Westminster. Holly had crossed the river on Vauxhall Bridge and weaved his way east of Buckingham Palace, across the Mall to St James's. Once, faint in the distance, he had heard the sound of sirens. Security near the palace had been noticeably stepped up.

The Royal Overseas League in Park Place had served as Tom's club for well over a decade now. It suited him well enough: neither too smart nor too stuffy, it was inexpensive, an important factor for a man on an SIS salary with no independent income, but respectable enough for his occasional informal meetings with friends and contacts. It lay almost exactly equidistant between the Foreign Office and the Egyptian and US Embassies. Men and women were admitted without distinction. It was not a place where people would be readily recognized, but if they were, their presence would excite no comment.

Tonight's meeting was to be a little different from the usual. Tom would not want to be seen by the wrong people, would not want questions asked. A more clandestine venue might have been advisable, but he had decided against it. If he was being followed—and during the past two weeks his suspicions of the possibility had grown almost to certainty— an obviously secret rendezvous with Michael Hunt and Ronnie Perrone would be bound to invite closer scrutiny. Getting together in the ROL, they would just be three old friends sharing an evening of drinks and reminiscences. It wasn't much of an alibi, but he wasn't in much of a position to throw it away.

Michael was waiting for him in the foyer wearing an old, creased raincoat that must have been brought out of mothballs for this London trip, shoes that were much too light for the weather, hair that showed signs of gray where Tom remembered only deep black. Michael stood and smiled awkwardly as Tom came through the door.

"Michael, I'm so sorry. I should have telephoned. I had to walk. The whole city's snarled up." He glanced at his watch. It was nearly 8.00. "God, I'd no idea it was this late. Thanks for staying put."

"Nowhere else to go," replied Michael.

"Well, you could have tried the Ritz. It's just round the corner."

"Not my sort of place. As you well know."

They shook hands a little nervously. It had been three years. Almost four. Tom's smile faded as he let go of his friend's hand.

"I'm sorry, Michael. About your father."

Michael nodded. He had arrived from Cairo that afternoon. Tomorrow morning he had to be in Oxford, to attend his father's funeral.

"It's at eleven tomorrow morning. You going to be there?"

Holly nodded.

"I'd like to, yes. If Paul doesn't object to my being there."

Paul was Michael's brother, a Catholic priest who rather disapproved of Tom and his sometimes voluble atheism. He would be performing the burial.

"He won't mind. You're an old friend. Father liked you. Which is more than can be said for a lot of people. There won't be a crowd at the graveyard tomorrow."

"No. No, I suppose there won't. Look, Michael"— Tom had started removing his own dripping raincoat— "why don't we go in? We can have a few drinks first, then see about a bite to eat. Or are you very hungry?"

Michael smiled and shook his head.

"Excuse me a moment, Michael."

Tom turned and handed his raincoat across the wooden counter on his left, took a ticket, and spoke to the porter.

"Has a gentleman called Perrone been asking for me?"

The porter shook his head.

"Afraid not, Mr. Holly. Nobody but the gentleman you've just been talking to."

"I see. He must have been held up as well. When he arrives, show him up, will you? He knows the way. We'll be in the bar."

"Very good, sir."

Holly turned to go, then doubled back.

"What's the latest from King's Cross, John? Anything?"

The porter's face grew grim.

"Eighty-three bodies last I heard, sir. It'll be well over a hundred, by the time it's done. Like the blitz, that's what it's like. Only that was war. This is cold blood. Wicked it is. Worse than wicked. They should send all the Irish back home."

"Yes, it is worse than wicked, John. Very much worse."

Holly took a deep breath and turned back to his friend. How little wickedness the public really knew of.

"Ronnie Perrone's coming?"

"Yes. I'm sorry, I should have said."

"Not to commiscrate, I suppose."

Holly shook his head. His bushy reddish hair was thinning.

"No. We can do all that tomorrow. This evening's more . . ."

"A case of taking advantage of my being in town."

"Yes. If you like. Look, let's go on up, Michael. We can't talk here."

The cocktail bar was up a short flight of steps, on their left. It was almost empty. This was not a night for coming into town or hanging about after work. The twinkling of lights on red, green, and yellow bottles lent the room an air of forced jollity. In a corner by the windows overlooking the garden and the path beyond, a middle-aged woman in tweeds sat nursing a brandy. Darkness filled the little garden like a rich, unwoven cloth. The barman rose slowly from his stool and smiled uncertainly at Holly.

"Nice to see you, Mr. Holly. It helps to have a friendly face drop by."

"A bit quiet tonight."

"Yes, sir. Not a good night, sir."

"No." Holly paused. "Let's see, I'll have a Glenfiddich and a drop of ginger."

"American, is it, sir?"

"No, just the regular."

"Of course, sir."

Tom turned slightly.

"Michael, what about you?"

"What? Oh, make mine a Campari and soda. No ice."

"Twist of lemon, sir?"

"Yes, why not?"

Drinks in hand, they retired to a table as far away from the woman as seemed polite. Tom noticed that his friend's hand shook a little as he laid his glass on the table. The effects of grief . . . or something else?

He remembered Michael at MECAS, the British-run Middle East Center for Arabic Studies. That had been in the old days, when the school was situated at the village of

Shemlan in Lebanon, in the Shouf mountains overlooking
southern Beirut. The days cramming Arabic grammar, the
jussive of *yaiya* and the imperative of *itta'ada,* the nights
with girls from the city in Mukhtar's cramped café perched
on the edge of a high cliff, the crumpled memories of kisses
mixed with the scent of bougainvillaea. *Songs of Love and
Hate* on the turntable at midnight, Michael restless for love
or deliverance. The confidences, the revelations, the discreet distances they had formed, the little, half-constructed
shells each man had built for himself, the beginning of a life
that was not a life. And in the hillsides all around them a
darkness gathering, heavy, stained, tense, a marketplace for
bloodshed.

"Drink up, Michael. You won't be getting any of that
stuff in Cairo by next year."

Michael sipped his bitter drink and raised an eyebrow.

"You'd know better than I, Tom. I don't have your inside information any longer."

"Come on, Michael. You live there, you know what's
going on. Nobody needs inside information."

Michael shook his head slowly. He was a tall man,
loose-limbed, almost carefully put together. His features
were Egyptian, his mother's gift to him. A Coptic Christian
from Asyut, she had married his father in 1952, two days
after a mob burned down Shepheard's Hotel in Cairo. Mar-
rying had seemed a foolish thing to do. Foreigners were
packing their bags and leaving Egypt: Greeks, Armenians,
Levantines, British. Nasser's revolution had taken place six
months later. It had been a marriage of inconvenience.

The newly-weds had stayed on. Michael's father had
had no choice. A signals officer with D Squadron of the Life
Guards, he would be one of the last British soldiers to leave
Egyptian soil. Michael had been born in Cairo's Coptic Hospital in 1953, his brother Paul the following year. Less than
two years after that, in March 1956, D Squadron had
boarded ship at Port Said along with the 2nd Battalion of

the Grenadier Guards, and watched Egypt slip away from them forever.

Michael grew up in Oxford, an English boy with Egyptian eyes and Egyptian skin. At boarding school, a few boys nicknamed him "the Gippo" until he gave them reason to think better of it. Most years, from the age of five, his mother took him to Cairo to stay with relatives. He learned to speak Egyptian Arabic like the native he was in part. He attended classes at the École des Frères and made numerous friends. But his father never accompanied him, never returned to a country he felt had betrayed and rejected him. Major—later Colonel—Ronald Hunt had loved an Egyptian woman but hated Egypt.

No, that was not quite true. He had loved the pyramids at dawn and felucas on the Nile, the scent of spices in a dark bazaar and camel jumping at the Gezira Club. But, his wife apart, he had cordially despised the Egyptian people. It had been the thing to do, his class and his ruined Empire had demanded it of him, a perverted test of loyalty. He called them all "niggers": Egyptians, Greeks, Turks, Armenians, Jews, they were all mashed together out of one substance in his eyes. Quite how an Egyptian woman had come to inspire passion in such a man was a matter for conjecture. But Michael's mother had been very beautiful. And her family very rich.

"I only know what I see and hear. I know nothing of what goes on behind the scenes. If you've brought me here in the hope of getting privileged information, you're wasting your time."

"Why are you so touchy, Michael? I only said something everybody knows. It's just a matter of months, a year at the most, before the fundamentalists take over in Egypt."

"I wouldn't say it was that certain."

"Yes, Michael, it is. Things are speeding up. Ahmad Badri held talks last week with Yusuf Othman."

Michael glanced at his friend with interest.

"Othman? The head of the Muslim Brotherhood?"

Holly nodded.

"There's been nothing in the papers," said Michael. "Not even *al-Itissam*."

Tom shook his head. He poured a little ginger onto his whiskey.

"This isn't exactly public knowledge, Michael. I should have thought you'd realize that. When two old enemies in the fundamentalist camp bury the hatchet, we can bet it's the start of a wider coming together. There are rumors of a coalition strong enough to overthrow the government by the end of the year."

"Why are you telling me all this, Tom? It must be classified."

Holly shrugged.

"Something's going on, isn't it?" demanded Michael. "And you want to get me involved. That's it, isn't it?"

Michael put down his glass. Slowly, he rose to his feet.

"Whatever it is, Tom, you can count me out. I'm serious. I left MI6 five years ago. That's one move in my life I've never regretted. Never. If you need help, if you want information, you'll just have to find somebody else."

Tom Holly put a finger to his lips.

"Put a sock in it, Michael. That's Ronnie Perrone coming through the door. He'll want to know about your father."

3

Perrone asked for an Aqua Libra "with a touch of ice, dear." Coming back to the table, he patted his stomach gently.

"Got to watch the flab," he complained. "A bad time of life. The tummy can take over if you let it. Develops a life of its own."

No disinterested observer would have guessed. Ronnie Perrone was thirty-seven, but he possessed the face of a twenty-four-year-old and the superbly conditioned physique of an athlete in his prime. He seldom worked out; there was no need, his metabolism did it for him, that and an occasional stint on the wagon. The stints never lasted more than a few weeks, and it never seemed to matter one way or the other. Drink was his only vice, he used to say. Well, he would concede in the right circles, drink and boys. But never the two together, that was altogether too risky.

"I thought you'd be tanking up, Ronnie. I've just been explaining to Michael here about the way things seem to be going back home."

Perrone had become British Chief of Station in Cairo after Michael's resignation. He sat now with a glum expression on his smooth face. He glanced up once at the woman in the corner, then away again.

"My dear, I don't like to think of it." He shivered. "Like exile to Jedda or Tehran, but with memories of better days staring you in the face on every street corner. I shall have to be careful with the boys as well. They aren't too fond of that sort of thing—not the boys, the chaps with the beards."

"I was just going, Ronnie," Michael apologized, standing.

"But my dear Michael . . ."

"Michael's father died." Holly's voice was flat, uninflected, as though a man's father might die every day without it mattering.

Ronnie looked up blankly. "Good God, I'm so very sorry, Michael. Me prattling on here like a great old elephant. I'd no idea, no idea at all."

"No, of course not. No way you could have, Ronnie. He died the day before yesterday. Heart attack, very sudden. We didn't even know he was ill. Well, Mother knew, of course, but she didn't want to worry us. You know how it is."

"You must be dreadfully shocked."

"Yes, we are. Mother's taking it badly, even though she knew. So Paul tells me."

"You're going down?"

"Yes, the funeral's tomorrow. I'm going to Oxford tonight. I've got a hire car."

"Well, stay and chat for a while. No need to run. I haven't seen you for months anyway. And old Tom here can't have set eyes on you for years, I imagine. Have you, Tom?"

"No, Ronnie. Not for years."

"Well, then, that's settled. I'll give up my lonely drive on the wagon and down a few glasses in loving memory. The old buzzard would like that."

"You met him once or twice, didn't you, Ronnie?"

"Met him? Of course I did. You can't have forgotten that ghastly little dinner party you gave. You and Carol, when you were living in that squalid little flat in al-Azbakiyya. You were still with the old firm then, of course."

Ronnie had been Michael's junior then. They saw one another infrequently, in the way ex-pats in the same city tend to do, attending some of the same parties and receptions, rubbing shoulders at seminars at the American University, where Michael taught politics. And Ronnie Perrone was likeable in his ghastly way, even if he did bring back memories of times and people best forgotten.

"Actually, I thought your father was a decent old stick," Ronnie went on, beckoning to the barman. "I don't think he approved of me, though."

"No, I suppose not. Father was army all the way through. He had a deep suspicion of intelligence people. He never forgave me for making my move sideways."

Michael had spent two years as a captain attached to the Military Intelligence HQ at Ashford before someone had suggested that, with his appearance and his fluency in Egyptian Arabic, he might be of more use working for the SIS. His father had always regarded Michael's defection as akin to desertion. The Intelligence Corps had been a bad enough choice in the first place—"pansies resting on their laurels" he had called them, in allusion to their rose and laurel-wreath insignia—but to get mixed up with civilian practitioners of the same black arts was beyond his comprehension.

"I think he had other reasons for disapproving of me," said Ronnie. He turned as the barman approached him. "I've changed my mind," he said. "Take this rabbit's piss away and bring me a strong G and T."

"With ice, sir?"

"Put anything you like in it, just as long as the gin drowns the tonic and not vice versa."

The barman smiled, picked up the Aqua Libra as though it were something vaguely obscene, and slipped away.

"Actually, I don't think Father had the foggiest idea you were gay, Ronnie."

"You disappoint me. I'm flamboyant."

"You know that's not generally true, Ronnie. But you'd have to have been the world's most roaring queen to have got Father's attention. He was an innocent man. More than was good for him. His view of the world was terribly black and white. There simply wasn't room in it for moral ambiguities."

"Are you calling me a moral ambiguity?"

"To Father you would have been, yes. To tell you the truth, up until a few years ago, I don't think he really believed there was such a thing as a homosexual. He thought gays were just a lurid fantasy dreamed up to warn young subalterns off what he used to call 'nancy behavior.' It all came as a great shock to him when you people started coming out of your closets."

"Poor man. It must have been terribly hard on him," Ronnie said, with only a trace of irony.

Michael looked soberly at his old friend.

"In a way, yes, I think it was. Sometimes we forget what his generation had to endure. They were born with such illusions about the world. To have all that taken away . . ."

The barman deposited a large gin and tonic on the table. Ronnie sipped, nodded, and relaxed. He raised the glass. The woman in the corner glanced across at them. She was reading a book, a thin novel by Anita Brookner. She did not seem riveted.

"To your father, Michael," murmured Ronnie. "May he find an eternity of innocence. In a heterosexual paradise."

"Without Egyptians or Jews or uppity women," added Michael, raising his glass.

Tom looked at him.

"Aren't you being a bit hard?"

"I'm sorry, Tom. It hasn't sunk in yet. None of it has. And I'm sorry if I was a bit abrupt earlier."

"No need to apologize. And if you want to know the

truth, you were partly right. I didn't arrange to meet you here just for the sake of commiserating with you. I'm sorry your father's dead, but it's . . . I saw an opportunity. That's why I called Ronnie in. He came here on a flight just after yours.''

"Yes. I'd rather imagined he must have done something like that. Too much of a coincidence for him just to have happened to be in town." Michael leaned back in his chair. "Suppose you just tell me what possible use you can have for someone like me. I don't have access to any information you can't get in a hundred easier ways, and in considerably greater depth. I don't have the ear of anyone very important. You've got Ronnie, you've got your agents, your sources, a whole lorryload of compromised civil servants. You don't need me."

Tom looked at Ronnie Perrone.

"Why don't you tell him, Ronnie?"

Ronnie put his G and T on the little table. He fished out the lemon and put it between his lips, sucked on it hard, and laid the rind on the coaster. It was an old habit that still set Michael's teeth on edge.

"We have no agents, Michael. There is no network."

" 'No network'? What the hell do you mean? I set it up for you. For God's sake, it was the best network in the Middle East."

"About two weeks ago," Perrone went on, as though Michael had not spoken, "someone began putting the network out of action."

"Out of action?"

"Dead or in prison, Michael. It didn't happen overnight, but by the end of last week I was left with a radio operator and a mole in State Security. For all I know, they may be gone by the time I get back."

"How did this happen?" Michael looked at each of his companions in turn.

"Would we be talking to you about it if we knew?" Tom leaned forward. "Michael, security was good. The best. We used the system you developed when you were CS, almost without changes. Even if there had been a leak, a couple of leaks, it could never have led to more than two agents. Ronnie kept no lists. The network was either in his head or in the main computer at Vauxhall. Do you understand what I'm telling you?"

"You mean either Ronnie sold his own network down the river, or someone in Vauxhall shopped them for him?"

"That's about the size of it, yes."

"What about the CIA? MOSSAD? Haven't you asked them for help?"

Tom raised his eyebrows.

"You want me to pop across to Grosvenor Square, shake hands with Bob Grossman, and say, 'Hey, Bob, somebody in Vauxhall has just blown our entire Egyptian operation. How about helping us out?' I can just see his reaction. They don't trust us as it is. MOSSAD have more or less stopped talking to us. You've been out of circulation too long, Michael. Give me a break."

"And you have no idea who it could be in Vauxhall?"

Tom shook his head. He had already given the matter deep thought.

"No," he said. "At least . . . Well, it has to be someone quite high up. A Desk Head at least, possibly higher. Only someone like that would have had access to the files in the first place."

"You're sure?"

"No, of course not. But security has been good for years now. Percy Haviland ordered a complete overhaul after he became DG."

"What about one of the other intelligence units? Defense, for example."

"You must be joking, Michael. What earthly motive could they have?"

"What motive could anyone have?"

Tom shook his head.

"Ronnie?"

Perrone shrugged and shook his head as well.

"Has it happened anywhere else?" Michael asked.

"Not as far as we know," answered Holly.

"You've asked around?"

"Discreetly, Michael. Very discreetly. For God's sake, this isn't information I want to get out."

"You mean you haven't told anyone yet?"

Tom shook his head and looked sullen.

"For heaven's sake, Tom, you'll have to tell someone."

"Ronnie's been faking reports. Well, not faking exactly: more updating old stuff."

"He can't keep that up indefinitely. Can you, Ronnie?"

Ronnie frowned and shook his head once.

Michael looked from one to the other.

"I don't see how I can help you. I've no contacts in Vauxhall, there's nobody I can speak to. Why don't you just go straight to Percy, ask him to set up an inquiry?"

"I will in the end, Michael. If it comes to it. But I need hard evidence. Ronnie thinks he may know what it's all about. He needs someone to back him up. Someone who knows what he's doing. A professional."

"I'm an ex-professional."

"You're better than most of the people we still have in the field, Michael. We don't have time to train someone else."

"I'm out, Tom. I had reasons for getting out. You know that better than anyone. I shouldn't have to explain my reasons to you."

"Yes, Michael, I know your reasons. I respect them. I never stood in your way before, you know that. But I need you now. Something big is going on, I'm sure of it."

"Big?"

"Ronnie, I think you'd better explain."

Perrone took a large swig from his glass. An elderly man came into the bar and ordered beer. From outside, across the stillness of St James's Park, the sound of sirens flecked the night with urgency. Ronnie shuffled in his seat.

"I had a source in Alexandria," he began. "A source called Barnabas. Barnabas was middle-rank *mukhabarat*, not an intelligence officer, just a senior filing clerk. But he knew how to come up with good material. Bits and pieces, but all of it the highest quality. Tip top.

"About a month ago, Barnabas slipped me something more than usually interesting. A *mukhabarat* officer with special responsibilities for the surveillance of fundamentalist groups had uncovered evidence of a link between a Jama'at cell and a German terrorist organization. The curious thing was that a meeting had taken place between representatives of the two groups. Not in Germany. Here in London."

Holly broke in.

"Ronnie faxed me a copy of the report right away. I checked through all the relevant back files for the date in question, cross-checked with Germany desk, and came up with nothing. I found that hard to believe. If the Egyptians knew about the meeting, the Germans and ourselves must have had wind of it. I made discreet enquiries from the Bundesamt für Verfassungsschutz. They knew all about the meeting, of course. As far as they knew, we had a record of it as well. That was when I first started getting suspicious."

Ronnie looked anxiously at Michael.

"Tom and I talked about it and decided to say nothing for a while. It could have been a simple mistake. But if not, we didn't want to go alerting the wrong person. I put my people onto the connection and waited to see if anything came up."

"And did it?"

Perrone nodded.

"Not a lot, but enough. There was more in Alexandria. There'd been meetings there as well, and a few in Cairo. Some with Germans, some with French, some with Irish. And different fundamentalist groupings each time. There seemed to be no obvious link. Then a name came up. Abu 'Abd Allah al-Qurtubi. Ever heard of him?"

Michael shook his head.

"No. Should I have?"

"Not necessarily. I don't know exactly who he is myself. He appears to be the leading light in a group of religious radicals, but I can't even get a name for them. There's something . . ."

He hesitated, frowning. In the corner, the woman was reading her novel. The old man sipped his beer. There was a sound of people climbing the staircase to the Wrench Room. Some sort of function.

"There's something not right about al-Qurtubi," said Ronnie. "My prime source in the *mukhabarat* clammed up when I mentioned his name. Said he'd never heard of him. But he was lying. I started asking around. That's when the killings started."

Holly broke in again.

"He has connections in this country, Michael. I think he has a friend in Vauxhall. Maybe friends in other places. Don't ask me why or how. But I need to find out. I need you, Michael. I need you in Egypt."

Michael finished his drink. His hand was shaking slightly. There were too many memories. He didn't want this. He had never regretted his decision to leave the service.

"I'm sorry, Tom. Ronnie. I'm sorry, but I just can't afford to get involved again. You know why I left. I can't go through that again."

"I'm not asking you to. I'm only . . ."

"It isn't on, Tom. I'm really sorry, but that has to be my answer."

Tom said nothing immediately. He glanced at Ronnie. Ronnie was sipping his gin. He seemed deep in thought. When he looked up, his expression had changed.

"They're trying to put the fundamentalists in power, Michael. That's what this is all about. You know what that means, you know as well as I do. It's what we've been trying to prevent for years. If it happens . . ." He paused. "Please, Michael—just think about it. Do that for me, will you?"

There was a seriousness about Ronnie's appeal that

Michael did not quite understand. As though for a moment the poseur had been stripped away. Leaving what? Though he could not be certain, Michael thought he had seen a badly frightened man. But frightened of what?

"I think I should go," said Michael. He hesitated, then turned to Perrone. "I'll think about it, Ronnie. I don't want to let you down. But I have myself to consider. You understand that, don't you?"

"Yes. I understand, Michael. But please give it some thought."

Tom Holly placed a hand on Michael's arm.

"Michael, is there any chance of your coming up to town tomorrow evening?"

"If it's just to talk about this, I'd rather not. I'd like to get the funeral out of the way before I start doing any hard thinking."

Holly shook his head.

"Take your time, Michael. Give it all the thought you need. But I'd like to see you tomorrow if you can possibly make it. It's quite important. Quite a different matter. There's someone I'd like you to meet."

"I can't promise, Tom. Can't it wait till Sunday?"

"Afraid not. Tomorrow night will be the last chance. If you hadn't happened to be here I would never have thought of it. There's a reception at the School of Oriental and African Studies. In the library. Seven o'clock. Please, Michael, try to be there."

"I'll try, Tom. Honestly I will. But no promises."

They got up together. Tom signed for the drinks and they left. It was still raining outside. In the bar, after they had gone, the middle-aged woman in tweeds drained her glass and put her novel down. She opened her handbag and applied lipstick and powder to her face with care. Closing her pocket mirror, she took out a portable phone and gently punched in a number in Vauxhall Cross.

4

The day of the funeral dripped and dripped. In the cemetery, the trees were already turning leafless; beads of rainwater lay on their branches like tiny buds rushing spring into autumn. A gray light saturated granite and marble, the tops of funeral urns and the wings of broken angels. It fingered the gold-lettered names of the dead, it rustled among the dull petals of dried and withered flowers. The gravel paths were lined with weeds and pitted with small, irregular pools of water. Michael walked to the graveside like a pilgrim whose quest has ended, but for whom fulfillment seems as far away as ever.

He had arrived in Oxford the night before. Getting out of London had been a nightmare. There had been jams on the M40; he had forgotten what it was like driving in England. He had spent a little time with his mother before bed. She spoke quietly in Arabic, finding comfort in words and phrases from her past, flooding Michael with memories of a time that was as dead as the man she had been married to. They managed their grief so differently here, she said, they left her wordless and tearless and sunken. None of her Egyptian family would be at the funeral, though there had been phone calls and telegrams, some from people she had almost forgotten. She was a stranger in a strange land, and never before had her exile ridden her so hard or with so little forgiveness.

There were, as Tom Holly had suggested, very few mourners at the funeral. Ronald Hunt had not been the most popular of men. There were barely flowers enough to cover the coffin while it rode in the hearse. One wreath lay at its foot, a creation in roses and white carnations depicting his regimental badge. But only a few old comrades-in-arms were at the graveside to see him buried. Apart from them, there were some relations. Carol was there.

It would have been unlike Carol to forgo such an opportunity, Michael thought. But an opportunity for what exactly, he could not say. To make mischief of one kind or another, he supposed. To intrude on his grief with her own imagined sufferings, to scorn whatever it was he thought he had become since leaving her.

She looked good, she had not let herself go to pieces since the separation. That would not have been her way, of course. Her fine blond hair was tied back and tucked up hard beneath a black silk headscarf. She wore a dark cashmere coat without ornament, her Bruno Magli shoes were immaculate even after the short walk to the graveside. She had arrived at the house unaccompanied. She still lived alone, or pretended to: a slip in visible standards would not have suited her. Carol was still a mistress of the double life. Throughout their long marriage, Michael had never guessed at the full range of her infidelities, never suspected the easy vigor of her duplicity. She and Michael had driven to the funeral in the same car. Paul had seen to that.

Paul performed the funeral service as planned. Tall, angular, in a black cassock silvered by rain, he stood by his father's open grave as though at the gaping mouth of any death, a priest rather than a son. His perfectly modulated voice rang out among the gravestones without hesitation. It shook just once, when he spoke his father's name. There were no visible signs of grief on his face or in his manner. And yet, Michael knew, Paul was the most torn by his father's death, and the most abandoned.

He and Michael had had very little opportunity to speak on the previous night. For almost a year now, Paul, too, had been living in Cairo, and the brothers saw one another from time to time. Though far from close, there was no enmity between them. Just a distance, a falling apart that both regretted and neither knew how to bridge or mend. They had flown in to Heathrow together, but Paul had gone straight to Oxford while Michael remained behind in London for his meeting with Tom Holly. When he had mentioned Tom's name on the plane, Paul had said nothing, but Michael had sensed his disapproval. And something else. Something a little like fear, or apprehension.

Throughout the service at the graveside, Michael held his mother's arm. She was old and frail now, and he thought she would follow his father quickly. Without him, what was there for her in this cold, unwelcoming place, in this England that was not the England she had been brought to all those years before? For a moment, Michael thought of suggesting she return with Paul and him to Cairo. She still had family there, she could live out her days in some sort of peace. But he quickly saw that it would be useless. She had made her peace years ago, had chosen to cut herself adrift from a country that had never really wanted her. And, if Tom Holly was right and a fundamentalist regime did come to power in Egypt, it would be even less a place for an old Christian woman to live out her days in. She would stay with their sister Anna and her husband; it had already been arranged.

They walked back to the cars together, Michael and Paul on either side of their mother, each holding an arm. She was tiny between them, her thin gray hair stuck out uncontrollably from beneath her hat. Carol came behind them with Anna, keeping her distance. As they walked away, they could hear the rain dropping steadily on the wooden lid of the coffin.

"Your father never liked the rain," said their mother. "He used to say we should go back to Egypt to live. Well, we'll never do that now."

"He'd never have gone anyway, Mother," said Michael. "You know how he felt about the place."

She nodded.

"He was lonely," she whispered. "Very lonely. Nobody ever came to visit him. Almost nobody."

The journey back took place in silence. Carol, moody, stared through the window. When she turned to look at Michael, he would turn his face away. He knew she was trying to make him feel guilty: for walking out on her, for staying away, for refusing to overlook her infidelities. The long car purred its solemn way back to the little house in Headington. There are so many kinds of death, so many kinds of burial.

When they were inside, Paul took Michael aside.

"Please, Michael, it's very embarrassing if you insist on ignoring Carol. She made an effort to be here today. At least think of Mother."

"It's not that easy, Paul. Or that simple. You know that."

"I only know you have a problem to solve and that you don't seem to be looking very hard for a solution."

"That's easy for you to say. You know nothing about marriage."

Paul reddened and lowered his eyes. Behind him, the sound of strained voices came from the living-room. Everyone was trying desperately to be polite, to put up a good show, to avoid the very subjects that were on all their minds.

"You don't have to remind me, Michael. It's a subject priests try to steer clear of. But I am a priest, and you are my brother, so I have to try. You loved Carol once. I know that better than anyone. You never tired of telling me about her, about how wonderful she was. You lived together as man and wife for fifteen years. Surely that's time enough for a couple to learn to put up with one another's faults. I know Carol could be difficult, but surely . . ."

"I stopped loving her in the first year, Paul. By the time we split up, I'd hated her so long I couldn't even remember what loving her had been like. If I'd found someone else, God knows I'd have left Carol much sooner."

Paul winced.

"You know I can't comment on that, Michael."

It is hard to talk about love with your brother when he is a priest. Michael had never found it easy to call his younger brother "father," or to think of him as anything but the child he had known, as though they had never grown up or grown apart. Time passes. God introduces spaces into the lives we have known. Or we introduce them ourselves, out of boredom or hope or the drift to suicide. Michael shivered.

"You can't comment as a priest? Or as my brother?"

"Please, Michael, don't start this again. You know it gets us nowhere."

"As my brother, then. I don't want your blessing. I want your understanding."

Paul raised his eyebrows. He had inherited more of their father's looks than his brother. For all that he was younger, he seemed the older of the two. His hair was light, almost fair. The eyes were cold, without Michael's intensity: all around them, small wrinkles insinuated themselves into his cheeks and forehead. Not laughter lines, but the toll of years of study and concentrated prayer. Pathways of intellect and faith gouged day by day through his skin, tokens of yet deeper scars. Paul Hunt was a Jesuit by training and a man by afterthought.

"My understanding?" he said. "Don't you mean my love?"

Michael looked at his brother without speaking. Then he nodded gently. "Yes," he said, "I suppose so. I suppose I mean your love."

Paul seemed to have made a decision. He stepped forward and took Michael in his arms. Then, disconcertingly, he began to cry. Michael held him as though, inexplicably, his little brother had been transformed into an ungainly man in black robes, as though, in the midst of a game of make-believe and dressing-up, their mock solemnity had turned to real tears, and to a grief beyond their years.

Slowly, Paul's tears subsided to gentle sobs. He pulled himself away gently, not looking at Michael, as though embarrassed to be caught out in his vulnerability. Sometimes, Michael thought, his brother wore his clerical garb like armor, the way some doctors wear white coats or soldiers regimental badges. Paul was a Jesuit, a priest of the intellect, highly trained and highly thought of. Before his posting to Cairo, he had spent several years at the Vatican, working for the Secretariat of State. Whatever his weaknesses, he had long ago succeeded in keeping them out of sight.

"I'm sorry," he murmured at last.

"There's nothing to apologize for," whispered Michael. "I wish I could feel the way you do."

Paul did not answer.

"Let's go into the garden," Michael said. "I need some air. I think the rain's over now."

As they passed through the kitchen, they heard a snatch of news from the radio, which had been switched on by one of Anna's children. The death count at King's Cross had reached one hundred and nineteen and was still likely to rise sharply over the next few weeks as more of the victims succumbed to their injuries. Paul hesitated, listening, before going through the door. He seemed to take a special interest in the broadcast.

When they were both little, the garden had seemed a vast realm of unexplored possibilities. It had changed little since then. The old summer shed still hung crookedly on its rusted rail, the elder tree still bent over the wall at the bottom, there were rows of earthenware pots stacked up alongside the greenhouse as there had always been. Would the changes begin now? Michael wondered, in the wake of their father's death. Would that event, which would have seemed so cataclysmic thirty years ago, strip away the leaves and uproot the grasses, bring the garden to ruin and weed at last?

Or had the real changes begun in them in adolescence, as they turned their energies away from the lawn and the dark, evergreen shrubs, out towards the world? The garden seemed so much smaller now, so much narrower in its compass. They made their way to the shed and stepped inside, like schoolboys playing truant. But today it was death, not school, from which they were hiding.

Paul talked about their father while Michael listened. A torrent of reminiscences and regrets. There were incidents Michael remembered, others from which he had been excluded or had excluded himself. Briefly, in the damp shed, full of the dark smell of leaf mold, their father came vividly to life.

"You never really knew him, did you, Michael?"

Michael shook his head.

"You tried though, didn't you? I think you tried very hard. Joining the army, serving your country, all of that. You were trying to be like him."

"I suppose so, yes. Or to be liked by him. But it never worked. I enlisted in the wrong regiment, I opted for intelligence work, I joined the SIS. Nothing I did ever pleased him."

"I think you pleased him more than you ever realized, Michael. He was a little jealous of you; did you know that?"

Michael glanced at his brother, puzzled.

"I can't imagine that."

"It's true. You had brains, you got the postings you wanted, you were a popular officer."

"I always thought he despised brains in a soldier."

Paul laughed.

"That was just part of the front he put up. I think that had a lot to do with what went wrong between you, the fact you never understood what an old fraud he was. You took him much too seriously, Michael. He used to play you up, and you'd rise to his bait like a suicidal perch. No, he admired what you did. He used to boast about it to me." Paul hesitated. "He never really understood why you left the intelligence service so soon after getting your desk job in London. None of us did."

Michael looked into his brother's eyes.

"Didn't you?"

"You never explained."

"No. No, I don't suppose I did. It wouldn't have been easy. It still wouldn't be very simple. There's not much to say, really. I had to betray someone. Someone I was close to."

"A woman?"

Michael shook his head.

"No, a man. Another agent. An Israeli." He halted briefly. "I can't tell you the details. But I had to choose between giving him away to the Egyptians or letting a lot of other people die. It was a harder choice than you might think. I knew his wife and children well. And there was the situation with Carol on top of it all. I needed a break, a fresh start. A whole new life, I suppose."

"And have you found it?"

"No, not really. You can change your clothes and your home, even your taste in music; but you stay the same inside. Don't ask me any more about this, Paul. Not at the moment." He smiled. "Not while you're dressed like that anyway."

"I'm glad we've talked."

"Yes, so am I."

"Michael . . ." Paul hesitated. "Look, I don't know what it is Tom Holly wants you to do, and I know it's none of my business anyway. But . . . Try to think twice about it, whatever it is. Let things stay as they are. It's better this way."

"How do you know so much about Tom Holly all of a sudden?"

"We don't spend all our time in prayer, you know. The Vatican is a clearing-house for all manner of information."

Michael stared at his brother.

"What exactly did you do there, Paul?"

Paul smiled and pressed Michael's hand. Without answering the question, he stood.

"I have to go back in, Michael. Mother must be wondering what's happened to us. Are you coming?"

Michael shook his head.

"I'll stay on here for a bit, Paul, if you don't mind. I have something I need to think over. We'll talk again. If not here, when we're both back in Cairo."

Paul nodded and left the shed. Michael watched him stride back up the leaf-strewn path, a man whose only outlet for human pain was in the confessional, and perhaps not even there. For the first time, Michael realized that his brother's world was even more secret than the one to which he himself had, until a few years ago, belonged, and to which he felt himself being sucked back against his will.

He knew he should be back at the house, talking with relatives, sharing memories of his father, looking at old snapshots, cutting slices of cake for guests. But at this moment he needed to be here alone. The shed was more to him than a place of memories. He had always come here as a child and teenager to think things over. His first fears, his first moral dilemmas, his earliest temptations. He looked at the cobwebbed, unpainted walls, trying to think through the implications of what Tom Holly had told him. Darkness was moving through the air.

A soft voice spoke behind him.

"I thought I might find you here."

When he looked round, Carol was standing in the doorway, smiling down at him.

5

"You've been ignoring me all day, Michael. You haven't even made eye contact."

"Eye contact." He guessed she had been taking a course in counseling or something similar. Carol had always had an insatiable capacity for courses of self-improvement of one kind or another.

"We've nothing to talk about, Carol. We've been over it all before. Dozens of times. It's too late now."

"It's never too late to enter into communication with someone, Michael. And we have no choice. We're still married. I'm still your wife, even if you refuse to have anything to do with me."

She had already pressed in through the doorway and was standing beside the chair Paul had lately vacated.

"You don't mind if I sit down, do you, Michael?"

"Suit yourself," he said. "The place is yours. I was just leaving."

"You can't keep running, Michael. You can't just walk out on all of life's little dilemmas. Me, the service . . ."—she hesitated—"your father."

"I don't think this is the best time to score points about me and my father."

"Why not? You haven't exactly been griefstricken. Well, have you? Emotions never were your strong point, Michael, were they? But I'm afraid you're going to have to come to terms with some of them. I don't intend to go away, Michael. I'll stick to you like glue. If necessary, I'll come after you to Cairo."

"You're wasting your breath, Carol. Let's just get on with our separate lives. It's better that way."

"Is it? Maybe for you, but not for me. You left me in limbo. You're a Catholic, so you won't let me get divorced, you won't let me marry anybody else. I've spoken to Paul about an annulment, but he says it wouldn't be possible. For God's sake, Michael, we can't go on like this. It isn't natural."

"What do you want me to do, Carol? Do you want me back? Is that what this is about?"

"Don't be so fucking stupid, Michael. That's the last thing either of us wants, and you know it."

"What, then? What do you want? If it's money, I don't have any. I don't even earn what I did when I was working for the service."

"I'm pregnant, Michael."

She let her bombshell drop almost without premeditation, as though the fact of her condition had just occurred to her as an afterthought. For fifteen years she and Michael had tried unremittingly to have a child. The effort had become their marriage, had transcended even the lack of love between them, had thrown them together time and again in a lust for fertility.

"That's impossible," he said.

"Why? Because the fault could never have been yours? You make me want to puke, Michael."

Somehow, he believed her.

"Who was it, Carol? Was it someone I know?"

"I wouldn't let any of your friends get within a mile of me. If you must know, his name is Simon, and he runs a

restaurant in Hampstead. And you needn't look at me like
that either.''

"Like what, Carol? How do I look at you?''

"I don't know. With that little snide look, that 'let's-put-
her-in-her-place-and-show-her-who's-boss' look. Well, you
can forget all that, Superman. Little Carol's got her own life
to live. I want a divorce, Michael, and you're fucking well
going to give it to me.''

"You don't have to swear." He paused. "Couldn't you
have used contraception?''

She erupted in fury. "You always were a hypocritical
little shit, weren't you? 'I'm a Catholic, you can't get divorced.' But now it's, 'couldn't you have used contraception?' What a tiresome prick you are.''

He closed his eyes. The scene felt disgustingly familiar.

"What sort of restaurant is it?''

"What?''

"What sort of restaurant? He doesn't sound Italian or
Chinese. Something up-market and trendy, is it? With faux
marble pillars and subdued lighting? A clientele of advertis-
ing executives and their rapacious wives?''

"What the fuck has that to do with anything?''

"Calm down, Carol. I want to know about this won-
drously fecund man of yours, this latest acquisition. This
man who achieved what so many of us had not. Is he married? Divorced? Does he have other children? Several
dozen, I should imagine.''

She took a deep breath, fighting back anger.

"Yes," she said, "he's divorced. He has two children, a
girl and a boy. One's fifteen, the other thirteen. His wife
went off with one of their chefs.''

"No doubt she wanted a high standard of personal cui-
sine.''

"Look, I didn't come here to have you make snide re-
marks about Simon. He doesn't come into this.''

"I rather thought he did. I rather imagine he's come

into you more than once . . . Or was it a one-night fling and now you're calling in your debts . . ."

She struck him, a hard blow, thick against the cheek. He did not flinch, though he had expected it and seen it coming. It stung, but inside he hardly felt it. She had drained him of his capacity for pain long ago. And love too. All of that.

"Don't bother apologizing," he said.

"Michael, I need a divorce. So Simon and I can get married. We owe it to the child. And his other children. At least think of the child, Michael."

"I am thinking of the child. I will always think of the child. If you want a divorce, why don't you file for one?"

"It's not that simple. You know it isn't. I need your consent. We've been separated over two years. If you don't contest, we can have it fixed up straight away."

"You won't need my consent in another two years anyway. Why not just wait? The baby won't know the difference."

"Other people will know. We'll be a laughing stock."

"So that's it. That's what it comes down to. You're afraid people may laugh at you and lover-boy."

She grew angry again.

"Why are you like this, Michael? You don't even believe in God! What difference can it possibly make to you?"

"I can't divorce you because it would kill my mother. My father's dead now, so he's spared all this, thank goodness. I have to think of my family."

"Your family? You mean your fucking brother, the priest. He was daddy's favorite, so you have to suck up to him just to prove you're one of the gang. You may not believe in God, but you're a good Catholic all the same. That's the message you're giving out, isn't it?"

"That's enough, Carol . . ."

"No, it's not enough. Your motives aren't high enough, Michael. Maybe I'm no saint, but at least I'm consistent. Don't worry, I won't embarrass you. I'll say my good-byes to your sweet mother and leave. I don't know if you plan to stay in England for very long. But if you do and you decide to talk this over properly, like a civilized person, you've got my number. And don't worry, you won't have to speak to Simon, he spends most of the time at his fucking restaurant."

She turned abruptly and was gone. Her perfume lingered for a moment, harsh against the damp autumnal smells of the shed. Michael recognized the scent, a Guerlain perfume, Jicky or Jardin de Bagatelle. It was as though spring had caught the garden unawares, throwing all things in it into disarray. The sharp odor brought back memories he preferred to keep well buried.

He stepped out of the shed. All about him, the afternoon was growing slowly dark. He wanted to be back in Cairo, where autumn could not tear your heart open with such subtle force. He looked at his watch. There was still plenty of time to make it to London.

6

It had been a couple of years since Michael's last visit to SOAS. If he remembered rightly, it had been to hear Pierre Cachia lecture on modern Arabic literature. During his year at Vauxhall House, he had come to Bloomsbury regularly to attend lectures and seminars, and to use the excellent library facilities.

For all that, he felt out of his depth the moment he opened the door into the room where the reception was being held. He recognized a few people from the Foreign Office and a couple of diplomats from Arab embassies, including some Egyptians. Among them milled a motley crowd of academics, drawn from universities in Europe and the Middle East, with a few rather obvious Americans tucked in for good measure. The seminar, Michael had noticed on his way through the foyer, had been devoted to "The Amarna Rock Tombs of Huya and Meryre' II," a subject about which he knew absolutely nothing.

As he tried to secure himself a glass of cheap Bulgarian wine from the buffet, he was pinned against the table by a balding Japanese professor who had just seen off two Danes, an Italian, and a graduate student from Milwaukee.

The horn-rimmed spectacles seemed to have been supplied by a firm specializing in Second World War costumes. A hand gripped Michael's arm tightly.

"Professor Jurgens making very serious error, you not think? He is ignoring my paper on the West Wall of Huya tomb. Wall has dated inscription to Year Twelve, quite correct. But inscription has Re-Aten form of name. So tomb must be dated to period after second half of Year Eight. Also consider painting of six daughters on East Wall of Meryre' tomb. In Huya tomb, is only four daughters. But . . ."

"Excuse me, but I have to take Professor Hunt off your hands."

Tom Holly's voice had never sounded so welcome.

"You were just in time, Tom," Michael sighed as they weaved their way through clumps of earnest archaeologists. Behind them, the Japanese scholar was already looking around predatorially for his next victim. Michael was balancing a glass in one hand and a cocktail stick bearing tinned pineapple chunks and mousy cheddar in the other. Tom steered him expertly to an empty space in the middle of the hall.

"Michael, I'm so very sorry. I simply couldn't make it to the funeral. Something came up at the last moment, I just couldn't get away. You must remember how it is."

"That's all right, Tom. I didn't really expect you."

"You got my wreath all right, did you?"

"Wreath? Oh, yes. The lilies. It was very tasteful. Mother liked it very much."

"She's all right?"

"Well . . . She'll get through this part. It's afterwards I worry about. She depended on Father an awful lot. Not just for company, but . . . He was her world, Tom, after Egypt. There was never any going back for her. Not then, at least, not when they first arrived in England. Maybe later, in the seventies, for a while; but it was too late by then. And it's too late now."

"I don't recommend her going back, Michael."

"She wasn't really thinking . . ."

"I'm serious, Michael. Take my word for it. It's going to get hard for the Copts. Very hard." He paused. "Did she really like the wreath?"

Michael shook his head.

"She hardly knew what was going on. I read your card, all the cards, but they didn't register. There weren't very many of them. They've been kept for later."

"Thanks, Michael. Thanks for coming. I'm sorry I had to ask you to come tonight."

"To be frank, I was glad to get away."

Tom frowned.

"Carol? She didn't turn up, did she?"

Michael nodded.

"What a pity. She'd have done better to have stayed away. But then Carol was never one for tact."

"She's pregnant, Tom. She wants me to give her a divorce."

Tom registered the news patiently. He had first met Carol soon after Michael and she had started going out together. At first he had been jealous of his friend's success with such an attractive and sophisticated woman. It had taken some time before he learned the truth, or as much of it as he ever did learn.

"Are you going to?"

"Divorce her? You know that's impossible, Tom."

"Is it? I'd think about it, Michael. I'd give it very serious thought. It could be the best move you ever made."

Michael changed the subject.

"You said there was someone you wanted me to meet. Suppose we get on with it. Has he arrived?"

Tom glanced anxiously round the room.

"This way, Michael. Over in that corner by the potted plant."

Near a parlor palm in the later stages of what had undoubtedly been a slow and unlamented decline, a little cluster of Arab academics stood talking vociferously. The subject, Michael noted as they drew near, was not archaeology, but politics: to be precise, the threat posed to civil liberties by the fundamentalists. There were three men and a woman. She seemed to be arguing with one of her colleagues.

"They are still our best hope of throwing off the baggage of colonialism," the man was saying. "The Nasserists failed to implement half their policies. In the past ten years we've become more tied to the West than ever. If we want genuine independence, we have to take radical steps. The Jama'at are the only people with a clear program. We'll have to throw in our lot with them, otherwise . . ."

"It's easy for you to say that," interrupted the woman. "You're not a woman. You don't face the possibility that all you've worked for, all you've achieved, could be snuffed out in an instant by some piece of retrogressive legislation."

As she spoke, one of the men next to her leaned back against a table, and Michael saw her properly for the first time. He felt himself grow still, and the room, and the voices in it. It was as if he could not breathe, as if it did not matter whether he breathed again or not. The moving shadows of people, smoke curling from cigarettes, the gestures of hands and faces, laughter, the fluttering of napkins, the lifting of glasses, all grew perfectly still, or so it seemed. His tongue touched the roof of his mouth, once, very gently, infinitely softly, and fell away again. Her face was the only moving thing, her mouth was the focus of his attention, he could hear her voice and nothing else.

She looked up and caught sight of him, and he reddened as her eyes stayed on him without moving. He was sure she could read his thoughts. He felt as though he was standing naked in the middle of the room. Then she looked away and continued speaking.

"They won't make you wear a veil," she said, "or stay at home to have children and cook meals. But what about someone like myself? I . . ."

"Dr. Manfaluti . . ." Tom caught the speaker's attention. He spoke in Arabic. "I'm so sorry to interrupt, but I wanted to introduce you to Michael Hunt from the American University in Cairo. You may remember I mentioned him to you a couple of days ago."

The woman stopped speaking and turned, frowning. Then, as she caught sight of Tom, her face lightened. She changed to English.

"Mr. Holly. You were able to make it after all. I'm so pleased."

Turning back to her companions, she made her apologies.

"I'm so sorry, but Mr. Holly here has some matters he needs to discuss with me. Maybe we can continue our conversation later."

The men parted, allowing her to escape. She came straight for Tom and shook his hand warmly.

"Thanks for getting me out of that," she whispered. "There's nothing I hate more than professed liberals backing the religious zealots just because they think it suits their own purposes. My God, you'd think they'd have learned their lesson after what happened in Iran."

They were well out of earshot by now.

"Dr. Manfaluti, this is Michael Hunt. Michael, A'isha Manfaluti."

She smiled and reached out her hand. She was not as beautiful as Carol. Not as tall, not as perfumed, not as well-dressed. Not, he thought, anything remotely like Carol. He thought he could have looked at her for hours without once blinking or turning his head away. He felt her hand in his. She was looking directly into his eyes, slightly amused, he thought.

"Mr. Hunt. I've heard a lot about you."

"Oh? What's Tom been telling you? You know he's a notorious liar."

"Tom? Oh, you mean Mr. Holly. He's told me very little. Isn't that right?" She smiled at Tom. "But I've heard things about you from friends in the American University. I have my spies everywhere. You know Riaz Wahba, don't you?"

Michael nodded.

"And Nabil Faraj?"

"Yes, of course. They're both in sociology. We've shared some courses." He noticed that she had not let go of his hand. His mind was in the sort of whirl he remembered only too well from his teens. As though he had never looked at a woman in his life before.

"Are you here doing research, Mr. Hunt?" She drew her hand away, very slowly it seemed to him. His skin felt electric from her touch.

He glanced at Tom.

"I'm sorry, Michael. There wasn't a chance to . . ."

"My father died. I came to England for the funeral. It was this morning."

Her face fell. Not as Carol's would have fallen, in mock sympathy, but quite naturally, as though they had been good friends for a long time. Almost, he felt, as though he had known her all his life.

"I'm dreadfully sorry. I didn't mean . . ."

"There's no need to apologize. It's over now. He was . . . We were never very close."

He wondered why he had blurted that out in front of someone he had only just met.

"All the same. It can't have been easy."

"No," he said. "It wasn't."

Her hand went to her forehead, pushing back a lock of falling hair. He noticed the ring on her finger and felt something cold turn round inside him.

"Look, why don't I leave you two alone together?" suggested Tom. "There are some other people here I'd like to have a word with." He paused. "I'll see you later, Michael. We'll have a drink. Don't let Dr. Manfaluti captivate you too much. We still have that other matter to talk about. When you feel ready."

Before Michael could stop him, Tom was off, leaving

them together in an empty corner. He noticed that she had nothing to eat or drink.

"Can I get you something to drink?" he asked. "Wine? Or there's fruit juice."

"That's very kind. Yes, please. But not fruit juice. They always have some nowadays for the sake of the believers. I came to London to get away from all that. I'd like a white wine, please."

He fought his way to the buffet and returned with a glass he had filled from a cardboard box labeled "French Dry White."

"It probably tastes like paintstripper."

"Always does," she said, taking the glass. "It's part of the charm. The price we academics pay for all our other privileges. Thanks."

"What privileges?"

She smiled and sipped the wine.

"Not paintstripper. Heating fuel possibly." She paused and looked at him. "Well, Mr. Hunt, what did you want to see me about?"

"What did I . . .? Did Tom say I'd asked to see you?"

She nodded.

"Did he get it wrong?" she asked, a little bemused.

"I don't know. He just said there was someone he wanted me to meet."

"I see. No doubt he has his reasons. You do know who Tom Holly is, don't you?"

"Tom? He's just an old friend. We met on the Arabic course at Shemlan. He . . . works for some department or other in Whitehall."

She laughed softly.

"Tom Holly works for British intelligence," she said. "Don't tell me you didn't know that."

Michael reddened.

"Well, I . . ."

"You had your suspicions." She laughed again. It was the loveliest laugh he had ever heard. He had not thought it possible that, at his age, in such a moment, at the onset of winter, he could be so arrested by a woman's laugh. Or that, on a day of mourning, he could feel life at the edge of things.

She did not pursue the topic of Tom and his ancient profession. Michael she appeared to take at face value. As he talked about himself, she seemed to sense his awkwardness when speaking of the past, letting him steer away from it towards other matters.

For much of the evening, they talked about the political situation in Egypt and the Middle East generally. He discovered her passionate about the threat to liberalization, a keen defender of the rights of women and religious minorities, blithely lacking in respect for convention and what she considered the false morality of the religious leaders and the extremist groupings.

"For an archaeologist, you take an unhealthy interest in the present," he joked.

"It's all that matters. I only study the past for the light it can shed on things here and now. Otherwise I'm not interested in it. Egypt's a land of tombs. You must have been to the City of the Dead in Cairo. Poor people actually living in tombs, because there's nowhere else for them to go. We have to break free of all that."

"You should have been a politician," he said. "Egypt could do with more women in parliament."

Her face changed abruptly, and she looked away from him for the first time.

"I'm sorry . . . Did I say something wrong?"

She shook her head, still staring at the floor.

"No," she muttered. She looked up, smiling. "It's all right. You just . . . reminded me of something."

The longer they talked, the more he felt himself ensnared. She was, as Holly had implied, captivating. He registered every gesture, caught every nuance of her smiles and frowns, watched every movement of her head. But every so often he would glance at the ring on her hand and feel a lump form in the pit of his stomach. The next time he met her, in Cairo, she would be with her husband. And she would hold her husband's hand and smile at him delicately, and tell Michael with a winning smile how much she loved him and how much he loved her. There was no point in thinking anything else, not even for a moment, because in Cairo it was not merely imprudent to harbor such thoughts, it was actually dangerous.

The reception began to break up. People started drifting away, singly and in groups. In a few minutes, the room would be empty and it would be time for him to go as well. Tom Holly was sitting alone, waiting for Michael.

"It's been lovely meeting you," Michael began.

"No, don't say that," she reprimanded him. "That's what people always say at these things, when it's time to leave. They don't mean it, not really. It's just a form of words."

"But I have enjoyed meeting you. Very much."

"Well then," she said. "We must meet again. When we're both back in Cairo."

It would come now, he was ready for it: "You must come round for drinks some night, meet my husband and children." But she did not say it.

"Have you got a piece of paper?"

He found an old envelope in his pocket. She wrote on the back of it, an address and telephone number in al-Azbakiyya.

"Get in touch when you get back. If you'd like to, that is . . ."

"Yes," he said. "I'd like to very much."

She shook his hand, waved to Tom Holly, and was gone. He watched the door swing closed behind her. When he turned at last, he and Tom were the only ones left. The room was huge and echoing and empty, full of discarded glasses and half-eaten food that nobody had really wanted in the first place. Michael closed his eyes, remembering his father in a place without echoes or light.

7

"She's very lovely, isn't she?"

They were walking past the British Museum, in search of somewhere to eat. It had been Tom's suggestion. Michael did not feel in the least hungry.

"Who?"

"Oh, don't be such a jerk, Michael. You know very well who. A'isha Manfaluti."

"I suppose so."

"You suppose so! You couldn't take your eyes off her."

"Why did you introduce us, Tom?" Michael stopped walking, forcing Tom to do the same.

"Why? You must be having me on, Michael. She'll have told you that at least."

"She told me nothing, Tom."

"What did you two talk about for God's sake? Her latest dig?"

"We talked about that a little, yes."

"But at least you know who she is."

"Who she is? Her name's Dr. A'isha Manfaluti. She's—what?—about thirty-four years old, she works at the Egyptian Museum, her specialty is tomb architecture of the nineteenth dynasty. Her father was a lawyer attached to the mixed courts. She has no brothers or sisters. She . . .''

"We're not interested in any of that, Michael. I'm talking about her husband, all of that."

Michael did not answer at once. Confirmation that she had a husband was like a blow, soft and sickening.

"Husband? She never mentioned a husband."

"She . . .? Christ, Michael—if you hadn't been so interested in her bone structure, you'd have worked it out at once. Are you telling me you really don't know who A'isha Manfaluti is?"

Michael felt himself go cold. He had begun to sense that this had been no casual introduction, that a great deal hung on it for Tom Holly. Of course, he had known there would be a price to pay. But now he began to think it might be a high one. He said nothing. Behind them, the great gray stones of the museum measured themselves against the night.

Tom took a deep breath.

"A'isha Manfaluti's husband is Rashid Manfaluti, the leader of the al-Hurriya party. Do you know what I'm talking about now?"

There were shadows, echoes all around them. The night clamored. Michael felt very cold.

"I don't understand. Wasn't . . . Wasn't Manfaluti kidnapped?"

Tom nodded gently.

"Five years ago. He was snatched shortly after he made a speech in Cairo condemning the religious right. They'd just forced through a law banning marriage between Copts and Muslims. Nobody knows the identity of his kidnappers, but there have been educated guesses. He's never been seen since the day of his abduction. No photographs, no videos, not even a letter. Some people think he's dead, but the consensus is that his kidnappers are keeping him alive as an eventual bargaining chip in the event of a government clampdown. Some of the older reactionaries remember the camps Sadat set up for the Ikhwan in the sixties. They don't want things to go back to that."

"What use would Manfaluti be to them?"

"Quite a lot. His name is still a rallying point for the country's liberals. He had a reputation for being uncorrupted. A lot of ordinary people would give him their vote in an election. He's against the extremists, but he keeps an open mind on religion in general. He's a Muslim whom the Copts feel they could trust. If anyone could stop the fundamentalists getting into power, it would be Rashid Manfaluti."

"If he's still alive, yes. In which case, wouldn't his kidnappers have done better to have killed him?"

Tom shrugged.

"Maybe. But I don't think so. If it got out that they'd been responsible, there'd be a hell of a backlash. It could be worse than having the man himself at large again."

"Where does his wife come in?"

Tom began walking again. Michael followed close behind. They headed down Museum Street, past the illuminated windows of bookshops.

"The party has been trying to persuade Mrs. Manfaluti to stand for parliament at the next election, in January. With her husband's name behind her and her own abilities on the platform, she's an obvious choice. If she were to get in, she could do a lot of damage to the fundamentalists. She could win a large percentage of the female vote. There's only one snag."

"What's that?"

"She doesn't want to stand. She's passionate about political issues, but she has absolutely no interest in being a politician. No, it's more than that. She has a positive aversion to the idea."

Michael remembered with embarrassment her reaction to his clumsy suggestion that she take up politics.

"Why didn't you tell me about all this?"

"I'm sorry. I assumed . . . I thought she'd tell you her-self, if you didn't already know. It seems I was wrong."

"What's your interest in her?"

"I should have thought that was obvious."

"Tom, I've been out of touch for over four years now. A lot of things can change. I'm not sure if I know exactly what our official policy in Egypt is these days."

"We keep the fundamentalists out of power. With Is-lamic governments in control now in Iran, Iraq, Algeria, and Sudan, and with several other countries teetering on the edge, we can't afford to let Egypt slip out of control. If an extremist regime exercised power over the Azhar Univer-sity, they could have enormous influence throughout the Islamic world. The Azhar's almost the last institution the majority of Muslims have any respect for. It would be a mas-sive step backwards for the region."

"Would that matter to us? It didn't stop us supporting Saddam Hussein when Iran was the enemy. Or Iran when we decided Saddam was the greater evil."

Tom shrugged.

"I don't make the policy, Michael; you know that."

"And what about A'isha Manfaluti?"

"I'd like you to keep an eye on her, Michael. That's all. It shouldn't be too hard to do. Rather a pleasure, I'd have thought. See no-one's taking an unhealthy interest in her. Make friends with her. See she doesn't get into trouble."

"What sort of trouble? Another kidnapping—is that what you're expecting?"

"Something like that, yes. It's a possibility."

"Then she ought to have a round-the-clock body-guard."

"She's been told that, but she won't listen. It would be too much like giving her a role. She thinks she's safer with-out protection because that implies she's not a commodity worth protecting. Important people have bodyguards, im-portant people get kidnapped. And, of course, people who have bodyguards will be treated as though they were important, which is precisely what she does not want."

"She could be right. About people with bodyguards getting kidnapped."

Tom nodded.

"Perhaps. But we can't afford to take that chance or to let her take it. If the time comes, we'll need her as a symbol, if nothing else. Unlike her husband, she's no use to us dead or as a hostage. I just want you to keep a friendly eye out for her, Michael, that's all. There aren't any other trained people I can ask."

Michael stopped again.

"She knows about you, Tom. Who you are, what you are."

"Of course she does, old son. She's very sharp and she's been around."

"She knows you introduced us. I don't think she's going to fall for the poor but honest academic routine for long."

"I expect not. But it doesn't really matter. She doesn't like westerners interfering in Egyptian affairs, but she's also enough of a realist to know we have to get along together. You've got legitimate reasons to get to know her. That's all I'm asking."

"Do you expect me to go to bed with her?"

"Please, Michael, you know me better than that. I never worked that way. How close your friendship becomes is entirely up to you."

"You want me to look for Manfaluti as well, don't you?"

"I never said that."

"But you'd like it."

"Yes, of course, if you get any leads." Tom paused. "Michael, about this other business. I need an answer soon. When can we talk?"

Michael sighed. On New Oxford Street, a crowd of

lager louts paraded to the sound of jangling cans and loud cries without meaning.

"There's no need, Tom. I've had enough time. I'd like to fly back to Cairo on Wednesday. I'll need a full briefing before I leave."

8

Colonel Ronald Hunt's will was read on Monday morning at his solicitors, Ephraim, Rainbow, and Gillespie. Their offices were on St Giles, just past Pudsey House, in a building that looked as if it would have leather patches on its elbows, if it had had elbows.

They were a small and subdued group: Michael, his mother, Paul in a tweed jacket and polo-necked sweater, Anna, her husband Andrew, and their teenage sons. Michael had been worried that Carol might put in an appearance; worse, that she might take the chance to make a scene. The reading of a will can be an occasion for the acrimony of years to throw off its polite concealment, and Michael knew how little reason Carol ever needed to make her feelings naked.

Benjamin Ephraim was a man who had struggled to create a Dickensian dimension to the otherwise tedious life of a provincial solicitor. He had very nearly achieved it. His room might have served for a set in some BBC production of *Bleak House,* book-lined, dimly lit, cluttered with worn leather chairs capped with antimacassars, it exuded an atmosphere of chestnuts and dumplings, old clay pipes and sweet sherry in red decanters. Ephraim himself apparently belonged to a circle of self-professed eccentrics who chose to appear in public dressed in Victorian garb, looking for all the world like extras in search of a Sherlock Holmes or a Nicholas Nickleby to give them some sort of purpose.

In a lugubrious voice he read the will through clause by clause. It was not a long will, nor did it contain any surprises. No skeletons had hung in the narrow cupboard of Ronald Hunt's life, or, if they had, he had tied them up well with string and sealing wax, so that they would not rattle and disturb the children. Most of the money—what little there was of it—went to his widow for the remainder of her days. There were small gifts to his grandsons. No-one's life would change. It had only been a very little death, with ordinary consequences. The three children shook hands with Ephraim and left his office insignificantly richer than they had gone in, and just as sad.

They took lunch together in the Randolph, a family that was a family no longer. For some reason, the conversation turned to love. They spoke of it by turns as something to be sought or won or struggled for, something that could be held or lost like a possession, like a reward for goodness or faith or tenacity. Michael said nothing, listening to them chatter, surmising this and that. He knew that, if he spoke, it would only be to their embarrassment and, perhaps, his own.

For he knew now that love was not like that, was not bought or bargained or struggled for, did not arrive as the result of patient prayer or endured longing. It descended, quite simply, quite formlessly, as if from a great height, it burned you, it consumed you utterly, it was uncontrolled, uncontrollable, and strange. And once it was there, once it was in you, nothing you could do could chase it away, not ever.

"Are you all right, dear?"

His mother was looking at him anxiously across the table. They had reached the dessert. He noticed that he had hardly touched his plate.

"Yes, I'm fine, Mother. I was just . . . thinking."

"You've been preoccupied all day."

"I'm sorry. I haven't meant to be."

"Why don't you stay home a little longer, love? You need a rest. They won't need you back yet. I'm sure you can find someone to fill in for you."

"Yes, Mike," Anna said, always ready to support their mother in any little project. She was the only one who ever called him Mike. "Do stay. We've scarcely seen you. The boys have so few opportunities to spend time with their uncle. Isn't that right, boys?"

The boys nodded dutifully and returned their attention to their rice puddings. Michael had brought them silver-mounted daggers from Cairo, but they had shown only polite interest; their hearts were not in beauty, they wanted computer games and videos.

Michael shook his head.

"I'm sorry," he repeated. "It just isn't possible. I've promised someone I'll be back on Wednesday. A friend. He has important work for me."

Paul glanced up sharply. He seemed troubled.

"That wouldn't be Tom Holly by any chance, would it, Michael?"

"Please, Paul. Not over lunch."

"Very well, not now. But I'll be back in Cairo next week. Call on me, will you? Promise?"

Michael nodded.

After lunch, they split up. Anna and Andrew went back home, the boys returned to school for the rest of the afternoon. Paul said he would drive their mother home.

"What about you, Michael? You don't have anything else to do, do you?"

"If you don't mind, I'd like to be on my own for a bit. I'll be home later."

When they had gone, he found a taxi and asked to be driven to the cemetery where his father had been buried. He had no particular motive for visiting the grave so soon, unless it was that he would be leaving Oxford tomorrow and wanted a chance to say a farewell alone.

Over the weekend, wind had disturbed the flowers the grave-diggers had laid on top of the grave. A plain wooden cross recorded the number of the plot and the identity of its inhabitant. Michael stood for a long time, trying to connect the amorphous mound of earth with the father he remembered. And it shook him to discover how few memories there actually were, how hard he found it to recall his father's face or voice or mannerisms. He had tried so hard to please him and achieved so little. It had been Paul—Paul with his vocation, Paul with his rejection of the military— who had won and kept their father's affection. Michael did not call it love, did not think of it as love.

A funeral party arrived out of nowhere, driving slowly through the lines of graves towards the spot where he stood. He noticed an open grave next to his father's, the soil piled high beside it, waiting for the next in line. As the first car drew alongside, he stepped away and headed for the gate.

As he left the cemetery, someone opened the door of a car parked immediately opposite the entrance. He was about to turn down the pavement when a voice softly called his name. Looking back at the car, he saw that the door still hung open and that the driver was looking in his direction, waiting for him. He crossed the road.

She did not say anything. She did not have to. He got into the car beside her in silence, looking at her, not quite believing, unable to call a halt to what was happening. He thought that, if he spoke so much as a word, the spell would be broken, that she would vanish into thin air, leaving him as he had been just moments earlier, alone, without memories, in search of a way back to a place that no longer existed, that perhaps had never existed.

9

A'isha drove straight to the Randolph and parked the car. Michael went inside and asked for a double room. The hotel was hushed, filled with autumnal scents. The public rooms were almost deserted. In the corridors, the air tingled with tiny whispers. As they walked along the passage that led to their room, they could barely hear one another's feet on the carpet. They touched then for the first time, holding hands gently, fearfully.

She turned to him as they reached the door.

"I've never felt so nervous before," she said. "What about you?"

"No," he said. "Never."

And he put his arms around her and pulled her close to him, holding her silently, her cheek against his, for a long time. Then the lift came, followed by a sound of voices, and they drew apart. He opened the door, blinking in the soft light that fell through the high window.

The door closed softly, shutting off everything, shutting the past firmly behind them. It was like a dam holding back torrents. In an instant, the room was, as it were, closed off. It was as if they had immured themselves in a remote chamber of a secluded monastery or gone up into high mountains miles from any human habitation. The walls, the ceiling, the furniture, all seemed peculiarly alive. Just to feel the air touch his skin filled Michael with electricity. Just to breathe made the whole room vibrate.

A'isha crossed to the window. On the other side of Beaumont Street stood the Ashmolean Museum. She had spent so many hours of her life there, surrounded by glass cases and figures of stone, watched by hard eyes of glass and faience and alabaster, survivors of a past she knew only in stuttering fragments, as though it was a tune she could recall in snatches. Not once had she thought that this room might be here, half a minute's walk away, waiting for her, waiting for them both. And she thought of her own past, and how it too was known to her only in fragments, in broken shards and faded inscriptions. Above all love, and the memory of caresses, and the touch of another's skin. How fragmentary all that became, how like a misremembered tune. She reached for the curtains on either side and drew them hard together, shutting out the light.

Michael switched on a lamp by the bedside. She had hardly spoken since he stepped into her car. There had been no need. He watched as she unbuttoned her coat and tossed it over the back of a chair. She lifted a hand and swept a strand of dark hair from her face. He noticed that she had removed her wedding ring.

She was dressed simply in a parchment-colored sweater and a long skirt the color of white wine. Around her neck she wore a short silk scarf, a burgundy scarf shot through with cream. With deft fingers, she untied it and laid it across the coat. In a few moments, he knew, he would see her naked for the first time. She would remove the sweater and the skirt, step out of her underwear, walk towards him, her flesh between light and shadow, into the shadows of his overwhelming loneliness. He closed his eyes as though in pain.

When he opened them again, she was beside him.

"Poor Michael," she whispered. They were her only words. She lifted her hand to his cheek and touched it softly, as though wondering at the nearness of him. He put his own hand over it, holding her palm flat against his cheek, feeling her warmth enter him. With her other hand, she unbuttoned his coat. He shrugged it off and let it fall to the floor.

They were wordless, like castaways who have been so long adrift they have forgotten the use of speech. He wanted to tell her that he loved her, he wanted to endear himself to her with praise and flattery. But he had no words fit for any of that. He touched her instead, first with his eyes, then with his fingers, and at last with his lips, gently against hers. Each impression was fresh, as though he had no memory, no recollection of love in other places, at other times. This was all there was, all there had ever been.

So she stepped away, and undressed, just as he had known she would. There were still no words. No explanations, no apologies, no lies. She lay on the bed and listened, not for speech, but for a fullness of silence for which she had longed for years. And when he finally came to her and his body touched hers, the silence grew, and the room seemed to fill with giant wings, beating the air without a sound, the wings of giant birds, the wings of angels without measurement or dimension, pounded the gilded air silently, tearing every word, every memory of every word, every shadow of utterance, tearing it and throwing it into the still air, into the silence, the silence that encompassed everything.

"How did you know where to find me?" he asked.

They were lying side by side on the bed, their bodies barely touching, their fingers lightly linked. Outside, rain had started falling in a steady patter against the window-pane.

"I called at your house. Your brother was there. He told me where you'd be."

"Paul? But I never told him . . ."

"No. He said that. But he knows you very well, I think."

She paused, turning to look at him. "Are you glad? Glad I found you?"

He rolled sideways and looked at her for a long time. Softly, he stroked her left breast, then bent to kiss it.

"I wanted you very much," he said.

"And is it all right now? Was this what you wanted?"

He kissed her.

"Yes," he said. "Better."

"Better? How?"

"You ask a lot of questions."

"I need to know. I've always felt . . . inadequate. With men. You don't know what it's like. If you aren't a virgin or a wife, you're a whore. There are no in-betweens. Sometimes I think there are no happy women in our country."

She sat up, leaning back against the headboard.

"I've never done this sort of thing before, Michael. Gone after a man, waited for him . . . I was taking such a chance. I thought . . . you might laugh at me. Or despise me."

"But you knew all the same, didn't you? That I wanted you."

She nodded.

"I thought so, yes. But how could I be sure? We'd hardly spoken."

"I'm glad you took the risk."

"Yes," she whispered. "So am I."

"This isn't a momentary madness, then?" He smiled.

"Not for me, no. I don't know about you. Maybe you're an opportunist. The sort lying in wait for innocent girls like me. My mother used to warn me about them."

He shook his head.

"No," he said. "I think it may be very serious." He paused. "When are you going back to Cairo?"

"I was supposed to fly back today." She laughed and glanced at her wristwatch. "My flight left just over an hour ago."

"I'm leaving on Wednesday. Maybe we can fly back together."

She frowned and shook her head.

"Not on the same plane, love. I would like to, but . . ."

"Your husband. Is that what you're thinking of?"

"In a way, yes. Did Tom Holly tell you about him?"

Michael nodded.

"It isn't simple, Michael. There are people . . . I'll be met at the airport, driven back to my apartment. They watch me. I'm supposed to be . . . I'm supposed to play the part of the faithful wife. If word got out . . ." She stopped.

"What would happen if word got out?"

She hesitated.

"I think . . ." she stammered, "I think they would have me killed. Because I had brought shame on Rashid's name."

"I see." He began to wonder what he was getting himself into. He looked at her hesitantly.

"Do you love him?" he asked.

"Rashid?"

"Yes."

She did not answer at first. As he watched, her face betrayed a range of emotions, as though she was engaged in a difficult inward struggle.

"We were married ten years ago," she said. "I was very young. A virgin. What else? The marriage wasn't arranged in the usual sense; but it was set up for me by his parents and mine. He was not so eminent then, of course. I was allowed to continue with my studies. He was very kind. He'd seen me at a wedding once and fallen in love with me, that was how the whole thing came to be arranged in the beginning. After a while, I started to love him, I think. Rashid would have done anything for me. He was a good man, a man who really meant the things he said. I admired him, and the longer we were together the more I admired him."

She paused.

"Michael, it isn't easy to answer your question. I did love him, I did care for him very deeply. But . . . It wasn't like this, not even when we made love. He was . . . a good friend, a kind husband.''

"And later, when his kidnappers release him—what will you do then?" He knew it was a stupid question. Premature, presumptuous, even dangerous. But he had to ask it.

She did not answer. Almost at once she seemed uneasy, as though perturbed, not so much by the question as by something else. Slipping off the bed, she walked to the window and drew the curtain aside. Light flooded the room. Michael watched her, naked against the window, staring into the street below. Rain streamed across the glass. The sound of traffic came up to them, drifting and incomplete.

"I want to tell you something, Michael. But you have to promise me that you will not say a word about it to anyone else. Least of all to your friend Tom Holly. Will you promise me that?"

She turned and looked at him. It was a sad, sad look, a lost look. He nodded.

"You must tell me," she said. "You must say it."

"I promise. Whatever it is you have to say, it'll be safe with me. I swear."

She nodded and turned her face back to the window. Rain trickled down the glass, a fat drop followed by dozens of lesser ones plowed a smudged path from top to bottom.

"About a year ago," she began, "I was given information that led to the discovery of a nineteenth-dynasty tomb on the Giza plateau, not far from the pyramids. It was a little tomb belonging to a priest called Nekht-harhebi. It had been built for him and his wife Teshat sometime around 1300 B.C., in the reign of the first Seti, the pharaoh Menma' atre'. He was the fourth pharaoh after Tutankhamun, if that means anything."

He said nothing, so she went on.

"The tomb was not intact. It had been robbed quite early on and re-sealed. But just beyond the main burial chamber we found eight bodies, all mummified, all in a poor state of preservation. We had them shipped back to the museum and asked the trustees for permission to unwrap one of them. Surprisingly, they gave the go-ahead, provided we didn't hold a public unwrapping. That would have stirred up trouble, you see. With the beardies.''

She took a deep breath, then hurried on.

"My colleague Ayyub Megdi and I were given the task of unwrapping the body. I was the one who performed the actual unwrapping, under his supervision.''

She turned round again, looking into the room, but not at him. Her eyes were fixed in his direction, but she was seeing something else. Not a hotel room in Oxford, but a cellar room in a museum in Cairo; no tangled sheets on which she had just been making love, but the bandages she had stripped away from a dead man; not Michael, but the man on the table, lifeless, dressed in a modern tie and suit. She remembered the tie, she had bought it herself.

"It was Rashid. It was my husband. They had wrapped him in bandages and left him there as a present.''

10

The Bentley slid to a halt immediately opposite the door. A servant was already waiting at the foot of the steps, but the man in the rear seat did not move. The servant would not open the door for him until he had been given the signal. The next moment the car carrying the visitor's personal bodyguards drew up behind. The guards got out, checked the driveway, the steps, and the front of the house. All seemed safe. One of them spoke briefly into a handset, then nodded. The servant appeared at the car door with a large umbrella.

Al-Qurtubi stepped out. He almost regretted the umbrella. This was his first time in England, and he had rather looked forward to enjoying some autumnal weather. Where he came from, the leaves did not turn golden before they fell. There was summer and there was winter, and what lay between was barely noticeable.

Sir Lionel Bailey was waiting at the top of the steps. Al-Qurtubi recognized him from the photographs with which his intelligence people had supplied him. The aristocratic bearing and lordly manner did not, in fact, go back much more than two generations, three at the most, as al-

Qurtubi well knew. His own nobility stretched back fourteen centuries. But it was not breeding he sought, after all, it was power. And power was something Lionel Bailey and his friends possessed in abundance.

There was no need for an interpreter to perform the introductions. Al-Qurtubi spoke English very well. Not that either man really required an introduction. Each knew who the other was and what each expected from the other. In his full beard and flowing robes, al-Qurtubi made an incongruous figure, standing on the steps of a country house in Kent. His host, waiting to receive him, scrutinized his guest carefully. Was this indeed the man they had been waiting for? Would he be capable of delivering what they wanted, and in the measure in which they required it?

"Mr. al-Qurtubi?" Sir Lionel exclaimed, stretching out one hand in welcome, yet remaining firmly fixed on the top step. No need to get himself wet on account of the little wog, was there? "I'm pleased that we meet at last."

The rumor was that their guest was not an Arab at all, but an Italian or Spaniard or something of that ilk. A Catholic who had converted to Islam in his youth and gone on to become a leading light among the zealot population. All that was speculation, of course. What mattered to Bailey was that al-Qurtubi headed one of the least compromising fundamentalist groups in the Arab world, that he exercised unquestioned authority over an extensive network of devotees, including many in Europe, and that he was willing to sup with the devil—in this case, Sir Lionel and friends—in exchange for their assistance in the achievement of his own goals.

"And I, Sir Lionel. I hope this will be the first of many meetings."

Sir Lionel pressed his best smile onto his lips. Not if he could help it, it wouldn't. He had no intention of becoming bosom pals with a darkie fanatic or his grubby cohorts. Their alliance was purely for reasons of self-interest on both sides.

They chattered on about nothing in particular for a few

minutes. Bailey had kept his wife and daughters out of sight, partly in deference to what he supposed would be his guest's prejudices, partly because he wanted knowledge of today's little chinwag to be restricted to as tight a circle as possible.

"If you're ready, perhaps we can proceed to the conference room, Mr. al-Qurtubi. My colleagues are waiting for you in the library. They're most impatient to set eyes on you at last."

The library had been built less to house books than to flatter the aspirations of those who owned but—let it be admitted—seldom if ever read any of them. The English aristocracy has never indulged in the intellectual pretension of their Continental cousins, but they have always been suckers for the charms of large rooms lined with leather and furnished with heavy armchairs of the same material.

Bailey normally reserved the room for business meetings. He could not see much other use for it. A long oak table of somewhat ornate design, with room for eighteen guests at a sitting, took up most of the center of the floor. Twelve of its chairs were now occupied. As Bailey entered, followed at once by al-Qurtubi, the entire assembly rose to its feet, as it had been primed to do. A log fire burned in the great hearth, throwing sharp shadows all round the room. Sir Lionel showed the guest of honor to a chair at the head of the table, then introduced him to each of his fellow guests in turn.

Al-Qurtubi knew who each one was. If the truth were known, he probably knew much more about any one of them than Sir Lionel himself. His intelligence operation was subtle, discreet, and more efficient than that of any medium-sized Western state. Had he not been convinced that these men could offer him precisely those benefits he could not easily obtain elsewhere, he would not have been in this room or even in England. Apart from Sir Lionel, three of the men around the table were English; two were French, two German, one Italian, one Spanish, two Dutch, and one Austrian. They were all either middle-aged or elderly: well-traveled, serious, dedicated men. They had not come here to make money or to win prestige or to seek personal advancement. All those things they already possessed, insofar as they wanted them.

When all was quiet, al-Qurtubi was invited to address the gathering. He did so in a quiet, unhurried voice, the voice of a man accustomed to being listened to in perfect silence. The only sounds other than his voice were those of sparks flaring in the broad chimney, of an occasional log cracking, of ashes settling in the spacious grate.

"Gentlemen," he began, "thank you for inviting me here today, and for having the patience to listen to me. You have been exceptionally kind. In another place, at a different time, I believe we would be enemies. Perhaps we shall be enemies in the future, it is still too early to say—nor would it serve any purpose. Suffice it to say that, whatever our differences, they are not as great as our present common need. And let me say too that it is my conviction that, should we resolve that need, we will resolve those differences as well, insofar as they immediately affect us. Am I understood?"

He looked at their faces, one by one, testing, probing, looking for clues. But they were too experienced and too clever to give much away.

One of the Englishmen leaned forward.

"I think, Mr. al-Qurtubi," he began, mispronouncing the name as though its first letter was spoken as "kw" and not simply "k"—"that, before we proceed to any resolution of differences, my colleagues and I are entitled to a few answers about what happened in London last Friday. I have no wish to question the basic principle involved. We are all agreed that incidents of this kind, however regrettable, are necessary for the creation of a proper public awareness of the dimensions of our problem. And I have no desire to impugn the professionalism with which your agents carried out their work. Nevertheless, I am uneasy about the . . . scale of the event. Surely it is possible to instill terror in people without going quite so far, without so many casualties."

Around the table, a few heads nodded in agreement. Others revealed nothing of their feelings, whether they agreed with the speaker or not. Al-Qurtubi listened impassively. When the speaker had finished, he leaned forward a fraction.

"You don't think I wept on Friday night? You don't think I've been praying for the souls of the victims and the healing of their poor families? Do you really imagine that my heart has never bled for the innocents my people and I have slaughtered before this, or that it will never bleed in future? I am all compassion, my friends, I am flooded with compassion and pity. Believe me, if I could restore a single life of the lives that have been lost, don't you think I would do so? I never asked for the burden that has been placed on me. It compels me to actions for which I have little stomach, to actions in which I have no pleasure. But it is God Who has laid this on my shoulders, it is God Who drives me. I am merely an instrument of His will. You, though you may not acknowledge it, are also nothing but His instruments."

He paused, looking round. They were listening. Did no-one ever talk like this to them?

"It is His will that the peoples of Europe should rise up against the Muslims in their midst, and it is His will that I should open Egypt to them and give them refuge. But how is that to be achieved? By administering pinpricks, as the Irish have been doing for generations without success? By toying with violence under the restraint of compassion? By frightening a little, but holding back in the end?"

He paused, holding them with his eyes and voice alone.

"You must understand," he went on, "that we stand on the verge of incomprehensible darkness. If mankind is to be rescued, if our several destinies are to be fulfilled, the action we take must be brutal and uncompromising. What would you ask a surgeon to do if you came to him with a tumor? 'Operate gently, please, and don't cut too much away?' Or if your leg was gangrenous, would you ask him just to take off the foot but leave the rest, you might have some use for it?

"I beg you to consider this very seriously. Well over one hundred people died last Friday. Before we have finished, as many as three or four thousand will have died, perhaps many more. Does that seem excessive? Are you tempted to call everything off because of the pain that will cause, for fear of a few nights without sleep? But just consider. If we do not act, if we do not create terror in the very heart of this darkness, what will happen? How many will die then? Ten thousand? Twenty thousand? A million? Ten million? I leave the computation to you. This is a matter of sums, that's all."

A profound silence lay across the room. He had touched their deepest fears, as he had meant to. The fire flickered. A log crumbled to ash. On the hearth, a golden retriever twitched its ears in sleep.

"May I be permitted a question?" It was the Italian, Alessandro Pratolini, who spoke. Al-Qurtubi nodded. He was in control of them now. They would do his will, he could sense it.

"It is this. I have responsibility for the situation in Italy. We do not have the same numbers of immigrants as France or Germany or England, but we are under heavy pressure from countries like Albania, and our economy is less able to cope with the influx. Unless we stem the tide soon, there will be disaster in both North and South. But we must carry the Vatican with us. In a matter like this, we could not act without the Pope's blessing. But the new Pope is much too concerned about promoting international understanding to give a sympathetic ear to our complaint. Next year, he plans a conference in Jerusalem. He has to be convinced that you pose the greatest threat to the peace he wants to negotiate, and that your demands must be met if he is to be successful. I need to know what you propose to do about this problem."

Al-Qurtubi smiled for the first time.

"Surely this has been explained to you," he said. "You have nothing to fear. The Pope has been taken care of. He knows of me, though he still does not know who I am. What is important is who he thinks I am. Who he fears me to be. When the time comes, he will give no trouble. You have my word on that."

"Can you give me details?"

"Certainly. We will speak later, you and I, and I will answer any questions you may have. *Ma in fondo, non sarà un problema per noi. Mi creda.*"

Bailey glanced at al-Qurtubi. He would have to check with Pratolini later, whether he thought the man was indeed Italian. It was the sort of thing intelligence should have checked on long ago.

The meeting continued. Al-Qurtubi answered questions about his organization, his state of preparedness, his plans for action in Egypt and Europe. Each of the men present had at least one question, and al-Qurtubi seemed capable of answering them to their satisfaction. More than an hour later, Lionel Bailey glanced around the room.

"Well, gentlemen, are there any further questions?" He waited. "No? Very good. In that case, I'd like to ask Mr. al-Qurtubi whether he has any questions he'd like to put to us."

Al-Qurtubi did not respond immediately. They had probed and questioned him to the best of their ability, and he had given away nothing of substance. But still they were not entirely his, still they hesitated to place themselves and the forces they controlled entirely at his disposal. He would have to reel them in more tightly still.

He reached inside his robes and brought out a small packet, which he laid on the table. It was a thick envelope. Out of it he took several photographs and two cassette tapes. He laid the photographs side by side on the table in front of him. They were six by tens, black and white, crisp and well-focused.

"The man you see here"—he pointed to the first photograph—"and here, and again here, is Kurt Auerbach, director of the Middle East desk of the German Bundesamt für

Verfassungsschutz. These photographs were taken last week in Berlin, in a café on the Unter den Linden. These are close-ups. There are other photographs showing the wider situation. The man in this photograph . . . and this one"— he indicated two others—"is a senior official working for the EATC, the European Anti-Terrorist Commission. His name is Zwimmer. These two photographs are samples of several taken four days ago by means of a high-resolution telephoto lens in Bern, Switzerland."

He paused. They were all listening intently. One more than the others, he imagined.

"There is, of course, a third man who appears in all these photographs. You will have no difficulty in recognizing him. He is sitting two seats to your left, Sir Lionel."

The man thus indicated was Paul Müller, one of the two German representatives. He had gone gray. With a visible effort, he turned to al-Qurtubi.

"Does this mean that you have had people secretly following me and photographing me without my permission?"

"It would appear so, yes."

"Then I must protest. What you have been doing could place us all in jeopardy. Contact with these men is an essential part of intelligence-gathering for our organization. Details of my conversations with them will be made available as always in my monthly report. I . . ."

"There is no need for that," said al-Qurtubi. He held up the cassettes one at a time. "These tapes were made at the time the photographs were taken, using a spike microphone. You can play them in full later, if you wish. For the moment, here is an excerpt."

Taking a tiny cassette player from his pocket, he placed it on the table and slipped one of the tapes inside. He pressed a button and at once the room filled with a slight hissing sound that exploded moments later into words. The conversation was in German. Not everyone around the table spoke the language, but several did, and that was enough.

Müller's face changed rapidly from gray to white. Al-Qurtubi pressed a second button and the tape stopped.

"I think we have heard enough," he said.

"For God's sake, you can't allow this . . ." Müller started to protest.

"Shut up," snapped Bailey. Then, turning to al-Qurtubi, he said, "If these are genuine and Mr. Müller has indeed passed on what he knows, our entire operation may be at risk. You understand that, don't you?"

"It seems," said al-Qurtubi, "that I understand it rather better than any of you. My people have been watching Herr Müller very closely for several months now. Last week was his first attempt to—what is the term you use?—to 'blow the whistle.' When you have listened to these tapes or read through the transcripts I have had made, you will see that he did a very thorough job."

"Then that's it," said Bailey. "It is, I suppose, only a matter of time now."

"Not quite. As Herr Müller himself will tell you, no-one else in either the BfV or EATC was informed of these meetings. Müller wanted to do a deal, and he knew he would get a lot further if he made his confessions to single individuals in the first instance. That, however, was a serious mistake. It was not a very difficult task to ensure that neither Auerbach nor Zwimmer reached his office the following morning. The matter has been taken care of. Your security remains as tight as it ever was. The problem remains what we should do with Herr Müller."

"We'll take care of that."

"No, I don't think so." Al-Qurtubi's voice was sharp and his tone definite. "I could have no confidence in that. All this talk of compassion makes me nervous." He stood, pushing back his chair.

Lionel Bailey felt the hairs rise on the back of his neck. Things were no longer going as he had planned. The little Arab was getting above himself.

"I think . . ." he began, but al-Qurtubi cut him off with a single, withering look.

"This is absurd," protested Müller. "I was the last person who would have betrayed you. You know that. He has faked the whole thing. Those tapes are forgeries. You can test them. There are tests, you know."

Müller was a fat man. His breathing came and went with difficulty, and as he grew more agitated, his lungs had to labor harder and harder to bring air in and push it out.

"You are only making things worse for yourself," said al-Qurtubi. He had moved close to Müller now. "It is not enough that you have tried to betray us, but now you accuse me of falsehood in the eyes of honest men."

No-one moved. It was as though al-Qurtubi had hypnotized them. Perhaps he had. He took another step, bringing himself close to the German. The room was filled with a terrible sense of expectancy. From his pocket al-Qurtubi took something that resembled at first glance a long pencil. On closer inspection, it revealed itself to be a pointed metal rod about a quarter of an inch thick and nine inches long.

Müller tried to back away from him, but al-Qurtubi reached out and pulled the German towards himself by the front of his collar. The fat man whimpered but said nothing. Al-Qurtubi raised the rod and inserted it, point inwards, into the hollow of Müller's ear.

"Does that feel uncomfortable?" he asked.

Müller nodded awkwardly.

"Ye . . . yes," he muttered.

"The tapes are no forgeries, are they, Herr Müller?"

The German whimpered again. Al-Qurtubi pushed the rod a little further in, hard against Müller's eardrum.

"I said, they are not forgeries, are they?"

"No," whispered Müller.

"They are perfectly genuine recordings. You betrayed us, did you not?"

Silence. The rod twisted further, causing Müller to

wince with pain. A trickle of blood ran from his inner ear onto the lobe.

"Did you not?"

"Yes, yes. Of course." Müller was sweating pints now, moisture poured down his forehead and cheeks and dripped onto his expensive suit. "But it's been taken care of. No harm has been done."

All around the table, silence floated down like threads on still air. No-one breathed. Al-Qurtubi smiled with pity.

"Yes," he murmured, "it's all been taken care of."

With a single action, he pushed the long rod home, deep into Müller's skull. The German jerked once, violently, then fell away from his executioner's grasp and toppled heavily to the floor.

Al-Qurtubi returned to his seat without a word. They were his now, to do with as he wished. Müller's confession had been a bonus. After all, there had been no need. Not when he knew that the tapes were, indeed, forgeries, that the German had been, as Müller himself had protested, quite the last person who would have betrayed them.

11

Vatican City
11 September

Tomaso Albertini paused to stretch his back. It was acting up again, and he knew it would not be long before he had to go back to the hospital for treatment. They would tell him, as they had told him so many times before, that a man of his age should take it easy. If he had to work, they would say, he should find a job that did not involve so much manual labor. But that would mean leaving the Vatican and finding work elsewhere. The very idea terrified him. He was sixty-one, he had worked in the Vatican since he was a boy, just like his father before him, and he knew he would never find a job that did not involve hard physical labor. What did doctors know? Even if it killed him, he would go on working here.

Pushing his ancient cleaning cart in front of him, he headed wearily across St Peter's Square to begin his day's work. It was five-thirty and the air was still freezing. All around him, a deathly hush squeezed the city tight. No rushing cars, no blaring horns, no tourists. Just an old man with his brooms walking slowly through the cold and dark.

He looked up to his right, to the complex of buildings above Bernini's northern portico. It was all so familiar, he could see it in the dark: the great square, the curving pillars, the obelisk, the twin fountains, the awesome dome towering over the world. But he was not interested in any of those things. One thing alone drew his attention: a lighted window on the top floor of the Apostolic Palace, in the section devoted to the Papal Apartments. The light was in the Pope's bedroom. Tomaso crossed himself devoutly as he did every morning. It reassured him to know that the Holy Father was, like him, awake. It comforted him to feel that, even before the sun rose over the dome of St Peter's, the Vicar of Christ was already up and praying for the souls of men.

He pushed his cart, shivering a little in the bitter cold. His back could wait another couple of months. He had more worrisome things to think about: his grand-daughter Nicoletta and her unfortunate marriage to that Sicilian; his wife's operation; the money he had managed to save towards a little Fiat. Preoccupied, he did not notice the light go out on the top floor of the Apostolic Palace.

The Holy Father looked tired, thought Paul Hunt. Tired and gray, as though weighed down with the worries of the world. He had known the old man when he was bishop of Dublin: Martin O'Neill, the simplest and the best of men. And he had rejoiced when he was elected Pope: the first Irish Pope, bearing the regnal name of Innocent XIV. But now he was not so sure. The very qualities that made him so loved by the faithful and so admired by non-Catholics were destroying him. He was, Paul thought, simply too sensitive for the burden of the Papacy. In a gentler age, he might have been a great Pope, perhaps a saint among Popes. But today, in this harshest of ages . . .

They were in the little private chapel near the Pope's bedroom. Normally the Pontiff would stay here alone until seven o'clock, when he would be joined by other members of the Papal household, including his secretaries. But this morning was different. This morning, instructions had been given to admit Father Hunt to the Pope's private apartments before anyone else. The Swiss Guard at the top of the stairs of the Third Loggia had been ordered by the Pope's personal secretary to permit him to pass.

The two men were sitting together quite informally at the rear of the chapel. On the floor beside them stood a stack of files. The Pope's head was bowed, resting on his thin hands. On one finger glittered a huge ring bearing his Papal seal. When Innocent died, it would be taken from his hand and broken in half by the Papal Chamberlain. So quickly did the trappings of majesty disappear.

Paul sat upright, staring at the red light flickering on the little altar. All around them, the centuries sat watching.

The Pope lifted his head. He was dressed simply in white vestments. On his feet he still wore the plain blue slippers he had put on by his bedside. Thin, gold-rimmed spectacles rested on a narrow nose. His eyes were the eyes of someone who has known suffering but has never acquiesced in it: sad eyes clouded with anger. But this morning, the anger had almost entirely gone. In its place was a look of apprehension.

"I'm very tired, Paul," said the Pope. "Sometimes I think I have always been tired." The soft Irish accent drifted through the dimly lit room, almost out of place among the Italianate fittings.

"I'm sorry, Your Holiness. Perhaps I can return later. It is still very early."

The Pope shook his head and smiled briefly.

"No, no. I asked you to come at this hour. It is the only time I have to myself. In just over an hour I have to meet with the Tardella to go over preparations for the Holy Year. It is a very heavy burden, to be Pope in such a year."

Paul looked sorrowfully at the old man. What he had to tell him would greatly add to his burdens. Had he the right to do so? Had he the right not to? He remembered Martin O'Neill well from the year he had spent in Dublin, attached to the nunciature. The bishop's commitment to peace, his willingness to speak with anyone in the hope of encouraging dialogue, his burning vision of an Ireland free from hatred.

And he remembered the fusillade of machine-gun fire that had torn into O'Neill's car one Sunday afternoon on a visit to Belfast. He had been there, in the car behind, he had seen the blood and the pain, he had traveled in the ambulance holding the bishop's hand. How long ago it seemed now. Long ago and far away.

"Do you still intend to visit Jerusalem?" Paul asked.

The Pope nodded slowly.

"Yes," he whispered. "I have no choice."

"It may be dangerous," said Paul.

"I am no stranger to that."

"I know that very well, Your Holiness. I intended no disrespect."

"None was taken. I am too old to worry about such things."

"Then let me tell you frankly that I believe the projected visit to Jerusalem to be . . . unwise. Not only for you, but for the region. You know what is happening in Egypt. Passions are inflamed. These recent terrorist outrages in Europe have stirred up bad feeling everywhere. There is a possibility that the recent terrible killings in England were the work of Muslim extremists. Certainly, there are already rumors to that effect. There may be retaliation against Muslims. Your own condemnation of the outrages has had a mixed reception. For a Pope to visit Jerusalem at this time . . ."

"It's the holiest of cities, Paul. Even holier than Rome. And next year will be the holiest of years in any of our lifetimes. It will mark the beginning of the third millennium since our Lord came to earth. It is the city where He was crucified. Where He rose from the dead. I have to go."

"Even in the face of protests? You know that *fatwas* have already been issued . . ."

The Pope raised his hand.

"I know all about the *fatwas,* Paul. Your people have kept me well informed. I have even been sent translations: 'Should the so-called Vicar of Christ set foot in al-Quds, he will do so as the chief of the oppressors and the lord of the crusaders.' I know them very well."

"Then you know there will be trouble."

"I will go there as a healer. Mine is a healing ministry. To all men. If I cannot bring peace to Jerusalem, where can I hope to bring it?"

"Jerusalem is not Belfast . . ." Paul caught the flicker of pain that passed across the Pope's eyes. "I'm sorry, Holy Father. I should not have said that."

"Why not? What you meant is that I did not bring peace to Belfast, that they are still killing one another there. I know you are right. I know I can hope for very little. But I still must go."

"They were killing Christians in Cairo three nights ago."

There had been an attack on Coptic shops in the north of the city. Six people had died.

"You do not have to remind me."

"They will soon be killing Muslims in Marseilles."

The Pope bowed his head, then glanced up at the little statue of the Virgin standing in a niche in the wall in front of him. She was a costly figure, decked in precious stones, a fine piece from the school of Bernini. Put up for auction, she might have fetched millions. Would that money serve to drive away some of the fear? Some of the hunger? Some of the desperation? He wished it were so simple.

"What do you really want to say to me, Paul?"

"It is not what I want to say, Holy Father. It is what I have to say."

"Then say it . . . I would like to hear what you have to tell me yourself. I may not have time to read all the files you have brought me."

"Your Holiness, you must promise me to keep them at all times in your private safe. No-one else must have access to them. I do not wish to appear as if I am giving you orders. But these files . . ."

"Is it as bad as that?"

"Yes," whispered Paul. He looked at the Pope. "Al-Qurtubi has been in England. We think he was there to meet with the leaders of a right-wing coalition group known as Z-19."

"Z-19? Have I heard of them before?"

"Possibly not, Your Holiness. Not, at least, under that name, though you will certainly know of some of its constituent groups. You'll find details in one of the files. Not very many, I'm afraid. Very little is actually known about them. Nevertheless, we think they may have been implicated in several terrorist attacks; never directly, but always through intermediaries. Z-19 itself is probably a very small band of influential individuals from several countries, each of whom will have both direct and indirect links with larger neo-fascist or racist groups. The figure 19 may possibly be a reference to their actual number, but we have no way at present of confirming that. We've been unable to establish the identities of any of them. However, the rumor is that they include top government officials and one or two extremely wealthy businessmen."

"To what end?"

"They're one of the groups that grew up in the wake of German reunification and the collapse of Communism in the east. They want to keep western Europe pure, or as pure as they can. That means keeping out Czechs, Poles, Albanians, and any other riff-raff they don't want to share their lives, wealth, and happiness with. It also means clearing out all immigrants from outside Europe—North Africans from France, Turks from Germany, Pakistanis, West Africans, even Chinese from Great Britain."

"To send them where?"

Paul shrugged.

"Back home, I suppose. That's usually what they say. Whatever it means."

"Does it mean anything?"

"Not a lot. Certainly not to second- and third-generation immigrants, the ones who were born and brought up in

Europe. Not to the countries of origin, who have neither room nor food for them."

"What would al-Qurtubi want with Z-19? Surely he doesn't believe he can charm them into mending their ways."

"No, I'm sure he isn't that naive. I rather suspect he wants to encourage them in some way. An anti-Muslim backlash in Europe would, in many ways, play into his hands."

"Again, to what end?"

"I'm not entirely sure. I think he may have helped them engineer the recent terrorist outrages in England. That would make some sort of sense. It would be in their joint interest to promote widespread instability. A breakdown of security would be certain to lead to draconian legislation and a police crackdown. If Z-19 could implicate Muslim terrorist cells, they might get a long way towards their objective."

"But that still doesn't explain what al-Qurtubi hopes to get out of it for his own cause. He'd be taking an enormous risk with his followers."

"We're still doing our best to infiltrate his organization, Your Holiness. But that isn't easy. And it's even harder getting close to him personally. I have one man who may be able to do it, but he's reluctant, and I'm wary of pushing him."

The Pope nodded.

"Yes. Yes, I understand. You've achieved a great deal, Paul, there's no need to apologize." The Pope hesitated. His eyes rested for a moment on the Virgin. "Tell me, Paul: what about al-Qurtubi himself? Have you reached any conclusions yet? Is he who we think he is?"

Paul closed his eyes. For the longest moment in his life, for the longest moment in the life of the Church, he held his breath. The Pope watched him, knowing how much hinged on his reply. An entire world, millions of souls.

"Yes," said Paul. He opened his eyes. "I believe that is exactly who he is."

A long silence followed, a silence filled with the tiny, human sounds of the city coming to life outside. The faint light of dawn scraped at a tiny window high up above the altar. The Pope looked into Paul's eyes, the eyes of a man in very deep pain.

"Help me to the altar," he said.

Paul helped him out of his wheelchair, held him firmly as he limped to the low steps and knelt down. Few people guessed how much pain the old man endured merely to kneel. But Paul knew, Paul had been in the hospital, Paul had seen them cut away the trousers, had seen what the bullets had done to the bishop's legs. He knelt beside him.

No-one came. The Pope had left instructions that he and his visitor were not to be disturbed. The sound of voices from the rooms beyond came faintly to their ears. They ignored them and continued praying.

Paul looked up once and caught sight of the crucifix above the altar. And for the hundredth time that week, his thoughts returned to the prophecies of St Malachy.

Malachy had been an Irish priest of the twelfth century: Abbot of Bangor, Bishop of Connor, finally Primate of Armagh. He had died in 1148 at Clairvaux, in the arms of St Bernard. In the middle of the sixteenth century, a Benedictine historian called Wion had revealed a string of prophecies made by Malachy, prophecies that foretold in roundabout fashion the identities of the next one hundred and twelve Popes.

For those who believed in the prophecies—and there were many in the Church who did—the election of Innocent XIV had been a momentous event. Malachy allowed for only one hundred and twelve successors to the See of Peter, the last of whom was to be Petrus Romanus—Peter the Roman. According to the order of the prophecies, Innocent—referred to by Malachy as Gloria Olivae, "The glory of the olive"—would be the last Pope to reign before Petrus. With the second millennium drawing to a close, it would soon be time for the fulfillment of the saint's last words:

"In the final persecution of the Holy Roman Church there will reign Peter the Roman, who will feed his flock among many tribulations; after which the seven-hilled city will be destroyed and the dreadful Judge will judge the people."

Paul shivered inwardly, wondering how long this frail old man seated before him would live. How long it would be before the "dreadful Judge" appeared and Rome was made a ruin.

At last the Pope finished his prayers. Paul got to his feet and helped him back to his chair.

"I think it is time to go," the Pope said. "People are waiting. They get impatient if they have to wait too long. Even for a Pope."

He smiled. The old, winning smile, the smile that had won so many to his side.

Paul stood and went behind the wheelchair.

"I had the dream again last night, Paul," whispered the Pope. Paul felt his heart skip.

"I too," he said.

"The black pyramid. I was deep inside it, very deep. I think he was close. Much closer than before. I am afraid that I shall soon see his face."

There was a dreadful silence. Paul started and turned. He thought he had heard, high up, the rustling of wings. And he knew they were not the wings of angels.

II

"I will make the land of
Egypt desolate in the midst
of the countries that are
desolate, and her cities
among the cities that are
laid waste shall be desolate
forty years: and I will scatter
the Egyptians among the
nations, and will disperse
them through the countries"

EZEKIEL 29:12

12

Cairo
Monday, 22 November

For the second year running, winter lay on Egypt like a curse. Wild-eyed men walked through rain-soaked streets like Jeremiahs, prophesying destruction. Frost undermined the foundations of old buildings. Snow settled further south than it had ever been recorded. At times, the Nile was hidden in mist, at times the desert sparkled with ice. And the voices of goats echoed on high escarpments, there were omens in everything, the horizon was full of blood.

He saw her almost every day. Most nights they slept together, though they kept separate apartments, for the sake of appearances and to reassure her watchers. Appearances had become increasingly important in Cairo since the summer. As winter deepened, so too did the mood of the people. Every day there were long processions in the streets. Men and women in black clothes chanted slogans until they were hoarse, then returned the next day to chant them again.

In the bazaars, Rushdies were on sale everywhere. A "Rushdie" was a rag doll in the form of a bearded man. It came in varying sizes and costumes. The doll had cute little horns on its temples, and red eyes, and it came suspended by the neck from a miniature wooden gallows. On the doll's forehead the Star of David was sewn in blue and white. People hung their Rushdies in their windows or propped them up in the backs of cars. They had become popular presents. Children loved to play with them. They would take turns at being executioner.

Michael and A'isha got on with their lives, knowing that, at any moment, the Rushdies might no longer be dolls or the gallows tinderwood. He taught his courses at the university to dwindling classes. His views were increasingly unpopular with the students, and more than once he got embroiled in bad arguments with intense young men in beards who decried him as an imperialist stooge. He never knew how to answer their jibes.

A'isha went most days to Nekht-harhebi's tomb, where she and Megdi were still working. They had kept the identity of the mummy secret. Megdi and his assistant, Butrus Shidyaq, had disposed of Rashid Manfaluti's remains in the museum's furnace-room. The substitution of a rather nondescript mummy from the store-rooms had allowed them to conceal the discovery from the Board of Directors. A'isha still kept knowledge of the death hidden from her husband's supporters, who needed to believe in his eventual return from captivity, as though he were some sort of messianic figure, a Christ or a Hidden Imam. She knew better, but said nothing. She didn't think telling anyone would help. There had been "leaks" in the press about Rashid's imminent release, in return for the lives of fundamentalists under sentence of death in Tanta, where they had assassinated seven members of the local Council. Someone, somewhere was playing an elaborate game.

It was a cold day, with a threat of snow in the air. There had been a power cut late in the afternoon, and the city was without lights. People huddled around kerosene or gas stoves, eating by candle-light or listening to news that was not news on battery-operated radios.

Michael and A'isha were walking hand-in-hand by the river. There was no-one near them, they were sure A'isha had not been followed. The darkness concealed them. In spite of difficulties, the feeling between them had not passed or diminished. In the time they had been together in Cairo, it had grown stronger, beyond their capacity to resist or change. Michael had never thought it possible to talk so openly, with so little concealment, to anyone. Thoughts and feelings had poured out of him: in bed after making love, over meals, during walks, in cafés and restaurants. His entire life had been turned upside down and inside out for A'isha's inspection, as though he craved her approval for his actions and inactions, not only those he contemplated, but those of the distant past. Now only one thing remained, and he was afraid to reveal it, for fear it would turn her against him, that it would blight their relationship forever.

"What is it, Michael? I've not seen you like this before."

"Like what?"

"Moody. You haven't said a word since we got here. We've been walking in silence. Don't tell me you're really operated by electricity."

"No," he laughed. "I carry my own batteries."

"What is it, then?"

She held his arm tightly. Above them, clouds scudded across a half moon. On the river, small boats bobbed up and down without a sound. The only lights were the lights of cars weaving through the darkened streets.

"Do you remember when we met?" he said. "We were introduced by a friend of mine called Holly. Tom Holly. I told you I thought he was a civil servant or something, and you said he was nothing of the sort, that he worked for British intelligence. You were quite right, of course. Tom Holly is the Desk Head for Egypt within the Secret Intelligence Service. MI6. He's been with them for a very long time. Before he was promoted, he worked here in Egypt. I . . . The thing is, love, Tom and I were colleagues. That's to say, I used to work for MI6 myself. All the things I told you about posts at British universities, about research trips—it was all lies."

"I know."

"What?"

"I've known since the beginning. Or guessed. I could never be sure whether or not you were still working for intelligence. Something made me think not."

"I resigned four years ago. Before that, I was Head of Station here in Cairo."

"So how come you never heard about me?"

"Oh, I'd heard about you all right. But your husband wasn't my responsibility. He belonged to my deputy, a man called Ronnie Perrone. Ronnie's the new Head of Station. You figured in his reports from time to time, but never prominently. I never made the connection when we met. Not until Tom told me."

"I see."

"You aren't angry?"

"Angry? Why?"

"Because I used to be a foreign agent. Your husband worked so hard for real Egyptian independence. People like me would have been anathema to him."

She shook her head.

"Not entirely. Oh, he would have had you expelled if he'd been in power and found out about you. But we all have to do what we think is right. He would have sent Egyptian spies into Israel or Libya."

"There's something else," he said. He felt cold, uneasy, as though confessing to an infidelity, as though their honeymoon was over now and the innocence of their affection irredeemably tainted.

"After we met," he went on, "Tom and I talked. He asked me to keep an eye on you. You're important to them, they want to keep you alive. I don't think they know about Rashid's death. Anyway, I agreed. I said I'd watch out for you."

"I know."

He looked at her, puzzled.

"You can't know."

"Of course I can. I do. It was obvious: why should he have introduced us? I probably knew before you did."

"And you still came for me that day? At the graveyard . . .?"

She nodded. He could barely see her do so.

"Yes," she said. "I'd fallen in love with you. And I knew, or thought I knew, that you felt the same way. So what did anything else matter?"

"Didn't you worry that I might sleep with you just in order to carry out my duties?"

She stopped and found him, slipping her arms around his neck.

"Yes," she whispered, "I was afraid of that. But only at the beginning, before we went to bed. There are some things it's not possible to fake."

"You're an attractive woman. It wouldn't be hard for a man to feel aroused by you."

She kissed him softly on the mouth.

At that moment, the lights started to come on. All along the riverside white globes hung suspended in the blackness, their ghostly shapes reflected in the water below.

"It's all right, then?" he asked.

"All right?"

"For me to love you."

"Do you?"

He looked at the river. An image of the moon hung suspended in the black water and a moment later was scrubbed out by a passing cloud. He drew her tightly to him. For thousands of years, he thought, lovers had been coming here to stand like this beneath just such a moon. Perhaps his mother and father had come here on a night like this, in the middle of the storm that would drive them from Egypt forever.

"Yes," he said. And he shivered as he said it, for he knew that another storm was coming.

13

Tuesday, 23 November

He stood on a raised marble platform placed precisely between the desert and the sown. At his back lay a river red with blood, in front of him the open sands. At intervals of ten or fifteen feet, two lines of huge black sphinxes ran back into the depths of the desert. One by one, they turned their heads to look at him, then looked away again. They were carved from basalt, their eyes were rubies, and they were garlanded with deep red flowers.

He knew that he had to walk down the long avenue, but for some reason he was reluctant to do so. As he hesitated, the bloodstained water of the river lapped around his heels and started rising over his feet. Nervously, he stepped forward in the direction of the sphinxes. Each one was about fifteen feet high. They towered above him as he walked between them, and he could hear them whispering together, though he could not make out the words.

He walked for a long time. Night came, then it was day again, and the desert had filled with heat. Curiously, snow was falling gently on the broad backs of the sphinxes. It lay stark and cold on the surface of the basalt. Not one flake fell upon the sand. He looked up and strained his eyes towards the distance. On the horizon he could make out a shape, a dark shape, like a mountain.

Suddenly, he was closer, much closer, and he could make out what lay ahead of him. A huge black pyramid rose towards the sky. It had been clad in marble, black marble polished until it shone and trembled with reflections. The avenue of sphinxes continued right up to a causeway leading to an entrance high in the pyramid's side. The whispering voices were much louder now. He could almost understand what they were saying. Almost understand, almost understand . . .

"Michael, are you all right?"

He woke with a start into semi-darkness. A'isha was holding him. He shivered and realized he was covered in a cold sweat. The room was icy, but he had thrown the covers off. Gently, A'isha replaced them.

"You were calling out," she said. "You were frightened."

"I . . . was dreaming."

"I know. What about?"

"I can't remember. My . . . my mind's a complete blank."

"You're all right now. Go back to sleep."

He sat up.

"It's cold," he said. "What time is it?"

She glanced at the clock.

"Nearly six o'clock. It'll soon be dawn."

"What time's my first lecture?"

"You should know."

"I can't even remember what day it is."

"Tuesday."

"Christ, I've got to talk about the bloody Ayyubids at nine. Half the buggers won't be there: I'm not exactly flavor of the month."

He reached for her. She was naked and warm beneath the sheets.

"Not now, Michael. I'm not awake."

"It'll wake you up."

She punched him on the shoulder.

"I do love you, you know," he whispered, still trying to pull her towards him.

"No you don't, you lust after me. It's not the same thing."

"Yes it is. I . . ." He stopped in mid-sentence.

"What's wrong?"

"Shhhhh."

She fell silent. For a moment she could hear nothing but the faint sound of her own breathing. Then, out of the morning, out of the dim sounds of the slowly waking city, she heard it: a deep rumbling sound like heavy stones rolling down a hill without force.

"What is it, Michael?"

"I'm not sure." He swung himself out of bed and crossed the room to the window. They had gone to his apartment in 'Abdin the night before. The bedroom window looked out into Muhammad Bey Farid.

Michael drew back the curtain softly and looked out. A pale dawn light had crept across the city and was struggling to push aside the darkness. He opened the window onto the chilly morning air, shivering. The sound came more loudly now; it was growing or coming closer, a roaring sound like heavy engines. He looked along the street both ways. He knew exactly what the sound was; he had heard it too many times in his army days to be mistaken. Tanks moving in formation through broad city streets.

Even as recognition dawned, he saw lights to the south, from the direction of Shari' al-Nasriyya. He waited patiently as the lights advanced slowly. He knew where they were heading, and he guessed what they were up to. The presidential palace was only a few streets away to the north. A little further to the west lay the parliament building. Throughout 'Abdin were scattered municipal and national government offices.

The tanks reached his window. They were M1A1 Abrams, US imports intended to defend Egypt against the possibility of Libyan attack, presents for Egypt's support during the Gulf War. Michael could not be certain whether they were moving on the palace to defend it or take it over.

"Turn on the radio," he said.

A'isha was standing just behind him. She went to the bedside and switched on the set, which was already tuned to a local station. Loud music filled the room. She turned the dial, and again the sound of an Egyptian dance band blared out at them. It was the same at every station.

"Keep it tuned to the main station."

"Do you think it's a coup?"

"Of course it is. We've got to find out quickly whether or not it's been successful."

He paused briefly, then closed the window. Still shivering, he found his dressing-gown and slipped it on. A'isha dressed quickly in the clothes she had been wearing the night before.

"Can you contact one of Rashid's people, someone in a position to tell us what's happening?"

She nodded.

"I think so."

"Then ring him now."

"Will it be safe? To use the telephone, I mean."

"I see no reason why not. The security people will have too much on their hands at the moment to worry about listening to wire taps."

She picked up the phone and punched in a number. It rang for over a minute before anyone answered.

"Samir? Is that you? This is A'isha."

"A'isha?" came the voice on the other end. "Where on earth have you been? I've been trying to get hold of you for the past two hours!"

"That isn't important, Samir. But I want to know what's going on."

"Going on? Good God, you mean you don't know?"

"Why do you think I'm ringing you?"

"The fundamentalists have taken control of the army and air force. It happened overnight. They're already in command of the radio and television stations, the telephone network, the airports, and the railway stations. We don't think there's much real chance of pushing them out. It was very well planned, much better than anything we imagined. Some troops loyal to the government are putting up a resistance in the provinces, but it looks like it's all over in Cairo.

"Listen, A'isha—we've got to get you into hiding. I'll send some men over. Where are you?"

"I'm sorry, Samir, but I'm not going into hiding."

"A'isha, it's more important than ever that we keep you safe. If they let Rashid out of captivity, . . ."

"Samir, Rashid won't be coming out. He's dead."

There was a brief silence on the other end. Then the voice resumed.

"You can't be sure of that. There's still a hope that . . ."

"I saw his body, Samir. I'm sorry I didn't tell you this before. Please, tell the others. It's too late to do anything now. Promise me."

"A'isha, this is just madness. You . . ."

She hung up. For the first time in her life, she hung the phone up on a man. For a moment she stood, her hand resting on the telephone, breathing deeply, her eyes shut fast. She had closed an important door behind her.

Opening her eyes, she turned and repeated to Michael what she had just been told.

"He was right, you know. You will have to go into hiding."

"You too? There's no need. They've got what they want. I'm no threat to them, and they must know about Rashid's death. Surely I can stay here at least. They'll have no reason to disturb you. Will they?"

"I'm not so sure. They may feel there are old scores to settle. But you should be all right for the next few days." He paused. "Will you stay here this morning? I've got to go out."

"Out?"

"I have to see Ronnie." He started dressing. "Before it's too late."

14

It was a short walk to Ronnie Perrone's. Ronnie lived in a cramped but elegant apartment in al-Azbakiyya, a series of rooms that had once formed part of an Italian-style *palazzo* built in the reign of Khedive Tawfiq and inhabited until the 1950s by a wealthy family of Greek hoteliers. Its faded grandeur and high ceilings were a canvas on which Perrone, a man of aristocratic tastes and civil service income, painted the little fantasies of *la vie élégante* around which he constructed his egg-shell existence.

Ronnie's cover was that of a dealer in antiques and fine art. He had learned the trade from his natural father, Reggie, who had run a small emporium on the King's Road, dealing in chinoiserie and souvenirs of India brought back to Bournemouth and Brighton by children of the Raj. Little Ronnie had been reared among jade and soapstone, porcelain and ivory. His first toys had been *okimonos* and *netsukes,* he had dressed up in Chinese shawls and Kashmir robes, he had played at soldiers wielding Mughal swords and the inlaid pistols of maharajahs. In time, his own tastes had turned to Islamic glass and metalwork, and after his recruitment to the service, his hobby had become his front. He dreamed of retirement to a real shop in a real street in England, with a strong man who would love him for himself.

When Michael let himself in, he found Ronnie already up, sitting on a gilt chair in his ornately chintzy drawing-room. He was dressed in an intricately patterned Georgina von Etsdorf dressing-gown, smoking a carefully rolled joint that he had placed incongruously in a long ivory cigarette holder.

The boy who had opened the door made himself scarce. Ronnie seemed to be in a foul temper.

"Michael. About bloody time. I've been trying to get you on the blower all morning."

"No, you haven't, Ronnie. I only left my place about twenty minutes ago."

"Well, I'm glad you've come. Take a seat."

Michael dropped into an armchair stuffed with horsehair-filled cushions. It was a good deal less comfortable than it looked.

"I take it you know what's going on, Ronnie."

"Know? I know sweet fucking nothing, Michael old son. No network, almost no contacts. I must be the last person in Cairo to know what's going on."

"Doesn't Loomis keep you in touch?"

Loomis was the CIA station chief at the US Embassy.

"Jesus, Michael, don't mention that man's name to me."

"I thought you and he were friends."

"I thought so too. I used to buy him birthday presents. He invited me to Christmas lunch last year. For God's sake, Michael—do you know what the bastard told me last week?"

Michael waited.

"He told me his own network was taken out round about the time they rubbed out mine. Can you believe that? They lose an entire operation and pretend nothing's wrong. He says he was under orders to say nothing. Orders? What sort of orders are those? Who ever heard of anybody giving orders like that?"

"I have, Ronnie. Often. So have you. You've given orders like that yourself."

"They were feeding us with false information, Michael. So we wouldn't guess they'd gone down. Didn't want the Israelis to get wind of it. Can you believe that? The Israelis!"

"Yes, I can believe it very well. You yourself were feeding false reports to Vauxhall until recently. However, that's not the point. I need to know just where this leaves us. If the people at Center know what they're doing, they'll have you out of here and picking up rent-boys on Piccadilly within twenty-four hours."

Ronnie made a pained expression.

"You don't have to be crude, Michael. In any case, there's no chance of that. I'm staying put."

"I don't think they'll give you much of a choice. Tom won't leave you here waiting to have your brains picked."

"They can't afford to pull me, Michael. I'm all they've got, barring Shukri and Rif'at; and neither of them is likely to be of much use at the moment."

"You're forgetting that Tom has me working for him again."

"And can't tell a soul about it. Forget it, Michael. As far as the top brass are concerned, I'm it. I've still got a good cover. If they'd been onto me, they'd have bumped me off when they cut off the network."

"I wouldn't be too sure about that, Ronnie. They may have had their reasons. And this coup could provide them with reasons to finish the job."

"I reckon I'm safe for another week or two anyway. Don't you think?"

"Have you been in touch with London yet?"

Perrone shook his head.

"Waste of time, Michael old boy. Still early days. No guarantee it'll stick."

"The way I heard it, it was sticking pretty hard."

"Possibly. But I want some degree of confirmation before I start anything rolling at that end. I'm expecting Shukri to get in touch. He's a good man. First-rate source. Never had a piece of pie from Ahmad that went off on me yet."

"I'd rather you left him out of it."

"Out of it? Ahmad? Why on earth? Not because of the woman, surely?"

"Yes, because of her. Precisely because of her."

"He is, Michael, as my ex-friend Mr. Loomis would no doubt say, 'my main man.' In fact, he's just about my only man. After Ahmad, it's street peddlers and little whores on the make. Not much of substance there, I can assure you. I promise you I won't let her get compromised. Tom's given me strict instructions about that." He paused. "How is she anyway? Have you checked?"

"She was with me last night."

"I rather hoped so. She'll have to go into hiding, of course."

"She doesn't intend to. You're not the only grade one lunatic in this city."

Perrone smiled wanly.

"I haven't offered you a smoke, my dear. Prime quality. Fresh in from Marrakesh last week."

"No thanks, Ronnie. I've got to keep a clear head."

"No better way."

"Honestly."

"Well, I'll have Abdi bring you in some coffee."

"No, just leave it for the moment, Ronnie. By the way, I think I'd watch little Abdi from now on, if I were you."

"I watch them all, dear; believe me. Always have done."

"Nevertheless, Abdi could be trouble. If this thing has come off, you'll be extremely vulnerable. To blackmail if nothing else. They'll be hanging your sort."

"What's new, Michael? That's all there's ever been. Do you think I've never been blackmailed before, never made a payoff to some rude little guttersnipe as eager to get his hands on my wallet as my cock? You'd be surprised how little it takes to send them on their way. You'd think it quite pathetic. Really, one only has to call their bluff. They'd have to lay an accusation in person, and who's going to do that? Eh?"

"All the same, Ronnie, do be careful. You've got a reputation. I don't like the look of young Abdi. Things won't be the same now. An anonymous tip-off is all it will take. Don't give him any reason to resent you."

"Would I do that, my dear?"

"Yes, Ronnie, you would. Just take care, will you?"

Ronnie nodded.

"Michael, let's leave my personal peccadilloes for the moment and turn to matters of greater moment. You've not been getting very far with your enquiries into al-Qurtubi's group, have you?"

Michael shook his head.

"I've never seen people clam up so quickly, Ronnie. Nobody's ever heard of him, except that you can see right away that they have. All the other lines I've been following have trickled out the same way, here, Alexandria, one in Tanta."

"Well, I'd like you to slip back to Alexandria, if you can manage it. Today or tomorrow if possible."

"You must be joking, Ronnie. There's just been a coup."

"Nevertheless. I'm serious, Michael. Something's come up. Do you remember that incident just after we got back to Cairo? Where some gunmen killed virtually all the passengers on a 225 headed for Edinburgh?"

"Of course I do. Why?"

"There were half a dozen survivors, all of them badly hurt, none of them able to remember very much. Except one. A broker of some sort called Blair. Lives in Edinburgh. He was in first class when it all started, in the first compartment. They left him for dead, but the bullets all missed vital organs. He won't walk again, but his brain's apparently in fine order. They've patched him together now, and a few days ago he started talking. Seems he got a good look at two men up his end who were part of the team. He remembers where they got on, what they were wearing, all that sort of thing. And . . ."—Ronnie paused—"best of all, he's identified one of them. A good ID, Michael, nothing half-baked about it. Blair's been in the TA, he's got a good head on his shoulders, he'll make a star witness. Defense won't be able to budge him a millimeter off track, or so I'm told. Solid gold."

"So?"

"The man he identified is a certain Eberhard Schwitters. Like the artist."

"Never heard of him."

"A Dadaist. You wouldn't like his stuff."

"No, I meant the terrorist."

"Well, as a matter of fact you have. Eberhard was one of the Germans who visited Alexandria last year to meet with members of al-Qurtubi's group. Remember now? In fact, he's been there at least twice, as far as we know."

"That doesn't take us much further forward. We know all about that meeting. Your man's description just gives us a link to the train shootings, that's all."

"Not quite. There's more. The anti-terrorist people did some back-checking on the ammunition and magazines used in the attack. They also did some work on the explosives used at King's Cross the week before. Customs and Excise did some digging about of their own. They found some entries that didn't quite tie up. A series of shipments from an operation calling itself the Misr Manganese Mining Company. The shipments in question left Alexandria between March and June this year on ships belonging to the Adriatica line. They consisted of parts for mining equipment, ostensibly on loan to an Italian subsidiary. All the shipping manifests were in order. The parts were delivered to Venice, moved by rail to Naples, where they were recrated by an Italian company called the Compagnia Mineraria de Napoli. The next step was to give them an Italian origin and fly them into Manchester, for delivery to a firm of mining engineers in Hull.

"Obviously, we have no firm evidence that the MMM shipments were tied to the incidents at King's Cross and on board the train; but the identification of Schwitters makes it much more probable. I want you to go to Alexandria and find out what you can about MMM."

"This all sounds to me a bit like shutting the stable door, Ronnie."

Perrone shook his head.

"I don't think so, Michael. I don't think our horse has bolted yet. I think he's still in the stable, pawing the ground and waiting to come out at a gallop. And the door is very far from bolted."

15

Michael and A'isha spent most of that morning listening to the radio. Television wasn't even on the air. Broadcasts recommenced shortly after nine, beginning with a long session of readings from the Qur'an. At half past ten, the supreme shaykh of al-Azhar, Muhammad Fadl Allah Hasanayn, came on the air with a pious sermon alluding to the duty of the believers to obey whomever God had set in power over them and to avoid all forms of civil disturbance as an evil as great as unbelief itself. There then followed more Quranic recitation, delivered this time by Shaykh 'Abd Al-Rahman Yusuf Hamuda, Egypt's leading exponent of the art.

At eleven o'clock precisely, the presenter introduced "his excellency 'Ali Nadim, head of the revolutionary command council and president-elect." Nadim had been the outlawed head of an extremist group known as the Difa' al-Nabi, "Defense of the Prophet." He spoke quietly and deliberately, but all the time they could sense how hard he had to struggle to keep a note of raw triumph from sneaking into his voice.

A group of Muslim officers had taken command of the

armed forces. The chiefs of staff had been arrested shortly before dawn and executed for the joint crimes of treason against the state and waging war against God. Their true punishment, intoned Nadim without emotion, would lie in the fires of hell.

Others were now in prison awaiting trial. The military and selected bands of Muslim activists were now in command of key installations throughout the country. All ports and airfields had been closed, and telephone communications with the outside world temporarily suspended "in order to allow the nation sufficient time in which to prepare itself to ward off the treacherous attacks that will, sooner rather than later, be launched against it by the forces of the imperialist, anti-Islamic powers, the Zionists, and the Freemasons."

Ex-President Sabri had been apprehended while attempting to flee the country with millions of dollars that he had stolen from the oppressed and long-suffering people of Egypt. He was currently under house arrest and would in due course be tried and punished for his multifarious crimes against Islam, against the Egyptian people, and against humanity in general.

"That's very sad," said A'isha when she heard the news about Sabri. "He was an honest man. He would never have stolen anything." She told Michael how she had met the ex-president more than once, and how she had admired him, even liked him. He had tried his best to bring prosperity to a country floundering in poverty and constantly paralyzed by the forces of reaction. Her husband Rashid had admired Sabri while decrying certain of his policies. He had once told her that, should he ever succeed in becoming president himself, there would always be a place in his cabinet for Abbas Sabri. The president had written to her privately after Rashid's disappearance, expressing real sympathy and promising to do all in his power to find him and secure his release.

Sabri's real crime, she knew, had been his passionate opposition to the constant religious interference in political and legal matters. She knew he would pay for that mistake with a rope round his neck.

Nadim promised retribution for the sins committed against God and His people. There would be a settling of accounts, a universal putting to rights. All should now examine their consciences and consider how they might best make amends for their past behavior. The best, the safest course of action, he said, was for those who feared they had done wrong or given offense, to hand themselves over to the newly established religious police, the *muhtasibin*. Towards those who repented and were prepared to mend their ways, the state was prepared to be generous. "God's arms are open wide," he said, "wide enough to embrace even the most hardened of sinners. Give yourselves up to His mercy. Do not expose yourselves to His wrath."

Having made his debut in history, Nadim set off to fulfill whatever destiny he thought was in store for him. There were more readings from the Qur'an, long Medinan *suras* devoted to the fate that lay in wait for the enemies of the Prophet, exhortations to the believers to lay down their lives and their belongings in God's path. Shortly after twelve, a man described as the Head of the Religious Police for Egypt came to the microphone. His name was 'Abd al-Karim Tawfiq, and he spoke in a flat voice, a voice from which all traces of individuality and humor had been mercilessly excised. It was like the voice of a surgeon talking about an amputation he is about to perform, who knows his audience is squeamish, but who does not really care.

He reiterated what Nadim had said about the benefits of giving oneself up before a squad of *muhtasibin* arrived at the front door. Then he proceeded to read out a long list of God's enemies whose fate had already been decided in their absence by secret religious courts set up for the purpose many years ago. These offenders would be arrested, arraigned before those same courts—now operating publicly—and properly sentenced. Though he did not say so, it needed little imagination to guess what their end would be.

Michael switched off the radio. The room filled at once with a tense, shivering silence. He stood and went to the window. Outside, nothing moved. The entire city was suspended, watchful, vibrant with fear. He could feel it creeping across the streets, a tangible, nervous force that slipped through dark alleyways and slithered past doors and windows, doors and windows behind which an entire population lay huddled with stale, bated breath, waiting for a knock.

He turned to A'isha. There were tears in her eyes, large, wounded tears that she struggled to hold back.

"Darling," he said, "I can't tell you what you should or shouldn't do. What happens now is your decision. But I'm worried that your life may be at risk. You aren't named in that list, but that's no reassurance. You can bet that's not the last list he's going to draw up. There are probably dozens of others already in circulation."

He paused. She said nothing, still stunned by the rapidity and extent of what had happened. Many of the names on the list were friends of hers, people she loved and admired.

"There's something I have to tell you," he said. "When I was with Ronnie this morning, I agreed to do something for him. I said I'd go back to Alexandria. There's something there that has to be investigated. I'm the only person who can do it. But I'm afraid. And I'm frightened to leave you here alone."

"I'll come with you, then."

He shook his head.

"No, that wouldn't be wise either."

"Why not?"

"It's out of the question, A'isha. Don't even ask me."

"Because it's dangerous?"

He nodded reluctantly.

"It would increase the danger for us both," he said. "Above all for you."

"Why are you allowed to take risks and I'm not? Who ever said it had to be like that?" She was growing flushed and angry. He was treating her the way every man had ever treated her since she had been a child. "Because you're a man and I'm not. That's what it comes down to, isn't it?"

Her anger troubled him.

"No," he said. "I don't think like that. It's because I'm a professional. I've been trained to look after myself. You haven't. It has nothing to do with maleness and femaleness. If you were a man, I'd still leave you behind. But if you were a female agent and I needed help, I'd take you with me. It's a dangerous mission, and I can't afford someone who may make mistakes. About whom I'd have to be worrying all the time. I . . . I don't want you to be killed, A'isha."

"Then why do you have to go at all?"

It wasn't easy to explain or justify, even to himself. But he tried. He told her about the bombings, about the train with its dolls and paperback books smeared with blood, about the mole in Vauxhall House and the untold harm he could do.

"Not just in London, A'isha, or in England. Here as well. Perhaps here more than anywhere. Whoever this man al-Qurtubi is, whatever he is, I think he may be infinitely more dangerous than any of the people behind this coup. We're already living on borrowed time here. Nobody's going to send in the cavalry to sort this out. These people aren't a threat to the West's oil supplies; they don't have nuclear weapons. All they're going to do is kill a lot of Egyptians and make life unbearable for a lot more. Nobody's going to go to war over that."

"No," she said. "That would be too easy, wouldn't it?" She paused. "Will you be gone long?"

"I don't know. I may be able to find out what I need to know in days; or it may take weeks. But I can't do it at all unless I know you're safe."

"I'll stay in my apartment. Rashid's people will keep an eye on me. There's . . ."

He shook his head.

"No, you won't be safe there. And I don't want any of

Rashid's friends to know your whereabouts. There are bound to be informers within a group like that. You won't know whom to trust. Isn't there anywhere else you can go, somewhere they won't think of?"

She thought for a while. They would look for her at her parents', at the homes of relatives.

"What about Megdi?" she said at last.

"The professor?"

She nodded.

"I know I can trust him," she said. "And he knows all about Rashid."

Michael nodded. That made sense.

"You're sure he can be trusted?"

"Absolutely."

"And you think he'd take you in?"

"I'm sure of it. He lives quite near here. In Imad al-Din."

"Fine. We'll go there later, once things settle down a bit. Stay here for now. We'll have something to eat. We ought to keep our spirits up."

He smiled and reached out a hand to stroke her cheek. Her skin felt cold. She did not move her head, but let him stroke her, like a cat that barely tolerates its owner's touch. Michael let his hand fall away slowly.

"We can't let this come between us," he whispered.

"Rashid used to talk like this," she said. "He didn't understand either."

"Understand what?"

"That duty isn't everything. That you have to find your real life in the cracks between the things that seem most important. It's what's responsible for all this killing. People putting the important things first, putting them first so often that, in time, there only are the important things, and nothing else matters. But it's the little things that make our lives. Rashid could never see that, so he got himself killed. This man Nadim, all these fanatics, they can't see the things that really matter to people. I wonder what they tell their wives and children. And you, Michael, you're just the same as them. You have to save the world, you don't care what happens to people like me who are just trying to make sense of little things."

"I don't care about the world," he said. "I care about you."

She looked up. Her tear-stained face was pallid, not from fear, he thought, not from anger, but from an incomprehension so intense it left her shocked and breathless. She was shivering, the room was cold, there was winter in everything.

"Do you?" she asked.

Outside, the day grew steadily colder. A bitter wind set in from the north. There was a smell of frost or of snow. The first car-loads of prisoners, their frightened faces concealed beneath sacks of cotton cloth, were driven stealthily to their cells.

In the street below, a man walked past slowly. As he passed, he glanced up at the window of Michael's apartment, then, taking a thin notebook from his pocket and a pen from another, he jotted something down. Replacing the pen and notebook, he walked on.

16

Monday, 29 November

Michael had been gone a week. To A'isha, it seemed more like a month. In the time they had been together, they had not been apart for more than a day at a time, and she took the separation badly, like an abandonment. She spent her days in Megdi's apartment like a caged bird, restlessly peering through half-shuttered windows onto streets that had only half returned to life.

Megdi went to the university every day, as had been his custom for over thirty years, when he was not working at the museum. Each time he brought back bad news. The new regime had lost no time in settling grudges. They had started clearing out the universities and colleges, places they associated with the western crusade against Islamic purity. At the American University and Cairo University, as well as at lesser institutions throughout the city, large numbers of teaching staff had received letters instructing them that their services were no longer required. Subject areas like sociology, anthropology, philosophy, and European culture had been closed down entirely. Others were being radically reshaped to suit the requirements of the new ideology. Teachers of Islamic sciences—the Qur'an, Traditions, hermeneutics, law—were being drafted in from mosques and Qur'an schools throughout the country.

All this was serious enough, but more disturbing was the news of the arrests of both staff and students on and off campus. Arrests and, if reports were to be believed, executions. Megdi checked discreetly at the museum for enquiries about A'isha, but it seemed that she had not as yet attracted the attention of the authorities. Her absence from work had been noted, and she would soon have to make up her mind about whether to return or not. To stay away too long would look like an admission of guilt of some kind.

Once, she went outside to telephone Michael at the Cecil Hotel, where he was staying. They found themselves talking about unimportant things and were briefly comforted by it. He told her nothing of his work or how it was proceeding. No-one knew how many phones were tapped.

This morning, Megdi had gone in to the university as usual. He was due to deliver a lecture on the Kushite Viceregency at 10.00 A.M. At 10.30, he was back at the apartment.

"It's all right, A'isha," he called out as he entered. "It's me, Ayyub. I've come back early."

She came into the hallway and stopped short. The professor was leaning against the door, his eyes tightly shut, his body limp. He was breathing heavily, and clearly agitated. His white hair was disheveled, the sleeve of his coat torn. He looked as though he had been in a fight.

Hearing her, he opened his eyes.

"They're shutting us down," he muttered, his voice gravelly and indistinct. She had never seen him like this before. Taking his arm, she helped him walk to the livingroom.

"What happened to you? What did they do?"

He sank into a chair and fell forward, burying his face in his hands.

"Are you all right, Ayyub? Shall I call a doctor?"

He shook his head slowly, then began to straighten up.

"Turn on the radio," he said.

It was part of their arrangement that, whenever he was

out, A'isha had to preserve a strict silence. When he was around, they would talk in whispers or in soft voices while the radio played music in the background. She switched the set on and found a music program. They were playing classical pieces for the *oud*. Popular songs had been banned.

"I got into an argument," he said. "There was a disagreement. A group of these *muhtasibin*. Religious policemen! Such a stupid concept. Some of them were former students of mine. Can you believe that? You remember Salim Ahmad. Did a Ph.D. about five years ago. On Nubia."

She nodded. She remembered.

"He was one of them. A leading light, from what I could gather. He told me . . ." The old man shivered. His face was ashen. "He said I was an enemy of God because I'd spent my life resurrecting the past. *Jahiliyya,* he called it, the age of barbarism before Islam. I was glorifying it, he said, giving it a glamor it did not deserve. Digging up the bodies of unbelieving kings, putting the figures of false gods in glass cases for the public to see and worship. He reminded me of what the Prophet did when he conquered Mecca and smashed the idols in the Kaaba. They would do the same, he said, they would do the same. And this time they would show no compassion."

She sat beside him. Her heart was sinking, she had started to understand.

"What did you mean, 'they're shutting us down'?"

He looked at her with anguish in his eyes.

"The department. Archaeology is a proscribed subject. No, that's not quite true. Islamic archaeology is to be encouraged. But the study of *jahiliyya* must end. The . . ." He stumbled, as though his tongue was rebelling against the words. "The museum is to be closed down and its contents sold or destroyed."

"But . . ."

"Everything, A'isha. Everything we've ever worked to rescue or preserve. The ancient sites are off limits. I think . . . I'm really afraid they mean to destroy some of them."

"Destroy them? What would be the point of that? Surely . . ."

"They're talking about cleansing the country of all traces of *jahiliyya,* of whatever is un-Islamic. Physically and in the mind. There's no knowing what they're capable of. They see the world with such a narrow vision."

She brought him a drink, a large brandy in a crystal glass. He drank it eagerly and began to relax.

"We'll have to go sparingly with this stuff, my dear," he said between sips. "They're pouring all the booze in Egypt down the drain. There must be some very tight rats in the sewers."

She laughed and shook her head.

"Now, you know that isn't true, Ayyub. All the rats are above ground."

"You mustn't say things like that, A'isha. It'll get you into trouble."

She looked round the walls of the room that were shutting her in like the walls of a prison.

"I think I'm in enough trouble already," she said.

"Can't your young man get you out of this?" Megdi asked. "I'm not so lacking in worldly wisdom not to guess that he must have contacts in useful places. Why doesn't he get his people to have you taken out of Egypt? There are always ways."

"His people?"

"The British. Don't tell me they wouldn't be glad to have you. Once a viable opposition movement gets started in Europe, you could be immensely useful. You could help build up a moderate wing. I think you should give it some thought."

She looked away.

"You know that's not what I want," she said. "And as for the British, or anyone else for that matter—who knows what they may want? If they decide they can do business with this regime, they'll just go straight ahead. Anybody likely to cause them embarrassment will find himself on the first flight home. The new immigration laws in Europe make it very easy to get rid of political misfits.''

"You could demand political asylum. Not many people would have as good a case as yours."

She shook her head.

"My case would only be as good as current foreign policy allowed. They might let me in one day and ship me out the next."

"Why don't you and Mr. Hunt get married, then?"

"You know that isn't possible."

"Why? Because of Rashid?"

She nodded.

"Then you are taking a political stance."

"Perhaps. Ayyub, I don't want to talk about this any more. It's too early to come to any decision."

"You may not have the luxury of very much time in which to think it over."

"I'm sorry. I'll find somewhere else to stay. This is only making things difficult for you."

"I didn't mean that. You know you can stay here as long as you like. I enjoy having you here. If we stick to the rules we set ourselves, no-one will guess you're here. No, I just meant that things generally are likely to get much worse. Staying here only postpones your finding some sort of solution."

"I know. And what about you? What are you going to do now? How will you live? Did they offer you some sort of pension?"

He laughed.

"You know what that little prick Salim Ahmad said? He told me I should buy some brushes and polish, and set myself up as a shoeshine boy, so I could be of some benefit to society for once in my life."

"Didn't you ask him what he'd done a Ph.D. for?"

"That was the start of the argument."

"What about right away? Do you have anything in mind?"

"Oh, yes," he said. He stood and picked up his coat from the chair onto which A'isha had thrown it. He glanced ruefully at the torn sleeve, then slipped the coat on.

"I'm going to Giza," he said. "I overheard one of them saying something about work they had in hand at the pyramids. After what they said about destroying ancient sites, I'd like to see for myself what they're up to."

"You're crazy. You can't go out there. The site will be cordoned off."

"Perhaps. But I have to see for myself. If they are defacing the monuments, somebody has to get word out. Start an international protest through UNESCO."

"I'll come with you."

He shook his head.

"You'll do nothing of the sort. On my own, I can get away with it. If I had you with me, there'd be trouble for both of us. Stay here. When I've seen what's going on, we can talk about what to do."

He switched off the radio and kissed her lightly on the cheek.

The door closed, shutting her in to the silence, to the thoughts that circled like flies through her head. In the streets below, out of sight, she could hear the soft feet of God as He prowled the city on the search for sin.

17

By two o'clock, Megdi had not returned, and A'isha was growing anxious. She knew him too well to think that he would have taken foolish risks; but it took so little nowadays for someone to be arrested and hauled up before a revolutionary court.

Half an hour later, she slipped quietly out of the apartment. Several radio reports had mentioned new dress regulations for women, and Megdi had, accordingly, brought back for her a heavy ankle-length coat and black headscarf. Feeling tense and awkward, she set off to find a taxi.

It took a long time to find a driver willing to take a single woman as far as modern Giza on the other side of the river. She would have to walk the rest of the way to the pyramids "like everyone else" he said. She did not think to ask what he meant.

He left her on the western edge of the city, a little bit away from the Shari' al-Ahram, the broad tourist road lined with nightclubs that leads to the pyramids. She paid what he asked—an exorbitant sum—and set off for the road.

As she drew near it, she became aware of a loud humming noise, like the sound of bees fussing about a hive.

Then, coming around a corner between low houses, she saw that the road was thick with people, men and women in black robes. They were walking with their heads bent, shuffling along in a single direction, walking from the city westwards. Round their foreheads they wore bands of white cotton cloth bearing religious slogans, verses from the Qur'an or exclamations of piety, nothing more. Some walked in silence, others mumbled low prayers, moving their lips incessantly.

She stood by the roadside and watched them for a while. No-one turned to look at her. No-one talked. The only voices were those reciting prayers, a discordant mumbling from a thousand tongues. The shuffling of feet and an occasional cough were the only other sounds. Up here, close at hand, A'isha saw that there were children among the crowd, some too small to walk, being carried on their parents' shoulders. A few cried, but the majority were silent, cowed into impassivity by the funereal atmosphere around them.

She thought at first that that was what it was, a funeral, a huge procession for people who had died in the coup. But there were no corpses, no biers, no carts. The line stretched back as far as she could see, a vast black serpent disgorged by the city. Above, the sky was the color of old lead. There were no birds. However far she looked, A'isha could see no birds.

Without a word, she slipped into the crowd. A woman made way for her, but passed no remark and offered no greeting. Everyone seemed bent on his or her own thoughts. There was an intensity about the crowd, a seriousness of purpose that chilled A'isha to the bone. All about her, the murmuring of prayers rose and fell like a sea sound.

As they walked, she noticed people fallen by the side of the road, mainly old men and women. No-one stopped to tend them. No-one gave them so much as a second glance. She thought some of them were dead, that others soon would be. A'isha passed on without stopping. It was as though she was being drawn on by a tide, without volition or desire. The shuffling and the mumbling droned in her ears like an insanity. She wanted to lift her hands to blot them out, but she dared not draw attention to herself. She walked on, setting her pace by that of the crowd, wondering if she would ever be able to break free.

For some time now, she had been aware of a nagging uneasiness. Something was wrong, something that could not possibly be wrong. Then, as the procession turned a bend, she looked up towards her left. They should have been in sight of the pyramids long ago. The great bulk of Khufu's monument should be there, stark and stiff against the deserted horizon. But the air was empty. She looked again. Where the Great Pyramid should have been, a pale moon hung just above the horizon, insubstantial, like a planet in a dream. It might have been a trick of the light, but hard as she tried, she could see nothing but the moon.

Her heart in her mouth, she stumbled on. Somewhere, deep inside, she was beginning to understand. They had spoken to Megdi about the pyramids. The pyramids, those indestructible symbols of *jahiliyya*. She held her breath. There was frost in the air. There was a promise of rain.

As they drew near the Mena Palace Hotel, she moved to one side of the crowd in order to see more clearly. Ahead of her, on the plateau, was the largest of the three pyramids, or what was left of it. It had been demolished—or, rather, dismantled—to about half-way. Just over two hundred feet remained of the structure. Beyond it, she could see the corner of Khafre's pyramid, equally vandalized.

Without thinking, she turned to a woman on her right.

"I don't understand," she said. "Why are they pulling them down? What's the point?"

The woman looked at her as though she had just stepped off a spaceship.

"You don't know? Where have you been living? You must be the only person in the whole of Cairo who doesn't know about the *ahramat*. What are you doing here if you don't know?'' There was a flicker of suspicion in the woman's eyes.

A'isha stammered.

"I . . . I heard . . . there was work to do. That . . . that the government needed help.''

"Help?'' the woman sniffed. She was about forty, with a face that might have been soft if she had let it relax for just one moment. Her eyes bulged like little grapes in reddened sockets. There was a weight of sadness in them that threw the entire face into disarray. "They've got enough help. More of us every day now. This is my fifth day. They say we'll be finished by the end of the sacred month, but *Allahu a'lam*, God knows best.''

A'isha looked at the great mass that still remained. Finished? By the end of Ramadan? The month of fasting began in just over a week's time and finished twenty-eight days later. Five weeks to undo work that had taken decades?

"But why?'' she asked again. "What's it all for?''

"We're getting rid of *jahiliyya* for once and all. The pyramids, the temples, the idols. We're tearing down the false gods of Egypt. When we're finished here, we'll destroy the churches with their crosses and their icons.'' She paused for breath and pointed up the road ahead. "See those trucks? They're taking the bricks we pull down and carrying them off to build the wall.''

"Wall? What wall?'' A'isha began to wonder if the woman were not half-mad after all. Then she looked up at the half-dismantled pyramid and realized that any madness here was collective.

"The great wall we're building to protect us from the enemies of Islam. They say it will stretch around the whole of Egypt when it's finished and be ten meters high.''

As they drew even closer, she could make out a web of scaffolding on the east and north flanks of Khufu's pyramid, and pylons of heavy equipment being used to loosen the stones or load them into the waiting lorries. Most of the work was being done by hand, by hundreds upon hundreds of workers scattered across the faces of the monument. They covered it like an army of black flies battened on a corpse. And she alone among all these thousands was weeping.

Even as A'isha watched, a man high up near the much flattened top of the Great Pyramid lost his footing and plunged to his death on the rocks below, crashing and tumbling the whole way, taking at least three other men with him. A few people glanced around to register the accident, then turned back to the task of prising loose the bricks with what seemed like renewed enthusiasm. They would be martyrs, of course, the men who had fallen. Centuries ago, other men must have died in the raising up of the same bricks. A different age, different gods, but the selfsame futility, A'isha thought.

The procession had reached a series of check-points that had been set up at the point where the old Tourist Information Office had proclaimed the entrance to the pyramid enclosure. Some attempt was being made to organize labor at the site. A'isha supposed there would be food and drink later in the day, when the sun went down. Hastily erected sheds on the left, on the golf course, served, no doubt, as toilets, though very few people were coming or going between them. Beyond that, there did not seem to be any facilities.

As they arrived, most people were hastily assigned to work-teams on one of the three pyramids. Others were herded unceremoniously onto coaches that had been lined up along the branch road to Nazlat al-Samman. The woman told A'isha that the people on the coaches had been chosen for work on one of the several sections of wall already under construction, and that they would shortly be driven out to the desert in order to start work later in the day.

She said that A'isha would be assigned a face to work on at one of the pyramids, as well as a specific task. Women were employed chiefly in picking up fallen stones at the bottom and piling them into wicker baskets, which were collected every half hour or so by a refuse truck. Children of all ages in ragged clothes ran about fetching, carrying, stumbling on the naked rocks. For all that this was voluntary labor, many people seemed harried, a few distressed. A'isha noticed that armed men, whom she took to be religious police, were dispersed through the site at regular intervals. She wondered what would happen if someone took it into his head to throw down his tools and head for home. Somehow, she fancied it might not prove that easy.

She tried to hang back, thinking how best to get away from the crowd and make her way unobserved down to the southern field where the tomb was situated. She had an idea that Megdi might have headed there in some foolish attempt to rescue artifacts or equipment . . . But it was no good: the narrowness of the road and the surge of the people behind pressed her forward and into the jaws of a check-point. A *muhtasib* pinned a badge to her shoulder without once looking at her, and pointed.

"Follow the road around all the way to the right," he said. "You'll be at the small pyramid at the back. There are signs all the way."

"Menkaure"? Is that the one you mean?" she blurted out before she had time to think. She bit her lip.

He looked curiously at her, as though she had in some manner blasphemed.

"I don't know what they're called. We don't give names to the houses of idols. Get moving: there's no time to waste."

She felt herself pressed forward. Her badge bore a single number, "3," and by the roadside markers with the same number pointed towards the smallest of the three pyramids, the one nearest the southern field for which she was headed. That, at least, was one small mercy.

She had just reached a fork in the road, where one branch ran west and then south to the Khafre' and Menkaure' pyramids and another south-east for the Sphinx and the Valley Temple, when a man appeared out of nowhere and grabbed her fiercely by the arm.

"You," he said, "where have you been assigned?"

She pointed dumbly to her badge. He tore it away and threw it to the ground.

"You're needed elsewhere," he barked. "They've almost finished the little one, you'll just be left idle. I need more women to work on the wall. There's a coach ready to go. We've room for a couple more, but we've got to get moving."

And, keeping a tight grip on her arm, he began to pull A'isha in the direction of the line of coaches standing with their engines running on the ruined grass of the golf course.

18

They were perhaps fifteen yards from the coach when the man stopped and turned to A'isha. He drew her to one side and spoke rapidly in an undertone.

"Before you get on board," he said, "I'd like to check a few things. Are you carrying any money or jewelry?"

She looked at him blankly.

"Because if you are," he went on, "you'd better think fast. They'll take it away from you when you get out to the wall. They call it *tasfiyya*—purification. No-one working on the wall should bring with them any baggage from the world. We are all to depend on God. That's what they say."

He looked around. The last few passengers were boarding the buses. Engines were being revved.

"So make up your mind," he said. "Leave whatever you've got with me. I'll take care of it for you, skim off a few pennies for myself, hand it back to you when you're done. And . . ." He glanced at her more directly. "I'll see to it you don't have any heavy duties. I can see you're not bred to it. That sort of work can kill you if you aren't used to it."

A'isha thought quickly, as he had suggested. There might just be a way.

"I don't have any jewelry on me," she said. "But I know where you could find some. I'm . . ." She hesitated, wondering if this was wise. "I was an archaeologist. At the Cairo Museum. I was in charge of excavations out here in Giza. I know where you can lay your hands on a hoard of precious stones. We were digging a new tomb in the south field when the government closed us down. It isn't far. I can stay here and wait for you. We could go tonight."

He shook his head.

"How do I know where you'll be by then?" he said. "Are you telling me the truth? Are there really jewels out there?"

"It's a New Kingdom tomb, nineteenth dynasty, possibly from the reign of Seti I Menma' atre'. The owner of the tomb was a priest from the Amun temple in Karnak, Nekhtharhebi. We found several mummies and a chest of gold."

She could see the greed flicker in his eyes. Her evident knowledge had impressed him, made him alive to the possibility that she was telling the truth. And if she was not, she could see him calculating, she would be the one to suffer.

Without another word, he hailed one of the men standing beside the coach he was in charge of.

"Bilal, I've got something to check out. I won't be able to come on this trip. Explain to Tawfiq, will you?"

Bilal looked less than pleased at his commission, but he said nothing. He turned and jumped on the bus. A'isha noticed that it was filled with women. The driver and Bilal were the only males.

"Come on," said the coach organizer. He took her arm again.

"Which way?" he asked.

She pointed.

"We can take the road as far as the Sphinx," she said. "Then we can cut across country from there. But we'll need a light. The tomb hasn't been wired up yet."

He took her to a small hut where supplies were kept. In

a heap of assorted tools, he found an old oil lamp. It was about half-full.

It took them about fifteen minutes to reach the tomb. Away from the immediate area around the pyramids, a remarkable stillness hung over the site. A'isha could not hear herself breathe for the silence. Such an unaccustomed silence, louder than sound. The scuttling and the destruction seemed to be happening in a parallel world. The silence was an infection in the sky and sand. Out here, where the desert stretched away west almost as far as the Atlantic swells, only the past mattered. The pyramids were nothing now, just desolate, naked hills exposed to winter.

Her companion said nothing the whole way. He would not tell her his name, or anything about himself. Once or twice, she caught him giving her covert looks, as though sizing her up beneath her enveloping coat. She was acutely conscious of the risk they were taking, a solitary man and woman heading off into the desert alone. It seemed like an act of deliberate provocation, and her heart beat every time they passed near a *muhtasib*. But her companion had some sort of pass and a ready story about A'isha having been sent from the defunct Department of Antiquities to investigate the next phase of demolition.

They picked their way through piles of rubble, diggings, outcroppings. Twice A'isha stumbled, grazing her hands. The desert began here. Everything was parched and withered, a fit location for tombs and monstrous mountains of stone.

The exterior of the tomb was just as she remembered having left it. Her ability to find an entrance where no entrance seemed to be reinforced her companion's eagerness. He now believed her to have been telling the truth, he could sniff buried treasure, pharaonic loot. And maybe a little sexual recreation to round things off. He was hardly on his guard.

She let him go first. The boards that covered the way in had recently been dislodged. Once inside, it took her only seconds to find a rock big enough for what she had in mind. A week ago, she could not have brought herself to this; today, it seemed second nature.

He was standing at the top of the steps, holding the lamp high above his head, staring down into the blackness. Now that he stood on the threshold, a superstitious nervousness had come over him. He had heard stories of curses, of the dead wreaking a terrible revenge on the robbers of their tombs. He put the lamp on the ground, intending to go no further. He would send the woman in instead, she could bring the treasure out to him.

She brought the rock down hard just behind his right ear. He keeled over, almost toppling down the steps. Beside him, the lamp rocked once, throwing crazy shadows on the walls and ceiling.

19

In front of her stretched a straight, narrow passageway without embellishment of any kind. It had ended originally in a rough blank wall, as though the passage had in truth finished there, being no more than a false start, a trial shaft for a tomb that had never been finished. But robbers had seen through the deception centuries ago, as they had seen through so many others, and the traces they left behind had guided A'isha and Megdi to the mechanism that swung the wall and revealed a flight of steps leading downwards.

Today, the wall was wide open, the steps yawned black and threatening at A'isha's feet. She felt apprehensive, knowing what she had not know before: that someone had already been here several years earlier. Not robbers, but killers. For all she knew, they were still here, waiting for her. She called Megdi's name several times, but once the echoes died away there was only silence.

She stepped through the narrow opening, holding the lamp above her head. Darkness swallowed her up. Light was nothing here, or at most a gesture of defiance. What really mattered was the darkness. It was alive, it breathed and watched and listened, it reached out tangible fingers, it was heavy and full of flesh, it ate light, it grew fat on it, it slept and dreamed and woke again. She held her breath, passing a pit on her right, a deep shaft that they had not yet measured or entered. The walls of the passage had been gilded. As she passed, the mere movement caused whole panels of gold to flake away and flutter exhausted to the floor.

The passage opened into the antechamber in which they had found the mummies. It had been so clear in her memory, with the vividness of a dream: painted walls, gods in serried lines, scenes of harvest and hunting, the underworld receiving its latest guest, Osiris watching, the scales set, the heart of Nekht-harhebi in the balance, First Prophet of the House of Set.

She looked around. Someone had got here before her. The walls had been mutilated. They had scraped the paint from them like decorators preparing to apply undercoat. Someone had taken a hammer and chisel to the panels of carved hieroglyphic inscriptions, defacing them beyond recognition. It was as though some ancient priest had come to life, determined to erase the name of his enemy, to wrest from him the immortality that name conferred.

For a long time she stood stunned and witless in the mess of the little chamber, unable to make up her mind what to do. She picked up a piece of plaster, as though it might somehow be reassembled to form a god's head or a word. But she knew the tomb had been destroyed beyond hope of restoration. The question that nagged at her was why.

All the way back to the city she worried at the problem without making any headway. She made a wide circle around the pyramid area, slipping into the village of Nazlat al-Samman after it grew dark. 'Abd al-Ghaffar, the foreman of several digs, had fed her and taken her back to Cairo in the beaten-up truck he used for picking up his laborers. He already knew that there would be no more work for him or his men; but when A'isha asked what they would do, he merely shrugged and said that God would provide. She hoped God would prove a better provider than the people who acted in His name.

He left her at the museum. It was a forlorn hope, but she thought Megdi might have gone there. A light rain had started to fall. In the absence of tourists, the museum seemed almost comical. Comical and sad, like a church that has just lost its worshippers.

She headed straight for her office. The door of the departmental secretary's office was wide open. There was a light on. A'isha popped her head round the door.

"Fatna? Is that you? It's me, A'isha."

The secretary looked up, startled. She was standing in the middle of the floor surrounded by bundles of paper.

"Dr. Manfaluti . . . I . . . Are you all right? We thought something had happened to you."

A'isha stepped inside and closed the door behind her.

"I'm all right, Fatna," she said. "I thought it was . . . wiser not to come in for a few days. Until things settled down. What are you doing?"

"We've been told to be out by tomorrow. Have you heard?"

"Yes, I've heard." She did not say how. "Where are you putting all these papers?"

"They have to be burned. Everything has to be burned. Gamal is taking stuff down to the boiler room. To be incinerated."

A'isha felt a tremor of disgust run through her. Incinerated? Generations of notes, of records, of irreplaceable files.

"But . . ."

"There's nothing anyone can do. We argued. Everyone argued. But . . . You don't know what they're like, these *muhtasibin*. They don't think like you or me."

A'isha looked around at the empty shelves, at the cartons of files at her feet. They would bring their books of law

here, their dusty volumes of tradition and commentary, their
unreadable sermons and impenetrable works of theology.
She shivered. She felt sad and angry and helpless.

"Have you seen Professor Megdi?" she asked.

Fatna shook her head.

"Not all day?"

"No, he hasn't been in. It's one of his university days.
But I think they're shutting them down there as well."

"I see. Thank you, Fatna."

She turned and went to the door. Hesitating, she
turned again.

"What will you do, Fatna? Where will you go?"

"I really don't know. My father says he'll find me a
husband, that it's time I was married anyway. That's all there
is now." She hesitated. "Dr. Manfaluti, someone was here
asking for you. A few days ago it was. I told them . . . I said
I didn't know where you were."

"Who was it? Did he say?"

"There was more than one. Religious police, I think,
but I'm not sure; it's all so changed nowadays. You never
know who's who."

"I see. Well, thank you. Take care, Fatna."

"Yes. You too."

A'isha headed for her own office. The door was unlocked. Even before she opened it, she guessed what she
would find. For all that, it shocked her, the sheer malevo-
lence of it, the careful wrath visited on the room, doubtless
by the same hand that had laid waste the tomb. They were
all missing: every paper, every photograph, every record of
her survey of the upper chamber of the tomb, the only one
they had recorded so far.

He had been here all day, but his watch had almost ended.
In another hour, he could look forward to a cup of coffee
and a pastry. He would have liked some beer, or even better,
a woman; but his new bosses were touchy, he still had not

got the measure of them. So he behaved cautiously. A little at a time, just like before, judging how far he could go before somebody started to notice.

If he played his cards right, he would be off the streets and into an office job, as he had always wanted. These people responded to a few well-chosen expressions of piety, a *salla 'llah* here and an *astaghfaru 'llah* there. He would soon have them where he wanted them, no doubt of it. And he had other irons in the fire. The Dutchman was solid gold, if he could just work him the right way.

But at the moment, he was bored, and he was tired, and he was cold, and all he wanted was his coffee. The woman hadn't shown up in days, let alone anyone else. It was obvious that she'd smelled a rat and cleared off. There was a lot of that these days, people smelling rats. Some of the rats had four legs and a tail, of course, but you weren't supposed to say that in public. The other rats were of the usual variety, of human origin. She had smelled one all right.

He looked up suddenly. The woman coming down the museum steps looked as if she might fit the description. She must have slipped inside while he was having his last break. Well, he'd needed to pee—what of it? No-one would know. As she passed under a light, he felt a flicker of recognition. Yes, it could be her.

He detached himself from the shadows in which he had been lurking and began to follow her closely.

20

London
Tuesday, 30 November

England lay under shadow. The deep shadow, the pinched darkness, the dull throb of midwinter in a time of making and mending. There were no fires on the hilltops, no bright lights in the dark centers of the cities, the shopping malls, the unguarded, unguardable silent suburbs. Against the folding and unfolding of a gray sky, the wings of blackbirds caught the first rains of the night. People stayed indoors, measuring their lives by the dripping of water as it leached from the eaves.

They watched "Coronation Street" and "Neighbours," and re-runs of "Dallas" for the little variety they offered. Nobody cheered the heroes, nobody booed the villains; nobody cared. They passed their lives in front of flickering screens: their dreams of love, their hopes of fulfillment, their fears of violence were pale white fish that passed in deep water behind a wall of sparkling glass.

On the Thames, the lights of the long embankments were caught and changed to ripples. The river moved uneasily between its banks, eager to be out of the city. Here and there, solitary passers-by dawdled on the shore, not really waiting for anything or anyone. There were no tourists, hardly anyone came down from the provinces, half the lights were broken. A pleasure boat went by with a party of early revellers. Nobody waved as they went past. The river and the night swallowed them up as though they had never been: bobbing lights and boorish voices and popping corks.

The tall glass and concrete tower of Vauxhall House rose high above the streets like a ship at anchor. On the ninth floor, lights shone in a row of uncurtained windows. The clerical staff had gone home for the night, leaving behind a tribe of radio operators, cypher clerks, messengers, and heavily vetted cleaners.

From the ninth floor you could see quite a long way, across the roof of the Tate Gallery, towards Belgravia. From up here, the city looked peaceful, almost beautiful, almost in a state of resurrection. The Houses of Parliament were cut down to size. Someone had once remarked that a man could feel like God up here, with all the world spread before him.

The Director General did not feel like God; he did not feel very much at all. Just elevation without grace, a gnawing doubt that there might not be much point to his life after all. He had dedicated thirty years to protecting England from her external enemies, and all the while England had devoured her own flesh from within. He turned away from the window and the night and looked at the room and the long table and the men seated at it.

"Gentlemen," he said. "Thank you for coming. I'm sorry to call a meeting at such short notice. I know that several of you have important work in progress. But this is entirely necessary, I do assure you."

Heads nodded. Percy Haviland had called a meeting of the Heads of all Desks for the Middle East and West Asia. There were no observers. They were all there, the Regional Desk Heads for the Middle East, North Africa, the Gulf, and the Sub-Continent (Pakistan), together with several Station Desks: Egypt, Turkey, Syria, Israel, Saudi Arabia, Iraq, and Iran.

Haviland had been Director General—"Control"—for

ten years now, long enough for anyone. In a way, he thought his appointment had been a mistake. He was a Cold Warrior, he had cut his teeth on the Stasi and the KGB, first at the Foreign and Commonwealth Office, then at Century as Desk Head for East Germany, Poland, and finally Russia. His appointment had coincided almost exactly with the ending of the Cold War, the breaking down of the Berlin Wall, and the re-emergence of the Middle East as the chief focus for world events. The Gulf War had followed two years later. He had felt like a man in control of a beast whose nature he has never mastered.

Were any of them masters of the beast? he wondered. Looking around, he thought it curious that no-one at the table was old enough to remember Suez or the Baghdad Pact, at least not professionally. They were all veterans of the Iranian Revolution and the Gulf War; the oldest went back to the withdrawal from Aden. They knew their Middle East, of course they did, they spoke fluent Arabic and Hebrew, Turkish and Persian. They spent their weekends with Oxbridge dons and their evenings attending lectures at the School of Oriental and African Studies. They were paid-up members of the British Society for Middle East Studies and half a dozen similar organizations.

But it worried him, that gap of memory, that short-circuiting of experience that forced even the Heads of Desks to rely on books and dossiers and newspaper clippings for their briefings.

"Gentlemen," Haviland continued, "you will not need me to remind you that we last met as a group one month ago, when we discussed Tom Holly's report on the virtual elimination of Ronald Perrone's network in Egypt. In a private communication to me, Mr. Holly very properly expressed his concern that there had been a security leak here at Vauxhall House. I do not have to explain why it was not thought prudent to mention that suspicion during our meeting. However, I would be very surprised if you had not all reached the same conclusion yourselves.

"Following Mr. Holly's letter, I instituted an inquiry by Internal Security. Very discreet, of course. No need for alarm at this stage. As you all know, the IS boys do their job thoroughly. No stone unturned is their motto, I believe. So you will all be as relieved as I was to learn that they discovered not a trace of any leak in this establishment.

"Now . . ." The DG paused and cleared his throat. He had never felt at ease in this sort of situation. His stilted speech and awkward manner were barriers he erected to keep others at a distance. Subordinates were, after all, just that: subordinates. He disliked the democratic slovenliness that was creeping through Whitehall these days. Positive discrimination in favor of grammar school boys and polytechnic graduates. My God, they even called polytechnics universities now! He winced inwardly and carried on.

"We have just received information to the effect that our American colleagues have suffered the same distressing loss, and at about the same time. It appears they kept the matter quiet for what they call 'reasons of security.' Nevertheless, we do wish they had let us know earlier. It might have saved us a great deal of trouble. We might have concluded well before this that, wherever the leak originated, it could not have been here in Vauxhall House. Unless there were two simultaneous leaks—a proposition which I must say I find wholly preposterous.

"Now, our task is to find a link between the two networks, or at the very least between Mr. Perrone and his American counterpart. I have asked Mr. Holly to set about a fresh investigation to that end. I wish you to give him every cooperation. He may need some of your own Arab agents. I know some of you are under pressure at the moment. Nevertheless, I do think Mr. Holly's case deserves priority, in view of the overall situation in Egypt.

"And that, I think, must be my cue to ask for your situation reports. I have to prepare a position paper for tomorrow's JIC meeting."

The briefing continued for another two hours. There

were detailed reports on the continuing impact of the Egyptian revolution throughout the region. The one place no-one knew anything much about was Egypt itself. Foreign embassies were still functioning, but under enormous pressures and subject to strict limitations on the movement and activities of diplomatic personnel. Most of their energies since the coup had gone into advising and rescuing British workers trapped in the country. Getting information out of Egypt was next to impossible. Tom Holly felt blind and deaf.

There would be a Joint Intelligence Committee meeting the following afternoon, attended by the heads of SIS, GCHQ, Military Intelligence, and the Security Service, with representatives from the Foreign Office and the Cabinet Office Joint Intelligence Organization; Haviland would represent the SIS as usual.

Only when the great and good had deliberated would a formula be reached on what the PM would really be told. That in turn would be diluted considerably for the Cabinet. By the time it reached Parliament, it would be mainly water. The great British public would as usual be told just as much and as little as Whitehall decided it needed or deserved to know.

When everyone was gone, Percy Haviland took a thin cigarette case from his inside pocket. He allowed himself six cigarettes a day. It had once been five, but he had decided that that was too metric a figure and moved to half a dozen. Lighting one, he inhaled the smoke deeply, then blew it out again in a long, thin line. Closing the case, he slipped it back into his pocket.

He went to the door and opened it. Above him, a fluorescent light flickered fitfully, like the aura of a coming migraine. At the far end of the corridor, a cleaner was beginning her rounds, swinging a polishing machine back and forth across a floor of pale gray linoleum. The machine hummed gently. Its long orange flex snaked behind it, disappearing around a corner. All through the hours of darkness, she would move up and down her long, empty corridors.

And tomorrow the dust would settle again. Haviland thought it a perfect metaphor for all that went on in the building, in all the other buildings like it across the world.

He returned to his desk and picked up the telephone. Moments later, a voice answered.

"Gordon? It's Percy. They've all gone. I'd appreciate it if you could pop in. Just for a little chat." He paused. "I think," he said slowly, "we may have found Hunt's woman."

PART III

*"there may be blood throughout all the
land of Egypt . . ."*

Exodus 7:19

PART III

21

17 Shari' al-Ruway'i
Al-Azbakiyya
Cairo
30 November 1999
21 Sha'ban 1420

Dear Michael,

It is very late and I am alone. There are stars tonight, the first in over a week; I have come up to the roof to look at them. Where are you when I need you, Michael? I rang your hotel, the number you gave me. They said you were not there, that you had checked out. Would you leave Egypt altogether, leave without saying goodbye? No, you would never do that. But you might be forced to leave, they might come for you at midnight and put you on a plane. They do that now, there are rumors, stories passed surreptitiously through the bazaars. I am frightened, Michael; I am alone and frightened.

I have not seen Megdi since this morning and with each hour that passes I grow more afraid for

*him. I am back in my own apartment now, but I
know it is not safe. I try ringing Megdi, but he does
not answer.*

*I am on the roof and I am cold and I am fright-
ened. Why aren't you here tonight? Down in the
street below me, nothing is moving. No-one is laughing, no-one is weeping. It is all stillness. Stillness
and apprehension.*

*Michael, it's not just words. They're wholly seri-
ous about this thing, about this destruction of jahiliyya, this purification. Nothing is safe, no-one is
safe. The streets are silent tonight. We have become
a frightened people, those of us who do not stand in
lines and pray.*

*Let me tell you what happened, what I
saw . . .*

As she wrote, she hummed softly to herself, a song she had
sung in bed at night when she was a little girl, *anta 'umri*,
you are my life, a popular ballad by Umm Kulthum. Then,
the darkness had seemed to diminish around her, she had
been lifted to a place of safety far above the sleeping city,
almost as far as the stars themselves. Now, twenty years
later, she looked up from the letter on her lap and saw the
darkness like a great tower all about, a tower that spiraled
upwards from the rooftops to the sky and beyond. There
was no place of safety anywhere.

When she was a child, her whole family had slept on
the roof every night in summer. Even in winter she had gone
there often to be alone and to watch the stars in a sky
blacker than obsidian. Tonight, led by a flawed instinct, she
had come here to look at the same stars, as though their
permanence could shore up a dangerously tottering sense of
what was real. Stale roses grew in pots by the roof's edge.
They had no smell. There was no perfume in anything tonight. Her instinct had misled her. The stars were too far
away to be of any use to her.

I keep shivering, I keep thinking of the loss, the emptiness it will leave, the stupid, senseless waste. It was like this when I found Rashid. They knew, of course, they knew or hoped or conspired that I would be the one, the one to do the unwrapping. He was their gift to me, their warning. I can still remember that moment, that moment when I took the last bandage away.

He was wearing a suit, a dark suit, his best Armani suit crushed out of shape by the bandages. He was a time-traveler, Michael, he had no right to be there. That's the way it seemed, he was someone who had gone back thousands of years to die and be buried in someone else's tomb. It wasn't that at all, of course. He'd died in his own time. We all do that, we die in our own time. Have I told you that I love you? That I am dead without you?

To the west, less than a mile away, the river shuddered against its own blackness. She could make out a patch of naked water just beyond the slums of Bulaq, its edges barely lit. There were few lights anywhere: cinemas, nightclubs, restaurants, grand hotels had been closed or were threatened with closure. No-one was driving out late to Sahara City, no-one was walking hand-in-hand beside the Nile. Not even dreams, not even dreams . . .

In front of her, to the left, a single red light flashed on top of the Cairo Tower, warning low-flying aircraft away. Immediately to its right, a necklace of lights on 6 October Bridge joined Gezira Island to the mainland. They had recently renamed the bridge: it was now called Kubri Sayyid Qutb, after the fundamentalist martyr and writer. A few streets away, on the roof of the Omar Pasha mosque, a garish neon sign spelled the name of God in four-foot-high green letters. From time to time, the name flickered. Did God flicker? Did He come and go like a light, making and unmaking galaxies as He flashed off and on? What would happen if His name went out for good, if it was swallowed up by darkness like everything else?

A handful of lights, then the darkness and, beyond, the desert waiting for the city to die. A'isha shivered. Something was coming, she could smell it in the air. Something ugly, something damned.

Are you being careful, my love? Do you say your prayers at night? I know you do not believe, but I think you should pray all the same. I would pray to your Virgin if I thought she would listen, that anyone would listen. Our God has ninety-nine names. The Sufis say there is a hundredth name, a secret name. They say what they like about Him, He couldn't care less. Sometimes I think I have a secret name too, that God is not unique. They would kill me for that thought.

They used a long strip of white cloth, Sa'idi cotton, the best quality, to blind him in his last moments. Perhaps he prayed, sought for the hidden name. He must not have found it. One of them wrote something on the cloth in Arabic: mawt al-jahiliyya. "Death in the time of ignorance." Is that how I should translate it? Or perhaps "Death in a state of ignorance." Somehow, I think the first is more correct. You understand, of course, you understand better than I.

We burned it afterwards, of course, along with everything else. Skin and bone, and a white blindfold with a declaration of war. That was what it was, of course, wasn't it? A declaration of war. What else would you call it, Michael? Hatred? A failure of understanding? A kind of bitter love, perhaps? Maybe it was all those things together, Michael. So much in so few words. Butrus put them all into the furnace and burned them. The words too, he put them in there as well.

I wish you were here with me, I wish I could hold you, hear your voice.

I'll post this to your hotel. Perhaps they have a forwarding address for you after all, perhaps you will call there in a few days' time, perhaps you will never see this but be back with me here in Cairo, having a baklava and coffee at Groppi's. Maybe you are here already, maybe tonight is just a dream.

I forgot: they won't allow men and women to eat together any longer. Not at Groppi's, not at Fishawi's, not anywhere. The taboos are spreading, there is a new one every day: "Do this, don't do that." We have become a careful people. We watch our smallest actions. Our thoughts. Our dreams. It is like a cancer, Michael, it is like a cancer eating the city. Or a virus. A plague virus. Please write, Michael. Please come.

A'isha.

She laid down the pen, let the letter and the board it had been resting on slide to the ground. Standing, she wrapped her shawl more tightly around her shoulders and walked slowly to the edge of the roof. She held the parapet tightly, as though a wind might take her and waft her into space. With half-closed lips, she hummed a few more bars of the song, finally limping to a halt, as though she alone in that vast city were alive and singing, as though the silence had at last overwhelmed her. She was secret and silent, and her eyelids were heavy with memories that were not quite memories, dreams that were not quite dreams.

22

Alexandria
Wednesday, 15 December

He watched a seabird brace its wings against a steep wind before dropping as though stunned to a broken sea. Wind, and a high scattering of water, a taste of salt in the air, the waves green and curling, boats on a slack anchor in the eastern harbor, the deep horizon plummeted in a dark and dangerous wash of purple, as though painted in watercolors, the sky falling, geese stalling on a turning wind, the white Bride of the Sea encircled, golden, jeweled for the brief moment before darkness, the past echoing in the drab mirror of the present, the slapping of colored ships rising and falling in the long, weary harbor, Qaitbay honeyed by the setting sun.

Michael Hunt turned his back on the sea and began the slow walk back home, buffeted by a gray wind. The light was almost gone. On the tops of minarets, little twinkling lamps glimmered, lighthouses for the coming night. The *adhan* rustled through the streets. Figures appeared, shuffling singly and in groups to prayer. Veiled women scattered before him, hurrying out of sight. It was the beginning of Ramadan. The month of fasting lay ahead of the city, time of penance and denial from the moment a white and a black thread could be told apart.

Suddenly, the streets seemed inexpressibly dull to him, the unpainted houses, the broken pavements, the shuttered offices. Only summer could bring the city to life, and summer seemed further away than ever. He decided to head for Taha's. He would spend the evening over a cup of coffee, then try ringing A'isha again. His concern for her was growing rapidly.

Several times over the past few days he had telephoned, but there had been no reply. She had not been in touch. He had tried ringing the museum, only to be told that it had been closed for repairs. Megdi's department at the university seemed to have disappeared.

Taha's was a dingy café in the Karmus quarter where Michael was allowed to make and receive telephone calls. In the old days, in the time of Taha's father, it had been the hub of a small intellectual and gay community, mainly Greeks and Armenians, with a sprinkling of northern Europeans and gray-faced birds of passage. Durrell had dreamed of Justine like a spent moonbeam reflected in its windowpanes. At its marble tables Cavafy had sat sipping cup after bitter cup of *qahwa sada,* writing tired poems on tiny slips of Greek paper. Taha's had been the "dark café" where the poet and his poor dead friend had gone: "A knife in his heart Was the dark café where They used to go together."

Now, Taha's was a sad and lonely junction without roads where old men played backgammon in silence or read ragged copies of *Al-Jumhuriyya* or smoked cheap *ma'assil* tobacco through the long stems of *shishas* or coughed away what little remained of their thin and joyless lives. Spring and autumn, winter and summer, a slow fan with heavy blades revolved patiently through its faded, smoke-filled air.

Michael had gone there first as a boy of twelve, a solitary youth arrived too late to taste the city's greatness. Taha had befriended him, taught him the argot of Bahri Arabic, introduced him to what remained of café society. Together, they had walked the dark streets of a city where nothing remained but gestures in the afternoon and stale, redundant silences. Five years later, Taha had procured for Michael his first woman, a dark-eyed girl from Tanta with tiny, surprised breasts, and small white scars that crisscrossed her back, and a tongue that moved like a fish deep in his open mouth. Now Taha had grown old, old like his city, like his café. Old and arthritic and vulnerable.

"Someone was asking for you," the old man said, slipping the cup of hot coffee across the table.

Michael lifted his eyebrows. He wondered how much Taha really knew of him, of what he had been once. A little, perhaps, but only a little. Taha was like so many others, part of the fabric of Michael's deception woven over many years.

"I sent him off with a flea in his ear. Told him he was making a mistake, I'd never heard of you. But he'll be back."

Michael knew what that meant. How could you lie in times like these, with people like these? They knew the old man, knew his past, his father's past, the tormented history of a café for lonely men. No-one was safe now, no-one could be trusted, not even old friends.

Michael glanced round.

"Is there anyone here now I should watch out for?"

Taha shook his head.

"They're all regulars. You'll be all right."

Michael nodded. But they both knew there could be no certainty. If there was money on offer—and there was bound to be money—any one of Taha's regulars might be tempted.

They sat together for a while talking, two Egyptians, an old man and a younger man chatting about old times. If the people asking about him thought they were looking for an Englishman, they would be disappointed.

He lingered until closing time, just after ten o'clock. Before leaving, he tried Megdi's number again. It rang and rang, but no-one answered. When he left, the streets were almost deserted. People would be in bed early tonight, in order to wake before dawn to fill their stomachs for the day of fasting ahead. A sea chill drenched the air. He wished he still had the comfort of a hotel, but he had left the Cecil before going underground. Since then, he had changed a seedy room in Muharram Bey for one even seedier between the railway tracks and the Mahmudiyya Canal. He had little comfort there. In bed he could hear the sound of trains passing nearby, a desolate sound that woke him in the empty middle of the night and stayed with him long afterwards, even as far as dawn.

Everything was still. Mid-winter held the streets and alleyways in its grip. The clanking of the trams had fallen silent early tonight. The wind had fallen to a quiet murmur between buildings.

The footsteps had been behind him for several streets now, growing steadily closer all the time. He did not look round, did not quicken his pace. Walking steadily, he watched for the first opening. A few yards ahead, there was an alley on his right. A large puddle of water slanted across it. Ducking inside, Michael pressed himself against the wall, waiting. The footsteps grew unmistakably louder, still coming in his direction. He held his breath. A freight train passed with a ragged, jangling sound that turned to a high squeal of brakes as it reached the sharp bend at al-Jabbari.

A man came in sight through the opening, tight against the side of the street as he skirted the puddle. He stopped and looked all round him, as though puzzled. Now Michael was sure he had been following him. He waited, poised to attack.

"Mr. Hunt? Mr. Hunt, are you there?"

The voice was familiar, but Michael could not place it.

"Mr. Hunt, I have a message for you. Are you there?"

Michael remained in shadow.

"Who is it?" he asked.

"Mahmud from the hotel. I've been trying to find you."

Michael breathed a sigh of relief. He had bribed one of the clerks at the Cecil to leave messages for him at Taha's. Mahmud had been paid more than enough to ensure unswerving loyalty. Michael stepped into the street. Mahmud turned, startled.

"Mr. Hunt. I've been following you from Taha's. I reached the café just after you left. You walk very quickly."

"What is it, Mahmud?"

The clerk reached out a hand in which he clutched a crumpled envelope.

"This arrived for you this evening. From Cairo. It had been delayed."

Michael took the envelope. He walked a few paces further along the street to a lamp. The envelope was addressed to him at the Cecil. It had been posted in Cairo two weeks earlier. The writing on the front belonged to A'isha.

23

The train for Cairo got into Sidi Gabr station almost one hour late. He had wanted the earliest departure, the slow train that normally left Alexandria's Misr station at ten past six. It should have got to Sidi Gabr several minutes later, but that morning all traffic between Alexandria and the capital was being delayed. There had been no formal announcement to that effect, but somehow or other people knew. A whisper here, a shrug there. A picture was forming. Something was going on. Someone, somewhere, was getting jittery.

The contents of A'isha's letter had alarmed him, and he had decided against his better judgment to get back to Cairo at once. During the long hours he waited at the station, he thought more than once about turning back. He was known in Cairo, would be a sitting target for Abu Musa and his men, if they were still operating. And, knowing Abu Musa, Michael had little doubt that he would still be around.

A light drizzle slanted limply from a slate-gray sky. Here, where the sea came sweeping in like a darkness against the coast, and Africa was just a trick of tired light against a bent horizon, the rains came every winter, flat and cold, with the bitterness of another world in their hard and their soft descent. Michael shivered, turning his shoulders to the cold air. The Gulf War eight years ago was wreaking its revenge at last: on top of existing climatic shifts, the long months of smoke and burning oil had brought deep changes to the ecology of the region. It was the second such winter. Perhaps they would all be like this from now on.

He was dressed in a threadbare gray suit whose thin lapels were stained with grease spots, quite different from the one he had worn to Alexandria. His papers described him as Yunis Zuhdi, a resident of the working-class suburb of Shubra, a graduate of Cairo University, now a private language tutor, an educated loser teaching an anxious generation who would be losers like himself. He wore spectacles of plain glass and smoked cheap local cigarettes that made him cough. His chin was stubbled with three days' growth of grayish beard.

To make sure of a place on the train, he had been waiting on the platform since two o'clock. He felt the intimate warmth, the complex pressures of too much humanity on every side. Like a tiny figure at the center of an ant-hill, he watched busy formic shapes move darkly all around him. The damp air carried a twittering of many voices, high-pitched and staccato, like the voices of insects.

Families huddled together in untidy groups, fathers and mothers with ill-wrapped children clutching their legs or perched on weary shoulders. Food vendors moved awkwardly through the clamor, the rank odors of *fitir* and *ta'-miyya* sandwiches an assault on the early morning air. It was not yet dawn, not yet time to begin fasting. A few feet away from Michael, a boy had set up a shoe-repair stand. Beyond him, a legless beggar slipped lugubriously through a forest of legs, propelling his thin frame on powerful arms. Close to the platform's edge, a stringy *fellah* sat on a high wire cage full of wild quail, provender for restaurants on the brink of closing.

A seagull swooped low across the tracks, gray feathers

stained with salt. Michael looked up, his attention drawn by the flicker of wings in a cold sky. He could smell the sea, the purple sea, in the wind and the sour rain.

The train pulled in at last, drawn by an enormous Hungarian cargo diesel, a *"maghari,"* that should have been decommissioned years ago. It was already crowded with passengers who had boarded at Misr station. The third-class compartments were almost full.

Women with baskets mixed promiscuously with men carrying sacks or tools. Everyone seemed to be carrying something. Michael felt empty-handed, almost naked, but without a bag he was unencumbered and free to push his way through. Miraculously, he found a space on one of the wooden benches, between a crate of chickens and an old man with the hacking cough of a lifelong consumptive. From somewhere came the crackling sound of a transistor radio, the thin jangling of an oud.

The train finally crawled out of the station twenty minutes later, leaving behind almost as many as had clambered aboard. Some were perched on the roof, others clung precariously to the windows, a few hung dangerously close to the wheels. Michael lay back exhausted, searching for a fine edge of sleep on which to take refuge from the noise and stench. He dozed off, was jolted awake by the train's sudden motion or startled by a burst of coughing from the old man beside him, until at last, worn out by a succession of sleepless nights and simple physical weariness, he gave way to a dark and fretful sleep.

The train was at a standstill when he woke. A steady sound of hissing steam filled the air like a nest of angry vipers. The rain had stopped falling. The radio had fallen silent. Michael wore no watch, had no means of telling the time. The light had changed, but it seemed to be still early morning. He looked around the compartment. All about him, people were whispering or had fallen curiously silent. Frightened eyes met and looked away from one another. Outside, voices were raised. Orders were shouted, blurred and unintelligible. They had not stopped in a station, but stood stranded in open fields, barely visible to Michael from where he sat.

He stood and pushed his way to the window on his left. Outside, white mist shivered over fields of cotton. People were milling about, the roof-riders and the other hangers-on. Michael caught sight of a tall man in a white *thawb* striding up and down beside the track. In one hand he brandished a long stick with an iron ferrule, using it to keep the passengers in line. Further back, soldiers stood uneasily on the margins of the fields, guns pointing at the train. The first man was joined by a second, identically dressed. Beyond the fields, a line of water was barely visible through the mist: either an irrigation canal or the Rosetta branch of the Nile.

They had been stopped by the religious police, the newly established *shurta diniyya* or *muhtasibin,* a force modeled partly on earlier Islamic guardians of public morality and partly on the infamous Saudi *mutawi'in.* In the short time since their establishment, their reputation had been passed from mouth to mouth until there was no-one who did not live in dread of them.

It was the *muhtasibin*'s sworn duty to implement the traditional religious precept to "command good and prohibit evil." Like puritans everywhere, rather more of their energies were spent on the latter. They took as their authority for action, not the limited legislation of the new Islamic parliament, but the *fatwas* of a small group of senior shaykhs at al-Azhar. They were ubiquitous and they were ruthless.

They snatched china dolls from the hands of little girls and chessmen from the fingers of their fathers: both were contraventions of the law against idolatry. They smeared excrement on boxes of liqueur chocolates and broke the arms of pharmacists whose cough mixtures included alcohol. In narrow streets and the cluttered aisles of supermarkets, they descended on women without headcoverings and beat them hard with sticks. Couples strolling together were stopped at random and their papers checked: if they were not married to each other, they were arrested and hauled before a judge. They supervised public burnings of blasphemous books, from Nadim al-'Alawi's translation of *The Satanic Verses* to the novels of Nagib Mahfouz.

Oblivious of his surroundings, Michael watched as little groups of men, women, and children were marched off the train and huddled into lines beneath the vigilant guns. That so many of his fellow-passengers might be considered sinners seemed to him at once unsurprising and outrageous. Systematically, the *muhtasibin* moved through the train, from air-conditioned first-class down to the cramped compartments of third. Michael had never known an Egyptian train so hushed or its occupants so cowed. He wondered if the *muhtasibin* were looking for him.

Two white-robed men stepped into the compartment, their sharp eyes already scanning the tangled rows of passengers, prying out sin amidst poverty. Michael thought he would be safe if he kept his head. The chief concern of the *muhtasibin,* as of all moralists, was visible innocence and visible guilt. They did not concern themselves with the invisible world of thoughts, they did not search hearts. Those were oceans in which they dared not swim. Michael's papers had been painstakingly prepared for him by 'Abd al-Farid Nassim, the most skillful forger in the whole of Alexandria. They had already taken him through more than one checkpoint. He felt sure of them. His face and dress would excite no comment.

"Ismak ayh?"

Michael raised his head: a tired man, a wounded man, a man it would be easy to forget.

"Your name?" repeated the *muhtasib.* Michael studied him warily from beneath half-closed lids. A hard mouth, dreaming eyes, the skin tense against the cheek-bones, thin and bright against the temples. Not a man for compromise.

"Yunis."

"Yunis what? What's your family name?"

"Zuhdi."

"Speak up!"

"Zuhdi, sir."

"Let me see your papers."

Michael reached inside his jacket and drew out a battered wallet. He extracted his identity card and other documents. In spite of the cold, in spite of his confidence in 'Abd al-Farid's superlative skills, he felt himself beginning to sweat. The *muhtasib* scrutinized the papers carefully. Michael wondered why he was being singled out. Had they circulated his photograph already?

"Address?"

Michael repeated the address he had memorized.

"Occupation?"

"Teacher. I teach English. For university entrance."

"In Shubra?"

"No, sir. People in Shubra can't afford tuition. I go mostly to homes in Misr al-Jadida. They have more money there."

"It says here that you have spent time abroad."

"Yes, sir. Two years in London. To improve my English."

"You realize residence abroad is now an offense?"

Michael felt a worm twist inside his stomach.

"Living abroad?"

"Outside Dar al-Islam. It has been made a punishable offense."

Dar al-Islam: the realm of Islam, all countries under Muslim rule.

"I'm sorry," said Michael carefully. "I didn't realize. Is it a new ruling?"

"Stand up."

"I'm sorry?"

The *muhtasib* grabbed Michael by his left arm and hauled him roughly to his feet. For a second, training almost took over, and he barely stopped himself moving in to counter the assault. Instead he staggered as he tried to find his balance. The *muhtasib* turned and gestured to a soldier positioned at one end of the compartment.

"This one," he snapped.

"What's wrong?" Michael shouted. "What have I done?" Dimly, he realized he was not the only one shouting, that others were being hauled to their feet and hustled to the door. He looked round. Those fellow-passengers who had not been picked on were looking away, at the floor, through windows, pretending to be deaf and dumb and blind.

Suddenly, the shouting stopped, as though a wand had been waved or a switch pulled. No-one moved. There was perfect silence. A moment later it was broken. A gunshot rang out, thin and etiolated in a vastness of white fields. It was followed a few seconds later by another. The shouting began again, intensified now and despairing.

24

The soldier took Michael roughly by the wrist and dragged him down the aisle. The crowds that had been jamming the passage gave way miraculously before them, like turbulent waters parting. Outside, two guns fired almost simultaneously. The soldier got behind Michael and pushed him through the door, down the steep steps to the cinders beyond the track.

There were two lines, one of men and one of women, and behind them a staggered line of soldiers with guns. In front of each line, Michael now saw for the first time, a low trench had been dug. Two *muhtasibin* walked slowly behind the lines, ignoring the cries of the women and the pleas of the men. Each held a pistol in his hand, which he would place at the base of the skull of his next victim. Michael saw a legless beggar shot where he lay and his body kicked into the open ditch. He saw a man dressed in the turban and robes of a religious teacher dragged to the edge and shot without pity, a verse of the Qur'an half-completed on his lips. He watched as a tall man was bayoneted and riddled with bullets.

Michael was pressed hard against a passenger from his

own carriage, a young man who looked like a student. On the ground at the youth's feet lay a paperback book, its pages ripped and torn. Michael looked closely. The title was just visible, stained with mud: *Qissa madinatayn,* an Arabic translation of *A Tale of Two Cities.* The young man was shaking like a leaf, unable to comprehend what was happening. As Michael was pushed in close, the boy took his arm.

"Can't we do something?" he pleaded. A shot rang out further along the row. They were getting closer.

"I don't understand what's going on," said Michael. "Why did they arrest you?"

The boy pointed at the book in the mud.

"For that," he moaned. "For reading that. They say it's part of *jahiliyya,* that I'm tainted, we're all tainted. I'm a Muslim, a good Muslim. I recited the *shahada,* but they wouldn't listen. It was just a book."

And in an instant Michael understood. He remembered Cambodia, what the Khmer Rouge had done, the eradication of all book learning, all urban taints, all foreign influences. Year Zero. The killing fields. The past wiped out in a blizzard of deaths like a landscape blotted out by snow.

In the mist, a white-robed *muhtasib* stalked up and down the rows, staring into faces, looking away again. Behind the lines, his companions carried on their grisly task. Blood seeped into the wet ground. The train got up steam and slowly started to draw away from them. Michael saw faces at the windows, both horrified and relieved, pale faces in a mist pulling away from him forever.

The executioner reached the boy. Michael felt him stiffen as the gun barrel touched the nape of his neck, felt a shudder pass through his body, heard the shot and its echo, felt him become nothing. Blood spattered the pages of the ruined book. Michael looked round and saw the train receding in the distance, a small red light swagging through the thickening mist, as far away as life itself.

The cold barrel of a gun touched his neck like early frost.

Those moments, watching the train slide softly into a bank of soundless mist, were the longest Michael had ever known. They seemed to stretch in front of him forever, they became lifetimes, fragments of eternity. He died and was reborn a hundred times. But his life did not flash before his eyes: only his death.

A voice rang out: "Not that one." Only long afterwards did he link the voice and what was said to himself. "Not that one. I want to speak to him."

Instead of the expected bullet, he felt a rough hand between his shoulderblades, pushing him forward. He toppled, thinking he must be dead and alive at one and the same instant. There was no pain anywhere. A gunshot sounded far, far away, and his body pressed down like a vast weight into the stinking mud. His cheek grazed the cheek of the boy they had shot for reading a book. The boy's skin was still warm.

A hand grabbed him by his jacket collar and hauled him forward.

"Stand up! You aren't dead."

He felt his knees beneath him, quaking, his feet slipping on wet earth. Everything was dark. All at once, he realized he had been screwing his eyes tight shut against the explosion that had not come. Opening them, he saw a man's shoes, black against the loose fabric of a white *thawb*.

The stranger hauled Michael out of the trench and set him on his feet. He was a tall man, with a smooth face and long, dim lashes over restless eyes. The eyes had been burned through with fever. Not physical fever, but a nervous inner heat that had left him scarred and angry: a ferocity of the spirit that consumed whatever it did not perfect. Michael expected thin lips, but saw instead the outline of a broad, sensual mouth, the lips fat and rounded, suffused with dark blood.

For a long time, no words passed between the two men. Michael stood shivering from cold, frightened to move. He knew his life hung in a balance. The *muhtasib* looked at him for what seemed an age, saying nothing, doing nothing. From time to time, a gunshot would carry through the imperfect stillness. The voices crying out were fewer now. Michael heard a child crying, an anguished, pitiful sobbing suddenly cut off. He had never felt such a completeness of anger before. Or of such anguished helplessness.

"I'd like you to come with me, Mr. Hunt," the *muhtasib* said at last. "We need to talk."

Michael opened his mouth to protest.

"My name is Yunis Zuhdi. I . . ."

"Your name is Michael Hunt, you are a teacher at the American University, you once held the rank of British Chief of Station in Cairo, and you are presently in my custody. My name is Yusuf al-Haydari, *Qa'id al-Muhtasibin* for Lower Egypt. Please don't waste time pretending. It is an insult to my intelligence, and it only demeans you."

"You must be making a mistake, sir. My name is Yunis Zuhdi."

For answer, the *muhtasib* took from his pocket a small photograph. He passed it to Michael.

"That is you, is it not?"

Michael shook his head.

"It's like me, but . . ." He recognized it. It had been taken several years earlier, at an embassy reception.

Haydari looked around uneasily.

"Mr. Hunt, we don't have time to fence. We can't talk here. Please come with me."

He turned and led the way to a crooked path that wandered through the desolate, sleeping fields down towards the river. Once, Michael turned and looked back. The *muh-*

tasibin had almost finished their work now, farmers in a winter field sowing a terrible crop.

Near the end of the women's line, a girl of about eighteen crouched above the waiting ditch. There was nothing in her face, nothing but a cessation of longing, a rapid dimming of life. In her arms she held a bundle of clothes, a baby perhaps. There was no comfort in her embrace. She looked up and caught sight of Michael, a man without a uniform walking away from the carnage. Suddenly galvanized, she leapt to her feet and held out her bundle, shouting wildly.

"My baby! Take her! In God's name, take my baby!"

The *muhtasib* nearest her lifted his pistol and shot her once in the neck. In God's name. Her wide eyes froze in astonishment, her mouth opened, but no sound passed her lips. Then blood appeared at her mouth, her legs gave way, and she fell forward, crushing her child beneath her as she toppled into the ditch. In the distance, just beyond the fields, the wheel of a *saqiyya* turned slowly, lifting water to the crops. The river shone like glass. Michael closed his eyes and continued walking. He had decided that he had to make a break for it at the first opportunity. If he did not make it, he knew there would not be a second chance.

They would want to question him, that he knew. But why out here, in the fields?

It was not far to the river. The water was calm, a dark brown color streaked with yellow, a little swollen, tilted at its extremities, where it touched the north and south horizons, a flat loneliness moving through brown fields beneath a gray sky. On the far bank, palm trees huddled together beside a pillar of carved stone. Far away, like a mirage, a white sail bent into a wind furling from the sea.

At this point, the bank rose no more than five or six feet above the water. Driven by a blindfolded cow, the wheel of the *saqiyya* revolved ponderously, dipping its wide-necked clay jars into the muddy water, lifting them to the irrigation channel it served, tipping the water into its waiting mouth. As it turned, the wheel made a soft plashing sound.

Haydari stopped and looked out across the water. He stood thus for a long time, thinking or praying, Michael could not tell which. Finally he turned.

"I am very tired," he said. "We are all tired, all exhausted. God drives us hard, just as the farmer drives that cow. But his fields need water."

"Or blood."

The *muhtasib* did not react as Michael had thought he might.

"Yes," he whispered. "Blood too. There will be an extraordinary harvest."

"I hope it chokes you. I hope you drown in it."

"And you, Major, have you never shed blood? Has England never shed blood in the world?" He looked around. "These fields are wet with blood shed by British soldiers."

"That's an exaggeration. You know it is. There was never . . . anything like that."

"Perhaps you would not be so weak today had you acted otherwise. We have our reasons, our responsibilities."

"Reasons? What reason could there have been to shoot that girl?"

"What girl?"

"The girl with the baby. The one who cried out. Why was she shot? What had she done?"

Haydari reflected for a moment.

"I remember now," he said finally. "She was traveling without a permit from her husband. Such permits are mandatory now. The child may have been illegitimate, the woman may have been a prostitute, how could we tell?"

"That makes it better?"

"That makes it possible."

Michael turned his face away. He wanted to strike the man, but he knew it was out of the question. Someone had to escape. Someone had to stay alive, had to bear witness to what had happened. There would be a reckoning. When that time came, Michael wanted to be there to tell the world what he had seen.

"Do you hate me, Mr. Hunt?"

Michael said nothing.

"Look at me. We are a people of love, how can you hate us? We want only the well-being of our people, of all mankind. How can you find it in your heart to hate that?"

"Why do you think?"

"Because of the blood?" The *muhtasib* sighed and looked back over the fields towards the railway tracks. It was silent in the distance now. The shooting had stopped. He turned and faced Michael again.

"The blood is necessary, Mr. Hunt. It is not an indulgence. Did you think that is what it was? Something for our pleasure?"

Michael listened to the sound of the river passing, a scarcely audible murmur of water, a fluting of wind on ice-cold waves.

"Killing may be necessary sometimes," he said. "But never to kill the innocent, the truly innocent. That is worse than an indulgence."

"None of those were innocent, Mr. Hunt. They had all committed crimes. Not the greatest of crimes, but not the least. And all equally punishable." He paused. "And now, Mr. Hunt, we come to you. To your innocence and your guilt."

Michael watched as the man settled himself to his purpose. He observed the niceness, the assuredness of body and intellect, felt the electricity of spirit.

"Your investigations in Alexandria did not go unnoticed, Mr. Hunt. I want you to believe me when I say I wish you well. Something is going on, and I am just as worried as you. But my hands are more tied than yours. You are free to go places neither I nor my men can go, ask questions we cannot ask in safety. I want you to go on. I want you to work for me. Find out more, find out all you can. And if you report to me, I will do what I can to help you."

Michael stared at him.

"For you? Why the hell should I do anything for you after all I've seen?"

"Your life is in danger, Mr. Hunt. I think you have opened more cans of worms than you realize. There is nothing I can do for you, other than give you this warning. Abu Musa knows something. Your file was sent to him several days ago. He has men on the lookout for you."

"Is that it? You dragged me out here just to tell me I'm being watched?"

In answer, Haydari took a small pad of paper from his pocket, scribbled on it with a stubby pencil, and handed the top sheet to Michael. It bore a name and a telephone number.

"Keep me informed," he said. "That number will be manned twenty-four hours a day. Give that name and you will be put through to me or to someone I trust. Do you understand?"

"You think I would do this for you?"

The *muhtasib* shook his head.

"Not for me, Mr. Hunt. For yourself. Come, I've had your train halted. I'll see you're put back on it."

Michael took the paper and put it in his pocket. He promised himself that, the next time they met, he would be carrying a gun.

25

Ramsis station was like a morgue. No trains were leaving. Those that came in were staying put. The familiar roar of voices and the rumbling of trains had given way to a strained and fragile silence. The ticket offices had been shut down until further notice. Everywhere there were hand-written signs saying that rail services had been suspended during the state of emergency. The notices were signed by 'Abd al-Karim Tawfiq, State Prosecutor and Head of the Religious Police for Egypt—the man Michael and A'isha had heard speak on the radio that first day of the coup. Hushed voices echoed and were lost in the vast, empty concourse.

On the platform, a line of *muhtasibin* supervised the disembarkation from the Alexandria train. They had not stopped at either Tanta or Benha as scheduled, but headed straight for Cairo in a silence broken only by weeping and the sound of clanking wheels.

As he stepped off the train, Michael could sense the fear. It was a palpable presence throughout the station. The *muhtasibin* surveyed the crowd with an arrogance born of unchallengeable power. They had only to glance at a man and he would shrink into himself, turn his eyes away, walk with his head bent, cringing.

These were the witnesses of a massacre, but no-one seemed concerned about letting them go free into the city. It seemed an act of recklessness, but when Michael thought about it, he believed he understood. It was far from reckless. After all, to what tribunal could these carriageloads of clerks and peasants, shopkeepers and washerwomen carry their witness? Let them talk instead to their families and neighbors, to their colleagues at work and their employers, to their customers and their casual acquaintances. They would talk; everyone talks. In a matter of days, Cairo would be a city of fear.

Like everybody else, Michael kept his head down and his eyes fixed straight ahead. He saw two men pulled out of the queue, just before they reached the platform exit. The culling was still going on. He had known he would be in danger the moment he set foot in Cairo. Al-Haydari's warning had only stressed what he had known already.

Turning left at the cafeteria, he strode out of the station onto Ramsis Square. It was like walking straight into a wall. He had to pause to catch his breath. Usually the station prepared him for this, the transition was not so marked. Today, the combination of noise and light and petrol fumes caught him off his guard. His thoughts were elsewhere.

A string of moth-eaten camels passed, stripes of dark red paint on their flanks, marking them for the slaughterhouse. On the far side of the square, a group of *zabbalin* in dirty clothes and straw hats followed donkey carts piled high with rubbish, on their way back to the great *maqlab,* the rubbish heap in the Matariyya slums. His hand held down hard on the horn, a bus driver passed them with only inches to spare.

He decided to walk to A'isha's, but not directly. If someone had set him up, they would have a man watching for him there. Shari' al-Ruway'i was just on the east of the Azbakiyya Gardens, between the bus station and al-Ahmar mosque.

He crossed the square and made his way by a series of

small miracles to the relative safety of Shari' al-Jumhuriyya.
Poverty was not the only thing that never changed in Cairo:
the volume and lunacy of the traffic were two other contend-
ers for permanent status. He kept on down Jumhuriyya,
heading south, leaving behind the clamor of the station district. Something was missing, something ordinary and familiar, but he could not place it. He walked on, glancing discreetly in shop windows and the mirrors of parked cars to
see if he was being followed. No-one. At least, no-one visible.

Azbakiyya had been Cairo's first truly Westernized
quarter, its long streets and elegant squares built in the nineteenth century, long before the brashness of Coca-Cola or
the puritanism of the Muslim Brotherhood. Shepheard's
Hotel had been burned down in 1952, the Opera House in
1971. The Europeans were long gone, the richest residents
had moved west to the Gold Coast and Zamalik, the streets
had taken on a faded, tattered air. A surprisingly large number of shops and businesses were boarded up or bore small
handwritten notices on their doors saying they were closed
until further notice.

Huge posters were in evidence everywhere, on walls
and doorways. They were of two types: solid text in *naskhi*
script, slogans expounding the aims of the revolution; and
enormous blown-up photographs of Islamic thinkers and
martyrs. Michael recognized the more prominent among
them: Sayyid Qutb, the fundamentalist thinker hanged by
Nasser; Hasan al-Banna, founder of the Muslim Brotherhood; Abu 'l-A'la Mawdudi, the Pakistani ideologue; 'Abd
al-Salam Faraj, the mind behind the Jihad group responsible
for Sadat's assassination; and Khalid al-Islambuli, the assassin.

An outsider might have wondered why none of the text
posters carried verses from the Qur'an. Had the holy book
not been declared the constitution of the new state? Was it
not quoted daily on radio and television and in the Revolutionary Council? But posters get torn, posters get defaced,

posters get splashed with mud and worse. The Word of God must be protected from abuse.

He found a newsstand on the corner of Najib al-Rihani. There were copies of *al-Ahram* on sale, thinner than usual and showing blank spaces where the censor's pen had left its mark. The banner headline read: "Revolutionary Council Declares State of Emergency." Beneath it was a sub-heading: "Shaykhs of al-Azhar issue a joint *fatwa* in support of the Government." Neither article told Michael very much he could not guess or did not know already.

He turned left at Sur al-Azbakiyya. The second-hand bookstalls were doing business much as usual, but it took Michael only a few seconds to see that almost all the stall holders were men he did not recognize. They wore the short hair and beards of the religiously observant. A couple of *muhtasibin* stood casually to one side. Nobody seemed to be buying any books.

Michael walked slowly past the stalls, picking up a book here, a pamphlet there. The titles were depressingly familiar, and almost all religious.

A five-minute walk took him to the corner of Shari' al-Ruway'i. He walked along the north side of the street to a little shadowed alley almost opposite the building in which A'isha's flat was situated. Taking the newspaper from under his arm, he stood in the cold shadows and began to read. Each time he lowered the paper to turn and fold the page, he made a slow survey of a different section of the street.

In spite of his impatience to see A'isha and his deepening anxiety for her, he forced himself to stay put. It might take hours to be completely certain that no-one else was watching. At the end of the first hour, he moved to a different position further up the street and resumed the stake-out.

These were familiar streets. He remembered walking here with A'isha when they first arrived back from England.

He was shaken from memories by the sound of the *adhan* for the noon prayer, spluttering from the loudspeaker on a nearby mosque. Cautiously, he looked round.

If there was a watcher, would he let piety distract him from his duty?

People began to trickle into the street from shops and garages, offices and workshops. Buses and cars stopped where they were or pulled in to the side of the road. Their occupants joined the crowd assembling in the roadway. It was not unusual nowadays for the city to come to a standstill while rows of men performed the midday *salat*. Michael watched carefully, keeping himself hidden in shadows.

That was when the watcher gave himself away. Michael saw a figure dressed in black detach itself from the cover of an archway about one hundred yards from where he was standing. Rather than join the large crowd now assembled in the roadway, the man remained on the pavement. He placed a stone in front of him to serve as his *sutra* and, as the prayer commenced, followed the actions of the crowd.

There was nothing wrong in his behavior: the only strictly communal prayer in Islam is the noon prayer on Friday. Today was Thursday. But praying alone meant that the man did not have to leave his post. If anyone came or went while the prayer was in progress, he would be able to see them.

The prayer came to an end and the street quickly resumed its customary pace. Michael watched as the man in black slipped back into his archway. He wondered if he should try to smoke him out. It was a foregone conclusion that they were watching for him, that the man had been given his description. But if Michael simply entered the building, turning around perhaps to make sure he was seen and recognized, the chances were that he would achieve nothing but his own arrest. The watcher would have instructions not to act alone. He would almost certainly be equipped with a pocket radio that would put him directly in touch with Abu Musa or one of his lieutenants.

Abu Musa had been the former head of the Egyptian *mukhabarat 'amma,* the secret police, a man publicly noted for his personal devotion to Islam and privately known for his devotion to himself. Michael did not doubt that he would have been transferred directly to the Islamic internal security organization immediately after the coup. He had scores to settle with Michael, important scores. The de facto amnesty that had operated previously was now null and void. Michael was fair game wherever he went.

If there was a watcher, it implied that A'isha might be in Abu Musa's hands. That greatly limited Michael's options. He would not for any consideration put her life on the line.

It was not until past four o'clock that he saw his opportunity. The sun had already set, and the street had emptied of people. Everyone who could be indoors had gone home to break the fast. The watcher came out of his archway, looked up and down the street impatiently, and glanced at his wristwatch. Michael guessed his shift had ended and his replacement was overdue. Five minutes later, a man dressed in the clothes of a Sa'idi farmer stopped alongside the arch. Michael saw his man come out, exchange half a dozen words with the newcomer, and take his leave. A few seconds later, he passed the front of the alleyway.

Michael stepped into the street. He let his quarry gain thirty yards, then began to follow him.

26

The man seemed in no hurry to get home. He headed down to the Shari' al-Muski, then east into threadbare skirts of the old city. Like someone stepping back in time, Michael followed him. This was a world of ghosts, a gray world flecked with memories. Its streets were vibrant, full of life and noise, but haunted. Dark, ghost-ridden streets that wore the past like scars on soft flesh.

The man walked at an unhurried pace, pausing every now and then to examine merchandise on a market stall. He entered a small baker's shop and came out again carrying a loaf of bread. After Shari' Bur Sa'id, he turned left, heading into the warren of streets and alleyways bordering the Khan al-Khalili. Here, all pretensions of modernity were stripped away. The living were overshadowed at every step by the overpowering presence of the past: the porticos of medieval mosques and *madrasas,* high buildings touching like lovers across narrow lanes, the delicate wooden latticework of *mashrabiyya* screens, broken and shabby, worn clothes strung on lines high across the narrow lanes like banners of poverty. Men in patched *jalabiyyas* passed bearing trays of sweetmeats precariously on their heads, donkeys squeezed by with inches to spare, weighed down with broad loads, unwashed children dashed in and out between a forest of legs. It had been like this forever.

They came to a tiny, empty square at one side of which a Mamluk drinking fountain lay broken and abandoned. The watcher hesitated briefly at the entrance to a small café, then plunged inside. Michael followed half a minute later.

The café was a medium-sized room with a handful of rickety tables and chairs. Its floor consisted of hard earth, covered in sawdust and beaten flat by generations of feet. There were no windows: what little light there was came from three or four weak bulbs suspended on wires from a low ceiling.

The man was already seated alone at a small table in the corner. Near him, a group of men in *jalabiyyas* were sharing a *shisha* while they played cards. Thin wisps of blue smoke escaped the bamboo mouthpiece of the *shisha* as it passed from hand to hand. The men looked up at Michael as he entered. A second group at another table stared at him. No-one said a word. Cafés were usually filled with animated conversation, but this one seemed immoderately quiet.

Unlike the chic establishments in town, these little neighborhood *qahwas* were not places for the casual passerby. Their patrons were regulars, they were more like private clubs than public establishments. Michael felt exposed, as though he had walked into a trap. The man he had been following glanced up briefly and looked away again. Michael did not think he had recognized him.

He found an empty table near the door. He could keep an eye on his man from here. He took his copy of *al-Ahram* from his pocket and pretended to read. The *qahwaji* was at the watcher's table now with a glass of strong tea. The two men seemed to know one another. As Michael watched, they began to converse rapidly using sign language. Michael glanced around. Another pair of customers were doing the same. It suddenly dawned on Michael that he had heard of such establishments, cafés for the deaf and dumb or blind. This must be one of them.

The *qahwaji* came over to Michael. He put aside his paper as the man made a quick movement with his hands.

"I'm sorry," Michael said, hoping the man could hear him. "I'm not deaf. I was passing and needed something to drink. I'm sorry if . . ."

"Ma'lish. You're perfectly welcome. What would you like?"

"A plain coffee, please. Hot."

"I've not seen you around here before."

Michael shook his head.

"No, I live in Shubra. But I had business nearby. One of my old students has come to study at al-Azhar." The great center of theological studies was only a few minutes away.

"You're a teacher?"

Michael nodded.

"You'll be looking for a new job soon, I expect."

"Why do you say that?"

The waiter shrugged. His expression suggested that he had raised a topic he would rather not pursue.

"A plain coffee, was it?"

"Yes."

When he came back, the *qahwaji* just left the pot and cup on the table without saying a word. Some things were better not talked about. The *muhtasibin* had spies everywhere, so it was said.

A few moments later, the door opened again. A wave of cold air entered the room. The door closed with a gentle click. Partly hidden by shadows, the newcomer seemed out of place. He wore a long white robe, over which was draped a heavy *'abaya* of black wool. On his head was a small, tightly wound turban of fine white cotton. Over his head he wore a thin shawl of camel-colored wool. His beard was thick but neatly cut, not black but dark blond. His age might have been anything from thirty to forty-five. Michael was certain he was a European or an American.

The room grew still. The man sucking the *shisha* held the mouthpiece at his lips as though turned to stone. Two men playing backgammon halted in mid-move, the pieces clutched in one man's hand. A man's flashing fingers froze in mid-sentence.

The newcomer seemed to notice none of this. Ignoring the other patrons, he made his way to the table where the man Michael had tailed was sitting. He greeted him in a quiet voice, not as an old friend, but as someone he had come to do business with. The little man acknowledged the greeting with a curt nod.

Softly, the café came back to life. The water-pipe commenced its thick, resonant gurgling once more. There was a series of clicks as one of the players made a run on the backgammon board. There was a hiss of steam from the *sarabantina* at the rear of the room.

The two men were facing one another across the table, the watcher with his back to Michael. In a low voice, the European was speaking with exaggerated lip movements, which his companion must have been reading. When he stopped, the other man would scribble something on a little notepad, tear off a sheet, and pass it to him. This went on for ten or fifteen minutes, in the course of which the conversation gradually turned into an argument. The European's voice grew louder and more heated, the other's scribbling more and more frenzied. No-one seemed to notice. Michael could make out isolated words and phrases: "promise," "broken your word," "Babylon," "betrayed," and, three times, "Armaggedon."

Suddenly, the European got to his feet and threw his chair back heavily. It fell to the ground with a loud crash, unnoticed by most of the customers. Only one or two men glanced up, their attention arrested by the sudden movement. There was a look of consummate rage in the blond man's face, something like disgust or fear in his eyes. For a moment, the eyes caught Michael's and held them, as though in some sort of challenge. Michael tensed, thinking the man might have recognized him. But the next moment, he looked away and stepped past the table on his way out of the café.

The door slammed. At the table, the little man sat hunched over, quite still, as though expecting a blow. Michael thought quickly. Should he abandon his original quarry and follow the man who had just left? Whoever he was, his dress and manner suggested someone superior to the nondescript watcher at the table. But his talk of broken promises and betrayal suggested that something else was going on. With the watcher, Michael could at least be sure he was on firm ground. He decided to confront him while he was still shaken by his argument and the other man's outburst.

He rose softly and moved across to the table in the corner, where the little man was still sitting morosely, head bent down, unmoving. Michael stooped and picked up the chair. Straightening it, he sat down facing the deaf man.

A thin trickle of blood ran from the man's mouth onto the table, where it had already started to form a tiny red pool. Michael jumped to his feet and moved round to the man's side. He drew back his head. There was no question: the little man's throat had been cut from side to side.

27

It was late afternoon. The streets were dark. It was growing cold. Michael shivered, pulling his jacket collar high about his neck. He would have to find some proper clothes before he perished of cold. For over an hour, he had watched the entrance to the café from a discreet distance, waiting to see who might turn up. He had half-expected Abu Musa himself, or at least one of his lieutenants. But so far the only officials to make an appearance were a couple of *shawish,* ordinary policemen called from the nearby station in Bab al-Khalq.

The weapon that killed the watcher must have been very sharp and the blow extremely rapid. Michael could not remember the slightest movement that might have delivered the fatal cut. He had called the *qahwaji* and told him to go for the police. While he was away, Michael had taken the opportunity to go quickly through the dead man's pockets, in the hope of finding something that might give him a clue to his identity. All he found was a plastic-coated identity card giving the victim's name as 'Abd al-Haqq Uthman and stating that he was employed as an agent with the *mukhabarat 'amma.* The card was pre-revolutionary, a relic of the days of Mubarak. God alone knew who he had been working for since the new regime came to power.

At the door of the café, a stirring of footsteps and a volley of pious exclamations accompanied a small group carrying the murdered man into the street. The body lay on a wooden stretcher, covered in soiled canvas sheeting. A huge crowd had gathered, with small boys in the majority. A woman cried out, her voice loud against the stillness of the night. Michael watched carefully. No-one followed the stretcher bearers as they made their way along the alleyway down to al-Mu'izz li-Din Allah. Slipping from his hiding-place, Michael followed them. At the corner of the Shari' al-Azhar, an ambulance was waiting. One of the stretcher bearers shouted "al-'Ajuza" at the driver: they were taking the body to the police hospital on the other side of the river.

Satisfied that no more was to be gained from the man who had been killed, Michael decided to return to A'isha's apartment. He made several stops on the way. The first was to buy a cheap overcoat at a small shop run by a Coptic *khayyat* on al-Muski. He would have preferred something heavier and warmer, but it was imperative that he stay in character as long as possible.

The second stop was for a quick meal of *makarone*. And the third was to purchase a knife. He had a gun at his own apartment in 'Abdin, but it was too risky to attempt going back there yet. By the time he got back to the Shari' al-Ruway'i, the snow was falling seriously.

Someone was still there. Michael could not be sure that it was the man who had changed places with the one he had followed, but that made little difference. He waited until he was satisfied the man was alone. Beneath his arch, the new watcher paced up and down, rubbing his hands together hard to raise a little warmth. At one side of the arch, he passed near a lamp, and as he did so his breath grew suddenly visible, white and ponderous on the frosted air.

Michael slipped through the shadows of the street, doorway to doorway, until he stood in the archway, inches from the watcher. The cold had rendered his quarry unalert. Lightly, Michael stepped beside him and thrust the knife hard into the small of his back, with enough force to jab through his thin *jalabiyya* into the flesh.

"You're a dead man if you make a sound," Michael whispered.

The watcher froze, stifling a cry that had risen as far as his throat. Michael leaned close and whispered sharply into his ear.

"We're going to walk together across the street and into the apartment building opposite, the one you've been watching for the past two hours. I'll be behind you every step of the way. My knife will be in your back. I don't want to spill your insides over the road, but I promise you I will if you give me the slightest reason. Once we're inside, I'll frisk you. I don't want any misunderstandings. Then we're going up to Dr. Manfaluti's flat. I want you to tell me that you've understood everything I've just been saying."

The man gave a jerky movement of the head.

"Tell me. Say it."

"I understand. I understand perfectly." The man could feel the wetness of fresh blood against his flesh, a little trickle that could so easily turn to a stream.

They crossed the road slowly, like two men fearing for their balance on the snow-dressed hardtop. Michael handed the man a key.

"Use this," he said. "It opens the street door."

The man's hand was shaking, whether from fright or cold it was hard to say. He pushed the door open. Michael prodded him inside and stepped in behind him smartly, closing the door with his free hand. It felt suddenly warm. The knife-blade caught a dull light just above the doorway and turned it aside. Beside the stairway, the watcher pressed himself nervously against the wall. He was a young man in his mid-twenties, inexperienced, afraid. He eyed Michael warily, like an animal in his first cage.

"Who are you?" he whispered.

"No questions." Michael made him turn and face the wall, hands high, legs outstretched. With his left hand, he frisked him rapidly, missing nothing. The man carried a gun in his inside pocket, a 9mm Helwan automatic, the home-market version of a Beretta 951. Plunder from the old 777 anti-terrorist squad, disbanded after the coup. Michael slipped a round into the chamber, cocked the hammer, and set the safety catch before putting the gun into his own pocket. For his present purposes, the knife was still more useful to him. It was silent, highly selective, and just as persuasive.

"OK," said Michael. "Start walking. It's on the fifth floor."

A thick silence pervaded the building, as though all sound had been cushioned by the snow outside. Michael was reminded of the café, of its deep, incomplete silence, the absence of conversation, eyes with the mute appeal of whipped dogs. The stairs were steep. Their shoes scraped and shuffled noisily on raw concrete, little explosions rocking the quiet. Michael remembered other silences on these same stairs, and the quick sounds made by a woman's feet.

A second key fitted the lock. The door swung back onto darkness.

"There's a switch on the left-hand side. Shoulder height."

Light came on in a green shade. Shadows formed. A large black and white photograph of the mummy of Seti I leaped out of the wall facing the door. The man jumped, startled.

"Not been inside before?"

The man shook his head.

"Turn right. The door at the end of the corridor. Move."

The man threw a nervous glance at the photograph, then followed Michael's instructions. Michael noticed that he wore badly fitting shoes that had leaked, letting in snow.

His feet must be freezing, Michael thought. His own were far from warm.

The smell was noticeable even before they opened the door. The cold weather had helped, of course, but the flat was not an ice-box.

"There's something . . ."

"I know, I noticed. Now open the door."

Michael feared the worst now. He knew what the smell was. He knew what he would find.

The man opened the door, but hung back, afraid to go in. Michael sent him ahead with a push, tottering into the darkness. He came behind, fumbling on the wall for the light switch. The stench was overpowering now, unmistakable. Michael could hear the man ahead of him retching. His own stomach was churning. He found the switch at last and flipped it down.

28

The room was a mess. Furniture lay heaped and broken everywhere. Lamps and vases had been smashed, paintings torn from the wall, books ripped from shelves and strewn across the floor. Hadn't the neighbors heard? Hadn't anyone called the police?

Michael did not recognize the body at first. All he knew, all he cared, was that it was not A'isha. Then it sank in. The body—if it could be called a body—was that of Megdi himself. The face was still recognizable. Just. And the white suit—what could be seen of it beneath the layers of dried blood—was very like the one Megdi had been accustomed to wear. The smell was appalling. Michael gagged and placed a handkerchief across his mouth.

Relief and horror and pity jostled in the pit of his stomach. He had not known Megdi well, but he had liked and admired him. The relief was short-lived. If Megdi lay dead in here, A'isha's body could be in one of the other rooms, could be almost anywhere.

She was at least nowhere in the apartment. They went through each room in turn. Nothing had been left undisturbed. The study in particular had been ransacked with exceptional thoroughness. But there were no more bodies.

"When does your shift end?"

The man shrugged.

"Look," Michael said, "I could do all sorts of things. I could hit you, I could use my knife on you, hold your head under a bathful of water until your lungs burst. But I don't do that sort of thing, and I don't want to start now. I'm willing to believe you don't know what's going on here. I'm willing to trust you. All I want in return is a little information."

They were in the small kitchen, on hard chairs beside the table. All around them, smashed crockery and glassware littered the polished floor.

"They'll kill me. Don't you understand? They'll say it was my fault." The man was shaking, not from cold now, but from fear.

"Nobody's going to kill you. If you keep calm, we can sort this thing through. Let me ask you again, when does your shift end?"

The man glanced at a cheap wristwatch he wore on his left arm.

"Less than an hour," he muttered. "Seven o'clock. They aren't always on time. Sometimes they keep me waiting. Two days ago, I had to wait over half an hour."

Michael nodded.

"OK," he said. "You'll be back in place long before that. When your replacement comes, you haven't seen anything, you haven't spoken to anyone. Let them find all this on someone else's shift."

"But who . . .?"

"That's what I want to find out. Relax, I'm not going to hurt you. All you have to do is cooperate. What's your name?"

The man hesitated.

"I don't . . . Hamid, my name's Hamid. Who's the . . . dead man in the next room?"

"You don't know? His name was Megdi, Professor Megdi. An archaeologist."

"An archaeologist? How's that? Why would an archaeologist be mixed up in something like this?"

"Something like what?"

Hamid shrugged. Michael noticed that he had dirty fin-
gernails. He spoke in a tense voice with a Sa'idi accent.
Michael guessed he had not been in the city long. The security services often recruited Sa'idis as foot soldiers. They
were deracinated, dependent, trustable.

"Something like what?" Michael repeated.

"I don't know. Security matters. You should know."

"No, I don't. I want you to tell me."

Hamid licked his lips. His eyes moved nervously, now
focusing on Michael, now looking away. It was warm in the
flat. The central heating had been left running. A tap was
dripping into the sink. In the apartment below, someone
had turned on a television set. The sound of a single voice
drifted upwards, the words indistinguishable.

"No. It's not my job to know."

"What were your instructions?"

"Keep an eye on this flat. See who goes in and out.
Report anything unusual to my superiors."

"You weren't watching the flat, you were watching the
building. You must have been told what to look for, who to
look for. You were watching for someone in particular. Was
it me? Were you waiting for me?"

The young man seemed startled. He shook his head
violently.

"No," he protested, "not you. I don't know anything
about you. I was told to look out for a woman, a young
woman. Here . . ."

He fished something out of the pocket of a jacket he
wore underneath his *jalabiyya*. It was a photograph, badly
crumpled but still recognizable. A photograph of A'isha.

"Who told you to watch for her?"

The man licked his lips again and glanced at his watch.

"If I'm not there," he said, "there'll be trouble."

"You've got plenty of time." Michael was starting to

wonder if Hamid was telling the truth about the time his shift was due to end. What if it had been six o'clock?

"Who told you to watch for this woman? Who gave you her photograph?"

"My . . . My boss."

"What's his name?"

Hamid pursed his lips.

"Is it Abu Musa?"

Hamid shook his head.

"I don't know any Abu Musa. I work for the *muk-habarat*. They gave me work when I came here three years ago. Steady work. Not much money, but there's a chance of promotion."

Michael was sure he was lying. He had seen the man's reaction to the name Abu Musa, noticed his hesitation before denying that he knew him.

"What were your instructions if you found her?"

"Report back to headquarters. Straight away."

"When did this stake-out begin?"

"I don't know. I was sent here for the first time last Sunday. Four days ago. I don't know, maybe we had some people in before that."

"Who was the man you took over from today?"

"Abd al-Haqq? He's well known. Been with the bureau for years. They say he was born there. Never been pro-moted, though, on account of his condition. Can't speak. Hears well enough, though, and he's got sharp eyes. They say he knows all there is to know about what goes on down at headquarters."

"Not any more, he doesn't." Michael explained what had happened in the café. "Have you any idea who the man who killed him was?"

Hamid was visibly frightened now. He tried to get up from his chair, but Michael pressed him back down.

"Do you know him? The European."

"No . . . yes . . . I don't know. Look, what are you

keeping me for? I don't know anything. I've got to get out of here. Let me out."

Michael kept his hand on the other man's shoulders. Small flecks of saliva were forming at the corners of his mouth. His fear was growing.

"He's called al-Hulandi: the Dutchman. That's all I know, I swear. I've only ever heard of him. But I've never met him. Now let me out of here."

Michael suddenly clapped a hand across the man's open mouth.

"Shut up!" he hissed.

The watcher's eyes grew wide. He struggled to get out of the chair.

"Keep quiet!" Michael whispered. "I can hear something. Someone's in the flat."

Quietly, he slid his chair back and stood up. With a rapid but silent movement, he crossed to the door, found the lightswitch, and plunged the kitchen into darkness. He could hear hushed voices in the passageway, two men. At least two. Cursing himself for staying, he reached into his pocket for the pistol. He prayed it was not just a toy Hamid had picked up to boost his ego. Carefully, he released the safety.

Grabbing Hamid, he pulled him back past the table, into a small opening behind the refrigerator.

"It must be my replacement," Hamid hissed. "He must have come early and got suspicious."

"Were you lying about the time your shift was due to end?"

"No, I swear . . ."

The door opened. Light from the passage ran across the room. The sound of someone breathing gently. A tentative footstep.

Without warning, Hamid stood up. He had his hands in the air, and in one he was holding his *mukhabarat* ID card. He had seen too many TV movies in which plainsclothes policemen waved their badges at villains. Too many movies in which the villains put down their guns and raised their hands. The man in the doorway did not even pause to read the card.

All Michael heard was the roar of the gun. A moment later, Hamid's body hit the floor. There had not even been time for him to cry out. Silence, then another footstep. Dim light washing the kitchen. A voice from another room, indistinguishable words.

There was no back way out of the kitchen. Michael could see Hamid's feet jutting around the edge of the refrigerator. The cheap shoes bore little flecks of blood. A shadow fell across the floor. Michael twisted, looking for the gunman's reflection in the window. He could just make out a tall man and the shape of a sub-machine gun in his hands, poised for firing. Michael held his breath. The man bent down and examined the body on the floor.

A voice at the door.

"What happened? Why did you fire?" The voice did not belong to an Arab. French possibly, Michael thought.

"This one's dead. He leapt out from behind the refrigerator." This one was Egyptian, from Cairo.

"Who was he?"

"*Mukhabarat.* See, he had an ID."

Michael felt sweat creeping into his eyes. His hand on the gun was wet. He was out of training, had not been on a firing-range in years.

"There's no-one else. The place is just as we left it."

"He must have been their watcher. Must have come up here for some reason. Maybe he got too cold. He must have had a shock, finding what he did."

"You think they'll look for him?"

"Reckon not. He's not worth looking for. They can't keep track of their agents these days. Leave him alone. They can add him to their list when they do get around to breaking in. Let's put these lights off and get out of here."

A moment later, the light was doused. The front door slammed. Silence scampered back, paused at the latest death, and settled down again.

29

London
17 December

Tom Holly shivered and looked through his window into the sleeping mews. The milkman had just started his rounds. Bottles tinkled softly in the crisp air. A salvo of birdcalls rang out in accompaniment.

He should not be here, he thought; he should be in Egypt helping Michael Hunt. But Desk Heads do not travel, Desk Heads do not jeopardize themselves or their knowledge or their ignorance. They do their watching from a distance, and if necessary they withdraw behind the veils the service has woven for them. There were seven veils to hide behind, just as there are seven in the dance: the veils of Honor, Discretion, Security, Diplomacy, Secrecy, Tact, and Bullshit. It is this last veil above all that stands between servants of the realm and total nakedness.

"Tom? What are you doing up so early? It's barely five o'clock."

His wife was standing in the doorway, her hair still tangled from sleep, a dressing-gown draped loosely over her shoulders.

"Is it? I'm sorry. I didn't realize."

"I woke up and you were gone. Come back to bed, love. It's far too cold to be sitting down here. You'll wake the children."

"You go on back, dear. I'll come up soon."

Linda came into the room. She could barely see him, it was so dark. He was just a shadow against the window.

"Shall I switch on a light?" she asked.

"No. No, thanks."

"Do you want to talk about it?"

She asked because she thought it was the sort of thing a wife should ask. One way or another, it was something she had been asking ever since they had been married. His answer was invariably no, but she did her duty and asked all the same. It would have been uncharitable of her not to.

"I think someone I care for is in very deep trouble," he said.

Startled, she came close to him and slipped an arm round his waist.

"Is there anything I can do?"

He shook his head.

"Nope," she said. "I suppose there isn't."

"It's Michael," he said, "Michael Hunt. He's not the only one, but it's my fault he's in the situation he is. He'd resigned, got clear of it all; and I dragged him back in. If it hadn't been for this damned revolution . . ."

"Where is he? In Egypt?"

"Yes."

"I suppose that's all you can tell me."

He nodded.

"And you want to go and find him. Get him out, or whatever it is you think you can do."

He said nothing for a while, just held her tightly.

"How did you know?" he said at last.

"Good God, Tom. I don't know why they waste a salary on you." She paused. "Do you really have to go?"

He hesitated. So much hung on that one small word, "really."

"Yes," he said finally. "I think so. I don't think there's any other way. Ordinarily . . . It's not just Michael. Something's going on. Something I don't like."

"I'm frightened, Tom. I'm frightened you won't come back. Don't you have people for that sort of thing? Younger people. People without families." They had three children, the youngest four years old, the oldest eleven.

He could not tell her about his suspicions, that he was unable to trust anyone connected with Vauxhall.

"Not for something like this," he said. "If anyone goes, it has to be me."

"Will they let you go?"

He shook his head.

"They won't know. I won't tell them."

"But they're bound to find out."

"Oh, yes; but it'll be too late by then."

She did not reply. For a long time, she held him to herself, shivering.

"People may come round," he said. "Asking questions. Making accusations. Do you think you can handle that?"

"I can handle that," she said, "but I can't handle your leaving."

"I'll not be gone long," he lied.

"No?"

"No," he whispered. And he took her in his arms and held her like that, imprisoned by his fear, until the first traces of dawn began to creep across the rooftops.

Percy Haviland owned an apartment overlooking Cadogan Square. He was there now. He had not slept. There had been shadows on his face all night as he struggled to stay awake, in conference now with this minister, now with that. He had spoken with the Israeli ambassador at 2.00 A.M., spending over an hour in a secure room at the embassy in Kensington Palace Gardens. The chairman of the JIC had phoned at a little after four o'clock and stayed on for more than half an hour, a very difficult half-hour at that.

The telephone buzzed. He closed his eyes and swore

beneath his breath. Several glasses of malt whiskey during the long night had done little to sweeten his thoughts or improve his temper. He reached out a well-manicured hand and lifted the receiver.

"Haviland."

The voice at the other end was slow but to the point. Haviland listened, muttered a terse "yes," followed by "thank you," and replaced the receiver. For several moments he remained motionless, his hand resting on the black plastic. Then he turned half around in his chair and spoke to someone seated near the window, his face partly concealed in shadow.

"That was Burton," he said. "Personnel. A good man: I put him onto that matter of the code."

The other man lifted his head with interest.

"You know which one I mean, of course," continued Haviland. He looked around his glittering room. It was like a prison. Or a circus tent.

The stranger said nothing, made no movement. But he was listening.

"I asked him to look through the personal files on Michael Hunt and Tom Holly, see if there was any record of a one-time code they might have shared. He just rang to say he passed it on to the people in crypto-communications. They decoded the two messages a few minutes ago. Someone's bringing them up now."

There was a knock on the door and a messenger entered. He handed the transcriptions over and left. Haviland put on his reading glasses and scanned both pages. When he looked up, his face was grave.

"It's what we feared. Michael Hunt has resurfaced. He wants to see Holly. Holly has radioed back saying that he plans to leave for Egypt today."

"Do you think he will get through?"

"I very much doubt it."

"You won't try to stop him?"

"Of course not. Why should I?"

"And if he does get through, what then?"

"He will wait for Michael Hunt at the rendezvous he has chosen."

"Do we know where that is?"

Haviland shook his head.

"That's to come."

"And if Hunt doesn't show up?"

"Holly will start looking for him."

"Will he find him?"

Haviland shrugged.

"Perhaps. If Hunt is alive."

The stranger stood and went to the window, where the morning was waiting. After a long silence, he turned and faced his host.

"This is a lovely apartment, Percy. I have always thought so. I envy you. You have been very fortunate."

"Yes. Indeed I have."

"Your knighthood should be along any time now, I expect."

Haviland nodded.

"Yes. I understand so. In the New Year list."

"It's official, then?"

Haviland nodded.

"No more than you deserve." The stranger paused and turned back to the window. Slowly, he ran a finger down the windowpane, feeling the cold abduct warmth from his skin.

"It will help us if they meet, will it not?"

For a moment, Haviland could not think whom he meant. Then he nodded.

"Yes," he said. "It will be very much to our advantage. It will confirm Holly as the mole in Vauxhall. In a conspiracy with Michael Hunt and the woman, Rashid Manfaluti's wife."

"And afterwards?"

"Afterwards? There will not be an afterwards."

The stranger took his finger away from the window. He had left a streak of condensation on the glass.

"No," he said. "You are perfectly correct. There will not be an afterwards."

PART IV

"No man might buy or sell, save he that had the mark, or the name of the beast, or the number of his name"

REVELATION 13:17

30

Cairo

The priest had nearly reached the end. He was saying a private mass for the father of a parishioner who had died two days earlier in Florence. This was not his normal function, but Father Dominic had been taken ill the day before and he had offered to stand in. Only about two dozen people were in attendance, all muffled in scarves and overcoats: the daughter of the deceased, her two daughters with their husbands, their children, and a few friends.

In the dim chapel, white candles burned unsteadily. The air was thick with incense, as though perfumed to keep a pestilence at bay. The priest shimmered in the trembling light, a tall, white-robed figure crouched before a tiny altar. The dead man had been old, disabled and remote. His grandchildren had seen him only in photographs, his sons-in-law had long since fallen out of favor. No-one much regretted his passing. No tears broke the soporific rhythm of the liturgy.

Like an actor performing a familiar role in a darkened theater, the priest went through the words and motions of the mass. From the wall above, a statue of St Catherine of Alexandria watched the familiar movements, mute, transcendent, crippled by paint and plaster. On his cross, the pale god closed his eyes in pain.

A visitor from abroad might have noticed an atmosphere about the mass, a sense almost of transgression or illegality. Ever since the coup, Egypt's Christian community had been tense, the Copts most of all. Memories of the dark days of 1980 and 1981 had not had time to fade. There had already been moves by the religious authorities to tighten up restrictions on the People of the Book. Rumors of the morning's killings were already being whispered in the *suqs* and alleyways.

In Minya, Asyut and other Christian enclaves, it was said that the young men were arming themselves. Lebanese Christians had ferried in guns through Jordan and Sinai. A US-based evangelical group called The Sword of Life was sending dollars and, it was rumored, ammunition for the guns.

The priest turned to face the congregation. As he did so, he noticed, scarcely visible in the shadows at the back of the side-chapel, a man standing apart from the rest. He had not been there at the beginning of the mass. The priest thought he looked familiar.

The mass continued, correct, evenly paced, without passion, without drama: an act of grace, nothing more. The congregation had not come here for passion, but for a stifling of conscience. What did it matter? thought the priest. He had more important things on his mind.

The last words, the dismissal, the shaking of hands. Words of comfort for those least in need of it. The priest spoke in fluent Italian, with an accent. Near the door, the interloper stayed in his place, watching and waiting for the congregation to leave. They glanced at him nervously and hurried out. When the last of them had gone, he stepped forward out of the shadows.

"It's a long time since I last heard you say mass, Paul. You haven't lost your touch." He spoke in English.

"Thanks. I try to keep in practice. What the devil are you doing here at this time? And what are you dressed like that for? I didn't recognize you back there."

Michael shrugged.

"We all have our roles to play. I wasn't followed here, if that's what you're worried about."

Father Paul was already taking off his vestments.

"You were a professional, Michael. I've every faith in you."

Michael's face grew somber.

"I'm in trouble, Paul. I need your help."

Paul hesitated.

"Why come to me?" He draped his chasuble carefully over one arm. Beneath it, he wore a cotta of fine lace.

"Because you're my brother. Because I can trust you. I have no-one else, Paul."

"Is your life in danger?"

Michael nodded.

"I thought you'd resigned, Michael. I thought you'd walked away from it all. Or was that just some elaborate game?"

"No, it was genuine. What I told you back in England was true. All of it. But you warned me then about getting involved again with Tom Holly."

"He talked you into something?"

"Yes."

"I see. Well, you'll have to explain it all properly. Let's go to the rectory—we can talk there without being disturbed."

"What about Father Dominic?"

"Hospital. He was taken ill suddenly yesterday. There's some sort of bug going around. Half the congregation seems to be sick."

"I'm sorry to hear that. Give him my best wishes, Paul. He's a sweet man."

"Yes. Yes, he is."

Paul's face clouded over briefly. Then he smiled, put his arm round his brother's shoulder, and led him out of the church.

. . .

St Savior's rectory was, like the church itself, a hole-in-the-corner affair dating from the high period of British rule. Situated at the southern tip of al-Azbakiyya, it served a shifting population of local Catholics and Maronites, some Italians who had stayed on after Suez, and a motley assortment of expatriates who found St Joseph's in al-Zamalik too fussy for their taste.

Paul had arrived in Cairo unannounced at the beginning of the year. His order had posted him to Egypt to carry out research of some kind. Every day, he drove to the nunciature in al-Zamalik, most nights he stayed at the rectory reading or writing. He seldom socialized, never relaxed. Michael had no idea what the precise nature of his work was. He thought it might have something to do with his academic specialty of Islamic studies. Paul had written the definitive study of a fourteenth-century theologian, Ibn Taymiyya, one of whose books Michael had seen on sale earlier that day. Paul's study had been published several years ago by the Pontificio Istituto Biblico, in their Biblica et Orientalia series.

Paul set out two small glasses and a bottle of Irish whiskey.

"I like mine with ginger," Michael said. "Remember?"

"I remember you liked ginger beer when we were kids. You drank gallons of the stuff. It made you wet the bed. Ginger isn't good for you. And I don't think Dominic keeps it anyway. There's something called porter if you want it. It's foul stuff, but Dominic swears by it. He calls it Beelzebub. 'I might have a pint of Beelzebub tonight,' he says. God knows where he gets it from. No-one in their right mind would manufacture that stuff. I think he makes it himself."

"It's all right," Michael said. "I think I'll stick with the whiskey, if you don't mind."

"Go easy on it. It's Dominic's bottle, not mine, and whiskey isn't that easy to come by these days."

Michael looked up at him. He closed his eyes momentarily, tightly. A look of pain washed over his face. He opened his eyes again.

"It isn't just me," he said. "There are other lives at risk. Some are dead already. A man called Perrone for one, Ronnie Perrone. You wouldn't know him, but . . ."

Paul looked gravely at his brother.

"Yes," he said, "as a matter of fact I do. I know Ronnie very well. You say he's dead?"

"I've just been at his apartment. Somebody strangled him with the cord of his dressing-gown."

Paul's hand moved quickly in the gesture of the cross.

"How did you know him, Paul?"

"Let's just say that we met a few times in the course of my work."

"Your work? As a priest?"

"No. My research on the fundamentalist movements."

"I see. You knew he was the MI6 Chief of Station here in Cairo?"

"Yes, I knew. The Church is not without resources, Michael. You'd be surprised at how little there is we don't know or can't find out."

"That's largely why I've come to you."

"Yes, I rather thought it might be." Paul lifted his own drink, a neat brandy. "You said there had been other deaths."

Michael told him all he had seen.

"I never knew this man Megdi," Paul said. "Was he mixed up in any way with you or Ronnie?"

Michael shook his head.

"A'isha was staying with him."

"A'isha?"

"Manfaluti."

Paul had met A'isha properly only once, not long after his return to Cairo from the funeral. He had remembered her as the woman who had knocked on his mother's door in Oxford, asking for Michael. She had impressed him very much, but his conscience as a priest had made it hard for

him to be more than polite. Some—some priests even—
would have said he was being old-fashioned to object to a
couple living in what he regarded as sin.

"I see. I'm sorry. Whatever I think of your relationship,
I can only be grieved that she's in danger. But you must have
known when you . . . when you met her that this was a
possibility. Her husband poses an enormous threat to the
new regime. Even she . . ."

"Her husband is dead."

"What? Manfaluti? How do you know that?"

Michael explained. He left nothing unsaid. As much as
anything, he was externalizing his fears. The small, book-
lined room had a cozy familiarity, as though they were
worlds away from Cairo. This was Paul's study for as long as
he stayed. On a small table, Michael noticed photographs of
his mother and father and, behind them, one of himself and
Paul. They were standing together in a caul of sunshine,
squinting towards a camera held by their mother. The photograph had been taken on their last family visit to Cairo, in
1975. Michael's own copy had been lost or destroyed years
ago. Or perhaps this was it, acquired somehow by his
brother and brought back to Cairo in a little silver frame.

Paul did not speak at first when Michael came to a
finish. He had fallen into thought, as though troubled by his
brother's story.

"You haven't told me yet why you went to Alexandria," he said.

"I told you, Tom Holly wanted me to do a job for him.
I had to go to Alexandria to get some information. That's all
there is to it."

Paul got to his feet impatiently. He went to the book-
case and took down a small, leather-bound book. He flicked
through it a couple of times before returning it to its place.
With a sigh, he turned and faced his brother.

"Michael, when you came here you said it was because
you trusted me. And yet here you are, treating me like the

local security risk and telling me a story that adds up to nothing at all."

"There are things . . ."

"No, Michael, there aren't. Not any more. Let me tell you why you came here tonight. You want me to put you in touch with Vatican intelligence here in Cairo. Isn't that right?"

Michael opened his mouth to protest, then shut it again.

"Yes," he admitted. "You're right. I don't have contacts any longer. I might not be believed. Or trusted."

"Very well. You want an introduction to our intelligence people. Now, I ask myself, why should my big brother want something like that? Why should he need it? Ronnie Perrone wasn't the sum total of British secret involvement in Egypt. Even I know that. It wouldn't take too long for the Americans to check you out, even if all the contacts you used to have at the embassy were no longer there. So obviously a great deal more is going on than you've been telling me. If you want me to help you, you're going to have to tell me all you know."

Michael hesitated. He had already had qualms about bringing his brother into this. But A'isha's life was at stake, if she were not already dead. Who would he be betraying after all? A string of dead men? A traitor high up in Vauxhall House? He told Paul what he knew.

When Michael finished, Paul sat in silence for a time, his head bent, as though in prayer. As a younger man, he had thought that becoming a priest would help with things like this. Well, with everything: with being alive, with being afraid, with being alone. The truth was that nothing seemed to help, that being a priest made you more exposed, more vulnerable. You could hold a chalice in your hand, and God's blood in it, and still be less than nothing. You could grant absolution and fall asleep at night full of sin, damaged by remorse. You could live your whole life for God and still be damned.

Without raising his head, he spoke quietly.

"Michael, are you certain that the man Tom Holly thinks is behind these killings is someone called al-Qurtubi? That was the name he used?"

"Yes, of course. 'The Cordovan.' It's an unusual name, not an easy one to get wrong."

"No, no it's not." Paul lifted his head.

"Michael," he asked, "how strong are you? I don't mean physically. But mentally. Emotionally." What he really wanted to say was "spiritually," but he thought Michael might take it amiss.

"You think A'isha's dead?"

Paul bent his head, shaking it gently.

"I don't know, Michael. I'm not psychic. God knows, I wish I were sometimes. But I know no more than you do."

For the first time, Michael noticed that his brother was going gray. He remembered Paul's beauty as a child, his strength, his simple pleasure in the workings of his body. Women had been attracted to Paul, more than to himself. Paul had played football, gone canoeing, climbed mountains in Scotland. He had paid a price for his pursuit of the mind and spirit. How lonely he must be. Michael wanted to reach out a hand and touch Paul's cheek. That must be the hardest of all things for a priest, he thought: not to be touched.

"What is it?" he asked. Why was Paul looking at him like that? A silence rested between them for a moment, a tight, anxious silence.

"I think," Paul said quietly, "I think it might be better for A'isha if she *were* dead."

31

Snow lay on Cairo like a perfect, opaque shell. From a distance, white-sheathed domes and crescent-topped minarets lent the city a Christmas-card appearance. Angels could have folded their wings and come to rest upon the rooftops. A star might have circled about the pinnacle of the Citadel. And on the ragged outskirts of the great metropolis, if anyone had been looking, shepherds in the clothes of scavengers were tending their flocks in winter fields.

At street level, however, nothing of the deception remained. People shivered, struggling through heaps of dirty snow and freezing slush. These buildings and these pavements were not made for weather like this, least of all here in the oldest quarters, in the slums of Misr al-Qadima.

Father Paul Hunt stumbled against a sharp wind as he walked along a dark street in Babylon. He could smell the pungent smoke that drifted across from the pottery kilns on the edge of the wasteland separating Misr al-Qadima from the City of the Dead to the east. The narrow, winding streets were pervaded by another smell, the odor of poverty. Snow and wind did little to erase it.

An old man held out his hand for alms. Paul stooped

and dropped a few coins into the wrinkled palm. For a moment, the man looked into his eyes, bringing his hands together round Paul's in a gesture of gratitude. *"Allah yubarik fik,"* the old man whispered. *"Allah yubarik fik."* On the back of his wrist was a blue Byzantine cross. Paul smiled and passed on.

Babylon—Bab 'Alyun or plain 'Alyun—had been the earliest settlement in what later became Cairo. It had been built on the site of an ancient religious settlement, Khery-Aha. The Greeks called it Babylon. The Roman Emperor Trajan built a fortified tower there and named it "Babylon of Egypt." And when the Muslims conquered the country, they built their first city around it: al-Fustat, the "Military Encampment." As the Islamic city moved northwards, Babylon and its environs became "Old Cairo," a walled enclave inhabited by Copts and Jews, a place of cemeteries and churches, monasteries and synagogues, incense and visions. A hidden, crumbling place, dark behind high walls.

Now, the Jews had gone and most of the Copts had moved to Shubra or, if they had done really well for themselves, to Heliopolis and Misr al-Jadida. Some of the churches had been renovated for the pleasure of tourists venturing a little off the beaten track. Priests and monks still huddled close to its battered walls, the old liturgy still sounded behind densely patterned screens, tendrils of sickly-sweet incense wandered through the Sunday morning streets. But the life was gone, the spirit long ago spoilt and rotten.

Paul felt depressed every time he came here. On account of the bleak, hungry streets and the dark, windowless walls. On account of the faces in which centuries of suffering were reflected. On account of the old saints decaying behind disused altars. But most of all on account of what he had learned here, what he knew lay hidden beneath the streets and the walls and the icon-heavy screens.

He had left his brother sleeping in the rectory, in Dominic's room, worn out by his recent exertions. Allowing

Michael to stay had been a serious breach of church regulations. It was, after all, not his rectory to do with as he liked. But he consoled himself by the thought that he had had very little choice. Michael was his brother, and he had nowhere safe to go. To have tossed him out into the street might have been to deliver him into the hands of enemies he did not even know existed. Paul only prayed that he did not attract them to St Savior's.

A local train rolled past, on its way to al-Ma'adi and Helwan. It stopped briefly at Mari Girgis station, then set off again. Paul came to an opening in the old fortress wall and stepped through. At the bottom of a short flight of steps, he found himself in a narrow lane that squeezed between the Convent and Monastery of St George. A black-robed priest passed, a breviary clutched against his chest, frowning and preoccupied.

At the end of the lane, Paul passed through a low archway: on its other side, at the bottom of some steps, lay the side door of a small church. For a moment he hesitated. What if the old man was dead? What if he had been lying, for reasons best known to himself or his Church? Or worse: what if he had been telling nothing but the naked truth? He took a deep breath and pushed the door open.

Abu Sarga was part darkness, part light, part imagination. The door closed heavily, shutting Paul inside another world. He closed his eyes and thought he could hear the voices of all the dead, century upon century of them, whispering. And angels folding and unfolding crumpled wings. So little space. So much darkness. The wings opening and shutting like the pages of great leather books. He crossed himself and opened his eyes and the darkness settled round him, thick and fat, like a darkness of the spirit.

The birth and the death of the Church were here together. The flowering of the monasteries and the coming of Islam. Death upon death, darkness like syrup, angels with wings the size of Africa. Every time, he thought, every time he set foot here the priest in him was brought into the heart of his own unruptured silences. He had entered the Church to escape them, to fill them with words, but here in the darkness of Abu Sarga only the silences remained.

He stepped through the narthex into the nave. The darkness here was sugared with tiny flakes of light that dropped soundlessly from hidden lamps. Pillars of granite flanked narrow aisles, rising into high shadows. It seemed as though, by a strange dispensation, they ceased at some point to be stone and continued forever upwards into places of endless music. They were almost bare, stripped long ago of light and color. Here and there, faint images of forgotten saints could be distinguished, faded and drained of vigor. On the walls, plaster had fallen away, leaving holes in the gold and purple of icons almost as old as the church itself.

He passed through the dusty curtain in the iconostasis screen. Father Gregory was sitting where Paul had expected to find him, on a low wooden stool, facing the central *haykal*. His head was bowed, spilling his long white hair forward across his knees. Paul knew that he came here every day, summer and winter alike, to pray and meditate. His joints would no longer let him kneel, so he sat on his stool instead.

Paul did not interrupt him. He stood nearby, whispering prayers of his own fashioning into the shifting shadows. A candle burned in front of an icon of the Virgin. The church was cold.

An hour and more passed before the old man finally raised his head. He did not look round.

"Is that you, Father Paul?"

"Yes. I've been here a little while."

"I've been expecting you."

"I only decided to come this morning."

The old priest chuckled.

"Last night," he said. "You decided to come last night."

Paul frowned. The old man knew too much.

"Something has happened." Father Gregory did not frame the sentence as a question.

"Yes," Paul answered, looking up at the faded paintings at the rear of the sanctuary. "Something has happened."

"Good. It is almost time."

Paul understood what he meant. He shivered. Not all the wings folding and unfolding in the darkness were angelic.

"I think I have a means of tracking him down."

"Yes?"

"I told you about my brother Michael. Do you remember?"

The old man nodded. He might have been aged anything between seventy and one hundred. His eyes were dulled with age, his teeth blackened stumps. But his mind was as sharp as ever, and his memory unimpaired.

"I remember," he whispered. "Go on."

"It is much as I thought," said Paul. "His people have made contact with him, persuaded him to work for them again. To find al-Qurtubi."

"You didn't want this, did you?"

"No. I tried to warn him, but he paid no heed."

"What was the point of warning him? Those whom God has chosen . . ."

"He is my brother. Chosen or not. He knows nothing of al-Qurtubi. They are all ignorant. To them, he is nothing but the leader of a terrorist organization, an organization whose name they don't even know."

"And only we know the truth?"

"Yes."

"Don't you think that may be a little arrogant of us? Perhaps it's time someone else was told."

"As you yourself just said, what would be the point?"

"You may have to tell your brother."

"He is not a believer. He would not believe me."

"Nevertheless."

"I'll think about it."

"Can your people help him?"

"I think so. Yes. They may succeed in finding al-Qurtubi."

"Can they do it in time, do you think?"

"Perhaps." Paul paused. "There is a complication," he said. "A woman. Her name is A'isha Manfaluti."

"The politician's wife?"

"She's been my brother's . . ." He hesitated. "Michael's lover. For a few months now. They met in England, just after my father died. They were introduced by a man called Holly. He is the Head of Egypt Desk in London."

"And what is the complication?"

"Manfaluti is dead. His wife is missing. I'm afraid al-Qurtubi may have taken her."

"Then may God have mercy on her soul."

"Yes . . ." Paul fell silent.

Father Gregory began to pull himself up from the stool. Paul bent down, taking him by the arm and helping him slowly to his feet. Suddenly, he looked around, as though he had heard something.

"It's nothing, my son. Ignore them. They are only shadows."

"I can't help it, Father. I feel frightened."

"It will pass. Remember, they are nothing. Now, I think it is time for what I told you about."

Paul said nothing. He could not shake off the fear. He had lived with it for eight months, it had become part of him. And here, so close . . .

Resting on Paul's arm, Father Gregory led the way to the northernmost of the three *haykals,* a tall apse on their left. Here, an opening led to a flight of steep steps. A small lamp stood next to it. Father Gregory indicated the lamp, and Paul lit it with a flame taken from a nearby candle.

"This way," said Father Gregory.

Paul led the way down, half turning to assist the old man in his descent. The steps were ancient, made smooth by the passage of generations of pilgrims. Paul had only been down here once, many years before, on his first visit to Cairo after entering the priesthood. That had been before he met Father Gregory.

How little Paul still knew of the Coptic priest. He had asked questions, of course, made enquiries from the patriarchate via the nunciature, but no-one had been able to tell him very much. He did know that the old man had been born almost ninety years earlier to an old Coptic family in a village near Minya. He had taken his vows at the age of fifteen and entered the Dair Baramus monastery in Wadi Natrun, where he had spent most of his long life. At Wadi Natrun, an ancient settlement in the desert just west of Sadat City, Gregory had gained a reputation for scholarship. Invited more than once to the most important monastery, Abu Maqar, he had remained at Dair Baramus with his books and a succession of pet cats that followed him wherever he went.

Later, much later, Gregory had left his bolthold in the desert. Pope Shenouda, the head of the Coptic Church, had himself requested his presence in Cairo. And that was when the difficulties began. For Paul had been unable to reconstruct Gregory's life over the past twenty-five years. There were gaps, mysterious silences, comings and goings that could not be explained. The old priest had been taciturn when asked about his activities. Paul knew he could not entirely trust him. And that he had no choice but to do so.

The crypt beneath the sanctuary dated back to Roman times. It was by repute the place where Mary, Joseph, and the child Jesus had stayed during their flight to Egypt. Joseph, tradition related, had worked on the tower nearby.

Father Gregory paused at the small altar, his head bent in prayer. Paul prayed with him. He had no faith in the traditions, no confidence in any of the sacred sites throughout the region where Christ had eaten or spoken or died. But in the darkness of the crypt, his little unbelief did not seem to matter much.

The old priest raised his head as though listening for something.

"Are you ready?" he asked.

Paul felt his mouth go dry. No, he thought, not for this.

From a pocket in his robe, Father Gregory took a heavy leather wallet. He opened it and took out a large iron key.

"There has only ever been this one key," the old man said. "It has been passed down for generations. Now it is mine for a while."

Paul felt his heart shake, like a small bird quivering in flight.

The old man indicated a stone slab in one corner.

"Here," he said. "Help me lift this."

Paul bent down and found a groove just wide enough to accommodate his fingers. To his surprise, Father Gregory bent down as well and took the other side. The slab moved quite easily. Underneath it was a wooden door.

The key fitted into a large lock. It opened slowly, as though reluctant to give way. When it had been unlocked, Father Gregory returned the key to his wallet and the wallet to his pocket.

He looked at Paul.

"You are shriven?" he asked.

Paul nodded. He had attended confession the day before.

"It would not be well to be in a state of sin. Not where we are going," the old man muttered. He found a round handle recessed in the door, just below the lock. With an effort, he pulled on it. The door lifted. Paul bent to assist the old man. The door came up. At their feet, barely illuminated by the lamp, a flight of ancient steps began their soft and giddy descent.

32

Michael woke with a splitting headache. For several moments, nothing made sense: where he was, where he had come from, what was happening were all conundrums for which he had no answers. His mouth felt unwashed, his stomach simultaneously sick and empty. The room he had been sleeping in was freezing. He suspected some sort of Jesuit asceticism and groaned out loud. Nobody answered.

Forcing his feet out of the bedclothes, he steadied himself before standing. The movement caused his head to swim, as though his brains had been slung forward into the backs of his eyeballs. He wondered when he had ever felt worse. But memory was returning, and with it a sense that he had more to worry about than a sore head. He got to his feet and staggered to the bathroom.

Having used the toilet, he made his way unsteadily back to the bedroom and crawled back inside the blankets, still shivering. He had called for Paul a couple of times, but received no answer. Lying restlessly on the hard bed, he began to drift off again into an uneasy sleep. And with sleep came dreams, dreams he could not fight off.

He was walking through darkness, unbearable darkness. All around him, he could hear a great roaring, and the sound of padding feet. He knew the sphinxes were walking, stalking him through the sightless desert, roaring like lions. The pyramid was close now, just ahead of him. If he did not reach it soon, they would fall on him and tear him limb from limb. Their deep voices, their padded feet, their tails threshing the still night air.

Suddenly he woke up, sweating, trembling. For a long time he lay motionless, unable to shake off the vision of the black sphinxes, the oppressive presence of the great pyramid, unseen but waiting in the darkness.

He looked at his watch. It was well after noon. His head was aching more than ever. Carefully, he got out of bed and looked for his clothes on the chair at its foot. They were just as he had left them the night before, cheap and ugly. He longed for a change of linen. For the touch of silk. For A'isha.

He dressed slowly and made his way to the kitchen. Bright sunlight stabbed his eyes as he opened the door. On the table lay a note left for him by Paul. His brother had been forced to go out on business, but he hoped to be back by late afternoon.

A wave of depression hit him. What was happening to A'isha? He felt helpless, bereft of choice, not knowing whether she was alive or dead, not knowing where to start looking for her. He found coffee beans and ground them, wincing at the noise. Five minutes later, with the first cup of hot black coffee inside him, he began to feel a little better. But the depression would not go away.

He found some cold remedies in the bathroom cupboard. They were nothing but palliatives, they would cure nothing. But the paracetamol might clear his head a little. He washed them down with more coffee. His stomach still rebelled at the thought of anything more solid.

He took the jug of coffee into Paul's study. If only he could think clearly, devise a plan of action, carry out some sort of investigation. Cup in hand, he browsed aimlessly through the rows of books on Paul's shelves. This must only be part of his brother's reputedly vast collection, he thought. The rest must be in Rome. He saw familiar names: Fanon, Said, Hourani, Gellner. But they were outnumbered by the works of writers he had scarcely or never heard of, some in French and Italian, most in Arabic. Fundamentalist tracts sat side by side with sermons by Shaykh Kishk and pronouncements from al-Azhar. On one shelf, he found a collection of books on New Testament apocrypha. There were books in Coptic, Greek, and Syriac. Below that, another shelf held titles on Biblical prophecy, including a number of popular works published recently in the United States. A Moonie publication on the appearance of the Lord of the Second Advent. A Jehovah's Witness tract about Armageddon. Michael marveled at the range of his brother's learning.

And yet, hard as he looked, he could not find a pattern. Paul must have selected the books he had shipped to Egypt with some care. They must relate in some fashion to his work here. He had told Michael it was a study of Islamic fundamentalism, but the books suggested more than that. Certainly, there was an emphasis on the modern period. With the exception of a Qur'an and two standard *hadith* collections, the books on Islam had all been written in the present century. But how did that square with the New Testament material? Or the books on modern American millenarianism? Was Paul doing a comparative study of Islamic and Christian fundamentalism?

Michael put a copy of Schneemelcher and Hennecke's *Neutestamentliche Apokryphen* back on the shelf. He turned, as though startled by a sudden noise or movement. But the room was silent, still. There was something about the books, the incongruity of their juxtaposition, the way they nestled together, that unsettled him. He shivered. His depression about A'isha was getting to him. There was nothing wrong here. What did he know about his brother's work?

At the end of one shelf he came across a large photograph album, squeezed in between a Bible Atlas and Webster's dictionary. It seemed familiar. Pulling it out he recognized it as the one in which his father had kept their family snaps. Paul must have brought it back here from Oxford after the funeral.

He took the album to the other side of the room, to a gilded armchair in the "Luwis Khamastashar" style favored by the furniture-makers round Bab al-Luq station. "Luwis Khamastashar" translated as "Louis XV," but the chair did not. It seemed out of place here, like the furniture in most rectories Michael had ever seen. He opened the album, remembering at once days of winter and fires burning in a small grate. With his mother, he had once sat leafing through memories that belonged to other people. And now his own were mingled with them: snapshots of himself and Paul, on the beach at Brighton; his mother in the garden at home, playing tennis with her sons; Michael with Uncle Jurji in the old family home in Cairo; Paul at his first communion, embarrassed, proud.

For some reason, photographs had been removed from many pages and not replaced. Only the old-fashioned snapshot corners remained to show where they once had been. Michael could not at first understand just what had been taken out or why, but after several pages it became clear: there were no photographs of his father, not alone, not with his mother, not with Michael, not with Paul, not with anyone. Quickly, Michael ran through the pages of the album. No, it was not a mistake: there were no photographs of his father anywhere.

For a long time after that, Michael sat unmoving in the inappropriate, uncomfortable chair, staring at tokens of the past that no longer quite made sense. He had known that Paul and his father had had disagreements, chiefly over the role of armies in the world and the concept of a "just war." But his father and Paul had always been close and he had always envied his brother that link with a man he himself had both admired and feared. Had Paul harbored other, more negative feelings about their father, that he should have attempted to erase him so wholly from his life?

He stood and went to the shelves to put the album back in its place. As he did so, he noticed the edge of something sticking out from behind the Bible Atlas. It looked like a large envelope. He put down the album and drew the article out. He was right. It was a thick manila envelope filled with what might very well be photographs. His father's? The ones Paul had removed from the album?

Michael carried the envelope back to the chair. Why had Paul concealed it behind a row of books when he might have kept it in his desk drawer? Had he been unable to destroy the photographs, yet wanted them out of sight? There was no inscription on the envelope, nothing to indicate what it contained. The flap had not been sealed. Michael opened it and tipped the contents out onto the floor.

Not photographs of his father. Not memories—or at least he hoped not. No, how could his brother, how could a priest have memories like these? Perhaps they belonged to Father Dominic, perhaps . . . Tagged, arranged in groups within small folders, in some perverse sequence or diabolical taxonomy, a heap of black and white and colored photographs spilled onto the carpet.

He picked one up. A head and shoulders of a man in his thirties, Arab probably, that looked as though it had been taken from a police file. Clipped to it was a second photograph, a larger one, a blow-up of the same man's face, quite clearly dead. A date had been scrawled across the foot of the second shot. There were several more groups after the same fashion, a man's or a woman's face, then a shot of the same individual after death. Beneath these were other photographs, all taken at the scenes of terrorist attacks, showing the results of the carnage in sickening detail, all with dates. Michael had seen photographs like these before, but it did not make it any easier looking through them.

He felt sick. In the bathroom, he threw up all the coffee he had drunk. It did not help. He returned to the study. With numb fingers, he scooped the photographs up and returned them to the envelope, then replaced it in its hiding-place on the bookshelf.

As he slipped it back into place, he noticed something else in the space behind the books, something wrapped in coarse cloth. He took it out and unwrapped it. It was a gun, a Walther P38, the long-time favorite of Italy's Red Brigades. A twist of paper held a dozen extra rounds. The paper was a letter. A letter from someone in the Vatican: a letter addressed to Father Paul Hunt.

33

He opened his eyes. He was in bed, in the rectory as before, except that it was dark now. Someone was bending over him, someone who seemed familiar, yet not familiar.

"How long have you been like this?"

Been like what? He tried to sit up, but a hand pushed him firmly back onto the bed. His eyes stung if he opened them too widely.

"Michael, are you able to understand me?"

For a moment, he thought it must be A'isha. But that was impossible. A'isha was dead. Dead or vanished, it made no difference. And the voice was a man's. There was something else too, something he could not place.

"I'm going for a doctor, Michael. You'll be all right, he's someone you can trust."

Of course, that was it. The something else. This voice was speaking in English. It must be Paul, his brother. He felt a hand on his forehead, solicitous, but . . . But what? He knew there was something he had to remember, something about Paul, but it escaped him. In an effort to draw it back, he reached out a hand. Someone held it firmly, then let go. It was like being cast adrift.

"I'll be back soon," the voice said. Paul's voice. Perhaps they were back in England, back home. Perhaps Egypt had all been a dream. He held out his hand for mummy, but there was no-one, no-one.

The dream began again, the dream of the black pyramid. He had clambered up the steep causeway and was now standing at the entrance. The doorway soared above his head, reaching unimaginable heights: fifty, sixty, one hundred feet. And yet, from a distance it had seemed a mere speck in the surface of the great structure.

A long corridor stretched away from him, flanked on either side by tall torchères bearing white flames in the dishes at their tip. He was more reluctant than ever to continue walking, but somehow he had been brought within the doors. There was a loud crashing sound behind him, and he knew he was enclosed within the pyramid. The corridor stretched ahead of him forever.

The dream faded and was replaced by others of which he could remember nothing. When he woke again, it was the pyramid that remained in his mind, sharp and disturbing.

"Mr. Hunt. Can you hear me, Mr. Hunt?"

He opened his eyes very carefully. There was little light in the room. He thought it must be the same room he had been in before. With Paul. That's right, he had been with Paul. Except . . . Except, there was something about Paul he had to remember.

"Paul . . ." He managed to whisper his brother's name.

"It's all right, Mr. Hunt. Your brother is here. He'll speak with you later, when you're stronger. Right now, I want to examine you. Please don't try to do anything. Just relax. I can do everything I want without disturbing you."

A light was shone in his eyes, first the left, then the right, blinding him. When it was withdrawn, it left bright spots in a cup of darkness. Soft hands palpated his chest, a stethoscope was pressed against his skin, cold and hard. He felt the pressure of a thermometer in his armpit, then its abrupt removal. A hand on his wrist, the fingers perfectly placed, as though holding a bird. The prick of a needle in his arm. Darkness.

A figure in a dim room, seated on a high platform. A man with a goat's head. Eyes like coals, watching him.

"A'isha," he whispered. "It's time to unwrap mummy."

"He's a little delirious." The doctor's voice. What was Doctor Philips doing here? And why was the silly man speaking Arabic? Didn't he know they were in England?

"Is it what we suspected?" Paul was speaking. But Paul was in Rome.

"It's too early to tell. We can only hope not. There have only been a few cases in the capital so far."

"Officially."

"Yes, I know. But even the unofficial reports are within reason. It travels slowly at first."

"How soon will you know?"

"About your brother? A day or so. It's very difficult without access to a laboratory. They've all been closed down, you know."

"Closed down? I didn't know that. What on earth for?"

"What do you think? *Jahiliyya,* of course. Western science, Western medicine. All anti-Islamic, all fit for the dustbin."

"What about Michael? If you do reach a positive diagnosis, can you treat him? Have you got drugs?"

A brief silence.

"No. Under ordinary circumstances, supplies would have been shipped in specially. But there's an embargo. The borders have been closed. However, I and a few others are trying our best. There are ways."

"Could we get him out? I can arrange transportation."

"I doubt it. Not in his present condition. Certainly not if he gets worse. But try not to worry yet. This could just be a result of anxiety and exhaustion. There's a danger of overreacting. Your brother has a fever at present, that's all. There are no other symptoms."

"I'll go back to the church now. I want to pray."

"Yes, do that. Pray for him. It may be all you can do. Pray for all of them."

"For all of us, doctor. I'll pray for all of us."

The dreams were never-ending, without pattern. Only the dream of the pyramid made any sense. He walked for what seemed miles through torchlit passages, bleak and smooth and shining. The further he went, the more he had a sense of age. Somewhere in the distance, he could hear a beating of wings, as though a great bird or bat were flying toward him down the echoing expanses of the vast building. And from somewhere else came the padding of great feet, as though a terrible beast were stalking him. Or a man with the head of a goat.

The doctor returned several times a day for three days. By the end, Michael was growing coherent again. Between bursts of delirium, he could hold brief conversations about how he felt. He tried to ask about A'isha and Paul, but the doctor would not let him pursue topics that were likely to be distressing.

On the fourth day, the doctor declared him on the road to recovery. He had had a minor infection, much exacerbated by the strain he had been under. Rest and nourishment would see him back on his feet in another week. But after that he would have to take things easy.

"As soon as you're fit to travel, we're arranging for you to get out of Egypt. Your brother tells me your life will be at risk as long as you stay."

"I've got to find A'isha. I won't leave without her."

"We'll talk about that later. Now you should rest."

"You haven't told me your name."

"Faris Ibrahimian," the doctor said. He was a little man, gray-haired, with a face lined with endurance or stubbornness. An Armenian name and features to match. "You don't remember me," he said. "I was a friend of your mother's. A good friend. You were just a child when we met."

"I think I remember now. I remember her mentioning your name. Our families were close."

"Yes," the doctor said, "our families were close. Until Suez. Things fell apart. Most of my family went to Europe. I stayed on. My skills were needed then."

"And now?"

The little man grimaced and turned aside to fiddle with a clutter of tiny bottles.

"How long have I been ill?"

"About four days. You've made a good recovery, I'm pleased with you."

"I remember . . ."

"Yes?"

"You were speaking with my brother. Or perhaps it was just a dream. I had so many dreams. But I remember something about an illness that had just arrived in the capital. You sounded worried."

The doctor did not reply at once. He busied himself with his bottles, sorting them and putting them away in a little bag. He had long thin hands, the fingers jointed with broad knuckles.

"Yes," he said. "You remember correctly. It was not a dream. You're out of danger now, so I can tell you. There has been an outbreak of plague. The first reports came from Upper Egypt about a fortnight ago. Conditions in the provinces have been getting bad. Disease vectors are increasing. No-one believed the diagnosis at first. Then there were more cases. The government tried to hush it up, of course. Then they tried to close off all regions where the sickness had been reported. They imposed a quarantine. But it was already too late. There have been cases as far north as Alexandria."

"Are people dying?"

"Yes, of course they are. The authorities refuse to let doctors use modern treatments. Medicine is part of the contamination of Western culture. So people are dying and will go on dying. Dear God, it could wipe out most of the population."

"Surely the World Health Organization . . ."

The doctor laughed.

"I told you, the borders have been closed. All airports, ports, land crossings. No-one is allowed in or out. They've declared Egypt Dar al-Islam and say the rest of the world, even the Islamic world, is now Dar al-Kufr: the Realm of Unbelief. There was an announcement about the plague on the radio this morning. God is testing the faithful. He is weeding out the *munafiqun,* the hypocrites.

"They are quoting the sacred Traditions. The words of the Prophet from al-Bukhari: 'When you hear that plague has broken out in a country, do not travel there. And if it breaks out in the country in which you live, do not leave.' That is their chief justification for the total blockade. It has played into their hands perfectly."

"And when believers start dying? The faithful. Members of the Council."

The doctor shrugged.

"They have that covered already. Al-Bukhari again. 'Whoever dies of the plague is a martyr.' They say God will deliver them. Perhaps He will."

For some reason, Michael remembered the figure with the goat's head, the wide-eyed stare, the dark, flared nostrils, the head turning slowly in the light of a thousand lamps.

"And if He doesn't?"

"A plague could be devastating. If it's a mutated virus, nothing will be able to stop it. I have my own doubts about the long-term effects of vaccination. It distorts the immune system. A plague mutation combined with an immunologically weakened population could wreak havoc. Even people who might normally be immune would succumb. Perhaps it's a blessing they've decided to seal the country off." The doctor paused. "We've talked enough. You're tired. You still need rest. Do you think you could eat a little soup later?"

Michael nodded.

"Will Paul be coming?"

Ibrahimian did not answer.

"I asked if Paul was coming."

The little doctor looked up.

"No," he said. "He won't be coming. I saw him last on the day he brought me in to look after you. No-one has seen him since then. He was supposed to say mass on Wednesday morning, but he didn't turn up. He hasn't been at the nunciature for days."

The silence that followed was marred by only one thing. Michael had remembered the photographs he had found in Paul's study.

34

**The Cathedral Church of Christ and Blessed
Mary the Virgin
Durham City
England
24 December**

The cathedral was hushed, plunged in semi-darkness, speckled with a few points of candle light. Someone coughed. Someone else sneezed. Above the congregation, the great stone vaulting of the Norman ceiling rose into shadow and became darkness. The nave and side aisles were full of people, the largest congregation of the year, as always. They had come for the festival of nine lessons and carols, in their woolen scarves and thick overcoats, their rubber boots and knitted gloves, their stale humanity. With them they had brought their children and their own memories of childhood Christmases.

There was a rustling sound at the massive south door, where the famous demon's-head knocker kept watch over Palace Green. Heads turned to catch a first glimpse of the procession. The choir began to sing, "Once in Royal David's City," a single voice at first, a boy's voice, very pure and very sweet, startlingly clear in the enormous emptiness, then others joining in, a plangent swell of sound, echoing and echoing. And in the darkness, candles, a stream of candles moving from east to west. In front, a tall silver cross, flanked by long candles, then the choirmaster, walking slowly backwards, his arms rising and falling gently as he conducted his charges, then the choir proper, all in white surplices, some wearing small crosses around their necks, on purple ribbons. And then, suddenly, the bright colored vestments of the senior clergy, the Canons of the Chapter, the Archdeacon, visiting clerics, the Dean, and, at the rear, the new Bishop, Simon Ashton. In his right hand, he held a wooden crook. A verger walked in front, an old man in black, carrying a short silver stave.

Many curious eyes fell on the bishop as he passed. He had been enthroned only three months earlier, and this was to be his first celebration of Christmas in his own cathedral, with his own flock. There were mixed feelings among the congregation about their new pastor. His predecessor had been controversial, greatly disliked by conservatives both inside and outside the Church, much admired by liberals. Ashton came from the Church's evangelical wing and had been a close associate of Archbishop Carey. He was opposed to the ordination of women, rejected the very idea of homosexuality among the clergy, and had dedicated himself to the revival of Christian influence in an age of materialism.

Shortly after his enthronement, the bishop had preached a sermon that had been widely quoted in the press and threatened to make him at least as controversial as the man before him. In Muslim countries, he said, Christian minorities, where they existed at all, lived under sometimes severe restrictions. International Muslim missions sought to convert Copts, Armenians, Syrians, Maronites, and others wherever and whenever they could. The bishop had condemned all such activities, implying that, if Christians were not granted full religious liberty in countries like Egypt, Iran, and Syria, British Muslims might find themselves enjoying fewer freedoms than hitherto. The sermon had been widely condemned by Muslim leaders in Bradford, Manchester, London, and elsewhere.

The choir had reached the fourth verse.

> *For he is our childhood's pattern,*
> *Day by day like us he grew,*
> *He was little, weak and helpless,*
> *Tears and smiles like us he knew.*

There was a movement somewhere around the middle of the nave, at the very point where the rear of the procession was passing. A man stepped out of a pew on the south side of the church and made straight for the procession. Only a few people noticed him at first. He stepped in front of the bishop, forcing him to halt. The choir, oblivious of what was happening, continued to process, song among stone, a harmony beyond earthly measure.

> *And our eyes at last shall see him*
> *Through his own redeeming love . . .*

"What is it?" asked the bishop. "What do you want? If you need to speak with me, come after the service. I have to continue in the procession."

The man shook his head. He was holding something in his right hand. Beneath his breath, he whispered something inaudible. The silence sucked the words away. In the nearest pews, voices were raised, a puzzled murmur, still muted by shock.

"Please," said the bishop, "you have to stand aside. I . . ."

There was an explosion, like a shouting of thunder in the great church. It echoed back and forth among the huge, patterned pillars of the nave. The voices of the choirboys straggled into separate silences. Someone screamed. The bishop had fallen to his knees, as though in prayer. There was a second shot, and he toppled backwards. He did not move again. No-one moved. For a moment, the church was a vast, candlelit tableau.

And the bishop's killer, with a simple movement, raised his gun, and slipped the barrel into his open mouth, and breathed once, and fired.

PART V

"I shall erect a mighty wall between you and them"

QUR'AN 18:95

35

They had reached the warehouse three days earlier. Things had settled down a little after that, but it was getting dangerous now and she knew they would have to move on again soon.

She had barely escaped in time that first night. Butrus had come for her long after midnight, through a rear entrance. He knew of Megdi's disappearance and the raid on her office. He had taken her back to his apartment, using a complicated route to throw off possible pursuers. She had not argued, not after what she had seen at the tomb and in her office.

Returning to her apartment in the hour before dawn, they had seen a light in the window and the shadows of strangers etched against the blind. The air had been full of thunder, she had felt it sink and settle in her breast. Butrus had held her hand almost like a lover, and they had slunk away into the shadows, looking for a place to hide.

That morning, they had not gone back to the apartment in Misr al-Jadida where Butrus lived. They headed for his parents' house, several blocks away, only to find it empty. Later, a friend told them that a party of *muhtasibin* had come in the middle of the night and taken the old couple away. They might be in jail, they might be dead: no-one knew.

She took a cigarette from her pocket and lit it. Her hand trembled slightly as she did so, sending a gentle ripple along the flame. She shook the match hard and tossed it to the floor. The sounds of the match grating against the box and the insignificant flaring of the little flame had been the first in over an hour. It was silent here, too full of expectation. No, not expectation: dread.

They had decided against the countryside. People noticed you there, no-one could remain safe for long from prying eyes or wagging tongues. She had relatives in the Delta, in a village called Tukh al-Aqlam; but even if they could be trusted, their neighbors could not. There were religious busybodies everywhere now, and many of the villages boasted imams who made it their business to poke their noses into everyone's affairs. In the countryside, they would not have lasted a week.

The city had the virtue of anonymity, but it demanded skill to remain in hiding and alive. Their good fortune lay in the fact that Butrus was a Copt and, what was more, one with contacts in the militant wing of the young Copt movement. He had friends who were willing to hide them for a day or two at a time. But always they had to move on, always they had to watch their backs.

She had not yet told Butrus about Michael—what he really meant to her, what she hoped for from him, if she hoped for anything at all. He knew of Michael, of course, and she thought he had always been a little jealous. Butrus was unmarried and, as far as she knew, unattached. During the three years they had worked together, he had never so much as asked her out. That was not surprising: Christian men kept clear of Muslim women as a matter of course. Such liaisons were not merely unwise, they were positively dangerous.

But she knew he watched her when he thought she was

not looking, observed her comings and goings keenly, re-membered her birthday, scrutinized her moods, knew just how she liked her coffee. That was why she had turned to him when she knew herself to be in danger. And she felt guilty for it, felt she was taking advantage of him, betraying the love or the lust or whatever it was he underwent for her.

Her love for Michael was not perfect, of course, it was not a barrier against all other affection or a wall against self-absorption. But at the moment it was all that stood be-tween her and some form of final desperation. That was all women like her had: despair of the past, with its veils and its coffins rushed to the grave without lamentation; despair of the future, with its choices that were not choices: marriage without love or fornication without security.

She smoked the cigarette slowly, savoring it, knowing it might be the last she would have for a long time. The ware-house belonged to a friend of Butrus, a painter called Salama Bustani, who used it as his studio and, on occasions, as a place to live. It had been a pickle store originally, and the sour odor of *turshi* still hung in the limp air, mixed now with the smells of oil paint, acrylic, and thinner. The floor underfoot was thick with the unswept shells of roasted wa-termelon seeds: Salama was not tidy in his habits.

The bare walls were festooned with his canvases, mon-strous creations that his few friends admired and his many detractors regarded as garbage. His inspiration was the im-agery of the Church, above all the icons of the saints, the staring eyes and the tense, unsmiling lips. In his paintings, pale martyrs and hermits took on bestial forms: they grew horns and tails and ragged wings, their eyes grew huge with lust, their gilded flesh was turned to clay. But they possessed a singular grandeur that A'isha was only now beginning to understand.

She had met the artist only once since their arrival. They had shaken hands and exchanged a few words. Now she wanted to see him again, to ask him why there was so much loathing in his figures yet so much tenderness in their eyes. Last night she had dreamed of Salama. The dream was still fresh in her memory. She had dreamed that he was naked, that they were both naked and gilded, and that he possessed her in a frenzy with his tail thrashing and his leather wings beating the silver air.

She shuddered and slipped the memory to one side. The door opened and Butrus came in.

He shook his head.

"It's getting worse," he said. "They're rounding people up. Last night they came for Marquis." They had been there just four nights ago, before coming to the warehouse.

"Do you think . . . ?"

He shook his head again.

"No, we're not what they're after. Anyone's at risk now. We have to stay here another night."

"Shouldn't we move on? You said more than two nights in one place could be risky. We've been here three already."

"I know, but I can't find anywhere else to go. People are jumpy. I don't blame them. Someone . . ." He paused, his eyes moving from her face to a spot on the wall behind. He looked troubled.

"What is it?"

"Someone's been asking questions about me. Wanting to know if anyone has seen me or heard where I might be staying. One of my friends said . . . He said they've been offering money—quite a lot of money—to anybody who might tell them where I might be found. They may be asking about you as well."

The news made her mind up for her, but she still hesitated. It was so small a thing, yet it seemed a full-blown betrayal. As though she were giving Butrus a hold over her. Over her and Michael both. But if she kept quiet . . .

"Butrus," she said, "we have to find Michael. He can help us find a way out of Egypt."

"That's easier said than done. All the borders are closed. No-one can get in or out."

"Then we have to get out illegally. Listen . . ."

And she told him everything. About Michael, about the face beneath the mask, what he had once been. Butrus listened impassively, but she could sense his disapproval. Like most young Copts, Butrus was a fervent nationalist, he loved Egypt and wanted her continued independence. He hated the present regime, hated any regime that discriminated against his people; but foreign agents on Egyptian soil were past detestation.

"He's not an agent any more, Butrus. He resigned years ago. But he still has contacts." She said nothing about what Michael had been doing in Alexandria. "He can help us, we have to find him."

He shook his head sharply. She could sense his anger, the warmth of it, and beneath the warmth, the coolness.

"I don't want help from the British," he said. "That was the one decent thing in our modern history, that we kicked the British out, that we took control of our own destiny. The Turks, the Mamluks, the French, the British—we've sent them all packing. We're our own rulers for the first time in centuries. And now you want to go begging for sops at their table."

His reaction stung. He did not understand. But she saw no point in arguing.

"That isn't important," she said. "Not now. What is important is that we get out, that we tell someone what we know. Or perhaps you think we should just forget the whole thing."

He said nothing.

She looked at him.

"Have you got a cigarette?"

"No, I . . ."

"God, I could use a cigarette. My nerves are shot to hell."

"There aren't any in the shops. They . . ."

She stood up abruptly and crossed to the wall. He watched helplessly as she crashed her fist against it time after time. It hurt him how much he loved her, how little he could do about it.

"You'll hurt yourself," he said.

"So what?" She turned and looked at him. Her hand was raw where it had struck the naked brick.

"Look at you," he countered. "You're a mess."

"You think I want to be a mess? You think I want any of this?"

He shook his head, his eyes fixed on the floor, on the clutter of watermelon seeds. After A'isha's husband disappeared, he had said and done nothing to declare his feelings for her. Every day he had expected news of Rashid's death and, with it, the possibility, the bare possibility that, in due course, she might feel herself free to love him. Once Rashid was dead, he had known she would need time, time to grieve, to come to terms with her loss. He had steeled himself to patience. And then, like a black cloud invading his calm blue sky, Michael Hunt had made his appearance and wiped out for good all his hopes and dreams.

He looked at her sadly.

"You're right," he said, "we have to get out." He paused. "Very well, then. Can you find Michael?"

She leaned against the wall.

"Just one cigarette," she whispered. "One fucking cigarette, that's all." She raised her eyes and shook her head slowly from side to side. "I don't know," she said. "I'm sorry, maybe I shouldn't have mentioned it. I wrote to him in Alexandria, but I never got a reply. Then all this happened. Maybe he's back in Cairo, maybe he's looking for me. I don't know."

"Then it's just a waste of time, what you've been telling me."

"I don't know. Maybe. But there is someone who might be able to help, someone who could find out where Michael is. It means taking a risk, coming into the open."

"Very well, we'll go to this man. Who is he?"

"Ahmad Shukri. His name is Ahmad Shukri."

"You know him?"

She nodded. She felt tired. Tired and sick.

"Yes," she whispered. "I know him, I know what he does."

Butrus waited. He could sense the fear and the loathing in her voice.

"Ahmad Shukri is my uncle," she said. "My father's brother. He's . . ." She stopped and looked at Butrus. "He's a colonel in the *mukhabarat*. His office is in the Security Headquarters in Maydan Lazughli. And he was the main source for British intelligence there when Michael was Head of Station in Cairo."

36

Sometimes he would lie in bed, listening to tiny changes in the world outside. He would send his thoughts out into the streets like scavengers, guessing what might be going on in the city. They came back to him empty-handed. Five times a day, he would listen to the call to prayer from the nearby Yusuf al-Shurbaji mosque, marking and re-marking the boundaries of piety and ungodliness. It took so little faith to enter heaven, as little as a grain of mustard-seed. And so little unbelief to enter hell, the shimmer and dip of a king-fisher's wing in shallow waters: the look of a woman's face, shimmer and dip, or the beckoning in a boy's eyes. Dip and shimmer. Michael had never known such deep despair.

Sometimes he sat on a chair beside the little window and looked out. There was a courtyard dark with cypresses, and peacocks on frosted grass where the snow had melted, and the shadow of a tall minaret slanting across the wall in the late afternoons. There had once been a fountain, a small bronze fountain that brought life to the courtyard, but it was dry now and choked with leaves and debris. If he listened very carefully, Michael could hear it murmur in the stillness. That was in his imagination. And it was in his imaginings that he entered the depths of his despair.

Why had Paul let him down? First his father, then Carol, now Paul. Betrayal ran through his family and his loves like a virus. He himself was not exempt. Which made Paul's treachery all the harder to bear. Like all unbelievers, Michael hoped for perfection in the godly.

Doctor Ibrahimian called regularly, bringing food and medicine. The little doctor's face and gestures were marked with the traces of some indelible sadness. The sides of his mouth were pulled down permanently, his eyes sunken, shadowed, dismayed. His sadness lacked grace and strength, lacked, above all, the perplexity that might have served as its redemption. He was an exile in his own country, a man without a home or the memory of one. His hands were cold, he was bereft of passion, at midnight he would wake and listen to his own breathing in a vast, empty room and think of nothing. Nothing whatever.

Michael questioned him about what was happening outside. Ibrahimian said he was frightened. They were rounding up doctors, anyone likely to challenge the official approach to the spreading pestilence. And foreigners: they were rounding them up and putting them in camps. The Copts were growing jittery. There had been trouble in Minya.

The doctor left a small radio on which Michael was able to receive local broadcasts. He would listen for a while, then grow tired of speeches and sermons, of endless Qur'an recitations and interminable prayers. There was very little news, and what there was had no substance, like spongy white bread. When he tired of the radio, he sat by the window, staring into the courtyard. He saw someone come and go several times, a stooped figure in dark clothes. When he asked Ibrahimian who it was, the doctor shrugged and said nothing.

On Sunday, no-one came to mass. Father Dominic was still in the hospital, Paul was still missing. Those few who wanted to attend were taken by car to the Church of the Holy Family in al-Ma'adi. Michael spent the day reading.

When he went back to bed that night, he could not remember a word of what he had read.

Ibrahimian did not turn up on Monday. Michael found a little food in the kitchen and made himself a meal which he threw up later. There was no news on the radio. Once, he heard the sound of someone crying outside, but when he looked there was no-one there. The *adhan* continued, five times a day, as before. Once, he heard children playing, their voices far away. They did not return. Ibrahimian did not come on Tuesday.

That was the night Michael decided to visit the church. He had heard sounds from that direction earlier in the day, and now, in the late evening, he was troubled that Ibrahimian had still not shown up. He was, of course, feeling restless by now. He resented being cooped up alone in a tiny room day after day. Perhaps those were not his only reason for venturing abroad, perhaps he was prompted to the church by other needs. To reassert a forgotten paradigm, perhaps, to look for some sort of calm in a world gone quite mad. He was vulnerable, of course he was.

Between the rectory and the church lay a patch of open ground traversed diagonally by a cracked concrete path. Michael crossed it quickly, heading for the side door of the church. In the sky above him, quick, nervous stars pulsed meaninglessly. The moon was in its twentieth night, a wasting globe still bloated with light. What was it he had once heard about a plague moon? Would the epidemic reach its height when tomorrow's moon grew thin and wasted?

To Michael's surprise, the church door was already unlocked. He replaced the key in his pocket and slipped inside, letting the door fall shut behind him. The familiar smells of wax and faded incense caught him unawares, throwing him back instantly to a childhood of hopes and delusions. The side door opened directly into a small vestry. Michael pressed a light switch by the door, illuminating the little room with the flickering light of a fluorescent lamp. An open cupboard held vestments. On a table, packets of candles were stacked in an uneven heap. A low shelf held a variety of missals in several languages. On one wall, a recent photograph of the Pope, the cheeks gaunt with the ravages of illness, kept vigil over the room's treasures.

He heard a faint sound from the other side of the door leading into the church proper. A small, scampering sound, rapidly hushed. Mice, he thought, or rats. The thought of the latter was disturbing. They were a major vector for the plague virus. He reached up and doused the lights.

He had brought his gun, the Helwan taken from the *mukhabarat* agent. During the day, he had checked it over and oiled it, using a small bottle kept for extreme unction. No doubt it had been a sin to use it for such a purpose, but Michael's first concern had been survival, not the avoidance of sin. The action was smooth, but there had been no opportunity to test-fire the weapon, so he was forced to take it on trust that it would do its job.

Holding his breath, he opened the door a crack, not knowing if it would creak. He had expected light or darkness, but nothing could have prepared him for what he actually saw.

For a moment, he thought the church was on fire. It was as though someone had taken the moon and torn it into pieces, scattering the fragments in a burst of madness all through the sleeping church. The naked, moving flames of a thousand candles shimmered on oiled wood and colored glass and the lambent trembling of painted gold. In every shadow, particles of light danced and sang. The church was filled with light, yet curiously dark, as though the candle flames were being taken gently into the darkness, into the night, to be snuffed out one by one. And the shadows were growing about the particles of light.

Michael stepped cautiously through the door. As he did so, he heard another sound, a scuffling of feet from the direction of the main doors. He swung round just in time to see a dark figure run out into the waiting night. Michael dashed after him, pulling the gun awkwardly from his pocket as he ran.

The door hung wide open. Outside, five steps led down to a short path running to a gate. The gate led into the street. It was pitch dark. Michael heard the gate crash shut. He ran to it and opened it, dashing into the street in time to see his quarry leap onto the pillion seat of a small motorcycle. The rider kicked the engine into life and the bike pulled rapidly away from the curb, out into the night.

The street was narrow and deserted. Michael sank back against the gatepost, cold and weakened by his sudden, pointless effort. Somewhere a dog barked, startled by the sudden roar. The rider gunned the engine, pushing it hard. It rose in pitch, then faded into the wider silences of the night. The dog went on barking for a little while. Others joined it, then they too fell silent. A woman's voice was raised. In a house nearby, someone was weeping loudly. Michael dragged himself from the gate and walked back wearily to the church.

In the darkness, the candles burned quietly. His eyes traveled round the church, sifting light from shadow, air from stone. He stepped forward gently, closing the door behind him, listening to his heart beat in the hollow of his chest. Something was wrong.

To his left stood a tall plaster statue of the Virgin and Child. Someone had painted her breasts bright red. He could not see her face, because they had placed a goat's head on top of the statue's. The horns were broad and twisted, the thin beard white and matted with blood. He wanted to look away, but could not. His gaze was held, transfixed as it were by the gross blasphemy. Or was it, perhaps, the quiet dignity of the white-robed figure beneath the butcher's head and the scarlet paint, the simple beauty of those robes, the child wide awake in the cradling arms?

He turned away at last. On the other side of the church, a statue of St John the Baptist had been beheaded. Someone had tied an animal's penis—whether camel or bull, Michael could not tell—by a cord round his thin waist. The light of the candles swayed across the headless torso, turning it to gold. One candle burned down to its socket and went out.

All down the center of the nave, speckled with fine pieces of candlelight, a trail of blood stretched unbroken to the altar. Michael felt his heart throb with a sudden onset of fear and certainty. Like a participant in a bizarre midnight mass, he walked slowly down the spangled aisle, while on both sides candles guttered and turned to smoke and wax.

On the white altar cloth, they had written a passage in Arabic, the second half of a verse from the Qur'an, speaking of the death of Jesus: *ma qataluhu wa ma salabuhu wala-kin shubbiha lahum.* "They did not kill him, nor did they crucify him, but one like him was made to appear to them in his place."

Michael looked up. Above the altar hung a crucifix. They had taken down the plaster figure of the wounded god and set up their own victim in its place. They had stripped him naked, but for a pair of bloodstained underpants, and lashed him to the cross with thick cords before nailing his hands and feet. On his head, they had placed, not thorns, but a crown of broken razor blades, rusted and smeared with dried blood. The head was bent, leaving the face invisible.

The ladder they had used was still propped against one arm of the cross. Wearily, like someone walking in his sleep or in the depth of a black depression, Michael set his foot on the first rung. It seemed such a height to climb, and he felt so heavy and so like lead. There was no sound, no sound at all. He reached the bleeding feet and kept on climbing. The ladder had become a mountain he had to conquer. At the chest now, his legs trembling and unsteady, the ladder rocking on the cross.

Michael rested one hand on the wooden arm, and with the other raised the man's head. Ribbons of blood had traced dark lines across the cheeks and forehead. Beneath, the stubble of three or four days' beard scraped Michael's hand. But he did not need to bring a cloth or razor to know whose face he gazed on. He bent down, spent, lost, aching, and gently kissed his brother's swollen eyes.

37

The worst thing, Michael realized later, was that he had no-one with whom to speak. He had friends and acquaintances scattered about the city, but there was no-one to whom he could turn in his present disarray. There were a few he trusted, but those he did not want to betray. The rest he might have depended on in ordinary times; but these were not ordinary times. Even on the most practical level, he could not think of anyone to whom he could report Paul's death. Not to the police, certainly. He had no way of getting in touch with Ibrahimian. And Father Dominic was still too ill in hospital to be disturbed.

In the end, he telephoned the papal nunciature directly. A tired voice answered, the tense voice of an Italian *addetto* who spoke poor Arabic. He took the message without comment, as though priests were reported murdered every day. In some parts of the world, Michael reflected, that might almost be the case. No doubt some papal diplomats became inured to tragedy. The *addetto* said someone would be in touch.

Two priests came in less than half an hour, thin, disheveled men without clerical collars, wrapped heavily against the cold. They were Belgians, Fathers Verhaeren and Laermans. Michael did not accompany them to the church. When they returned, their faces were ashen.

"Mr. Hunt," said one of them, he had no idea which, "we would like you to come back to the nunciature with us."

"If it's all the same to you, I'd like to stay here. Just for a little while, until I get over this . . ."

The priest shook his head. He had dark curly hair and eyes like a spaniel with rickets. Michael thought he seemed anxious about something. Not ordinarily anxious, not anxious as he might justifiably have been under the circumstances. No, there was something else. It was as if—Michael pondered—yes, as if the priest was trapped, as if he was clawing his way out from soil or leaves or spiraling sand, from a whirlpool that tried to suck him in.

"It isn't that," he said. "You must try to understand: it is not safe for you here. Not now. Your brother told us about you, about your work. You will be welcome to stay at the nunciature for as long as you need. But first there is someone who wants to meet you. Tonight. If you're ready, we'll take you there now."

"What about . . .?" He meant Paul, but he could not finish the sentence. His whole life had become an unfinished sentence. Words, just words.

"That will be taken care of. I am very sorry, Mr. Hunt. I knew your brother. He was a fine man. A fine priest."

Michael looked up. He had been staring at the floor.

"Was he?"

"Yes. I think you know that."

"I don't know anything."

"Please come with us."

Michael shrugged. What else was there to do? They had cut Megdi's throat, strangled Ronnie Perrone, crucified Paul and he did not even know who they were.

"The authorities," Michael said. "Are you telling them?"

"About what happened here?" The priest shook his

head. He looked uneasily at his companion. "No," he said. "I don't think so."

The priests had come in a small car, a Fiat. For the return trip, Michael sat in the back, feeling a little like a prisoner being moved from one jail to another. He looked out of the window, seeing Cairo for the first time in days. Because of Ramadan, the curfew of the coup's early days had been suspended, and moving about the city by night had become, if not exactly safe, at least a lot less risky than before. The streets were deserted and lit only in places. Tattered banners emblazoned with religious and political slogans hung limply across the main roads. *Al-nasr qarib* proclaimed one: "Victory is near." It had never seemed so far away. The covering of snow that had lent a crisp beauty to the city's thoroughfares a few days earlier had been stripped away, leaving gray stones and patches of cracked concrete.

As they crossed Tahrir Square, they caught sight of flames reaching high into the night sky, thrown up by a huge bonfire in its center. Hundreds of people were milling about the pyre, some singing, some just standing, staring aimlessly at the flames. Those nearest the fire were busy throwing objects into it, feeding the flames, sending sparks and trails of ash spiraling high up into the brightness.

"Books," muttered Father Verhaeren. Michael had established that he was the one at the wheel. "They are burning books. They are purifying Cairo of what they call *jahiliyya*. You are familiar with that term?"

"Yes," said Michael. "Yes, I am."

"Keep your head down. There's no knowing what they may do with foreigners at the moment. This plague business is stretching people's nerves. There's a rumor going about that the Americans have planted the virus, that it's the result of biological warfare."

Michael wondered if that was true. Anything was possible. After what had happened during the war in the Gulf, anyone seemed capable of anything. He glanced back once as they left the square, catching sight of a woman staggering towards the flames, her arms filled with books. Years ago, he had watched Christians in America sing and play as they burned records of the Beatles and the Rolling Stones. His father had told him of darker times, of the gleam of firelight on highly polished boots and ash on a high wind, the last white traces of words on paper before they crumbled and disappeared forever. *Permit me to introduce myself, I'm a man of wealth and taste* . . . The words of the song slipped into his head and as quickly out again.

"Where are we going?" Michael asked.

He had thought they were headed for the nunciature on Jazira island, but instead of turning right across the Tahrir Bridge, Verhaeren had kept straight on, heading south along the Shari' Qasr al-'Ayni.

Laermans half turned in his seat.

"I told you earlier," he said. "Someone wants to meet you. He was a friend of your brother's. An old man, a Coptic priest named Father Gregory."

They drove on through ever more desolate streets. Michael looked through the window. The night continued, drenched with stars. Somewhere in the distance, across the river, fires were burning, lighting the sky with a sickly orange glow. They reached Old Cairo and parked the car in a side street.

"It's not far," said Verhaeren. "We'll be safer going on foot."

They crossed beneath the railway track and entered Babylon between the round towers of the old Roman fort. The church of Abu Sarga lay on their left. They entered it by the side door, the main entrance having long ago been sealed against attackers.

Inside, the church was a web of thick darkness, its strands knotted and twisted between marble pillars and the painted ghosts of saints. Candles flickered. There was a movement of gold in the darkness, and the red of rubies, and a glitter of silver. In the rods of light, tiny motes of dust floated like clusters of stars in a distant nebula.

Their voices fell to tiny whispers.

"We'll wait for you here," said Verhaeren. Michael thought he seemed nervous. Surely here, in a church, there was no reason to be afraid.

There was a sound of footsteps. A dim figure appeared out of the gloom, a bent old man carrying an oil lamp in one hand.

"This is Father Gregory," Laermans whispered.

The old man reached them and stood a few feet away, scrutinizing Michael with rheumy eyes.

"Your name is Michael Hunt?" he asked.

"Yes," answered Michael. His voice sounded tiny and insignificant.

"Please come with me."

Without another word, the old priest led Michael through the incense-riddled gloom. This was only a church, these were only the images of martyred saints, that was only a breeze from the doorway that shook the candle flames; yet as Michael followed the old priest into the darkness, he felt fear pass through him with a light touch, oily and sickening. He thought he heard sounds among the shadows, and sensed that his companion had noticed them as well. He could not shake off a sense of malice, a feeling that unfriendly eyes were watching him, that the darkness was more than just darkness.

They halted beside the northern *haykal,* near the steps that led to the underground crypt. Father Gregory turned to Michael.

"They told me you would come." He came closer. "You are afraid of me," he said.

"Of you? No. But this place . . . No-one's explained what's going on, why I've been brought here. What do you want with me?"

"Your brother did not explain?"

"My brother? Paul?" Michael shook his head. "Paul told me nothing."

The old priest was silent for a moment.

"I see." He seemed to shiver slightly. "I think he intended to tell you everything before . . . before they killed him. He was here with me ten days ago. Didn't you see him after that?"

"I was ill. In a fever. He visited me and brought a doctor. After that . . ."

"I understand." Father Gregory hesitated. "What . . . exactly did you find?"

"Find?"

"This evening. In St Savior's."

Michael hesitated, then told him briefly. If possible, the old man's face turned grayer than it had been.

"This is dreadful news," he said when Michael had reached an end. "I'm very sorry. And I'm sorry Paul had no time in which to tell you what he knew. He had every intention of doing so. I will have to do it now instead."

Michael was feeling perplexed. Perplexed and angry. Part of him was ruined, he felt like a bird with a broken wing, limping through deep snow. He wanted no part of this huddled thing, whatever it was—this skulking in shadows, this whispering among the white flames of candles.

"You assume I want to know, and that I want to get mixed up in this, whatever it is." He thought of the photographs he had found, the strict recording of horrendous deaths, the gun wrapped up and set casually aside. "I found my brother dead tonight, and all you want to do is play some elaborate game. I have more important things to do."

He turned and started to walk away through the patterned darkness. His heart was empty, his mind a blank. Father Gregory did not move.

"Tell me, Mr. Hunt," he said, his voice unexpectedly clear, "have you had any dreams lately? Dreams that recur, dreams that go on haunting you after you are awake?"

Michael was already several yards away. He stopped

and turned round. Gregory's voice echoed a little in the hollow spaces of the church.

"Dreams?"

"You understand me. Dreams. A black pyramid. An avenue of sphinxes."

Michael took several steps back towards the priest.

"How . . .?"

"I have seen them too. Every night for fifty years. Your brother also. And before him, your father."

"My father? What is this about? People don't have the same dreams . . ."

Father Gregory raised his eyebrow.

"No? Sometimes they have the same nightmares. Sometimes . . ." He hesitated. "Please stay, Mr. Hunt. I mean you no harm. We need your help."

" 'We'?"

"Those of us who know what is going on. Who al-Qurtubi really is."

"Al-Qurtubi? What do you mean?"

Father Gregory said nothing in reply. He lifted the lamp and shone it on the stairway that led down to the underground chamber. There was so much darkness; the lamp felt heavy in his hand.

"You may see for yourself," he said. "Come with me. Let me show you."

38

She watched him work, watched the long, rapid brush-strokes, the gentle way he swept the palette knife across layers of paint, the fits of anger that forced him back, again and again, to the raw canvas. What he did was harsh and simple, it denied all metaphor, all spiritualization. He took dreams and made them realities. He carved himself into the fabric of things, a little bit at a time. He did waking what most men do asleep, he remade the world in the image of his own fears and temptations and illusions.

A'isha sat on a paint-smeared stool watching his long hands, the muscles in his arching neck, the shape of his broad back beneath the sweatshirt. Salama Bustani had seemed quite ordinary to her on that first meeting; but now, watching him paint, she felt his presence with an intensity that came close to physical desire. Work transformed him. He radiated heat and energy. She sat smoking the last ciga-rette from a box she had bought earlier that day.

She and Butrus had gone to her uncle's old apartment in the Tawfiqiyya district, only to be told by the *bawwab* that Shukri no longer lived there. Discreet enquiries had elicited no information other than that he had moved out a week or two before the revolution and that he had left no forwarding address. Their only hope was to wait for him the following day outside his place of work. He would turn up, if he had not been put in prison or executed for crimes against Islam under the previous regime. They both knew it was unlikely that they would find him still alive. But A'isha pinned her hopes on her uncle's indispensability, on the need Egypt's new rulers would have of men like him, with their files and photographs, their fingerprints and locks of hair, their bribe-takers and bribe-givers, their eyes and ears, their long, terrible, interconnecting threads, their hooks, their bait, their tongues, their blood-stained walls, their knowledge of vice and beauty, pain and ridicule.

She drew hard on the cigarette, watched the smoke rise towards the high warehouse ceiling, felt fear inside her, moving with living force.

Salama stepped back from the canvas, wiping his hands on a cloth.

"There," he said. "It's finished."

He was aged about forty. His frame was lean and knotted, he had thin, graying hair that fell back sharply from a balding forehead. All he wore were sandals, blue jeans, and a grimy sweatshirt. In spite of the cold, he was sweating heavily. Around his neck, a small Coptic cross hung incongruously against the stained fabric of the shirt, on which was printed the quasi-fascist logo of a heavy metal band whose music he had never heard and which he would have hated if he had.

"Finished?" A'isha stood and went closer to the canvas. "But how can it be? There's a whole section there you haven't even touched."

"You're an artist now, are you?" he asked sarcastically.

"No, of course not. I'm not criticizing, only . . ."

"This is the last painting I shall make," he said. "Everything has been left unfinished in Egypt. And now they have started to unmake her past. I've left that for them. To destroy what I did, they'll have to paint it."

"Why did you do that?"

"Do what?"

"Paint the eyes like that. And the rest like . . . something tainted."

The painting on the easel showed the tall, ascetic figure of a Coptic saint. Everything about him seemed entirely as it should. His face, his halo, the gesture of benediction that he made were all drawn directly and skillfully from the canons of conventional iconography. But on closer scrutiny, it became apparent that, beneath his robes, the holy man possessed a huge erection. From the moment this fact revealed itself to the viewer, it was impossible to tell whether the smile on the saint's face was one of piety or lechery.

"Is an erection tainted?" Bustani asked. "Is punishing the flesh holy? What do you want me to paint? We're surrounded by madmen claiming to be saints, claiming to act in the name of God. I can't fight them, I can't overthrow them. All I can do is to present them with various forms of defiance."

Butrus came into the room. He looked anxious and wound up about something.

"There's been more shooting," he said. "Didn't you hear it?"

A'isha shook her head.

"I think they're working themselves up to something," Butrus said. "There are too many Coptic houses around here. If there's violence tonight we'll be right in the middle of it."

"We're always in the middle of it, Butrus," Salama said flatly. "Where can you go to get out of it?"

Butrus said nothing in reply. Salama was partly right. There was nowhere to run to. Identity cards labeled their holders Copts or Muslims, there had been proposals to bring back the old laws that compelled Jews and Christians—Peoples of the Book—to dress in a distinctive fashion so that they could be singled out.

There was a smashing sound nearby.

"What was that?"

Another crash, then another. Suddenly, they could hear the sound of voices. Many voices, muffled by distance, but coming rapidly closer.

Butrus ran out of the studio area, followed closely by A'isha. They hurried up a flight of steps to the next floor. A window had been smashed. Near it lay a large stone, surrounded by slivers of glass. They could hear the voices distinctly now, the dull chanting of a mob on the rampage. A'isha ran to the broken window and looked out.

The street was filling rapidly with people, many of them carrying blazing torches or heavy sticks. A burst of gunfire cracked out several houses away. She saw a woman running, pursued by a small crowd, saw her stumble and fall, saw her disappear beneath the blows of their cudgels.

Someone below shouted and pointed up at A'isha. She drew back quickly, just in time to avoid a second missile. More glass shattered.

"We've got to get out of here!" shouted Butrus.

They ran back down to the studio. Salama was sitting on the little stool, surrounded by his canvases. There was a dull crashing sound where the mob was trying to batter down the heavy wooden door.

"Come on!" shouted Butrus. "Leave the pictures. We'll try the back way."

"You two go," said the painter in a calm voice. "It's me they want."

"Don't be stupid. That's a Muslim mob. They're killing any Copts they find."

Salama shook his head.

"No," he said. "I think you'll find they're Copts. Killing other Copts. Someone has told them my paintings are blasphemies. If they destroy them, if they kill me, they think God will love them for it and reward them with paradise. Their God is simple-minded, like themselves."

"Forget the paintings. You can still save yourself."

"Why should I? It's all a blasphemy. Copts, Muslims—

they all blaspheme against something. There are so many simple-minded Gods.''

There was a loud crash and the door fell inwards. A group of men rushed in, then stood stock still as they caught sight of the paintings ranged round the walls. Several of them were carrying flaming torches made from sticks and rags.

"Get out of here!" Salama shouted, not at the intruders, but at Butrus and A'isha.

They hesitated, thinking to help him escape with them. But the was already bearing down on his attackers, taking the initiative, as though he were a guide and they visitors to his art collection. One of the men rammed his burning torch against a large canvas bearing the likeness of a naked Christ.

"Blasphemer!" the man shouted. "Antichrist!" bellowed a second, setting another canvas alight. Flames rushed upwards, lightning-quick, lurid and spangled, blasphemies of light.

Butrus grabbed A'isha's arm.

"Let's go," he said.

She looked around once, then turned and followed Butrus up the stairs. Behind them, the sound of burning was already growing fierce. The smells of turpentine and pickle were subdued by choking fumes of black smoke. The warehouse was wooden, its walls caught fire like tinder.

They made it to the first story without pursuit.

"Over here!"

Butrus had found a disused gantry that had once been used for lifting boxes of vegetables from ground level. With a kick, he knocked open the twin doors of the bay. A dusty rope lay coiled on the ground, one end attached to the gantry. Butrus pulled hard on it. It held.

"Can you climb down this rope?"

A'isha nodded.

"Hurry up, then."

There was a sound of footsteps hammering on the stairs. Butrus took a pistol from his pocket and aimed it at the head of the stairwell. A head appeared, then a man carrying a long metal rod. Butrus took careful aim and fired. A'isha spun round.

"For God's sake!" Butrus yelled. "Get out of here!"

She swung out on the rope, kicking to find a hold for her feet. There was a crack as Butrus fired a second time. Her hands were burning on the rough fibers of the rope, she was spinning, almost out of control. She glanced down quickly. The ground was almost invisible in the darkness. Suddenly, a window beneath her burst open, gushing flames. As the rush died away, she let go of the rope and dropped the rest of the way to the ground.

Butrus was at the opening. He leaned forward, shouting down.

"Cover me while I climb down. Here!" He threw the gun down at her feet, then swung himself out on the rope.

A'isha picked up the gun and stepped back. She knew how to handle a pistol. Rashid had taught her years ago, insisting she be able to defend herself should the need arise. She looked up, squinting into the darkness. Butrus was barely visible, a bulky shadow against the dark wall of the building. Just above him she could see the space from which he had climbed, the jutting metallic frame of the gantry. A shadow appeared in it. She lifted the pistol in both hands, aimed, and fired. The shadow leapt back, whether hit or not she could not tell.

Butrus jumped the last ten feet or so, landing heavily beside her.

"Let's get the hell out of here!" he cried.

"Out of here? Where? Where do we go?"

He stepped close to her, taking the gun from her, his hand lingering fractionally on hers as he did so, a soft, awkward touch that he almost regretted.

"Where? I don't know," he said. "Just start running. There'll be time to think of somewhere to hide once we're clear."

They turned and began to run through the dark alleyway, their feet hard against the night. And even as she ran, A'isha knew there were no hiding-places left, no holes, no caves, no sanctuaries anywhere. Just the night and the city, dying all around them.

39

Together, Michael and Father Gregory lifted the slab that covered the wooden door. The air in the crypt was chill and damp. It felt as though no warmth had ever entered there since the beginning of time.

"You must understand where you are," said Father Gregory. "In Egypt, the living and the dead dwell in one another's arms. Only the sands shift. Between them, time is an oasis. Travelers come and drink and move away again, but nothing changes."

The priest stopped and looked round. At the shadows. At the lights. At the quiet shifting of the one into the other.

"The church of Abu Sarga stands on a more ancient site," he said. "Babylon was a holy place. They called it Khery-Aha. There was a small temple here, with chapels, courts, and a causeway that ran to the Nile. There were priests and temple-servants and oracles. They danced and sang and played instruments before their gods. And they dreamed dreams."

He paused to let the significance of his words sink in. Michael felt a cold shiver pass down his back.

"Khery-Aha was a place of visions," Father Gregory

continued, "a place for dreams and the shadows of dreams. Young men would come here to seek visions of their future, and they would leave years afterwards, bent and white-haired, having dreamed their lives to their end. Young women came for dreams of lovers and children, and when they left they carried death on their eyelids."

"How do you know all this?" Michael asked. He was sure the old man was making half of it up. The whole thing was a fabrication from beginning to end, or a fantasy that the old man had dreamed up.

"The old knowledge was not wiped out, not entirely. We burned their papyruses and defaced their temples. But some things are not so easily eradicated."

He reached into his pocket and brought out the key.

"Since Abu Sarga was built," he said, "there has been a custodian in each generation to watch over this place. The wooden door was put here in the twelfth century, after the restoration of the church by Hannah al-Abah. This key was made then too. It has been passed down under conditions of great secrecy since then. Only a handful have ever known of it: the custodian himself, the abbot of the Dair Baramus monastery, and the priest in charge of Abu Sarga. Since the sixth century the custodians have all been monks of Dair Baramus. I was selected when I was twenty-five years old. The key was passed to me by the last custodian on his death-bed. I have held it now for almost sixty-five years."

He held the key in the palm of his hand. It was heavy, cut roughly from brass, unpolished, ordinary. An old key that would only open a single door.

"Your brother was to have been the next custodian," Father Gregory said. There was a profound sadness in his voice.

He bent down and inserted the key in the lock. With Michael's help, he opened the door to reveal an ancient flight of steps leading into a deeper darkness beneath the crypt.

At the bottom of the steps, they walked through a long,

empty corridor. All about them, a silence as old as sleep clung to walls of ivory and gold. The light from Gregory's lamp fell over them in a milk-white pool. Their breath rustled across the silence like paper. It hung in the air like mist. Above them, in a ceiling of cobalt blue, tiny gold stars twinkled. All along the granite-flagged floor, wreaths of dried flowers lay, looking as though they had just been left there. Red and purple and yellow flowers, enough to fill a shop. There was a faint smell as of incense, barely tangible, ghost-like, a perfume unlike any other.

There was something unsettling about the reliefs carved into the walls on either side. Gregory paused and played the lamp on them. The same figure was repeated endlessly along the length of the dark corridor. A tall god with powerful limbs, dressed in the robes of a king. In his hand he held a long staff surmounted by a serpent. And his head was a goat's head. It was golden and shining, and his body was pure white. Gregory shivered and walked on. Michael followed. He felt numb, as though, waking, he had stumbled into an old dream. There were, he thought, some dreams out of which you never wake.

They walked on, flanked always by the creature with the goat's head, under a painted sky. The passage never deviated. It bored straight through solid limestone, twisting neither to right nor left. And it ended in a high door of beaten gold.

The gold was chased and figured with a tangle of lines and circles, ovals and parallelograms that coalesced at last into a contortion of limbs and faces, like a representation of an orgy. But it was not that. Michael had misread the whole thing. What he had taken for abandon was nothing but the agony of death. Body piled on body, limb heaped on limb, mouths opened wide in pain, a golden torment.

The doors opened gently to the priest's touch. They hung, unassisted, on the air, perfectly hinged, still poised and centered after the passing of centuries, without rust. There was no sound as they opened, only Michael's heartbeat within him, only his breath. And the mist of his breath hanging, droplets of cold white water, in the cradle of the long, naked light. He stood silent, his eyes moving slowly as the lamplight cut through the darkness.

Father Gregory lifted the lamp.

They had entered a low chamber with a vaulted roof. Across the entire expanse of the concave ceiling lay stretched a figure of the goddess Nut, her limbs surrounded by stars.

One of the flanking walls was painted with the giant figure of the god Anubis as a jackal stretched from end to end, a white scarf round his neck, his long pointed ears rising like flags towards the roof. The low light spread itself like a thin film of oil across the black and red paint. At the far end of the room, shadows crowded together by the wall, as though backing away from the light.

Father Gregory turned to face Michael.

"This was the heart of the temple. The chamber of sleep, where the priests came to dream their dreams. Afterwards they would return to the oracle chambers above, where they would interpret the dreams of pilgrims."

"Why have you brought me here?"

In answer, the priest raised the lamp and let it shine across the side wall. Michael stepped across the little room. His head almost grazed the ceiling. He felt crushed beneath the gently sloping body of the goddess. The jackal lay behind him, black, staring at eternity. Michael felt the hairs rise on the back of his neck.

On the wall facing Anubis, stretching from one end of the room to the other, an ancient artist had painted a scene that he recognized at once—though whether it had been painted from life or from the artist's imagination, he had no way of knowing. Out of the ochre expanse of a flat and desolate landscape rose a pyramid, its point sharp and un-compromising against a lacquered sky. A black pyramid. The pyramid of Michael's dream. A long pathway led to the entrance of the pyramid, flanked by two rows of basalt sphinxes, exactly as they had been in the dream. Michael felt a deep shiver pass through him.

Men and women passed in a somber file along the pathway and up onto a ramp that took them into the heart of the great structure. There were no musicians among them. No-one danced. No-one sang. Their heads were bowed as they walked, they wore the simplest of clothes: starched white kilts for the men and long dresses for the women, without beads or ornaments. They were like people going to their deaths.

He turned away and, as he did so, the priest lifted the lamp suddenly and shone it on the wall at the far end. The shadows fell away. As they vanished, the priest closed his eyes.

Stretching from floor to ceiling was the painted figure of a man seated on a throne, his hands resting on his knees. His head was the head of a goat. His skin was the color of lead. His eyes were bright with rage and torment and ecstasy.

"He is the Beast of Revelations," whispered the priest. His voice seemed to come from a great distance. "The creature you have seen in your dreams."

Michael could not tear his eyes away. The great naked chest, the powerful hands, and, above all, the whitened, haunted eyes held him fast. At every moment he expected the figure to rise and walk towards him, as in his dream. He wanted to turn and run and never sleep again.

No ancient Egyptian had painted the Beast. The hand was unmistakably late, from the early Christian period. Beneath the figure ran a lengthy text in black letters, all in Greek.

"Can you read it?" the priest asked.

Michael shook his head.

Father Gregory opened his eyes. The goat looked at him without blinking, as it looked at him every night while he slept.

"Let me read it for you," he said. He paused briefly,

staring with distaste at the image on the wall, then cleared his throat and began, reciting from memory a text as familiar to him as the Lord's Prayer.

" 'There are appointed two thousand and three hundred days and twenty and three days from the death of the goat spoken of by Daniel to the appearance of the Beast. He shall come from the West to the Place of Temptation, even unto Babylon, as one out of the sea, having great power. And he shall blaspheme forty and two months, as it is written in the Book of John. *Here is wisdom. Let him that hath understanding count the number of the beast: for it is the number of a man; and his number is Six hundred threescore and six.* In his own tongue, he shall bear the name of the beast. And he shall take a new name, that will be a blasphemy, and it too shall be the name of the beast, though he conceal it in letters no man has ever seen.

" 'When he appeareth, a plague shall cover Egypt and the Nile shall be choked with blood. They will ascend the high places and destroy them, stone from stone. A time, two times, and half a time will pass from his first appearance, between a birth and a death and the fall of a kingdom. These are the days spoken of in the Book of Revelation, let him who has eyes observe. And from his first appearance in the West, the book has established one thousand two hundred and ninety days. He shall raise an army of the unrighteous and his reign shall be seventy weeks. For *from the going forth of the commandment to restore and rebuild Jerusalem shall be seven weeks, and threescore and two weeks.* Wherefore, let the wise consider what is written here, and pray that he may not set eyes on him, as I have seen him in a vision from God. And let all who read this pray for me and for their children and for the generation of the last day.' "

Father Gregory's voice faded away. He looked at Michael.

"Well, Michael," he said. "Shall I tell you his name? The name of the Beast?"

"Qurtubi," Michael whispered. "That's it, isn't it? You think al-Qurtubi is the Antichrist."

Father Gregory shook his head. He seemed very old and very tired, a man who has lived too long and seen too much.

"No, Michael. We do not think. We know. Your brother identified him for us. That's why he was killed."

The old man coughed once and shivered. He glanced round. The crowded shadows jostled for room. Behind them, the figure of the Beast seemed to stir. Gregory looked again at Michael, at the long shadow that crossed his face.

"It's time to go," he said. "We have seen what we came to see. Now it is time to seek him in the flesh."

40

Smoke still rose from the ashes of the warehouse. It had burned easily, for over two hours. Now, all that remained was a heap of charred timbers. The sharp smell of pickles and paint had been replaced by that of burning. The ashes smoldered. Every so often, a blackened beam would crack and fall, sending up a shower of red and orange sparks into the thick night air.

The Dutchman stood about a hundred yards away. His men had emptied the street, dispersing the mob and clearing out the host of children and idlers who had come to watch. In the distance, he could hear the cracking of guns as the shootings continued.

There was a movement among the shadows. A figure appeared, limping slightly.

"Well?" enquired the Dutchman.

The new arrival shook his head.

"Nothing," he said. "We've gone through the place thoroughly. There's one man dead at the back. Abu Samir says it's one of his men."

"What about the artist, Bustani?"

"At the front."

"You're sure it's him?"

The man nodded.

"Abu Samir swears that's where he was when they killed him. The body confirms that, sir."

"Confirms it?"

The man hesitated.

"They . . . It seems they tore him to pieces, sir."

The Dutchman was silent for a moment.

"I see. And the other two? You're certain they got away?"

"Absolutely. Abu Samir wouldn't lie to us."

"No? He's let me down badly. We need to find her. Have Abu Samir shot. He's outlived his usefulness."

"Yes, sir." The man hesitated. "What about the woman? What do we do now?"

"Do? We keep our men in place. She'll turn up. She has no choice. Nowhere to hide."

"And Hunt?"

"Don't worry about Hunt. I'll take care of him."

"Where do you think he is? Do you have any ideas?"

The Dutchman shrugged.

"They'll have taken him to the old man by now. After that, I'm not sure. He'll try to contact England. We'll get him then."

"What if he doesn't turn up?"

"He'll turn up. Believe me. He has no choice either."

41

Even here, in the dark interior of the church, they could hear the gunshots: three quick cracks followed by the barking of dogs. Then two more shots. Michael and Father Gregory were sitting together near the back of the building. Now that he had seen what lay underneath, Michael felt more than ever the immense, brooding power of the place, the strength of its darkness, the fragility, the little, flickering candles that struggled to deny the night absolute mastery. He shivered as another fusillade of shots rang out.

When the uproar died away and the silence became absolute again, Father Gregory turned to Michael. His voice covered the silence like a hand.

"You know what is happening tonight?" he asked.

Michael shook his head.

"They are shooting Christians," the old man said. His tone was matter-of-fact, his voice calm. "It began tonight. Someone started a rumor that the Copts are carriers of the plague. They are outsiders, you see. Agents of the Americans and the British, allies of the Zionists, inveterate enemies of Islam . . . A few Copts are fighting back. There is talk of camps, of pogroms."

He fell silent. More shots stuttered inarticulately, tiny pops, mere echoes in the plain, uneducated night, ripples drifting across the innocent river.

"You said something earlier about my father," Michael remarked. "You said he had seen . . . the dream you talked about."

"It was a long time ago," Gregory said. "He came here before you were born."

"Here?" Michael looked at the priest in astonishment. "To this church?"

"To the church. And to me."

"I don't understand. Why did my father come to you?"

Father Gregory paused. The flame in the lamp flared up briefly, then sank.

"He had dreams," he said. "Just like you."

"The same dream? Of the pyramid?"

The priest nodded.

"Yes. He was one of the first. It was during the World War, just before the battle at al-'Alamain, when we thought the Germans would continue their push to the east. Your father came here with two of his friends, all of them Catholics. To visit the chamber where the Holy Family stayed. They were very tired when they came, they'd just returned from a raid on German positions. He thought . . . He told me they fell asleep. Sitting in the darkness down there, with just a candle or two, they dozed off.

"Soon after that, heavy fighting began. One of the three was killed. Your father and the third man returned to Cairo. A few days later, the third man killed himself. That was when your father decided to seek help."

"Help?"

"They had all dreamed the same dream, all three men. By the time they got back to Cairo, your father's friend was visited by the dream every night. He was under terrible strain. At night he was afraid to sleep. During the days he could not bear to see shadows walk across a sunlit room. In the end he put his service revolver in his mouth and took his own life. Your father was frightened that the same thing would happen to him."

"And he sought you out?"

Gregory nodded. In the shadows, something rustled. A candle flickered and grew quiet.

"But you were in Dair Baramus then. That's one of the monasteries in the Wadi Natrun. How had my father even heard of you?"

"Your father was a Catholic, a religious man in his way. He talked about the dream to his priest, an English padre with his regiment. The priest knew of me. He had met my family, and they had told him a little about me. They had told him among other things that I was interested in dreams.

"Your father was an uncomplicated man, Michael," Gregory continued. "He could not bear the complexity of his dreams, the horror they instilled in him. Somehow, he had an instinctive understanding of how the dream would progress. That, in the end, each dreamer would experience in his nightmare whatever it was he feared the most. He thought it would drive him mad, or that it would lead him to a fear of shadows, to death at his own hand, like his friend."

"And did he? Did he see what he feared?"

Gregory shook his head.

"I can't tell you," he said. "I don't know. He would never tell me what his fear was. But I think it never came to that."

Michael remembered now with terrible clarity the two or three occasions in his childhood when he and Paul had been wakened in the middle of the night by cries from their parents' bedroom. Their mother had come to reassure them that all was well, that it was nothing, their father had had a bad dream. And they had gone back to sleep in time and forgotten. But he could hear his father's voice distinctly now, rising in a thin wail of terror, the baffled babbling of a simple man trapped by things he could not name.

"Your father's dream differed in several respects from those that came later," continued Father Gregory. "The interior of his pyramid was carved with hieroglyphs containing figures very much like swastikas. And he saw naked men and women being herded into great chambers, from which they were thrown out dead. Later, when the war was over, when there were newsreels of German atrocities, he told me that what he had seen were the gas chambers of Auschwitz. He had seen his dream only months after the first gassings at Chelmno. But by the end of the war they had already begun to fade from his dream."

Father Gregory paused and looked round him at the quivering shadows.

"The dream changes, Michael," he whispered. "It changes from person to person, and from time to time. Above all, it changes according to what a man most fears."

The priest leaned close to Michael and placed a gnarled hand gently on his arm.

"We think it is a very ancient dream, that we are not the first to have dreamed it. But we think that it is coming to its conclusion."

"And you think Abu 'Abd Allah al-Qurtubi is the Beast, the figure with the horned head." Michael looked into Father Gregory's eyes. Had his brother talked about all this with his father? Had he known something all along? Michael felt shut out. He wondered what this old man really wanted with him.

There was a sound nearby. Verhaeren appeared from the shadows.

"I think it is time to go," he said. "We may have difficulty getting back to the nunciature. But I have strict instructions to ensure that you are both brought there safely."

Father Gregory stood reluctantly. He looked round the old church wistfully, knowing this might be the last time he would ever come here. He nodded once.

"Yes," he whispered, "it is time."

42

It was after midnight. Father Gregory had said goodnight and gone to bed exhausted. Before that, there had been a nightmarish journey to the nunciature, and even now Michael found it hard to believe they had come through alive.

Verhaeren was with him now. They were sitting in a small downstairs room lined with empty bookshelves. There were signs everywhere of frantic packing. Nuns and priests came and went through the corridors carrying boxes of files. Michael had noticed one bearing a small crate of wine bottles. There was an air of tension throughout the small building.

The priest made drinks for them, large whiskies. There was no ice.

"We don't expect to be here very much longer," he said. "It's only a matter of days before they give us our marching orders. Or lock us up in some desert camp. We're quite prepared for that."

"But surely you're all diplomats, you have immunity."

Verhaeren laughed drily.

"Immunity? As well say we're immune to this plague. They don't recognize diplomatic immunity as a valid concept. The Iranians set a precedent for that. The art of diplomacy is a Western trick, a means of circumventing the rule of law and the rights of native populations."

Michael sipped his whiskey.

"Who are you?" he asked.

Verhaeren looked away, as though embarrassed by the question, then back again.

"I'm acting head of Vatican intelligence in Cairo. Father Laermans is my deputy." He paused. "Your brother was our Chief of Station."

"Yes," whispered Michael. "I'd guessed that much. Or something very like it."

"Father Paul was appointed by the Holy Father himself," Verhaeren continued. "That alone is highly irregular. He was sent here for one purpose: to identify, track down, and, if possible, destroy the man we know as Abu 'Abd Allah al-Qurtubi."

The priest paused. There was a sound of gunfire, very distant, very faint. He went on speaking as though he had heard nothing.

"After the Gulf War in 1991, race relations in Europe reached a low ebb. Anti-immigrant legislation was passed everywhere. Europe was turning itself into a fortress, and inside the citadel feelings were rising against the minorities—Pakistanis, Bangladeshis, and others in Britain, North Africans in France, Turks in Germany. The right-wing parties started to win votes, enough to put them in power in some regions, where they remain today. For years, European governments had been cutting back on employment, dismantling their respective welfare states, and in the process they created a new underclass that responded to extreme right-wing propaganda. Now, instead of Jews, it was anyone with a colored skin or a foreign faith. Above all Muslims. It was in 1991 that Le Pen, the French National Front leader, called for a ban on the building of mosques, and for laws controlling the teaching of Islam in France.

"All Arabs, all Iranians, all Turks came to be viewed as

potential terrorists. Or actual. Some people became para-
noid, thought they were all out there in the streets planting
bombs—men, women, even children. Muslims were attacked in the streets. Just because they had beards, just because they wore strange clothes. Mosques were burned
down. But that only exacerbated things. There were more
bombings, more assassinations. Calls for *jihad* from Muslim
extremists."

"I know all this," said Michael. "Why are you telling
me?"

"So that you understand," the priest said patiently. His
hands lay quietly on his lap, his body was still, only his lips
moved. "I was working at that time with the Vatican Secretariat of State. We began to receive intelligence reports on
the situation. Grave reports, reports that gave us cause for
serious concern. We began to think things might degenerate
to a point of no return. There were fears of a second Holo-
caust. It was our duty to preach reconciliation. And yet
priests in their pulpits preached a new crusade.

"As you know, a new wave of violence began about
four years ago. It took everyone by surprise. Not just the
politicians—anything surprises them—but the rest of us as
well, even the security and intelligence services. For several
years, the European security agencies had been making real
progress against terrorism. Leading activists had been
rounded up in France, Italy, Germany, England, Holland—
anywhere you care to mention. Dozens were in jail, the rest
were either back in the Middle East or buried. The cells had
been broken up, airport and seaport security was very, very
tight, controls over arms shipments had brought in a mountain of guns and explosives. And then the bombings and the
shootings started again. I remember somebody saying to me
at the time that it seemed like cheating.

"Someone had taken over from Abu Nidal and Abu
Abbas. Someone had built a terrorist network that remained
invisible in everything but its actions. Leads dried up, lines of
enquiry turned into blind alleys. People were tearing their

hair out. There were quarrels, resignations, reassignments.

"About a year ago, Vatican intelligence started to get some leads. Real leads, leads that promised results. The problem was that they went in more than one direction. Some went to European countries, some to the Middle East. Several led to Egypt. For some reason, those were the best, the ones that made most sense. So it was decided that someone be sent to Cairo to bring all the leads together: your brother. There was a religious dimension, or so we thought, and Paul was one of the people best qualified to follow that particular thread.

"Your brother was a resourceful man. He was more than a priest, more than a scholar. You never knew him, not really. He had contacts you cannot imagine, not even with your knowledge of intelligence work. He went everywhere, spoke to everyone." Verhaeren paused.

"He found . . . Your brother found . . . a man. A man and a cause. The man's name was al-Qurtubi. Abu 'Abd Allah Muhammad al-Qurtubi."

The room had grown chilly. Beyond the window, the fires had died down. Shadows stumbled across the sky.

"That is not his real name," Verhaeren continued. "It is his Muslim name, the name he took when he converted to Islam. That was thirty years ago. Before that, his name was Alarcón y Mendoza. Father Leopoldo Alarcón y Mendoza, a Spanish priest."

The priest seemed nervous. He kept glancing round him, at the empty shelves, the shadows they contained.

"He converted to Islam about 1969. Thirty years ago. I don't know much about it, the why or the wherefore: it was never much talked about. Frankly, it was considered a major scandal at the time. The very idea of any Christian becoming a Muslim was unthinkable. But a priest! There was plenty of gossip, of course, but the Spanish hierarchy had it hushed up quickly enough. Most people wanted it buried. A file was opened, but they kept it locked away, out of reach, out of mind. Or so they thought.

"We never knew what became of him after that. Some thought he had gone to North Africa, to Morocco or Algeria, and joined a Sufi order. There was a rumor that he was in Saudi Arabia, studying under religious scholars in Medina. Another that he was here in Cairo, at al-Azhar. I don't know. Perhaps none of those were true, perhaps all of them at one time or another.

"But your brother did confirm that by the late 1970s he was living in Egypt. Not only that, but he had already acquired a reputation for sanctity. Some people regarded him as a living saint. I can believe it. He must have brought the same fanaticism, the same intensity to his new faith as he carried to the old. It's not uncommon: converts have a fire inside them none of the rest of us could ever ignite for ourselves.

"He gained his reputation in a mystical order, the Idrisiyya, but before long he moved on. He joined the Muslim Brotherhood, the Ikhwan al-Muslimun. But he was still restless. He found the Brotherhood too tame. He wanted more fire, he wanted to ignite fires all around him. Eventually he was drawn into the circuit of the more extreme groups, the *jam'at islamiyya.* He could speak and read Arabic fluently by now. He read voraciously. He met with the ideologues of the new Islam, the radicals, men like Shukri Mustafa and Karam Zuhdi. Finally, in 1981, he founded his own group. He called them the Ahl al-Samt."

"Ahl al-Samt? The People of Silence?"

Verhaeren nodded.

"I've never heard of them."

The priest nodded again.

"No," he said. "I would be surprised if you had. I would be surprised if as many as ten outsiders know of their existence. That's why al-Qurtubi chose the name. They were to be a secret organization within a secret organization. Their original aim was to work abroad, to win converts for Islam in the West, particularly among young Catholics. Al-Qurtubi gave them a sophistication they could never have had without him. He knew the arguments, understood the best approaches.''

''And did it work? Did they get converts?''

''Yes. More than you would imagine. But that was not all. They also made contacts. With the rootless, the dissatisfied, the angry. That meant, in the end, radicals, terrorists. It didn't matter to al-Qurtubi whether they were left-wing or right-wing, nationalist, religious: they were all just grist to his mill, fuel for his bonfire. By the early 1990s, he had his network in place.''

''And this network was made up of converts?''

''Mainly, yes. Muslims of Middle Eastern origin were targeted by the security services. But Europeans could come and go with comparative ease. On al-Qurtubi's instructions they stayed away from the mosques, mixed with no-one but themselves. They would come to Egypt and other Muslim countries for training, working as teachers, engineers, doctors. A bit like yourself, really.''

''But you know who they are, you can move on them.''

Verhaeren shook his head very slowly.

''No,'' he said. ''We know the Ahl al-Samt exist, that al-Qurtubi is their leader, and that they are behind the terrorist attacks in Europe. But that is almost all. We do not know where they have their base, what their command structure is, where their cells are located. If we move now, it will only serve to trigger an alarm. The results could be catastrophic, particularly . . .''

The priest broke off.

''Yes?'' Michael leaned forward.

''We think al-Qurtubi is planning something,'' he said. ''Something of great magnitude. One of his ex-followers has talked. He did not know much, but he had heard rumors. Rumors of something that would make the Western governments look up, something that would repay Islam for centuries of oppression. An act of final vengeance.''

The priest fell silent. He looked at the window, at the night beyond. So much darkness, such a strength of darkness, such silent, hideous strength. He could not bring himself to look at Michael Hunt, could not summon up the courage to tell him more than he had told him.

In the darkness, the people of silence were dreaming of dawn.

43

Jerusalem
Wednesday, 29 December

They came out of the Aqsa mosque into sunshine. The Dutchman squinted: his northern eyes had never quite adjusted to the harsher light of the Mediterranean. He glanced at his watch. It was just after noon, and they would soon have to return across the Allenby Bridge into Jordan. A military plane would be waiting for them in Amman, to take them back to Cairo and the final stage of this great undertaking. He had no worries about getting out of Israel as easily as they had come in. Their papers were in order, the Israelis had little anxiety about people leaving the country.

No-one knew that the man with him was Abu 'Abd Allah al-Qurtubi. And even if the Shin Bet had known the name, he doubted if they would know he was the most wanted man on whatever list they had. Not that they needed to worry. Al-Qurtubi had not come here to kill anyone or to initiate a wave of terror. He was here to hear for himself the startling information that had just come to light. There was no way they could smuggle the source out of Israel, and al-Qurtubi had insisted on hearing at first hand what he had to say. Then and only then would he decide on a course of action.

Al-Qurtubi turned to his companion.

"Listen," he said.

Now that the noon prayer had ended, a nearby church had started to ring its bells. Even as they listened, a second church, then a third joined in. The sound of chimes zigzagged through the narrow streets of the old city like a paper Chinese dragon twisting and turning in an old dance.

The Spaniard looked round him, at the domes and towers, at the Israeli military guards. "Do you remember?"

The Dutchman nodded.

"Yes, of course."

The bells awakened the keenest of memories.

"Do you ever regret it?"

"Regret it? No." The Dutchman was certain. He had no doubts.

"Sometimes I do. Especially around Christmas. When I was a child, I adored the crib—the camels and sheep and donkeys, the baby in its little wooden manger. And the sweetest of incense in the church for midnight mass." He paused. "It had such a richness."

"Isn't that why we left it? Precisely because of the richness. The confusion of God with smells and textures and the taste of wine. You can't miss that surely?"

Al-Qurtubi did not look at the Dutchman.

"The child in me misses it," he whispered. "There is so much I have had to crush. You will never know. No-one will ever know."

Gradually, the chiming of the bells faded until nothing remained but a single, lonely ringing that seemed to come from far up in the sky. And that too finally died away, until there was silence and the resonance of bells, as though their sounds had entered the fabric of the stone, as though their ringing was hidden in the heart of it.

"I don't understand," the Dutchman said. "You've always been much stronger than I. Harder. I've never seen regret in you before."

"I said the child regretted it. The man is as constant as ever. Nothing will make me hesitate."

"I never doubted that."

"Yes," said al-Qurtubi, turning and looking at his companion. "You doubted it just now. You know that I could have you killed for either offense: for doubting me, and for lying to me about it."

The Dutchman hung his head. He was afraid of only one man in the world—the man beside him.

"I apologize," he said. He knew al-Qurtubi never made an idle threat.

The space between the mosque and the Dome of the Rock was almost empty. Beyond it, they could see the city dipping and climbing in a tangle of towers and domes and flat roofs, a confusion of sunshine and shadow, belief and unbelief, truth and pretense.

"I think we should go," said al-Qurtubi.

The Dutchman did not reply. They walked on together, past the guards, down from the Temple Mount into the Old City. Heading north, they crossed the Via Dolorosa towards the Muslim Quarter. Streets full of priests and soldiers, nuns and shopkeepers, bedouins and tourists, all mingling promiscuously wherever they looked. Jerusalem was a brothel, and its whores wore uniforms of every description. God had packed His bags and stomped off long ago, leaving them to it.

The streets grew narrower and darker, until they consisted of little more than defiles between high brick walls in which heavy, studded doors were set at intervals. The stillness was oppressive. The air was filled with a rancid smell, a blend of despair and poverty, hatred and impotent regret. For years, al-Qurtubi had been coming here, breathing in the outrage, the injustice, the perplexity, choking it down with his spit, tasting it in his mouth for long afterwards, a sour, metallic taste he could never quite dislodge. There was no sweetness in anything while Jerusalem remained in the hands of unbelief.

They came to a low doorway and halted. The Dutchman knocked hard, sending echoes up and down the cul-desac in which they stood. Moments later, the door opened and they were admitted to a narrow passage, lit only by a dull electric bulb. They were welcome by a woman dressed all in black; there were too many shadows to be sure whether she was young or old.

"Are we expected?" the Dutchman asked.

"They have him for you downstairs," the woman said.

"Has he been made ready as asked?"

She nodded shortly. The light caught her face, dividing it into two halves, light and dark. She was young, she possessed a fugitive prettiness creased with anger. Her eyes looked inwards away from the light.

"Are you afraid?" Al-Qurtubi's voice was surprisingly gentle. She looked at him, puzzled, as though the question had been obscure.

"I don't understand . . ."

"Are you afraid of what you may have to do in two days' time?"

She let her breath go, as though relieved.

"Afraid of that? No. It's my duty. Why should I fear it?"

He looked at her intently, keeping her eyes fixed on his for the passage of long moments.

"We perform our duties from the strength of our volition," he declared, as though quoting one of his own sermons. "That is what gives them value. You aren't a puppet. None of us are puppets. It would be sensible to feel even a little fear."

The passage led into a small reception room. Al-Qurtubi went ahead of them and turned into an opening on his left. A flight of narrow stairs led downwards to an old cellar. The Dutchman followed, while the woman remained at the top of the stairs.

The cellar dated from the time of the Crusaders, if not earlier. It had been constructed from roughly hewn blocks of stone quarried nearby and its first use had been for the storage of wine. It was a dank, unhealthy place, never warm, never dry. Even at the height of summer, no-one would have come down here to get cool: the damp, cold air seemed to penetrate beneath both flesh and bone.

They could smell it as soon as they stepped into the cellar, even before they saw what was there: an odor of decay, a sickening perfume of sweat and vomit. Al-Qurtubi switched on a light. He had been here before, he knew his way. The cellar filled with an unsteady yellowish illumination without warmth.

A man lay crouched in one corner. He was neither conscious nor unconscious, but in a narrow world between. In spite of the cold and damp, he was completely naked. His skin was covered with dirt and sores; patches of dried blood covered him like dark rags. Both his legs lay at a peculiar angle: they had been broken, systematically, each in at least half a dozen places. In spite of appearances, most of his injuries were internal and fatal. Not the most skilled of surgeons could save him now.

He opened his eyes dully, looking without interest at the two men who had just joined him. Sometime earlier that day he had passed quite beyond fear. Knowing he would soon be dead, would soon be beyond the reach of his tormentors had made it easy. All he wanted now was to talk, to tell them whatever it was they wanted to know, so it might soon be over.

"What is his name?" al-Qurtubi asked the Dutchman.

"Eli Gal. Major Gal."

"MOSSAD?"

The Dutchman shook his head.

"Shin Bet. With special responsibility for Vatican affairs."

Al-Qurtubi raised an eyebrow.

"Do they need that?"

"There are eighty thousand Christians in Israel. A large percentage are Catholics. Conversely, a lot of Jews live in Catholic countries or in states with large Catholic populations. It's a matter of policy. There were fifty-one attacks on Catholic churches in Israel last year."

"How many of them were ours?"

"Thirteen. We don't have to do much to keep things on the boil."

Al-Qurtubi bent down. The Israeli looked at him without curiosity.

"You must be in a great deal of pain." Al-Qurtubi knelt close to the prisoner, his lips close to his ear. He spoke in English with great deliberation. "But by now you are thinking it cannot last much longer, that the worst is over, that you will either be released to your friends and family or killed. You have told them everything you know, everything you think they want to hear, but you will tell them more if they ask for it. You have cleansed yourself. And so, you reason, the pain must soon stop. They will toss you back to your kennel or they will shoot you; either way, you will be free."

He paused, watching the effect of his words. They were sinking in. Major Gal was starting to pay attention.

"Ah," said al-Qurtubi, "I see you understand me. Good. We won't have to waste time. It is all very simple. There are some things I need to know, things you haven't mentioned to anyone else yet, things you may have thought we did not even guess about. By now you're thinking that it will not matter anyway, that you are past hurting and past caring." He paused and put his lips a little closer. "But you are wrong. Very wrong."

Casually, the Spaniard took something from his pocket.

"I'd like you to look at this photograph," he said. "As you see, it was taken yesterday. Such a pretty woman, your wife. And such delightful children. It would be a pity if anything . . . unpleasant were to happen to them."

Eli Gal closed his eyes. He had thought himself far away, on the far edges of fear and pain, but they had suddenly dragged him back to the very heart of them. Blood was rushing unpleasantly through his arteries again, his head had started aching intolerably, he could feel the cuts and bruises as though they had only just been made.

"I don't . . . know what you want," he mumbled indistinctly. They had done something to his mouth, to his teeth. Speaking was pure pain.

"You don't have to worry. It's all there. You just have to trust us and tell us what you know."

"Dear God, I've told you . . . everything. Please . . . don't hurt them. They . . . don't . . . know anything."

"All you have to do is tell me what will happen on the first of January."

"January? There's . . . nothing. I don't . . ."

"I can have them brought here," whispered al-Qurtubi. "You can watch it all. You know what my people are capable of."

"I can't . . . remember . . ."

Sweat had appeared on Gal's brow.

"Please," he said. "Something . . . for the pain."

"The pain can be made much worse. Now, think. Think hard. Tell us about the Pope. Tell us exactly what he plans to do."

If there had been any blood left in the Israeli's cheeks, it vanished now. He shook his head violently. Al-Qurtubi picked up his left hand, drew the forefinger back and snapped it. Gal screamed.

"You are only adding to your sufferings. Unnecessarily. I can guarantee the safety of your wife and children, but only if you tell me frankly all you know. And do not forget that, if what you tell us turns out to be false, they will still be in our custody."

Gal took several shuddering breaths.

"He . . ." he began, "the Pope . . . intends to celebrate mass . . . at the Church of the Holy Sepulchre, in the Old City."

"We know that. He plans to inaugurate the Holy Year and the third millennium at the same time. What else? When does he arrive?"

The Israeli coughed spasmodically, then looked up at his tormentor. There were tears in his eyes.

"His plane . . . will land at Tel Aviv early in the evening of the . . . thirty-first. I don't know . . . how long . . ."

"Two days from now."

"He'll be taken . . . straight to Jerusalem. To stay with President Goldberg. On . . . on the morning of the first, he'll go to the church. There will be . . . no journalists . . . No tourists, no pilgrims . . . Just the Pope and . . . a specially invited congregation. After that, there will be an inter-faith conference. There will be representatives from each of the main religions in the region."

Gal fell silent. The pain was driving him to reveal what he knew, his training and what remained of his courage were like needles on his lips, sewing them tight.

He kept his eyes tight shut. Saw Hannah and Yigael and Rachel. Saw blood, in his eyes, in their eyes, blood slipping across the moon secretly and warmly, blood on the trees, blood on the vast receding western beaches, blood flowing across the sun like a dark, trailing veil. And he began to talk.

Once they were in the street again, al-Qurtubi smiled. He looked at the Dutchman.

"Will everything be ready tonight in Cairo?"

"No question of that. We already have the newspapers prepared for tomorrow's announcement."

"The foreign press?"

"We intend to release a statement tonight at nine o'-clock."

"Good."

"We can't let the Pope get as far as Jerusalem," he said. "He will have to be diverted."

"Will that be possible?"

"I think so. He believes in me. In who and what I am."

"That you are the Antichrist?"

"Yes. He knows what I am. And he is afraid of me."

They walked to the Lion's Gate. A car would be waiting on Derekh Yeriko to take them to Jordan. Passing the Church of the Flagellation, al-Qurtubi shivered. What if it was not just coincidence? What if he was, after all, the manipulated, not the manipulator, the Beast, not its Master? Looking round at the gray and the honeyed stones, at the weight of centuries, he said in a broken voice:

"Come away from here. Quickly, come away. This place is full of whispers. There are too many whispers."

PART VI

"I dare say, you wish to know how the Plague is going on at Cairo?"

KINGLAKE, *EOTHEN*

PART VI

44

The rain made thin, irregular patterns on the windscreen as it swept across the glass. It had blown in unheralded from the desert, carrying grains of fine red sand secreted in its drops, and as it fell in certain lights it seemed like blood.

Butrus made no move to switch on the wipers. It had been raining since noon, emptying the streets of pedestrians, and the absence of passers-by had left him and A'isha exposed and vulnerable. The car belonged to a friend, one of the few left to whom they could turn. Through the window on the passenger side, A'isha watched the entrance to the gray stone building on the other side of the little square. He always came this way, she said, heading for Shari' Mansur, down which he would walk briskly to Bab al-Luq station, where he took the Metro back to Helwan.

Lazughly Square—or, to be more precise, Lazughly Circle—lies almost midway between the Parliament buildings and the Presidential Palace. Its north-west flank is occupied by the Ministries of Justice. It is the ideal location for the Headquarters of National Security. Since the takeover, Security had been playing second fiddle to the hot young men of the *muhtasibin*. One way or another, most of the old guard had gone; but like all new regimes, the Revolutionary Council of Egypt's Islamic Republic recognized the value of its predecessor's internal security apparatus.

The rain played music on the roof of the little car, the only music now permitted in Egypt following the implementation of the centuries-old injunctions against song and dance. A'isha could not sit at the steering wheel: women were banned from driving. She sat motionless, hunched up in the passenger seat, wearing a long robe and a full black *hijab* that covered most of her face. She hated dressing like this, but put up with it because it gave her a perfect and unremarkable means of concealment.

Her fingers drummed nervously on the top of the dashboard as she waited, praying for her uncle to appear. She wanted to light a cigarette, but did not dare. Smoking had not been banned, but it was better to play safe.

It was almost four o'clock when Ahmad Shukri finally made his appearance. He carried a large black umbrella in one hand and a small briefcase in the other. A'isha recognized him at once: tall, lanky, stooping. As a child he had always reminded her of a stork and she had feared he might take wing when the sky above grew gray and empty.

She knew all about it: his loneliness, the empty years since his wife's death at the age of twenty-five, his childlessness in a society that valued children above all other possessions. His work had been less public than his suffering, and, until now, of little interest to her. He was a civil servant, nothing more, he always used to say in unprompted moments of self-defense: just one of Egypt's great army of pen-pushers and rubber-stampers.

A'isha did not think her uncle had ever been the faceless apparatchik he made himself out to be. The whole family knew he held a position high up in the secret police: it had been their security, the little something they held back for a rainy day. Uncle Ahmad was a man as valuable as he was to be feared.

They followed him slowly as far as the corner of Majlis

and Mansur, well out of sight of the square. He did not look round as the car drew alongside to match his pace. Most people would have. A'isha pulled the veil away from her face and wound down the window.

"Uncle Ahmad. Please stop, I need to speak to you."

Shukri halted abruptly and looked round.

"A'isha! For God's sake, what are you doing here? Don't you know . . ."

"Please get in, Uncle. We can't talk in the rain."

Shukri looked round nervously, like a man whose conviction of invulnerability has suddenly been stripped away. A'isha opened the rear door and let it swing out. She looked imploringly at her uncle.

"Please," she said. "I need your help. And Michael—he needs help too."

"Michael?" He looked as though he really did not understand.

"Michael Hunt." She pronounced the name without inflection.

Shukri looked startled. He glanced around as though frightened, then stared at A'isha for a moment. Finally, he made his mind up. He climbed into the car, shutting his umbrella and shaking it. Butrus did not look round.

"Where to?" asked Butrus. They had not talked about a destination.

"My place," said Shukri. He turned to A'isha. "I've got a new apartment. I suppose you looked for me at the old one."

She nodded.

"I thought it best to move outside the city," he said. "I'll show you the way. If I'm going to be abducted, at least I want to be taken somewhere comfortable." He hesitated and looked round, trying to see through the rear window. "Take the Corniche," he said. "You'll find it easier to see if we're being followed. And switch on your wipers or you'll have us all killed."

Butrus let out the clutch and they set off towards the river.

In a doorway on the street they had just left, a man dressed in a long black *galabiyya* spoke quickly into a handheld radio transmitter.

The river sparkled with rain. On their right, the southern tip of Jazira island trembled, alight with greenery. All along the bank between the Tahrir and Fontana bridges, people had congregated in large numbers. Men and women mingled promiscuously, children wept or ran about uncontrolled, and at intervals Coleman lanterns had been hung on poles, their white light flickering on the faces of the crowd.

A'isha wound down her window and strained to see through the sheets of falling water. From all directions, she could hear a sound of lamentation.

"What are they doing?"

"Look," said Butrus. "Look at the river."

Bobbing, rising, dipping as the current took them, an armada of what seemed to be small boats drifted darkly on the surface of the water as they headed downstream between Jazira and the eastern shore.

"What is it?" asked A'isha. "Surely these aren't boats."

"They are coffins." Her uncle's voice sounded strained. "Every day now, people come here to dispose of the dead. They're afraid to bury them in the graveyards, for fear of contagion. Neither the authorities nor the shaykhs at al-Azhar will let them cremate them, out of religious scruple. So they set the coffins adrift on the Nile. They believe the river will carry them to the sea."

"And does it?" They were drawing away from the crowds now.

"No, of course not. Most of them sink before they reach Warraq island. The rest drift ashore. Farmers find the bodies trapped in reeds. The crocodiles take what's left. More and more corpses are coming up from the south, as the plague spreads. What can we do? What can anyone do? They say ten thousand people are dying every day in Cairo now."

They drove on, leaving the river behind. Above, the sky grew dark. A scrap of pale moon stood its ground behind a veil of sand and water.

As they reached Helwan, the rain eased off. Shukri had not spoken once since leaving the riverbank. He had stayed in the back of the car, staring through the windows at the gathering of night.

His new flat was part of an apartment block put up by the Cairo *Muhafaza* in the early sixties under Nasser, one of hundreds intended to provide low-cost housing for workers in the local factories. Since then it had lived under a pall of smoke from those same factories, its only concession to beauty or to art a huge mural painted on its eastern wall by a pilgrim returned from Mecca.

Each day he came home and saw the crudely drawn boat, the shrouded cube of the Kaaba, the figures of Abraham and Ishmael beneath the outstretched wings of Gabriel, Ahmad Shukri felt a terrible pain inside him. He had been on a pilgrimage once, he thought, a private pilgrimage on which he had embarked a long time ago; but somewhere, somehow, at some unspecified moment in his life, he had stumbled and lost his way.

He let them in, still silent, almost as though he had lost the power of speech. A'isha remembered the old apartment where she had often gone as a child until, in later years, her uncle's taciturnity and unexpiated guilt had driven her away. Her father had told her once that his brother unreasonably blamed himself for his wife's death, that he had stitched up the wound she had left, but gone on bleeding inside. From that moment, whether rightly or wrongly, A'isha had thought of her uncle as a man of blood. The apartment was almost identical.

. . .

"A long time, A'isha," he said. His eyes were unfocused, as though he were dreaming.

"Yes," she said. "A long time." Eleven years. Just after her graduation, that was the last time she had seen him.

"What did I do that you never came to see me?"

"Nothing," she said. "You did nothing."

"Your father tells me you don't see much of him or your mother. Is that true?"

"I visit them from time to time. It's enough. I can't cope with their dislike of what I've become. They brought me up to be independent, to think for myself. And now . . . Now, it's 'the Qur'an says this,' 'the Qur'an says that.' "

"You should try to make your peace with them."

"You can say that now? Or is that what you believe as well?"

He shook his head.

"You know what I believe. All the same, I'm sorry this has happened. Sorry for you and sorry for them." He paused. "I meant to get in touch with you. When your husband disappeared. But I thought . . . It might have seemed clumsy, you might have thought I was involved, interpreted my sympathy as guilt."

"Were you? Involved?"

"Of course not."

"Do you know who was?"

"No. We still don't know. But perhaps now these people are in power . . ."

"Rashid is dead."

"Dead? How do you know?"

She told him, the way she had once told him her troubles as a little girl. And he looked at her the same way, without amusement, treating her troubles with the utmost seriousness. And she wondered what sort of man he was, that he could be bloody and yet so caring.

When she finished speaking, Shukri said nothing. He sat plunged deep in thought, tapping a fingernail nervously against one tooth.

"I can't help you," he said at last. "The people who killed Rashid are beyond your reach, believe me. It's better you forget. Better we all forget."

A'isha shook her head.

"I didn't come here for that," she said. "I'm not looking for revenge, much less for justice. We're here because Michael told me about you. That I could trust you. He said you used to be his chief source in Egyptian intelligence."

"What are you talking about, A'isha? Who told you this?"

"Michael," she said. "Michael Hunt."

"I'm sorry," he said, "you must be making a mistake. I don't know anyone of that name."

She had not thought he would lie to her, not to her. The lie, so cheap, so ineffective, yet spoken with such conviction, sank to her stomach like a weight.

"Why are you lying to me about this, Uncle? My life depends on your honesty. You reacted to Michael's name when I mentioned it earlier. There's no point in lying: Michael told me about you, who you are, what you used to do for him."

"Why would this man—Michael Hunt—tell you anything about me?"

"Don't you understand? My life . . . my life depends on getting to Michael. But I can't do that directly any more. There are men watching his flat. He went to Alexandria over a month ago, but when I contacted his hotel he had gone. I have to find him. He can help get us out of Egypt."

"It's you who don't understand, A'isha. You and your friend here. You both understand so little, so very little. And you take that little understanding and twist it into a rope, and if you aren't careful you'll end up hanging yourselves with it. Please believe me, you are getting involved in things that can only get you into even greater danger."

A'isha shook her head.

"Don't you know? Don't you know about Michael and me?"

For the first time Shukri looked genuinely puzzled. Puzzled and frightened.

"About you and Michael?"

"That he and I are lovers. Surely your mutual friend Ronnie Perrone would have told you that."

She could see at once that he had not known and that his ignorance troubled him.

Shukri stood and crossed to the window. He stood leaning against the window-frame, staring into the darkness. They knew nothing, he thought, nothing. The country was on the brink of war, the municipality was filling secret vaults with plague victims, extremists were already threatening to tear the revolution from its moorings.

He turned and looked at A'isha, at the miserable young man by her side.

"You should have told me this at the beginning," he said. "It alters everything."

"Can you find him?" she pleaded. "Can you help us?"

Shukri nodded.

"Yes," he said. "I'll help you. I'll take you to him tonight."

45

Qasim Rif'at ran a small bookshop on the Shari' al-Sabtiyya in Qulali, the north-east sector of Bulaq, not far from the railway station. The shop was called the Dar al-Adab. It specialized in Arabic literature and philosophy. Like many small bookshops in the city, it doubled as a publishing house, and Rif'at had over the years issued numerous prestigious volumes of poetry and translation.

It was late when they set out. They were stopped once at a *muhtasibin* check-point on al-Sadd al-Barrani. Shukri was driving, with Butrus in the passenger seat and A'isha behind. In the darkness, uneasy men with guns stood around the car. A few yards in front, a man and woman had been ordered out of their vehicle and were standing silently in the cold. Shukri rolled down the window and produced a green laminated card from his pocket. The effect was instantaneous. The *muhtasib* in charge nodded once and waved them past. As they drove away, the woman at the other car glanced up once, lifting her hand in a gesture that was not hope and was not despair.

There was a power failure as they reached Bur Sa'id, the third that day. The only lights were those of cars and buses rushing headlong through the darkness.

Passing through Ahmad Mahir Square, they caught sight of a long procession of men heading south. They were carrying candles, tall white candles of dripping wax the height of lances. Their clothes were black, long black robes that reached to their feet, and round their foreheads they wore broad white bands on which slogans had been written in red ink.

A'isha guessed where they were headed.

"Why don't they stop?" she exclaimed. "All this destruction—it's completely senseless."

"Not to them," said her uncle. "They're tearing down the pyramids in order to build a wall. They're finished at Giza now. These people are going to finish work at Dahshur and Saqqara."

"I've seen them at work. But I still don't understand. They said it was to keep out the enemies of Islam. They can't keep the world out with a wall."

Shukri shook his head.

"It isn't the world they're trying to keep out. It's the plague wind, the wind that carries the plague into Egypt. If they build the wall high enough, they'll be safe."

"Have we all gone mad?"

Shukri said nothing. He pressed his lips together tightly and drove on in silence, staring through the windscreen at the trail their lights laid across the darkness.

They stopped a couple of streets away from Rif'at's. Shukri turned off the engine but made no move to get out. He sat staring through the windscreen for a long time, gazing into the night. Finally he spoke in an uninflected voice, picking his words with care.

"Someone is looking for you," he said. "A man called al-Hulandi, a Dutchman who converted to Islam and came to Egypt several years ago. I don't think you know of him."

A'isha shook her head, saying nothing.

"But he knows of you. He came to my office about three weeks ago, asking about you: where you might be found, who might be with you. He knows you're my niece, of course—everyone knows that."

"What did you tell him?"

"Nothing. I said I hadn't seen you in years. Then I ordered him out." He paused and looked steadily at her. "Then I picked up the phone and had men go out to your apartment."

"Why was that?" A'isha had sensed the nervousness in her uncle's voice, the hesitation that suggested he was holding something back.

"Please, uncle. Why did you do that?"

He looked round, and all the years seemed to strip themselves away from him. She remembered sitting on his knee during the Id al-Kabir in a season of dry weather. On her head she had been wearing a silken scarf the color of new grass. She had just had her first period. Unlike several of her friends, she had been spared the agonies of circumcision. Even now, she could remember their frightened faces. And yet, absurdly, she could also remember her own jealousy. "A woman is not a woman," they had told her, "unless she has been circumcised." She had had dreams of blood for months afterwards.

"Because he is dangerous," Ahmad said. "He's a killer. A cold man, nervous, always prowling the streets. He could snap you in half with his bare hands. I wanted to . . . protect you."

"Couldn't you have arrested him? This Dutchman. Surely, if you knew he . . ."

"You don't understand, A'isha."

"What don't I understand?"

"He's beyond my reach. Untouchable. A man with friends in high places. Very high places." He paused. "His real name is Jan Van der Veen. He's a native of Leiden, where he studied Arabic at the university. Fifteen years ago, he came to Cairo to study Islamic jurisprudence at al-Azhar. Some say he is the most brilliant thinker in the field since Ibn Taymiyya."

"Why would he be interested in me?"

"He has connections with a number of extremist organizations."

"Then surely he's . . . ." She struggled for the word.

"Respectable?" Shukri shook his head. "Only on the surface. He's an achievement, you see, a conquest. A Christian who has become not just a Muslim but a jurisprudent. Some people resent that, but others regard it as a blow against the West. We can't match them on their own terms, with planes or tanks or guns. But we can win souls, one at a time, gently at first, then terribly, once it begins to hurt.

"So al-Hulandi has his value. But he also has his price. He is linked to people we have been trying to find for years, people who make Islamic Jihad seem like children. The *muhtasibin* want them as much as we do."

"That still doesn't explain what he wants with me."

"I don't think it's you he's after. You're a threat to some people, but not big enough to interest a man like this. I think they're after Michael, and they want you as a means of getting to him."

He paused.

"I wanted to tell you this," he said, "so you could understand."

"Understand?"

"That if you find Michael you will both be in the greatest possible danger."

He opened the door and climbed out of the car.

46

Rif'at's shop was closed. A metal shutter had been rolled down to cover the window, and the door was padlocked. There were no signs of life. Across the street, lights were lit in second- and third-floor windows, but the floors above the Dar al-Adab remained dark.

"He has rooms upstairs," said Shukri. He seemed nervous. A'isha noticed him glancing around frequently, not, it seemed, from the force of training, but out of fear. "He lives alone with his mother and his books. She does the shopping and cooking, he stays home and prepares the catalogues."

"It looks deserted," Butrus said.

"Perhaps." Shukri was pensive. He looked up and down the street warily. Not far away, the voices of hired mourners wafted through the strained night air. A dog howled. Shukri reached into his pocket and drew out a bunch of keys. Fumbling in the darkness, he selected one and tried it in the lock. It would not fit. He tried a second.

"Tell me if anyone comes," he whispered. "The *muhtasibin* have orders to shoot looters on sight."

"Surely no-one would loot a bookshop," Butrus protested.

"Who knows?" whispered Shukri, trying a third key. "It's all that's left. Perhaps someone would like to steal a little wisdom before he dies."

The next key turned softly in the lock. The padlock fell open and Shukri withdrew it carefully from the hasp.

The door opened silently into a pitch-dark room. A'isha had brought a flashlight. When they were all inside and the door firmly shut behind them, she switched it on.

All around them they saw empty shelves, shadows, the ghosts of books. The beam swung in a wide arc, revealing nothing but the nakedness of shelves stripped bare. High up, a single forgotten volume caught the light, the gold lettering on its spine gleaming briefly before the beam passed on. A'isha turned the light on the floor. Paper was strewn everywhere in hills and valleys, a white landscape piled up between the denuded walls. Page after page had been ripped from its binding, torn, and tossed aside. Here and there, empty bindings lay gaping like gutted carcasses.

She bent and picked up a sheet at random. It was a page from Ibn Hazm's *Tawq al-Hamama,* from the eleventh century. Her eye caught a passage in the middle of the page: "Life holds no joy for me, and I do nothing but hang my head and feel utterly cast down, ever since I first tasted the bitterness of being separated from those I love. It is an anguish that constantly revisits me, an agony of grief that ceases not for a moment to assail me."

She let the paper slip from her fingers, let it fall to the floor out of the light back to the darkness. Sometimes she thought she would die like this, never seeing Michael's face again, never touching him, not even one more time, not even waving goodbye from a distance. She would die huddled in a dark, miserable room, in an unassuming darkness, on a day like any other, scarcely noticed, without love, with memories scattered like litter, like white pages, like torn, white pages on a dirty floor.

Shukri touched her shoulder.

"He may be inside," he said. "Let me go first."

There was a door on the other side of the shop, a rough door badly in need of a fresh coat of paint. A piece of paper tacked to it read "Private: No Entry." The letters were faded, the paper yellowing and curled at the edges. Shukri turned the handle and pushed the door open.

At first he could see nothing but mound upon mound of books, some reaching almost to the ceiling. Then he saw that light was coming from somewhere further inside. Treading carefully, he squeezed his way through the tottering heaps. A smell of paper and leather filled his nostrils. And another smell, far less pleasant.

Rif'at had made a fortress for himself among the fallen towers of his trade. He was sitting on the floor in the light of a little candle that was almost at its end. On his lap lay a large book from which he was silently ripping pages. Around him, yet more torn paper had piled up, covered in candlewax. Pebbles of bright red blood spattered the paper. In one spot someone had been profusely sick. The bookseller looked up as Shukri stood over him. He looked very ill.

There was no recognition at first, just blankness in the eyes. Not fear. Rif'at had become immune to fear. Or so full of it that there wasn't the least room for any more. His eyes were bloodshot and sunken, his unshaven cheeks were thin, haggard, drained of color. Thin hair lay smeared across his head with sweat. On his neck a broad purple blotch spread from just below his chin to his collar.

And then he recognized Shukri. As he did so, he was wracked by heavy coughing. They watched him helplessly, convulsed, hacking, his whole being digging deep into the cough, deeper and deeper, fighting, struggling, wriggling desperately for a moment of breath and air. It took a long time for the coughing to subside. When it was over, Rif'at leaned to one side, supporting himself precariously on a trembling arm, and spat a heavy gout of blood and saliva onto the floor. He sat for a while catching his breath, his eyes darting from one to the other of his visitors, as though he were trapped and seeking a way out.

"Qasim," Shukri said, bending down. "How long have you been like this?"

The bookseller looked up. His chin was wet with blood. His eyes were blank; the recognition once more vanished.

"Like this? Always like this. My whole life like this." The words came thick and slurred, dribbling from his mouth.

"How long have you been ill?"

"Not ill . . . Just tired. Need to . . . sleep. But afraid . . . of dreams. And books . . . So many books to hide. They mustn't find them here."

Automatically, his hands reached for the book on his lap and began tearing pages from it. Shukri noticed that it was a copy of the *Diwan* of al-Mutanabbi. Poems from it lay bloodied and streaked with sputum all around. Shukri looked at Rif'at more closely. He was no expert, but he guessed the bookseller did not have long to live. If he had contracted pneumonic plague, he would be highly infectious. Every time he coughed, he spread airborne bacilli through the room.

"I'll get a doctor," Shukri said. "There are still ways to find one. It may not be too late."

"Too late," Rif'at repeated. He closed his eyes suddenly and creased his mouth in pain. Shukri reached out his hand and touched Rif'at's cheek. In spite of the pallor, the skin felt hot and dry to the touch. At a guess, the bookseller had been seriously ill for less than twenty-four hours. From what Shukri had heard, the incubation period was around six days. After that, people went downhill quickly. There appeared to be several different strains of the virus at work simultaneously, with bubonic infection turning rapidly to pneumonic. He gave Rif'at a day or two at the most. Thinking it, he remembered the bookseller's fear that he might die of AIDS.

"Qasim," he said. "We're looking for Michael Hunt. Has he been here? Has he tried to use the radio?"

Rif'at looked at him blankly. He picked up a volume of modern poetry, Mahmud Darwish's *Awraq al-zaytun*. He pulled it open, breaking the spine, tearing it in half, snapping each half apart again. Shukri bent down and took the pages gently from him, letting them fall to the floor.

"We need to know, Qasim. We have to find Michael. Do you understand?"

Recognition dawned again in Rif'at's eyes. Tears formed and started to trickle down his cheeks.

"Michael," he stammered. "Michael was here."

"When? When was he here?" A'isha pressed forward eagerly, but Shukri held her back. Rif'at ignored her, his eyes focused now on Shukri. He grasped the older man by his sleeve, drawing him near. Up close, the stench was almost unbearable.

"This afternoon," he said. Then he paused. "Or perhaps yesterday. I . . . I don't know, don't remember . . . I . . ." He began to panic, terrified that he might be losing his grip over time.

"It's all right," Shukri murmured in a soothing voice. "Don't worry. You'll remember. Think hard, what did he do when he came? Did he use the radio? It might help you remember when he was here."

Rif'at shifted uneasily, still on the verge of panic.

"Radio? No, no radio. There's no radio."

"Qasim, listen: you don't have to be afraid of me. I'm Ahmad Shukri, your friend. I know about the radio. I was the one who brought Michael to you. Don't you remember that?"

Rif'at looked all round, at his tottering towers of Babel, at the candle burning perilously low.

"No, I don't remember," he said. "I don't remember anything."

Shukri was growing nervous now. He knew they should not spend long here. He wanted to get his information and leave.

"Please, Qasim, think hard. When Michael was here, did he use the radio to contact London?"

"I . . . don't know. Maybe . . . Yes, I think so. Upstairs, he went upstairs."

That was where the radio was kept.

"And did he tell you his address, where he is living?"

A guarded look came over the bookseller's face, a sly expression. From somewhere in his mind, old fears were surfacing.

"Michael has gone," he said. "Back to England."

A'isha felt as though someone had kicked her in the pit of the stomach. Could that be true? Would Michael really have left without her? She came close again and knelt down facing Rif'at. Shukri did not attempt to stop her now.

"Please," she said. "Please look at me." She had to take his head in her hands, turning his face forcibly to look at her. His skin was hot and unpleasant to the touch. The glands on his neck were swollen.

"I don't know you," he whispered. "Don't know you . . ."

"My name is A'isha," she said. "A'isha Manfaluti. Perhaps Michael mentioned me to you."

Rif'at looked at her bleakly, shaking his head slowly from side to side.

"I have to know," she said. "I have to know the truth."

He looked at her again, then burst into another fit of uncontrollable coughing. She let him go, feeling her own fear, her own abhorrence mount. More blood. A knot of slippery revulsion in her stomach. And the dread that she was alone, truly alone. The coughing subsided.

"Coming back," he said. "Midnight tonight. For the reply."

He reached inside his shirt and drew out a dirty, crumpled envelope.

"I have it here," he whispered. "To give to him tonight."

His words were uttered with real lucidity. A'isha felt relief wash over her. When she looked round, Butrus was watching. What was he thinking? she wondered. There was something in his eyes she could not read. Jealousy? Regret? Opportunity?

A crashing sound came from the next room. Someone had thrown the front door back hard against the wall. Feet sounded, loud, then suddenly soft on a carpet of poetry and prose. Someone barked an order.

Shukri acted quickly. In part, he had been expecting something like this. He swiveled, grabbing A'isha by the upper arm and pulling her to her feet. As he did so, Rif'at reached out and handed the envelope to her.

"Find him!" he murmured. "Give it to him."

"Quickly!" Ahmad cried, dragging A'isha round and all but throwing her towards a door to the left. "That way. Upstairs, the room on your right. You can get onto the roof from there. I'll do what I can to hold them off here." He reached into his inside pocket and pulled out a gun.

"But you . . ."

"Get going." He turned to Butrus. "You too. For God's sake hurry!"

As Butrus moved for the door, Shukri bent down and blew out the candle. At that moment, the door opened. At first, nothing happened. There was darkness, a terrible stillness, an expectation. Then someone began to scream.

47

Michael looked at his watch. It was time to make his move. Rif'at had insisted on midnight for the meet, in the naive belief that darkness would shield them. Michael had tried to dissuade him, but the bookseller had been more stubborn than usual. Rif'at was ill, seriously ill, and Michael had promised to bring him medicine. The nunciature physician had passed on a supply of streptomycin and tetracycline that morning, after giving Michael himself a single dose of attenuated vaccine. There had been enough vaccine to spare Michael half a dozen more doses. He was going to need them more than the doctor.

The clamp-down at the nunciature had come sooner than expected. The Vatican had been notified of the massacres of Christians in Egypt, and at mass that morning the Pope had issued a scathing condemnation of the violence. True, he had not accused the Egyptian government of direct responsibility or outright complicity in the pogrom, but he had not minced words when he said that they had chosen to turn a blind eye.

The regime had reacted immediately by instructing the nuncio and his "fomenters of discord" to pack their bags at once and head for home on a special flight laid on by the Egyptian Air Force. The nunciature, that "Center of the Crusaders and Evangelists in Egypt" was forthwith designated a Dar al-Da'wa devoted to the expansion of Islamic missions abroad.

By then, Michael was already safely installed in a nondescript furnished apartment off the Shari' al-Husayniyya, just north of the old City Wall. Verhaeren had taken him there the night before, after their conversation. He had seen nothing of his neighbors as yet, though he had heard them more than once: footsteps, calls in the night, the breaking of a window, a child crying after sleep.

He had other neighbors who were less noisy: through a grimy window he looked out onto Bab al-Nasr cemetery. Old graves, old expectations, old appeasements. At times he could hear the high voices of mourners tremble over the stones like the warbling of strange birds.

He had woken, exhausted, about eleven o'clock and gone straight to Rif'at's, where he had radioed a message to Tom Holly. Tending to the bookseller as best he could, he had returned to the apartment and spent the rest of the day reading systematically through the numerous papers Verhaeren had given him, the nunciature's treasure-trove of information on al-Qurtubi and the Ahl al-Samt. Most of it had been compiled by his brother Paul.

He put them all out of his head: Paul, Verhaeren, al-Qurtubi. Tonight he had something else to settle. He had to know whether or not his bolthole via the coast was still open. Open for himself, open—in what now seemed an absurd hope—for A'isha.

The street was quiet. Such a stillness held the night, a stillness and an expectation. Closing the street door, he paused, patting his pockets like a man who has forgotten something. Out of the corner of his eye, he watched for the tell-tale movement that would reveal that someone was watching, waiting to tail him. Or kill him. He took a deep breath. All was still.

Pulling the collar of his cheap coat up round his neck, he stepped out into the night.

Shukri grabbed Rif'at's arm, pulling him through the darkness behind a pile of book-filled boxes. He had calculated the distance before blowing out the candle. Fear held the bookseller's tongue. Shukri could feel him trembling beneath his hand. He wondered who had screamed. His own breathing was far from steady.

In the next room, someone swore loudly. Then a woman's voice cried out in pain. Rif'at struggled to get to his feet.

"My mother!" he exclaimed. "They're hurting her."

Shukri shoved him back down, fumbling to cover his open mouth. He could smell him, the fever and the fear mingled.

"Shut up," he hissed in Rif'at's ear. "You'll have us both killed!"

Why weren't they coming? What were they waiting for? Shukri strained to make out the doorway, but his eyes had not yet adjusted sufficiently to the darkness. Rif'at was still struggling to get free.

Then, out of the darkness, a voice as smooth as silk.

"You're wasting your time, Ahmad. The building is surrounded. You are heavily outnumbered. Four of you against a whole detachment. It's up to you to draw the obvious conclusion."

Suddenly, Rif'at wriggled sideways and broke free. The next moment, he was on his feet, calling at the top of his voice, "Mother! I won't let them hurt you!"

He made it as far as the doorway. Shukri heard the blow and the grunt as the bookseller was taken. He could just make out a patch of light where the door must be. And what seemed very like a man's figure blocking it. He raised his gun and aimed at the figure. The shot exploded through the room like a stroke of thunder. Someone cried out.

He threw himself back behind the pathetic rampart of cardboard boxes. A fusillade of automatic fire ripped through the room, tearing plaster from the walls, scything through the boxes just above his head. Shredded paper drifted like white confetti through the bruised air.

"I will give you a second chance, Ahmad. Just one. For old times' sake. If not for yourself, then for your niece. Throw away your gun and give yourself up. I promise you that no-one will be harmed."

Shukri twisted to the side of the barricade and fired another two shots. It was so long since he had been in action. So very long. The machine gun returned his fire, tearing the darkness into finer and finer fragments. The firing went on longer this time. When it ended, the woman in the other room was screaming terribly.

"I have Rif'at's mother. Every time you fire a shot, I shall make her suffer. It is up to you."

The screaming bubbled into sobbing. Shukri hesitated, then threw the gun aside. That was the trouble with life, he thought. The hard decisions were never up to the people with the big guns.

"And the others," said the voice. "Tell them to throw their guns away too."

"There are no others," Shukri called out. He sensed the hesitation on the other side. Then someone snapped an order. Light flooded the room.

They entered the doorway cautiously, their automatics poised, ready to fire. Two men dressed in the garb of *muhtasibin*. Ancient costumes, modern weapons: how well they go together, Shukri thought.

He was standing by the boxes, arms above his head, a tired old hand playing a tired old game. They ignored him until they had checked out the room. Then one of them grabbed him roughly by the arm and hauled him into the empty room that had once been a bookshop. Abu Musa had taken the only chair. He was dressed in the robes of a *muhtasib*. Always a step ahead of the rest, thought Shukri.

About a dozen *muhtasibin* crowded the little room. They all wore beards, all bore the same sour expression on their faces. How he despised it all. It was their lack of humor that grieved him more than anything. He noticed with a twinge of satisfaction that he had done some damage: one man lay on the ground, groaning and holding his thigh where he had been wounded.

In one corner, his face concealed by shadows, a tall man stood watching. Shukri stared at him, trying to catch a proper glimpse of his features, but he drew back out of sight. Something about him seemed familiar, but Shukri's mind was in too great a turmoil to think who it might be.

An elderly woman was crouching on the floor attending to Rif'at. The bookseller was coughing, just coming back to consciousness. Better if they had shot the poor bastard, Shukri thought. Maybe he should have done it himself.

As he entered the room, Abu Musa was giving instructions to a subordinate.

"And take six men to cover the front of the building. You have my full authority," he was saying. "The others are to go round the back. The girl can't have got far. I want every alleyway and rooftop searched until you find them." He dismissed the man with a wave of one hand. As the *muhtasib* left, taking four men with him, Abu Musa turned his head and looked calmly at Shukri.

"Ahmad, my sweet angel. To find you in such strange company. To think that you inhabit such a world."

He was almost smiling. It was the happiest Shukri had ever seen him. He looked him over as though seeing him for the first time. Slim, intelligent, good-looking, nauseating. How old was he now? Forty-five, forty-six? He looked a young thirty-five. One of those types who flourish in their dissipation.

Shukri knew all about him, knew him better than he knew himself. Loathed him, feared him. If Abu Musa had not been so good at his job, if he had not been so handsome and so tractable, so well attuned to other men's guilt and other men's longings, Shukri would have had him dismissed from the *mukhabarat* years ago. Now he regretted his inaction. He felt a sick lump of fear rise in his throat.

"You've changed your uniform, I see. It suits you." He hoped his voice did not betray the fear he felt.

Abu Musa looked at him coldly. There was something in his manner that did not ring true, a nervousness, a self-consciousness that ought not to have been there.

"And you," he said, "are just the same pretentious little shit you always were. Too bad." He paused. His eyes held Shukri fast. He was playing him like a fish in water, reeling him in on a barbed hook.

"Ahmad," he went on, "do let me explain. I have been given instructions by 'Abd al-Karim Tawfiq to set up a Department of National Security within the Religious Police. In due course, it will become an independent organ of the Islamic state. Within the next month, we shall take over the functions of the *mukhabarat amn al-dawla*. We already control the anti-riot brigades and the regular police.

"But in the meantime, I have old scores to settle. Old scores fare best in new conditions. And how fortunate I have been. As long as I belonged to the *mukhabarat,* my hands were tied. I had suspicions, but whom could I share them with? It was you they loved, not me. You were all-powerful in that place, or very nearly so. But I suspected you and I knew that one day I would have you. So I held my tongue and I waited.

"And then . . ." A trace of a smile flickered on Abu Musa's narrow mouth. But not his eyes. There was no smile in his eyes. And the nervousness, the nervousness was still there. Shukri realized suddenly that it was on account of the other man, the stranger who kept his face hidden in the shadows. Abu Musa would glance around from time to time, as though making sure the other man was still there. Shukri looked into the corner, but he could still make out nothing but shadows.

"Just three weeks ago, my luck changed," Abu Musa

continued. "A watch was being kept on your niece, the lovely Miss Manfaluti. We've been keeping an eye on her ever since her husband disappeared. But then you know all about that. You may also know that, a few months ago, she became the lover of a former British intelligence agent. A man called Michael Hunt." He paused. "Oh, that little flicker in your eyes. You know the name, of course you do. Such a perfect triangle: a senior officer in National Security, his delicious niece, and a foreign agent."

"You're talking nonsense."

Abu Musa shook his head slowly, with conviction.

"No," he said. "Not nonsense. Several weeks ago, Michael Hunt went to Alexandria. He vanished there. And then, strangely enough, a routine check revealed that your niece had disappeared as well."

The unsmiling eyes held Shukri's. Such hard eyes. Behind them, Abu Musa was soaring. He had never risen so high before, had never felt such wings bearing him up. If only . . . He looked half round, felt the eyes watching him.

"Until this afternoon, that is. This afternoon, Miss Manfaluti and a man we assume to have been Michael Hunt were seen picking you up on your way home from the office. You were followed to Helwan and then again back to the city tonight. And where should you all end up but here, in a shop owned by Michael Hunt's radio operator?"

Abu Musa swiveled. Rif'at was fully conscious now, sprawled on the floor with his mother bending over him. She was an old woman, dressed in a faded headscarf and a loose-fitting dress, the sort of old woman one finds on every Cairo street, wrinkled, sad, meaningless. Shukri wondered what she feared most: the plague on her son's breath or Abu Musa. He suspected the latter.

"Pick him up!" Abu Musa commanded. One of the *muhtasibin* near Rif'at grabbed the sick man by the hair and pulled him screaming to his feet. The old woman clutched at him, crying out inarticulately. Shukri noticed that she was bleeding in several places. Bruises had formed across her face.

"Twice today," Abu Musa began, "radio transmissions between London and Cairo were intercepted by our communications center in al-Amiriyya. The first originated in Cairo, the second in Vauxhall House in London.

"I think Michael Hunt was here today, and I think he sent a message to his Desk Head. The return message will have been the reply. Both used a one-time code which we are unable to break. But you will appreciate that it is vital to our national security that it be broken."

He paused and nodded towards Shukri. That was all he did, that was all he needed to do. Two *muhtasibin* came behind Shukri and took him hard by the arms.

When he smelled the kerosene, he wondered why he had not noticed it before. Had he been too afraid, was that it? He could have guessed from the moment he laid eyes on Abu Musa: it was his trademark after all. He felt the knot in his stomach tighten.

"I know you too well, Ahmad, to think I can make you talk as quickly as I would like. I just don't have the time. I need results. So you will just have to serve as my example." His mouth formed a half-smile again. He turned and looked at Rif'at.

"Not much, is he? A little man in far over his head. He's frightened now, but he doesn't know just how frightened he can be. But you know, Ahmad, don't you? You know very well. Perhaps he won't be frightened for himself, considering his condition. But his mother, he will be frightened for her. Once he knows what I can do to her."

Shukri smelled the odor of raw kerosene on the night air, strong and sickening. Sweat broke out on his skin in spite of the cold. He closed his eyes, wishing the pain and the indignity away. His eyelids felt heavy with memories that were not quite memories, dreams that were not quite dreams. He remembered his wife. Not so much as he had known her, but as she had appeared to him in dreams.

Every night in dreams for year after tearing year. Until recently. Recently, he had dreamed of a pyramid in the desert. He opened his eyes and saw the blank, bookless room again.

Abu Musa snapped his fingers. A thin-faced man came forward, holding in his hands a long tube, a thin rubber tube, soft and flexible. He felt the grip on his arms tighten. He wondered why they did not tie him.

"You are making a mockery of your position," he said.

"More than you made of yours?" Abu Musa asked.

"Yes," said Ahmad, "more than I made of mine." It did not matter now. What did anything matter?

The *muhtasib* pressed the tube hard against his lips.

"Relax," he said. "Relax and swallow, it will make it easier."

Shukri fought against the tube, but the man forced it into his mouth all the same. It was obvious that he had had practice. He gagged, choking, but the man rammed it down his throat regardless. It was a form of rape.

When the *muhtasib* had finished, he took a wide-necked funnel and screwed it into the top of the tube. Shukri wanted to cry out, but he could not; only moans escaped him. Rif'at was watching, his face turned forcibly in Shukri's direction. Shukri could see the fear in his eyes. Which was more terrible, the plague or humanity?

The bookseller began to weep as they poured kerosene slowly into the funnel. Shukri felt it slip down the tube, filling his stomach like death. When they had poured enough, they removed the tube. Shukri coughed and choked and tried to throw up. His insides were already in agony. The *muhtasib* took from his pocket a roll of bandage, a small, tight roll.

"Swallow this," he said.

He held his mouth shut tight. It was too much, he could cooperate no further. Abu Musa nodded and the *muhtasib* broke Shukri's jaw with a single blow from his pistol. He forced the roll into his throat, keeping tight hold of one end.

Ahmad choked it down. It had been soaked in kerosene: the taste filled his mouth.

Rif'at stopped crying. Shukri looked into his eyes. Fear. Resignation. There had been nothing in his poetry, nothing in his philosophy to prepare him for this. Shukri shut his eyes. He saw a long line of sphinxes, a black pyramid towering into a sky full of circling birds. There was silence, dreadful silence. And at last the sound of a match being struck, the sound of a flame hissing, then growing steady. He opened his eyes.

At that moment the Dutchman stepped out of the shadows and smiled at him.

48

A'isha shook with cold and apprehension. If Michael tried to make contact with Qasim Rif'at tonight, he would walk straight into a trap. She had no idea who had led the raid on the shop, but the entire neighborhood was crawling with *muhtasibin*.

She and Brutus were crouched in shadows in a narrow alleyway that branched off the lane behind the bookshop. They had already seen two Jeeps pass, manned by religious police and marked with their symbol, a green crescent made up of the words *la ilaha illa 'llah*: there is no god but God. The streets had grown ominously quiet. No shuffling of feet, no coughing, no barking of unleashed dogs. Not even the sobbing of children in moments of frightened awakening.

They watched as a personnel carrier halted in the lane, disgorging armed men. Out of sight, an officer shouted orders: "Seal off the area. Don't let anyone in or out. Remember what I told you: neither the girl nor the man with her are to be shot, unless they put up a fight and you have to return fire. The Dutchman wants them alive."

A sound of running feet, then the APC moving off.

"We've seen enough," hissed Butrus in her ear.

"They'll put a cordon round al-Qulali, then close in." He looked up. On the roof of a house opposite, he could see a dark figure silhouetted against the sky. High above, stars jostled one another for space in the narrow opening. "They're all over the place," he said. "We've got to move quickly, back up towards Shari' Ramsis. If we can make it to the Coptic Hospital, I know people there who will take us in."

"And what about Michael?"

"Michael? What about him? You don't know where he is, which direction he'll be coming from—if he comes at all. We have to think about ourselves. If you won't, I'll have to do it for you."

"Don't patronize me," she retorted.

"I'm merely saying that I care for you, that I want to keep you safe . . ."

"Safe?" she snorted. "Just who is safe, Butrus? That pathetic little man we saw half an hour ago, tearing his books to shreds? Your Coptic friends? My uncle? Nobody's safe now. I have to stay, I have to find Michael. But if you want to, you can get away."

"Not without you."

She turned on him viciously.

"*Not without you,*" she mimicked. "What does that mean? You aren't my husband, my lover, my brother. I have to do this for my own reasons. Your reasons are different. If you have any." She turned her back on him, shaking.

He said nothing, but she could sense the hurt that filled his silence. They were worlds apart, could he not see that? Did love make you that blind?

"A'isha, you don't understand. I have no expectations from you. If you want to find Michael, go ahead. But you can't do it alone. Think about it. The religious police are all over the place. Even if you managed to catch sight of him before they did, you'd have no way of getting to him."

She turned to him again. The darkness hid their faces from one another. With a sudden stab of understanding, she realized that her face had always been hidden behind one kind of darkness or another.

"Then what do you suggest?"

He hesitated before answering.

"We go to them," he said.

"What do you mean?"

He pointed to the wall on the opposite side of the alley-way. "Help me get up there," he said. There was a barred and shuttered window about nine feet above ground level.

She hesitated for only a second. With her back to the wall, she made a fireman's lift for him. Awkwardly, he put one foot into it, then jumped, using the momentum of her thrust to reach the window. Across it someone had long ago stretched strands of barbed wire. They were rusty now and slack, but the points were still viciously sharp. Carefully, nervous of falling and tearing his hands on the spikes, he worked one end of the lowest strand free. He had just finished when A'isha could hold him no longer.

"I'm sorry," she whispered. "My arms were about to give way. What were you trying to do?"

"You'll see," he said. "We'll wait a few minutes, then I'll lift you up. All you have to do is break that bottom strand free at the other end."

"Why . . .?" She broke off as an engine sounded in the lane. They lay down, flattening themselves against the wall. A Jeep crossed the opening, pouring light into the alley from a lamp mounted on its roof. They held their breath. The Jeep crept on, its engine growing fainter then vanishing into the depths of the night.

He was about to lift her to the window when the still-ness was torn by a sudden, agonizing scream. It lasted in reality just a few seconds, but no-one who heard it would ever forget the sound. Whether it was indeed a human scream or the cry of an animal in the full horror of its death it was impossible to tell. It did not fade away, but ended in a jagged shudder. The air remained full of its echo long after-wards.

A'isha shuddered and put her arms round Butrus. He held her lightly, torn between his dread for what he had just heard and his bitter, congealed longing for her.

"You don't think . . .?"

"Rif'at? Or your uncle?"

"No, I . . ." She stumbled to a halt. She had not thought of her uncle at all. Her fears had been only for Michael.

"You thought it was Michael?"

"It's almost time. If Rif'at was forced to talk . . ."

He stroked her head. Drawn in to him, she felt so fragile that he might have crushed her. If it had indeed been Michael Hunt . . . He shuddered, remembering the scream, thinking how terrible it would be if his happiness depended on that, on another's death. And yet he was secretly pleased. If it had been Hunt . . .

A'isha pulled away from him.

"Do you think it was Rif'at?" What had they done to him? Or to her uncle?

"I don't know," Butrus said. "How could I know?"

She nodded. Speculation was worse than useless. Butrus clasped his hands again. She took a deep breath and placed her foot in them. He lifted her effortlessly to the barred window. In less than a minute she had snapped the rusted wire in two. He lowered her to the ground and she handed it to him without a word.

With his foot, he bent down the spikes on both ends. He was not trained to this: it would not be easy.

The first *muhtasib* was in the lane, about twenty yards from the opening where it met the alleyway. His white robe gave him away. In the end, their love of purity would betray them as it always did.

"You'll have to help me," Butrus said. "I can't do this alone."

"What do you want me to do?" She was beginning to understand what Butrus was up to.

"Talk to him. Get his attention. Tell him you have a sick

child, ask him to help. If you can, get him to come down here, into this alleyway.''

She shook her head.

"Why would he help me? I'll have to tell him I've found the man he's looking for. Where will you be?"

"I'll be waiting," he said. "Leave that to me." He hoped the little guerrilla training he had had with the Coptic Defense League would be enough for what lay ahead. And he wondered why he was doing any of this at all.

A'isha walked quickly down the lane. The *muhtasib* heard her coming when she was about half way. He spun, covering her with his gun, and for a long instant she thought he would shoot her where she stood.

She kept her arms well away from her body, making it clear she was unarmed. He kept the gun pointed at her, and when she was a couple of yards away told her to stop.

"I need help," she said. "There's a wounded man in the alleyway outside my house. Please come." She spoke in a Sa'idi accent, like a woman fresh from the country, guileless, unthreatening, bewildered.

"Get out of here," he ordered. His voice was rough, unsympathetic.

"He's bleeding," she said. "He said someone was after him. You've got to help."

He hesitated. She could see that the hook had caught, pulling him off balance.

"Where is this man?"

She pointed back towards the alleyway where Butrus was waiting.

"You go in front," he said. He was suspicious, uneasy, younger than he had at first appeared. Eighteen perhaps, at most nineteen: a boy surrounded by adult darknesses.

She walked cautiously, sensing his presence behind her, the automatic weapon that could rip her in two in half a second. Each footstep took an age. Somewhere, very far away, a voice cried out, attenuated in the vaster silence of the dying city. She held her breath. She could feel him, murderously close.

Suddenly, he stopped.

"Just a moment," he said. "What's your name?"

"Dunya," she said, giving her mother's name. They were looking for her, but she did not know whether they knew her name.

"Turn around," he said. "I want to see your face."

She turned, trying to shrink back into the shadows.

"Why are you out so late? Why didn't you call your neighbors for help?"

"They're all afraid," she answered. "They stay inside. Because of the plague."

"There is no plague in Cairo," he said, reciting official dogma. "Come closer," he said, "come closer." He had a flashlight in his hand, he was going to shine it in her face. He would never take her for a country girl.

She leapt at him before he had time even to lift a hand in self-defence, throwing him back heavily to the ground. Her tiny body was no match for his strength, but fury and grief and desperation drove her. He lay beneath her, bewildered, bellowing. Desperately, she thrust a hand over his mouth, muffling his cries. He was kicking now, recovering from the initial shock of her attack. She did not know how much longer she could manage to hold him. Her strength was ebbing rapidly, she had to struggle to keep him down. With one arm he rained blow after blow on her back and head, trying to dislodge her.

It seemed an age before Butrus got to them. Without a word, he bent down behind the *muhtasib,* throwing a loop of barbed wire over his head. With all his strength Butrus pulled hard on the wire, bringing the ends together and across one another, tightening the rusted metal round his victim's neck.

The man reared up, throwing A'isha off. Frantic now, he struggled to get to his feet, but Butrus kept him down, a knee on each shoulder. The spikes were digging into the man's neck, drawing blood. He tried to cry out, but only inarticulate sounds issued from his throat. A'isha watched with horror as he struggled for life, his limbs thrashing, his face contorted. More than anything, the eyes frightened her. There was no appeal in them, no desperate plea for mercy, just sullen outrage and thwarted anger. She looked away, speechless. When she looked again, the face had grown still, the tumult of limbs had changed to a last, spasmodic twitching that diminished in moments to the most perfect of stillnesses.

He knew something was wrong long before he reached Fajjala. The unnerving silence, the deserted streets, the echoes of distant voices suddenly stifled, all alerted him to the possibility of danger. Ordinarily, he would have turned back, but these were not ordinary times.

He kept a close watch all the way down al-Sabtiyya. In every cluster of shadows he fancied he saw enemies. Only a few street lamps were still lit, leaving whole stretches of the long avenue plunged in darkness. He walked carefully to avoid potholes and uncovered manholes, severe hazards at the best of times. He heard a rustling sound as something soft and nimble scuttled past, disappearing into deeper shadows. A large rat, the first he had seen.

The shop came in sight. There was a light in the upstairs window, and lights in other second- and third-floor windows up and down the street. He felt strangely reassured. But why was no-one on the streets? Had the curfew been reimposed after all? He would have turned back even now, but he needed his answer tonight. And he had to make sure Rif'at had his medicine. If it saved the bookseller's life, it would be small repayment for all he had risked for Michael over the years.

The door was open. Michael hesitated, wondering what he might find inside. He would never come here again, no matter what happened.

Footsteps sounded behind him. He turned and saw two figures coming towards him out of the shadows. *Muhtasibin.* He recognized the white robes. They carried automatic weapons and walked arrogantly straight towards him. He looked up and down the street. Was there any point in making a run for it? For the hell of the thing, as a last gesture? In either direction, the street stretched away like death.

49

Up until the last moment, she thought it would turn out to be a mistake. It would be another man, a stranger, someone of no consequence to her. Or worse, she thought, it would be someone who had come there looking for her, someone who would, in another instant, see through the disguise of the white *thawb* she was wearing and raise the alarm. And then he turned and there was a sheet of light that gave his face shape among the shadows, and familiarity, and her heart leapt, and the fear she had felt for herself was entirely gone and at once replaced by all-consuming fear for him.

"Michael," she whispered. "Don't be afraid. It's me, A'isha. Just stay calm and don't give any sign you recognize me."

He looked at her, startled, frozen by the improbability of it. He had thought he would never see her again.

"A'isha?! I don't believe . . . Is that you?"

"Yes, my love."

He heard the catch in her voice and caught in a momentary shift of light the lost and wounded look in her eyes. Involuntarily, he made to take her in his arms, but she drew back.

"For God's sake don't touch me or show you know me. This place is full of *muhtasibin*. We've got to get away as fast as possible. Butrus and I will arrest you. We will walk together for fifty meters that way, then head into an alley. Once we're inside, start running."

"How . . .?"

Butrus grabbed his arm.

"Let's go," he said.

A'isha took his other arm, thinking how very long it was since they had last touched, how their reunion had become a mockery. It was the hardest thing she had ever done, to hold him without affection, to pull him down a cold, dark street acting a part, waiting every moment for the alarm that would separate them forever. She was certain they were being watched, that someone would already be asking himself questions, and that in moments they would be thrown stunned and bleeding to the ground. Every breath was a physical pain, every step a lifetime.

His initial shock overcome, Michael played his part perfectly. He struggled against his captors, as though trying to break free. Butrus turned and struck him what looked to be a hard blow in the stomach, using the butt of his sub-machine gun. Michael stumbled and staggered along as though winded, throwing his weight onto his companions.

Ten meters.

The stillness held like an egg about to crack. They increased their pace, fighting the impulse to break into a run.

Twenty meters.

The shop was well behind them now. Silence like liquid, enveloping them, drowning them, their footsteps dropping into it like heavy stones. Nothing moved. No-one called out. The darkness waited. Silence upon silence, footfall upon footfall.

Thirty meters.

A'isha could see the opening to the alleyway on her right. The stillness stretched more and more thinly, tight, straining, taut as a violin string drawn to breaking point.

Somewhere a walkie-talkie crackled. Without warning, the darkness exploded into sound and light. A voice blared out, distorted by a megaphone, rupturing the silence. In front of them, a giant floodlight flared into life, tearing from their eyes what little vision they possessed, blinding them.

"Put down your weapons," boomed the voice. "You are surrounded. You have nowhere to go. You cannot run from God."

Michael scarcely stopped to think. He snatched the automatic rifle from A'isha, lifted it towards the light, and fired straight down the beam. There was a bang. Glass shattered. Someone cried out. Darkness swooped.

"Run," shouted Michael. "Run!"

They ran. Blind, guided by memory and instinct, their eyes still throbbing with light, their ears filled with the echo of the booming voice. A gun rang out, then another. Bullets plowed into the ground mere feet away. A burst of automatic fire raked the wall they had just passed, tearing lumps of masonry from it.

"Here!" shouted Butrus.

The entrance to the alley was on their right, barely visible as a shift in the darkness. They tumbled down it, desperately conscious of the racket their feet made on the hard surface of the roadway. But speed was essential if they were to get far enough away from the main grouping of *muhtasibin* stationed round the shop.

There was a shout: *"Qifu!* Halt!"

A figure detached itself from the shadows, a ghost merging with the phantoms of light in their eyes.

They ran on. There was a shot. Butrus cried out and staggered backwards, falling. Michael fired at the figure in white, a short, accurate burst that hit its mark. The *muhtasib* cried out once, fell, and lay perfectly still.

"Butrus! Are you all right?" A'isha knelt beside Butrus, raising his head.

"My . . . shoulder. The bullet hit my shoulder. I'll be all right."

"Can you get up?"

With A'isha's help, he got to his feet.

"Did the bullet pass through?"

"I don't know," Butrus winced. "I don't think so."

Gently, A'isha ran her hand over the back of his shoulder. There was no sign of an exit wound. The bullet must still be lodged in the shoulder. Behind them, they could hear engines coughing into life, brisk voices snapping out orders, footsteps running.

A'isha tore off the white *muhtasib*'s robes she had been wearing, then helped Butrus removed his. She picked up the gun he had been carrying and set off, Butrus beside her, cradling his left arm in his right. They followed Michael deeper into the alleyway. There was nowhere else to run: on either side high walls and locked doors hemmed them in, forbidding any hope of escape. They ran on, harried by the sound of pursuing feet.

"They're going to cut us off at the lane!" shouted A'isha. They were heading down towards the alley that ran along the rear of Kamal Sidqi, a passage wide enough to permit the movement of wheeled vehicles. Even as she spoke, a light flashed in the darkness ahead of them. Behind it, an armored vehicle rumbled into action.

They reached the corner. Michael pressed himself against the right-hand wall. Hurriedly, he glanced into the lane. As he pulled his head back, A'isha joined him.

Michael helped Butrus to his feet. "Quickly!" he cried.

They ran into the lane. A'isha was waiting for them a few yards further down, at the entrance to a much narrower passage.

"In here," she said.

They moved quietly on the balls of their feet, seeking safety in silence more than speed. Behind them, they could hear men shouting.

The alley turned and twisted, leading them into a maze of ever-narrower lanes and by-ways. Suddenly, they found themselves trapped in a narrow passage that ended in a ten-foot wall. As they turned to retrace their steps, the sound of footsteps echoed through the intervening alleyways. Their pursuers could not be more than a few hundred yards away.

"We've no choice," said Michael. "Help me up."

A'isha helped him scramble to the top of the wall. He lay along it, reaching down. Grasping Butrus by his good arm, he pulled him to the top, then helped him drop to the other side. The footsteps were almost on them now. A'isha reached up. Their hands met and for a moment they froze. Then Michael pulled hard and she scrambled up and over. Flashlights appeared in the opening to the alleyway. Michael slipped over the side and dropped gently to the ground. They held their breath.

The footsteps halted, hesitated, moved away. A grim silence. Darkness all round them, not a light anywhere, no-one moving. A rat scuttled across A'isha's foot, startling her. A large rat with a long tail. They huddled at the foot of the wall, taking shallow breaths, listening intently for sounds of pursuit. Thick, thick silence, as though the wall had marked the boundary to another world.

When five minutes had passed, they set off along the narrow passage. Blank walls rose on either side like the sheer faces of a canyon. Another rat ran past, then another. They weaved and twisted through bent and narrow lanes, hemmed in on every side by the tall, faceless walls. Something was wrong. There were no *muhtasibin* here, but the area through which they passed was as silent as a graveyard. They saw no lights in the windows, heard no voices, not even the distant clamor of television or radio behind closed doors.

The moon crept out from behind a cloud, throwing a dull, sickly light on the city. Light lay pasted on old, broken walls, crumbling buildings, abandoned homes. It was as if they had passed out of Cairo entirely, left all humanity behind, and come to a separate place, a ruined place, a dark garden set behind high walls, a city of the dead. Ten yards in front of them, a horde of long gray shapes scampered and scurried in the thin moonlight.

"Where are we?" Michael asked. He knew Cairo well. Never, not even in his nightmares, had he entered or heard of a place like this.

A'isha said nothing. Slowly, reluctantly, she had begun to understand. She reached out for him, her hand finding his in the darkness. She looked round: at the rats, at the diseased and perished walls, at the pieces of old rag fluttering in a foul-smelling breeze. And she understood.

Tenderly, she drew him close. His face shone in the moonlight, unnaturally bright. His eyes were not his eyes, he was a stranger she had tried to love. She kissed him with her eyes fast closed, soft at first, then eager, blotting out everything.

In the shadows, Butrus watched. His heart was beating fast, his shoulder was throbbing with pain, but he forced himself to watch. He had understood as well: where they were, what they would find as they probed deeper into this shattered region. He understood, but as he watched Michael and A'isha embrace, it did not matter to him in the least. Nothing mattered. Because he knew they would never leave this place alive.

50

The wall stretched in both directions as far as anyone could see. Every day it grew longer and higher. It was four feet thick and, when it was finished, it would be fifty feet high and one thousand three hundred miles long. All of pagan Egypt would go into the making of it: pyramids and tombs, temples and obelisks, the ruination of centuries, brick and stone, the sweat of the long dead and the blood of the living.

Gangs of men had labored with spades and bare hands to dig a trench in the sand, holding the crumbling sides fast with wooden planks, then filling the hollow with cement and stone rubble carried in from the smaller sites like el-Lisht and Maidum. This rough foundation had been flattened by further gangs, working day and night. All round the frontier, the process of laying the foundations still continued without interruption. The lorries came in carrying rubble and went away empty.

And on the foundation they built the wall. Unskilled hands laid brick on brick, plastering them in place with thick mortar mixed on the spot. The water was driven in in large tankers; even when the work-force gasped for refreshment, the tankers still rolled in from their bases along the river and emptied the contents into the giant basins in which the cement was mixed.

At night, arc-lights flooded the wall so that work could be continued without interruption. Those who had labored through the day tried to snatch a few hours of sleep in flimsy tents, their rest disturbed by the bitter desert cold and the dull thumping of the electric generators from which the lights drew their power. Work progressed along a five-hundred-mile front, with as many as eighty sections being completed simultaneously.

Each day more people died. Some from exhaustion. Some from exposure. Some as a result of falls. Most from the plague. The dead lay where they fell or were dragged off the wall onto the sand, out of the way of the ever-encroaching bricks. Those who were not dead were at best half-alive. Work would go slowly for a while, then fresh volunteers would be bused in from the cities or the countryside. Farms were falling empty as the *muhtasibin* scoured the country, urging everyone over the age of twelve to join the great pilgrimage to the wall.

No-one harried them, no-one whipped them on to work. But a great passion gripped them, a fearful urgency, and above all an overwhelming dread of the rapidly spreading plague. They worked until they dropped, and, if they were able to struggle to their feet again, they resumed working. No-one complained.

Tom Holly reached the wall shortly after midnight on the 29th. He had traveled slowly through the Libyan desert, on foot for much of the time, riding only when he could do so without drawing attention to himself. He had known they would be looking out for him, remembering the numerous trips he had made through this region as an undergraduate.

The moon laid crumbling sheets of white across the rough surface of ancient brick and slapdash mortar. This section had long been completed. Nothing stirred. There were no guards, no dogs, no alarms. What use would they have been? The wall had not been built against human intruders, as originally claimed, but as a bulwark against the infected wind that came from the West.

The wall was not as hard to climb as it looked. Its face was dotted with cracks and projections. As though in a dream, cocooned by moonlight, Tom rose lightly to the top, then clambered down the other side. There was nothing to say he could not as easily climb back and return the way he had come. But he knew that, in the mere act of crossing the wall, he had committed himself to the final round of the game.

PART VII

"They shall go down to the bars of the pit"

JOB 17:16

51

Cairo was exhausted, ringed with pyramids of the dead. Choked with corpses, the river broke the great city into two unequal halves, dark annexes of its troubled waters. In the deserted streets, dogs crept into doorways in search of shelter. Behind locked doors, the dying shivered with cold and burned with fever. The living sat in silence, staring into stained and cracked mirrors, searching for the first intimation of their own deaths.

The moon had gone back behind black clouds, taking its thin light with it. Rain fell, an unsteady drizzle, out of a bruised and violated sky. They thought the night would never end.

They sat in the abandoned hallway of a tenement, huddled against the hard edges of the cold and dark. A'isha's head lay quietly against Michael's shoulder, her bewildered hair tumbling across his chest, wet and tangled. Her eyes were tightly closed. She imagined that they were home again, safe in his apartment, or away from all this in France or England. Anywhere but Egypt, anywhere but Cairo, anywhere but this terrible place.

She tried to close her ears against the silence, but it

pressed in on her from all sides, like water on a drowning woman, inexorable and swift. The few fragments of speech she and Michael had exchanged so far had been worse than nothing.

Butrus lay a little apart from them, on the other side of the hallway, nursing his wounded shoulder, half asleep, half conscious of a nagging pain. A'isha had done what she could to bind his wound, but it needed no skill to see that he would soon require medical help. He stirred restlessly, his half-dreams volatile with pain and longing. Even in his conscious moments, he could not tell them apart.

They had not ventured up the stairs. A'isha had a torch, taken from one of the *muhtasibin* they had killed. She had used it at first to help them find their way, but after a while she had switched it off. The light had shown nothing but squalor and decay.

Dust lay everywhere in thick, tattered pleats and intricate folds: on stairways, thresholds, windowsills. There were rats everywhere. Huge, black rats with pink tails and glittering eyes. They had carved out pathways through the buildings, leaving their raw footprints all over the gray carpet of dust. They showed no fear, as though well accustomed to the presence of human beings. And everywhere they had left their dead to molder and decay.

She opened her eyes at last, blinking in the darkness. Her dreams had gone. There was no point in clinging to them.

"Are you listening?" she asked.

"Yes," he said. "I'm listening."

She paused. Would it not be better to leave him in ignorance, give him a few more hours of peace before the sun rose and he worked it out for himself? But he had asked her to tell him, and after so long apart, she could hold nothing back from him.

"They sealed it off," she said slowly, stumbling. "An entire sector of the city. We thought it was a rumor, just one of those meaningless rumors you can't get away from in

Cairo. You know how it is. I paid no attention to it. Not even they could be that stupid, I thought."

"You aren't making sense," he said. "Why did they seal it off?"

She hesitated before answering. Then it all came out in one word.

"The plague," she said. "They sealed it off because of the plague. It broke out in one area to begin with. Just one sector, Bulaq. No-one knows why. The rats, probably. If this outbreak followed the traditional pattern, there will have been an influx of them from the Black Sea region. *Pasteurella Pestis* is endemic among the steppe rodents. Infected rats must have made their way here, gone underground, bred, and then spread the disease to their human neighbors.

"Anyway, people started dying in large numbers, most of them in this quarter. So someone said, 'Why don't we impose a quarantine? Why don't we seal off Bulaq, build a wall around it, leave them to it? No-one goes in or out. Half of them are Copts, we'll be well rid of them. They're going to die anyway, most of them. The rest God will save if He wishes. That will leave us with just a handful of isolable cases in the rest of the city.'

"They thought that, they believed they could contain it, that God would help them build barriers against infection. They were wrong, of course; but they still sealed this sector off. They carved out an almost perfect rectangle, with the Corniche on the west, part of al-Sabtiyya to the north, then down sharply behind al-Qulali as far as 6 Uktubir, all down the west side of al-Gala, leaving the railway track untouched, and finally north-west along 26 Yuliyu. That left the radio and television building outside. They erected walls across all the streets, then blocked up all the doors and windows looking outwards."

She looked at him, at his dim, urgent shape in the darkness.

"We're in a cemetery," she said. "A plague cemetery."

"And people accepted it? They didn't try to escape?"

"They tried. That's what I heard. Some of them tried. But they had posted guards at all the possible escape routes. Nobody made it out alive."

"There were no guards on the wall we went over tonight."

"They must have taken them away after a while. There's no-one left to try to escape; what's the point of guards?" She paused. "But they'll put them back now. To wait for us. We're trapped, Michael. Guards on the outside, rats in here. Rats, and God knows what in the rooms up there." She shuddered. He held her to him without a word.

Eventually, she pulled away and leaned back against the wall. As she did so, she felt something in her pocket. The envelope Rif'at had given her. She drew it out and passed it to Michael, explaining what it was and how she had come by it.

"Let me have the torch," he said.

He opened the crumpled envelope and drew out a sheet of paper on which Rif'at had written in his own hand the text of the message from Century:

R84156/ED/29 12 99
Transmission begins: 1723
Source: EGYPTDESK, VAUXHALL c PH
Destination: CAIROSTATION
Operative: B9

TEXT

PH sends congratulations on your return from the dead. We confirm Santa Claus departed UK 17 12 99. Also confirm his message of same date and proposed rendezvous. Santa Claus will be at the Sugar Palace between 1500 hours and 2200 hours nightly 31st and 1st. Emphasize possibility of delay crossing hostile frontier. In reply to your request 29 12 99, we have been instructed to state that evacuation by sea is now impossible, repeat, impossible exclaimer. It is imperative you meet with Santa Claus. PH requests details of AM. Do you have news of RM query. He also wants details of your Alexandria investigations, top priority. Good luck.

MESSAGE ENDS

Transmission ends 1724. Offsign.

Michael crumpled the message slowly in his hand and tossed it to the floor. The torch laid a solid beam of white light across a litter of rat droppings. Santa Claus had been the code-name for Tom Holly. The Sugar Palace was their private slang for the Sukaria café in the Khan al-Khalili. A quick calculation revealed that Tom would be there waiting for Michael in two days' time, three at the most.

A'isha picked up the scrap of paper and unfolded it. When she had read it, she slipped it absent-mindedly into her pocket, then asked, "What's the Sugar Palace?"

"The Sukaria," he said. "We used to meet there: it was our local. Nobody annoyed us, we could sit over a single cup of coffee for a whole evening if we wanted to."

He closed his eyes. How the hell had Percy Haviland become so closely involved? And why was the old fraud so suddenly interested in what Michael had been working on in Alex? Something was amiss, he was sure of it.

But how on earth had Tom Holly obtained permission for a field mission to Egypt? Anyone knew it was the height of folly to send a Desk Head into his own territory, especially at a time like this. Had Tom done a bunk? Was that it? Had he acted on his own initiative, and now Vauxhall was trying to cover for him, make the best of a bad job? Was that what was going on? Or was all of this passing through the hands of the mole? With a chill, Michael asked himself for the first time whether the mole might not be Percy Haviland himself.

He opened his eyes and caught sight of A'isha. Silent tears were streaming down her face. She was shaking, but not from cold. Michael reached out and drew her to him.

"I thought you were dead," she whispered.

He said nothing. He felt so far away from her, he wondered if he could ever find his way back.

"I thought I would never see you again," she said.

He heard her, but he did nothing. He held her, but he might have been a stranger holding a stranger.

"Was it so long ago?" she asked. "It seems like years, but it can't have been."

"No," he said, forcing the words. "Not years."

There was a long, ragged silence. Michael shivered and held A'isha close, wishing the darkness and the silence would leave him forever.

52

The darkness lifted, but the silence remained intact. Michael woke out of a sleep that was turning fast to nightmare. He had seen the pyramid again, he had walked through endless corridors and watched the goat-headed god remount his throne. Waking on a gray morning after a dream so many shared, he felt diminished, a prey to fears he could not name.

A'isha was already awake. He found her by the foot of the stairs, changing Butrus's bandage. The Copt was feverish and in great pain. A'isha looked up as Michael came to her side.

"We have to get him out of here, Michael. The wound is inflamed. He needs proper dressings and antibiotics."

Michael looked around. In the daylight, the shabbiness and decay were more in evidence. Chunks of flaking plaster hung from the walls. There was broken glass on the stairs. At the top of the first flight, a huge rat sat facing them, red-eyed, staring, unafraid.

"You're right," he said. "But how do we do it? If what you say is true, they'll have this place surrounded. We won't be able to shoot our way out, not in daylight."

A'isha nodded. She finished tying the bandage and looked up. It was the first time he had seen her in proper light since their reunion. He thought she had aged.

"You look tired," he said.

"So do you."

He nodded.

"Paul is dead." He said it brutally, though he had not meant to. As if someone else had spoken.

A'isha caught her breath.

"You've told me nothing about yourself," she said. "About what's been happening to you during the past few weeks."

"I've been looking for you," he said in a flat voice. "Ever since I got your letter."

She looked at him. Was that true? Had he been looking for her all that time? There had been moments when she had doubted it, when she thought he had taken a boat and sailed back to England. She reached for his hand. It felt cold.

"Let's go outside," she said. "He may get a little sleep now."

They walked out into the silent morning, onto a long street of ragged and abandoned houses. A door banged somewhere, again and again, moved by a light breeze. On the other side of the street, a sheep's skull glimmered whitely in the pale sunlight. Everywhere, there was an odor of decay, a stench of corruption that made their stomachs crawl.

They walked slowly through the dead streets, past the shells of abandoned shops and uninhabited dwellings. And there was an emptiness in both of them, an emptiness that came, not from the streets or the buildings, but from themselves. For a long time they walked without speaking, without touching. Then, passing a banner proclaiming a new life for the nation, he took her hand. She felt so fragile, he could feel the brittle bones through her flesh.

Finally, they began to talk. She told him all that had

happened to her, of her escape with Butrus, of what had taken place the night before at Rif'at's.

"I'm sorry about your uncle," he said.

"He was a traitor. You paid him to betray his country. I don't feel sorry for him."

"Paid him? Did he tell you that?"

"No. But there must have been a price."

"A price, certainly. But never money. Nor influence. Nor promises. I gave Ahmad Shukri nothing. He acted out of a sense of duty."

"Duty?" She turned an angry face to him. "He betrayed his country. What duty leads a man to do that?"

Michael shook his head.

"He never betrayed Egypt. He wouldn't have dreamed of it. Ahmad loved his country. He agreed to help me because I was half Egyptian, because we shared the same hopes. Ahmad came to me because he was worried about contacts between the previous government and some of the less stable regimes in the region. His own organization had been heavily infiltrated by pro-Iraqi and other elements."

"He came to you?"

"Yes. He knew who I was, he sought me out. We were to help one another. Sometimes I passed information to him. Nothing else changed hands."

A'isha fell silent. They went on walking. As they turned a corner, they saw in front of them a horde of rats battening like flies on something long and ragged lying in the middle of the street. Hastily, they turned back and took another turning. It was only then that Michael noticed there were no cars or buses, no motor vehicles of any description anywhere.

"You haven't told me about Paul," she said. "You said he was dead. That's all."

Haltingly, he began to explain. The words poured out in a flood, almost incoherently, stabbing the silence, filling it with pain.

Suddenly, without anticipation, he found himself weeping. All his life, he had been cheated of tears: tears of shame, tears of regret, tears of anger. And now, in this wretched, ill-suited place, they came to him like a swarm of wasps. To his surprise, he found himself thinking of the girl he had seen through the window of the train, her pale face in the mist, the anguish in her eyes, the *muhtasib* with his pistol already bearing down on her. Ronnie's fate he could understand, his own if it came to it, Paul's even—but why that girl? Because of her, the other deaths made no sense, they were nothing, not even gestures against the basic pointlessness of things. Ronnie, Paul, people he had killed.

She held him until the weeping subsided. Her hands stroked him with the reflexive movements of affection and resignation. He was hers again, for a short time anyway. And she wanted him, wanted him so fiercely she had to bite her lip to stop herself crying out.

As his tears dried, he became aware of her again. He drew back his head and looked at her, as if for the first time. He thought she was beautiful and frightened and a little mad. When they first met, he had thought her aloof, almost icy. And then, in moments, she had melted. Her eyes were dark, he could see nothing in them. He felt her hand on his cheek. Without a word, he unbuttoned her coat and pulled it aside, reaching for her. His hand touched her breast and he saw her fill suddenly with the same need that had taken him. She let him pull the coat from her shoulders, reached close into him, kissed him, not caring that it was so silent or that the streets were long and empty and full of dust.

He laid her down, partly on the discarded coat, partly on the grime of the street. There was no elegance in the act or the intention. Through closed windows, the dead watched them, wordlessly. He lifted her skirt above her waist and undressed her and brought his fingers to her, lightly and perfectly, and she cried out as though in panic, and he quieted her with a kiss that grew to madness, while he tore her dress and brought his lips to her breasts, his wet mouth to her nipples. And as he kissed her he thought of Carol and her cheap passion, and Paul and his disapproval, and her breasts in his hands, Carol's breasts and A'isha's, and the first woman he had touched like this, and he parted her like silk, and she called his name. Unbuttoning, he lay on her. There was no silence now, their breathing and whispering had ripped it all to shreds, their cries were echoing through the city like gulls circling, he moved into her recklessly, into the depth of her, and they cried out together again, his hands were on her shoulders, steering her to the moment, she was seeking his rhythm, pulling him into her own, and his hands moved once across her breasts so that she reared up and raised her legs and laid them on his back, and all the time the silence lay on top of them like a blanket.

And it ended in the silence, as it had started, with her last cry tearing the sky from end to end. He lay across her with his eyes closed and his face in her tangled hair, then, as his weight grew insupportable, fell beside her. They did not know how long they lay like that, uncoupled, staring into each other's questioning eyes, or with their eyes closed, returning slowly to a world in which the deepest darknesses were man-made.

She watched them from a distance at first, then, as she saw that they were unaware of her, she drew closer. They were not the first pair she had seen copulating in the streets, though she still did not understand the purpose of it or the reasons for the change that came over them. Sometimes they would cry out like this, and sometimes they would remain silent from start to finish. Once she had seen thirty couples or more together, naked, laughing and crying, stumbling through dark doorways as they pawed each other. She had not liked that: their rough voices and wild looks had frightened her. But the quiet ones, the ones engrossed in themselves, both fascinated and repelled.

She wondered where these two had come from. She had not seen them before, they were not friends of her mother or father, not people from the neighborhood. Not that it mattered. Whoever they were, the sickness would take them and they would die like everybody else.

She sat down on a step and waited for them to finish. It would be nice to have someone to talk to after all this time.

53

Her name was Fadwa. She was nine years, three months, and five days old and she behaved as though she were three times that age. When they asked her, she said her mother's name was Samira and her father's Nabil and that she had three brothers—Samih, Rashid, and Khalil—and a sister, Fawziyya. And aunts, uncles, and cousins galore.

A'isha looked at the little girl pityingly. She showed no signs of illness, but she was thin, unkempt, and filthy. She must not have bathed or changed her clothing in well over a month.

"Where are your mummy and daddy?" she asked. She still found it disconcerting talking to a child who had just been watching her and Michael making love and who seemed to regard the whole proceeding with a total lack of interest, even boredom. A'isha guessed that this had not been the first time. She shuddered to think how quickly she and Michael had fallen under the spell of this dreadful place.

"I'll take you to them, if you like," Fadwa said.

A'isha bit her lip. Could there still be others alive in here?

Michael had been the more embarrassed to find Fadwa

watching. Her serious face and lack-luster eyes had seemed to him as though filled with reproach. He approached her softly and bent down. She was just a tiny waif, but he felt curiously vulnerable beside her. She looked up at him incuriously; he could not read the expression in her eyes. They were large and black, and they reminded him of the eyes of the girl on the train.

"Are they very far?" he asked.

She shook her head.

"It's just that we have a friend near here who is sick, and we don't want to lose him if we go too far away. We don't know this part of town."

Fadwa nodded sagely. She knew all about people being sick. And about people getting lost: she had lost her way many times at first, when they had all started dying and she was sent from place to place, carrying messages, scavenging for food, bringing news of who was alive and who was not.

"Where have you come from?" she asked.

"From outside," answered Michael. "From beyond the walls."

"Is it nice out there?"

"Yes," he lied. "Very nice. Haven't you been there?"

She shook her head.

"Not for a very long time," she said. "When I was small we went there in a car, a big car. I remember it was red and smelled of honey. It belonged to one of my daddy's friends." She paused. A troubled look crossed her face. "They took all the cars and buses away from here," she said.

"Why was that?"

"I don't know. Men came. Policemen. They had funny uniforms. They said we didn't need cars any more. They were right, because when people are sick they can't drive cars."

She stopped speaking abruptly, and for a moment looked like a little girl. A little girl who was very lost and very frightened. Then, drawing on resources that would have been beyond most adults, she lifted her head.

"We'll go to your friend first," she said. "Then I'll know where he is, so I can bring you back again."

A long rat ran past within inches of Fadwa's legs. She did not start or flinch.

A'isha glanced down and noticed that Fadwa was sporting a pair of man's boots several sizes too large for her.

"I stuff them with bits of rag," she explained. "They're not very comfortable."

And off she went, hobbling slightly, walking alongside them like a little woman, in the direction they indicated.

Butrus was still half awake. The fever had subsided somewhat, but the pain was no easier. They spent a little while with him, explaining their plan. They would find Fadwa's parents, perhaps other survivors, discuss the possibility of finding a way out. If they could locate a pharmacy, there might be stocks of painkillers that they could bring back. And they were sure Fadwa must have access to some sort of food.

They set off in a different direction this time, winding ever more deeply into the dark gullies of the ghetto, following Fadwa down narrow alleyways filled with the stench of rotting garbage. Rotting garbage and . . . whatever else was filling the air with a sweet odor of decay. They held handkerchiefs to their mouths. But Fadwa, inured, carried on as though the atmosphere was like that anywhere. In places, the stench became almost overpowering.

Once as they walked, Fadwa came to A'isha and, without looking up, slipped her hand into the older woman's. For all her self-possession, the little girl was living in a nightmare.

Suddenly she stopped.

"This is my house," she said.

The smell was all-pervasive here. A'isha and Michael exchanged glances. The house was a tall tenement with shuttered windows. Dark patches of urine stained the outside walls. A few blue and white tiles from the Khedival period remained on the plaster, cracked and dirty.

They ascended narrow stairs in deep gloom. Only a little light succeeded in penetrating the grime-coated windows of the stairwell. The carcass of a dead dog lay across one landing, its coat torn and shredded where rats had feasted on it. Fadwa did not give it a second glance. She did not tell them that it had once been her pet dog, that it had had a name.

The door to an apartment on the right lay partly open. Fadwa stepped inside. Hesitantly, they followed her. The stench was even stronger here.

Fadwa apologized for the gloom.

"There's no electricity here," she said. "We used to have it, but they took it away the same time they came for the cars."

She found a candle stub and a box of matches. With the little light, she led them into the living room. The room was musty and thick with dust. Empty tin cans and unwashed plates lay in profusion on the grimy floor. A heap of old Coca-Cola bottles glistened dully on a low table. In one corner, a smashed television set glowered at them, its aerial bent and twisted. On top of it, a doll with a broken arm and a dirty red frock sat like the idol in a temple dedicated to squalor. There were spiders everywhere. The room was thick with their dense webs.

"Are you hungry?" Fadwa asked.

Michael started to say they were not—the very thought of food was nauseating—but A'isha interrupted him.

"I'll go to the kitchen with Fadwa," she said. "We'll make something nice to eat." She glanced meaningfully at Michael. "You take a look around."

Fadwa found another stub of candle and lit it for Michael. With A'isha holding her hand, the little girl led the way out of the room into another. Michael hung back for a few moments, then stepped into the corridor.

The kitchen was in an even worse state than the living

room. Pots and pans, spilt food, broken crockery littered the floor. The walls were thick with grease. There were signs of a fire that had started and been quenched.

A'isha turned to look at Fadwa. The child's lower lip was trembling. She was at last on the verge of tears, tears she had been holding back for longer than she could remember.

"I . . . I tried to keep it nice," she quavered. "I did at first, when mummy . . . fell sick. I cleaned, and . . . Fawziyya and Samih helped me. Then . . . Then they got sick as well. They were all in bed, I had . . . nobody to help me. Nobody came . . . I was . . . all alone."

She broke down finally, absolutely, with such force that even A'isha, who had been waiting for it, was taken aback. Her sobs became tears, the tears howls of anguish so deep there were no words for it. A'isha put her arms round her, holding her fast, feeling the tears crowd her own eyes. And in a moment she too was a little girl, weeping for everything she had lost, everything she had hunted for and never found.

There was a sound behind them. A'isha looked up. Michael was standing in the doorway. She would never forget the look on his face, the terrible, haunted look that told her everything. He looked at her, he looked at Fadwa, then turned aside and was violently sick.

54

The tears made their task easier. They left Fadwa so wrung out that she was in no fit state to resist when they took her out. Lack of sleep and unremitting fear had weakened her tremendously. It was almost a miracle that she had not succumbed to some chance infection, whether the plague or something carried in the food and water on which she had been surviving.

A'isha dusted the broken doll and gave it to her. She was too big for dolls, or so she might have said, but she clung to it fiercely, as though to a talisman.

Her mother had died first, then her two oldest brothers, Rashid and Khalil, followed by her father, sister, and younger brother, in that order. She told it all between deep, choking sobs, unable any longer to deny the reality of what had happened.

"Do you still have the vaccine, Michael? I think we should give her a shot." They had taken theirs the night before.

He shook his head.

"She must have an unusually strong immune system," he said. "There's a risk the vaccine could compromise it, even trigger off the very infection it's been fighting against all along. We've got the antibiotics. If she shows any signs of developing something, she'll be better off with a shot of those."

A'isha looked unconvinced. She had been brought up in the belief that vaccines were a sort of Holy Grail, an answer to all ills. But she squeezed Fadwa's hand and smiled down at her.

"We have medicine with us," she said. "You don't have to worry if you get sick now."

Fadwa did not answer. She led them out of the maze of back streets into a short bazaar. The shops had been looted at some point, probably very early on; but whether by the inhabitants or the *muhtasibin* was not clear. They found a small pharmacy at the far end. It was worse than the others. They found a small packet of morphine at the bottom of a pile of empty cardboard boxes. There was little else of any use.

Fadwa led them to a grocer's shop a few doors away. The grocer had died guarding his shop. He was still there, sprawled on the floor behind the high wooden counter, bones and dried flesh held together by strips of rag. Fadwa showed them a huge old refrigerator containing bottles of Coca-Cola. They took some and found a cheap plastic shopping-bag in which to carry them. Michael added some cans of beans and lentils from a high shelf Fadwa had been unable to reach.

On the way back, they passed through a little square flanked by tall houses. A place full of shadows, and the sky above it so torn and mottled it might have belonged to another planet. From the upper stories of the dwellings around it, long white banners stretched to the ground. On them in large letters ran verses from the Qur'an, talismanic verses repeated like mantras.

They had brought their dead here at first in an attempt to burn them. A huge pyre rose up in the center of the square, a black tangle of charred wood and limbs. A faint smell of kerosene still hung limply on the air, overlaid with other, darker scents.

Skirting the edge of the square, they passed hurriedly into another maze of abandoned alleyways. Fadwa traced her way through them flawlessly. Only once did she show any sign of fear or apprehension. They had just turned a corner which led past a *hammam,* an old bath-house dating from the mid-nineteenth century. Next door to it was a wide grating that covered the entrance to the sewer system. Fadwa caught sight of the opening and backed away, then hurried past as though expecting it to open and swallow her up. Moments later, they were back in a jumble of narrow lanes that eventually brought them back to the street in which they had spent the night.

Butrus was asleep when they reached him. They sat by him, watching carefully, afraid to wake him. He was feverish, restless, his dreams broken by tiny whimpers. At last, turning awkwardly in the perturbation of sleep, he jarred his shoulder and snapped himself awake.

They gave him the morphine, a large dose, administered with one of the hypodermics Michael had brought. It soon began to take effect.

Michael opened the cans with his penknife and they feasted on pulses, using their fingers to spoon them into their mouths. A'isha tried hard not to think of the grocer whose body had lain only feet away from the stack of cans. Michael ate only sparingly: his stomach had not yet recovered from the effects of what he had seen in Fadwa's house.

While they ate, Michael told A'isha about al-Qurtubi, repeating what Gregory had told him. The basic facts of his conversion, his later studies, the establishment of the Ahl al-Samt. And the things Verhaeren had told him that night, or that he had gleaned from Paul's files.

"I think Verhaeren found it hard to make his mind up whether al-Qurtubi is sane or not. Apparently he was satisfied at first to be leader of the Ahl al-Samt. But after a while even that seems to have become too restrictive, too . . .

parochial. He began to get other ideas. Or else someone saw potential in him and egged him on. That part isn't clear.

"In 1989, al-Qurtubi began to study genealogy. His own genealogy, to be precise. He comes from an aristocratic family in Cordova. That's how he came to choose his Arab name, al-Qurtubi: the Cordovan. But his proper name is Leopoldo Alarcón y Mendoza. The family originally came from Granada. They rose to eminence in the early seventeenth century. Before that they had been Moriscos, secret Muslims who had outwardly converted to Christianity after the fall of Granada in 1492. One of his ancestors was a leader of the Morisco revolt of 1569. All that was conveniently forgotten, of course, and by this century the Alarcón y Mendozas were respectable sons of the Church. They've produced bishops and cardinals before now."

He paused. Fadwa ate slowly beside him, oblivious of all he was saying. In her world, none of this had any meaning.

"In 1989, a document came into al-Qurtubi's possession. It was a parchment that had been handed down from the days when his family still held their allegiance to the old faith, the faith which he, whether by accident or a stroke of destiny, had chosen for his own. The document is known as an *aljamiado,* a manuscript written in Spanish but using Arabic characters. Since his family had long since forgotten how to read the Arabic alphabet, they had been unable to decipher the *aljamiado,* and it had been passed down as nothing more than a curiosity. To al-Qurtubi, it presented no difficulties.

"Now, most *aljamiados* are simply manuals of Islamic law, or lives of the Prophet, or Qur'an commentaries—the sort of thing that might be useful to a beleaguered minority living under the Inquisition and in need of instruction. But al-Qurtubi's was nothing like that. It was a detailed account of his family.

"I won't bore you with the details. What counts is that al-Qurtubi discovered he was the last living descendant of the Umayyad caliphs of Spain. By his reasoning, that linked him by a direct line of descent to the first caliphs, the successors of the Prophet himself.''

A'isha shivered and laid her hand absentmindedly on Fadwa's head, stroking her knotted, unwashed hair, wondering what meaning any of this had for her or for the child.

"According to Paul, al-Qurtubi had already been obsessed by the problem of a lack of leadership within Islam. He wrote a pamphlet in 1985 entitled *Khilaf al-khilafa*, "The Dispute about the Caliphate." That was one of the first things that got my brother interested in him. He argued that the abolition of the Caliphate in 1924 by Atatürk was the greatest blow suffered by Islam in its entire history. By one man's action, Muslims all round the world had been left without a leader. Their present humiliation goes back to that betrayal.''

"Where's all this leading, Michael? We're surrounded by madmen. What's so special about al-Qurtubi?"

"Can't you guess? He's proclaimed himself the new Caliph. The rightful ruler of the Islamic world. If he can summon up enough support, he'll become the focus for a fundamentalist alliance from Iraq through to Morocco.''

"Just because he calls himself a Caliph?"

Michael shook his head.

"No, not just that. He has to have something to offer them, something no-one else can provide. My brother discovered what that is." He paused. So faint it might have been a dream, the sound of the *adhan* calling to the noon prayer wafted across the empty spaces to them out of the remote reaches of the city.

"He wants to turn back history," Michael said. "You know that there is a ruling in Islamic law which says that, once land has come under the control of Islam, it must forever remain Islamic territory. That's why the loss of Palestine was such a blow. Al-Qurtubi wants revenge for the establishment of the state of Israel. Compensation. A fair exchange. The Western powers have driven a wedge into the Arab world, now the Muslims will reclaim land that once belonged to them, land that was taken away by force. A bridgehead in Europe.

"He is no fool. He knows he cannot ask for all of what was once Muslim Spain. That would be unthinkable. But he intends to ask for the modern region of Andalusia, the rump of the last Muslim state. That means the provinces of Almería, Cádiz, Córdoba, Granada, Huelva, Jaén, Málaga, and Sevilla. Thirty-three thousand, six hundred and seventy-five square miles. That is almost exactly the sum total of the area that is either currently occupied by the state of Israel or which has at one time been occupied by it, including the Sinai peninsula.

"He has not yet put forward any demands. Before he does so, he will wage a terrorist campaign throughout Europe. He has called it *Fath al-Andalus*. The Conquest of Andalusia. Verhaeren is convinced that the Conquest of Andalusia will be the bloodiest terror campaign ever witnessed. Andalusia will soon seem like a cheap price to pay."

She was silent for a long time. Beside her, Fadwa sat in silence, puzzled by this adult game. She was waiting for them to die. Everyone died in the end. She had no hopes of anything or anyone.

"Who will live there?" A'isha asked at last.

"Refugees. You do not understand this man's mind. Paul's files revealed it to me in detail. It is a horror. There are eight or nine million Muslims living in Europe: North Africans in France, Pakistanis in Britain, Turks in Germany, other groups scattered all over. They are already a focus for racist violence. Many people are demanding their expulsion. By the time al-Qurtubi's bombing and shooting spree comes to an end, they will be welcome nowhere. He expects that. Expects it and wants it. They will be his first settlers. And then there are the Palestinians, still without a state: he will invite them into his Caliphate. Muslims from India, who feel threatened by the Hindu majority. Whole groups from the old Russian satellite states. He will fill his new Andalus."

"And the present inhabitants?"

"What happened to the Palestinians when the Zionists came? That is what he will say. Spain is a big place, he will say; Europe is rich, the Catholic Church is wealthy, Muslims have suffered long enough at the hands of their oppressors. He will offer the Christians the right to live as *ahl al-dhimma,* protected peoples, People of the Book. They will have better rights under Islam than Muslims had under the Inquisition."

"No-one will accept it."

"He is not asking for acceptance. He wants his horror to become the politics of the world. He wants God's Kingdom, and he is not particular what price he or anyone else may have to pay for it."

55

"How did your friend get hurt?"

Fadwa was kneeling beside Butrus, helping him sit up straight.

"He was shot." A'isha got up and went over to help her.

"Who shot him?"

"The police."

Fadwa looked anxiously at A'isha. "Will they come here?" she asked.

"The police? No, I don't think so. They're finished with this place."

Fadwa nodded gravely. By the look on her face, A'isha thought she was more frightened of the *muhtasibin* than of the plague.

"We have to get our friend away from here," she said. "He has a bullet in his shoulder. It has to be taken out."

"Will he die if it isn't?"

A'isha nodded.

"But he will get sick and die anyway."

"No, I told you we have medicine. Listen, Fadwa, you have to help us. We have to find a way out of Bulaq. People

. 367 .

must have tried escaping before this. Didn't anyone ever tell you of a way out?"

Fadwa shook her head.

"There's no way out," she said. "Not since they built the wall."

But something was wrong. The child looked frightened, as though the very mention of escape had awakened in her some barely repressed terror.

"What's wrong, Fadwa? Why does my talking about escape frighten you?"

"I told you, you can't escape. No-one can." But the child's voice was shrill, and she would not look at A'isha.

Something in her appearance reminded A'isha of the moment when, as they walked back from Fadwa's house, she had been frightened by something as they passed the bath-house. The bath-house and the sewer entrance.

Of course! That was it. A'isha wondered why she had been so obtuse. The way out lay through the sewer system. She bent down and reached for Fadwa's hand.

"You don't have to be frightened, Fadwa. Michael and I are here now; we'll look after you. There's nothing to be afraid of. But I need to know: did someone try to escape through the sewers? Did something bad happen to them? Is that what you're afraid to say?"

Fadwa tried to pull her hand away, but A'isha kept a firm hold. The little girl bent her head, shaking it wildly from side to side.

Michael got up and went outside. He looked up and down the street. He stared at the blank windows. He thought of Tom Holly waiting in a cold café, watching the door for a face that would never appear.

"They tried to get away through the sewer," Fadwa whispered. A'isha had to bend low to hear. It was as though the child were talking to herself, explaining her fears to her own heart. "People said they shouldn't go, that there were things down there. Things that creep. They told them they would be attacked, but they didn't listen. They did go. And they were eaten alive.''

A'isha did not smile. There could be a nugget of truth in the child's story.

"By rats? Is that what you mean?"

Fadwa shook her head fiercely.

"No, not rats. There are rats in the sewers, but they can't eat you unless you're already dead. I mean other things. I don't know their name. Giant things that creep along.''

"But surely a big girl like you doesn't believe in monsters.''

"They're not monsters. They're real.''

"Have you seen them?"

Fadwa shivered and shook her head.

"Who told you about them?"

"Daddy. He said I wasn't to play near there.''

"And you say the things ate the people who went down there.''

Fadwa nodded.

"How do you know?"

"Because they didn't come back again.''

"Perhaps that was because they got away.''

Fadwa looked startled, as though such a possibility had never occurred to her. She was not a child, not in her heart. To her, all things ended in death. Escape, true escape, the escape of the wounded heart, figured nowhere in her universe. Not in her dreams, and not in her waking.

"Sweetheart," A'isha said. "I don't think there are monsters in the sewers. There will be rats, but we can deal with them. If we could find our way through, we could get out of here. Would you come with us?"

Fadwa closed her eyes tightly and shook her head.

"We wouldn't leave without you, Fadwa. If you won't come with us we can't go. We'll have to stay here. Butrus will die. When our medicine runs out, Michael and I will die.''

Fadwa pressed her hands hard over her ears, still shak-

ing her head. A'isha had not meant to be cruel. She reached
out for the little girl, placing her hands over hers, gently
prising them from her face.

"No!" Fadwa screamed. "No, I won't go!"

She jumped to her feet and, before A'isha could stop
her, ran off into the street. A'isha leapt up, stumbled, and
set off after her. But, as she reached the doorway, she
halted. It would do more harm than good to chase the little
girl.

Michael was waiting further down the street. "Did she
tell you anything?" he asked.

"Yes. The sewers. That's the way they went. Fadwa
thinks they were eaten by things that live down there."

"Are we going after her?"

"No. We wouldn't find her. She'll be back again, I'm
sure of it."

"She's looked after herself pretty well until now."

"She had no choice then. But she's frightened and
lonely, Michael. She's just a little girl. Believe me, she'll be
back."

They walked back slowly. Neither spoke of the love-
making that had brought them together again. Love was so
fragile, it could not depend on lust renewed in a cold season
on a cold street. But they held hands and pretended love was
simple.

"Do you think you could find your way back to the
sewer entrance?" A'isha asked.

Michael nodded.

"I think so. I can try."

"Do what you can. Look for other entrances. But don't
stray too far. I'll stay with Butrus. Someone has to be here in
case Fadwa returns. See whether there's a way in. And if
you find a shop with torches and a compass, bring them
back. Some rope as well."

"Is that all?" He smiled. It was the first time she had
seen him smile since his return.

"No," she said. "I'd like some perfume and a new

dress." She tried smiling too, but her mouth would not obey her.

"I'll do what I can," he said. He bent down and kissed her. When they had been apart, there had been so many things he wanted to say to her. But now they were together again, his lips felt dry and his tongue paralyzed.

First he had to be sure there was no other way. By a combination of instinct and luck he found a path to the perimeter, where a high wall blocked off further progress. He could hear the sound of voices and engines beyond the wall, but it was too high to see over. Instead, he made his way inside the building on his right, a tall house backing onto the street.

A door on the third floor landing lay partly open. The same sweet sickly smell filled the air. He switched on his torch and slipped inside. There was no choice: he had to risk the light at first in order to find his way. And the thought of stumbling through that darkness blind filled him with horror. He could not have done it, not even for his life.

On his left the door to a bedroom stood open. The darkness inside was riddled with points and bars of light. Michael stepped inside.

Motes of dust hung in the air like tiny stars. Wands of pale sunlight lay gently on the floor, and the rear wall was dappled with little lozenges. Michael's eye was drawn against his will towards the bed, a tall bed with richly colored coverings, suspended in a cradle of sunlight. It was seething with maggots, pale, blind, in constant movement. Michael shuddered and looked away.

The window had been blocked by a heavy wooden casing bolted to the wall. He switched off his torch. Opening the window frame, he squinted through a large gap in the wood.

The street below was filled with soldiers. Half-tracks and Jeeps growled past in a long file. Others were parked at intervals along the roadside. He looked in the other direction and saw the same picture repeated. A'isha had been right. The way out above ground was closed. And he did not think it would be long before they tired of waiting and decided to move in.

56

Nuri Waffaq's hand shook as he straightened his tie. His office on the tenth floor of the tower block that was Cairo's Radio and Television Building, was in semi-darkness. His windows overlooked the river, the southern part of Jazira island, and the slums of al-Ajuza. With good binoculars, he might have been able to see the pyramids, though he had never thought to try. Now, he knew, it was too late. But that, like the plague and the camps and the daily round of executions, was something he could never mention on the air.

For weeks now, he had been living on a razor's edge. As Egypt's leading television presenter, he had been of immense value to the new regime, smoothing the way for its novice presenters and nervous spokesmen. His was a well-known face, a reassurance to people in the midst of change, and they had exploited him mercilessly. What was it the Americans called someone like him? An anchorman. Yes, that was exactly what he was: an anchor for a very restless ship of state.

But there had been a price to pay. The razor's edge. The not knowing from day to day which way official policy would shift, what facts would be acceptable, what changes had overtaken even recent history. He had seen half his colleagues carted off before tribunals, heard rumors that most of them had been shot. The female presenters had been laid off en masse on the first day: no women's faces were to be seen on the nation's TV screens, no female voices were to be heard on its radio waves. Incitements to debauchery and crime, that was what the new Broadcasting Minister had called them.

They'd known about him, of course: about his women, his drink, his cocaine. That was why he had agreed to work for them. He gave them an anchor in their storm, they left him alone. But each day it got harder to stomach, each day the lies and subterfuges stuck more grossly in his throat. He knew no-one out there believed a fraction of what was broadcast. So, where he could, he gave them hints of what to read between the lines. He made small alterations, alterations he hoped they would either not notice or would choose to ignore.

For "Rumors of an outbreak of infectious illness in Egypt are wholly without foundation," he had substituted "Reports of plague throughout the country are thought to be exaggerated." He didn't know whether anybody noticed, never learned whether anybody cared. And he knew that, at any moment, he would fall foul of the censors and vigilantes who patrolled the corridors outside his office, sniffing out heresy in every broadcast.

He was nervous about tonight. Things had moved rapidly in the new Republic. There had already been numerous moves between the top posts, sackings, and, it was rumored, more than one midnight execution. A few days ago, power had passed decisively to a shadowy group within the ruling junta. Tonight, the identity of the new president would be announced.

There was a knock on his door. A tall man entered, dressed all in black. One of the "bodyguards" assigned to him shortly after the takeover. His minder, a man called Wafa', nodded politely. He was always a little in awe of Nuri.

"They're ready in the studio now, Mr. Waffaq. The President's waiting in the reception room. He says he wants this to go out on time. No delays."

"I understand. I'll be there now."

Was there some significance in the timing? Nuri wondered. Were they afraid of another coup if they waited five minutes too long? How many more presidents would he have the honor to present to a hungry nation? Assuming he lasted the night himself.

The studio was hushed. All the checks had been run, all the cameras were in their places. The card that announced an important declaration was being televised. Waffaq walked directly to his desk, nodding at his producer, a new man they had brought in from Saudi Arabia.

A technician clipped on his shirt mike, they ran a quick check on the voice level, and a production assistant holding a clipboard in one hand started a silent countdown with the fingers of the other.

There was a burst of martial music. The emblem of the new republic, the name of God in Kufic letters inside a green crescent, appeared on the screen. As the emblem faded, the titles went up. And he was on camera.

"Bismi 'llah al-Rahman al-Rahim," he intoned, as instructed by his new masters. "This is a special broadcast on behalf of the Islamic government of Egypt. Good evening." He glanced up at his teleprompter and went on. "One hour ago, a lengthy session of the revolutionary command council ended in the Presidential Palace. For several days now, Mr. Ali Nadim, the president, has been confined to bed on the orders of his physician. His condition is stated to be serious, and it is expected that he will be forced to remain in bed for several weeks more. Earlier this afternoon, he declared himself reluctantly unable to continue to shoulder the burdens of the presidential office, and expressed his wish to step down in order to permit a more suitable candidate to take his place. At this evening's session of the command

council, a new president was chosen from among those deemed most worthy of that exalted position."

Waffaq paused. His mouth felt dry. To his left, off camera, there was a flicker of movement as a door opened. He glanced around once, then back at the camera.

"Noble people of Egypt," he read on, "people of true belief, people of Islam everywhere—your new president has just arrived in the studio. In a few moments, he will address you for the first time. May God be praised. I wish to present to you his excellency Abu 'Abd Allah Muhammad al-Qurtubi, the President of the Islamic Republic of Egypt."

The camera held Waffaq's face for a few moments longer. He went on smiling, knowing his life depended on it. The light went on on camera 2.

Al-Qurtubi looked straight into the lens. He used no teleprompter, he had no prepared speech in front of him.

"Bismi 'Ilah," he began.

PART VIII

"To him was given the key of the bottomless pit"

REVELATION 9:1

57

It was dark by the time Michael returned. He had found more food—tins of cooked macaroni and spinach, several bars of chocolate, boxes of roasted nuts. One of his pockets had been stuffed with packets of Camels for A'isha, another with matches. At the back of a little religious bookshop near the mosque of Mustafa Mirza, among a heap of boxed *mushafs* and white *'arraqiyyas* he had discovered boxes containing the little compasses that are used to determine the direction of Mecca. There had been torches and batteries in a hardware shop on Bulaq al-Jadid. And in a garage bright blue overalls. For Fadwa he found a small pair of boy's jeans and a yellow anorak.

To his delight, he had found a small shop selling wares for small boats on the Shari' al-Khadra, in Western Bulaq, less than a block from the river. From it, he had taken a length of rope, a pole with a hooked end, and—wonder of wonders—a small rubber dinghy barely capable of holding three adults and a child. If there was an emergency, it might just save their lives. He prayed they would not be forced to use it.

With it, there had been a single inflatable lifejacket. He

had scoured the shop for others, but could find none any-where. This was an old one, much-patched and well past its best. But he inflated it and it stayed full, so he placed it in his bag along with the other things.

Fadwa had returned as A'isha had predicted, just before it started to grow dark. She had been alone somewhere crying. Her eyes were still red, but she was calm again. When A'isha asked whether she had been home, she shook her head. She was afraid to go there now, she said. With A'isha and Michael's arrival, all pretense had gone. She knew what she would find in the old apartment.

Michael had found some toys in a little bazaar off 'Abd al-Jawad Square, cheap Chinese imports in bright plastic. He brought them out, thinking they would cheer Fadwa up: a dog with a nodding head and a wagging tail, a clown with a red nose that spun around. She fingered them disconso-lately for a while before returning to her battered doll.

While Fadwa played, A'isha drew Michael aside.

"Did you find an entrance to the sewers?"

"There are several ways in," he said, "but some of them are blocked and only the first one seems to have been opened. It still seems the best bet. I think it must have been chosen by someone who worked in the system. The lock on the grille had been opened with a key. I went in part of the way. There's no sign of flooding. We shouldn't have to go far: all we need to do is get beyond the Bulaq perimeter."

"What if there's flooding further in? There's been a lot of rain."

"We'll just have to be careful. If the water level is too high, we can't afford to wait until it subsides. We'll have to try going over a wall later tonight. The advantage of the sewers is in giving us the chance of getting out without rais-ing the alarm."

"Butrus can't swim, Michael. Not with that arm."

"He can wear the lifejacket. As long as his head stays above water, he should be all right. What about Fadwa?"

"I don't know. I haven't asked her. Someone may have taught her to swim in the river."

"If necessary, we can use the dinghy. But if it capsizes, we could all drown."

"When do we go?"

"As soon as possible. There's no point in wasting time. We'll eat now, then wait until Butrus's last dose of morphine wears off. He'll have to put up with the pain until we're safely out."

An hour later they set off. Fadwa took a great deal of coaxing before she would go with them. They walked silently through the deserted streets, a subdued and thoughtful band held together by just one thing: the hope of escape. From time to time they risked using a torch to check their position. Everywhere they passed, they saw the gray shapes of rats in the darkness, watching patiently. Glittering eyes, sleek bodies, razor-sharp teeth.

They carried almost no equipment. Michael wore the rope over his shoulder in a long coil. A'isha carried the dinghy, deflated in a small canvas satchel. They left the submachine gun behind. Above them, the sky was dark and lightless, threatening rain. Small, icy gusts of wind blew against their faces. Acres of loneliness surrounded them.

They came at last to the grille. It hung open as Michael had left it, revealing a gaping aperture that led into deeper darkness. Fadwa hung back, her former fears resurfacing now she was face to face with the focus of her terror.

Michael took out his pistol and handed it to her.

"This is a real gun, Fadwa," he said. "It fires real bullets. I promise you it will kill anything we find in there. You don't have to be frightened."

This had seemed to him better psychology than wasting hours in an attempt to disabuse the child of her belief in underground creatures.

She examined the gun solemnly.

"What will we find when we get outside?" she asked. "Is everybody dead there too?"

He hesitated. How much of the truth was it wise to tell her? He still had no idea what they were going to do with her once they got her out.

"Some of them, Fadwa. But not all. We're not going to stay in the city. You'll be quite safe."

"Will anyone be waiting for me?"

"No, sweetheart."

"Can I have a cat?"

"You can have lots of cats. And a dog too, if you want one."

A look of dismay clouded her face. She shook her head.

"No," she whispered, "I don't want a dog."

Too late, Michael remembered the tattered remains he had seen outside the child's apartment.

She made to hand the gun back to him, but he shook his head and pressed it into her hand.

"Hold on to it for me," he said. He thought the possession of a weapon would further strengthen her faltering determination.

Michael went first, holding Fadwa's hand tightly. A'isha followed, helping Butrus, who was conscious but in great pain.

A short stretch of tunnel walled with cracked and broken tiles led to a round hole in the ground, from which a heavy manhole cover had been removed. This was the opening to a vertical brick-lined shaft that descended out of reach of the torch's beam. A rusted iron ladder ran down one side, clamped flush to the bricks by heavy staples.

"Let's do this in the right order," said Michael. "I'll go first. A'isha, you come after me. I want Fadwa to follow you so she can keep an eye on Butrus."

Giving Fadwa responsibility for Butrus would help keep her mind off her inner fears. He was haunted by the thought that the child might freeze half-way through the tunnels.

They could not abandon her, but it would be difficult, perhaps impossible, to carry her all the way through by force.

"Butrus," Michael continued. "You'll have to climb down with just one hand. Fadwa will hold you steady each time you move down a rung. Just take it slowly. We've got plenty of time."

"I'm . . . afraid of heights," said Butrus.

Michael shone his torch on him. The man was white-lipped and trembling. Blood had already leaked through the shoulder of his overalls. He looked done in. Only sheer willpower had taken him this far, and that alone would get him to the other end. If there was another end.

"I don't think it's very far to the bottom," lied Michael. He had already been down there, he knew the ladder descended about a hundred feet. "Just concentrate on one rung at a time. That's all you'll be able to see anyway."

Butrus nodded and tried to smile. He could scarcely remember where he was. The bullet in his shoulder felt like a ball of fire. And why? Because he had been stupid enough to love a woman who cared more for someone else. But perhaps he could fix that. Perhaps he could turn everything to his advantage after all. If only his shoulder would give him a moment's rest.

Michael tossed the dinghy, mooring pole, and rope to the floor of the shaft. Disencumbered, he eased himself into the narrow opening and started the descent. This section of the system was old and in a poor state of repair. The brickwork of the shaft was of low quality, and there were frequent gaps where entire bricks had fallen out or where the mortar had crumbled away. Many of the staples that held the ladder to the wall had either been dislodged or were hanging halfway out. If this had been used as an escape route from Bulaq, it was likely that the ladder had been put under an unusually heavy strain. Michael warned his companions to keep well apart, all except Fadwa and Butrus, in order to place as little extra strain on the structure as possible.

Every sound, however tiny, was magnified and tossed

back and forth through the shaft: the scraping of their feet on the rungs, the grating of the staples holding them to the wall, even their breathing. Once, Butrus let out a cry of pain that echoed horribly in the confined space. They continued their slow descent. Above them, the high-pitched squeals of rats served as a reminder of what lay above.

Without warning, a section of ladder snapped just above Michael's head. The nearest staples were torn out of the masonry, ripping out the ones next in line as well. The ladder buckled and bent at a second weak spot about six feet underneath Michael, swinging back, throwing him hard against the shaft wall, almost breaking his hold with the force of the impact.

He cried out in pain, then again as his feet slipped from the ladder, leaving him hanging by his hands.

"Michael! Michael, are you all right?"

He could barely answer, so great was the strain on his arms and chest.

A moment later, the shaft filled with light as A'isha switched on her torch and swung the beam down towards Michael. It revealed him hanging by his arms from a narrow rung near the top of the broken section of ladder. The top end of the ladder had swung all the way back and lay wedged tightly against the wall behind him. It still held at the bottom, where his weight had pulled it back, but it was obvious that even a little extra strain might snap it and send him hurtling to his death.

"Get on top of the ladder, Michael! Twist round. If you can pull yourself up, I'll get hold of you."

With infinite care, he inched himself round slowly until he was sideways on to the ladder, though still gripping it at the center, by two separate rungs. The strength in his arms was ebbing rapidly, but he could afford no sudden, sharp movements. He took a deep breath and began to pull himself up, as though on a bar at the gym. Now he could risk slipping an arm over the top. A little further. The ladder groaned and slipped against the wall, almost toppling him.

He waited until it was steady, then brought his left arm around. With the last of his strength, he hauled himself as far as his chest, then edged his body over the ladder.

He was on top of it now, lying at an angle, facing upwards. He looked up and saw the light of A'isha's torch above him.

"When you're ready, Michael, give me your hand."

He shook his head.

"If I come up, none of us will ever make it. This is the only way down."

"There are other entrances. You said so."

"Somebody selected this one as an escape route, somebody who knew the system. It must be the safest way out. Maybe the only one with tunnels large enough to walk through. We can't risk losing it."

"Michael, don't be crazy. There's no way past. That section of ladder could give way any moment."

"I'm going down for the rope. Stay here. I'll be back."

Gingerly, he edged himself to the unbroken end of the ladder, then lowered himself from it onto the section below, praying it would hold. It did. Just. As he started to climb down, he could feel the ladder shake beneath him.

"Just hold on a little longer," he murmured, unsure whether he was addressing the ladder or himself.

There was still some distance to go. As he descended, it grew colder. A foul odor crept up from below, a mixture of sewage and river sludge, and something else that was indefinable yet disquieting. A thin, malodorous slime clung to the rungs of the ladder. Twice, Michael's feet slipped on it, leaving him swinging momentarily in the void.

At last, he touched the ground. For what seemed a very long time, he leaned against the ladder, resting. The air was thick and noisome this far down, making it impossible to take deep breaths. Gradually, his heart slowed and he felt his strength return. He switched on the torch and shone it on the floor.

The objects he had tossed down the shaft were lying

where they had fallen. The rope lay at his feet, still coiled, with the boat-hook beside it. But the dinghy had rolled a little away. As Michael turned the light on it, he saw that it had come to rest beside something. He stepped forward to see more clearly.

It was a human being, or what was left of one. Most of the flesh had been torn away in lumps. The skeleton had been dismembered and scattered in all directions. The head was missing.

It looked as though something had eaten him alive.

58

There was an arch and a short tunnel that led down to a low transverse culvert. Michael brushed the bits and pieces of the skeleton into it, using the mooring hook for a broom of sorts. He could not bring himself to touch them with his hands. The water level in the culvert was high, and the bones sank mercifully out of sight beneath its surface. He had scarcely had the stomach for it, but he knew that Fadwa might not go any further if she saw what looked like proof of her worst fears. He shivered as he returned to the ladder. Surely rats could not have done that to a human body. Even as he thought it, a large brown shape scuttled past on its way to the culvert.

For the moment, he put all thought of what he had seen out of his mind. He heard A'isha's voice calling to him from above.

"Michael? What's taking you so long? Have you found the rope?"

He called back, reassuring her that he was on his way.

Rather than tackle the ascent with the rope coiled round him, he tied one end about his waist and let the remainder snake out behind him as he climbed. The ladder creaked and groaned in places, but it held his weight. During the last twenty feet or so, A'isha lit his way with her torch.

"What's it like down there?" she asked.

"It seems all right," he said. "There's an arch through to a larger cross tunnel with a culvert. It's not very deep: we can wade through it."

"If we can get down."

"It's all right. The ladder's not too bad on this bottom stretch. I'm going to throw one end of the rope up to you. Tie it to the strongest rung you can find. I'll fasten the other end to a point just above where the broken section still joins the rest. Once that's fast, I'll push the broken end back up to you. Keep enough extra rope free so you can tie it fast."

It took several throws before A'isha caught the coil. Michael had to throw upwards awkwardly with one hand, scarcely daring to swing his body with the arc of the toss, for fear he might further dislodge the ladder from the wall.

When he came to force the broken section back up to the wall, it proved too much for the exhausted metal. But if the rope held, the ladder would still serve to get them down. Michael moved several feet lower and lit his friends' slow descent. The ladder shook precariously, but held. When they were safely on the lower section, Michael passed up a knife to Fadwa and told her to cut the rope as high up as she was able. Michael did not let it fall this time, in case they might need it again.

Butrus came close to falling more than once. But for Fadwa, he would have plummeted to his death. She talked him down like an adult, steadying him, making sure his feet were hard against the rungs before instructing him to let his single handhold go. It took them half an hour to complete the descent.

By then Michael and A'isha had been able to explore the next section. Choosing their direction would not be easy. They could not travel west: the river lay that way, and they could not be certain that the sewers would come out above water. A straight line east, north, or south would take them out of Bulaq, but they did not know whether the main tunnels went continuously in one direction. There were bound to be twists and turns, side tunnels and branch tunnels and dead ends. Without care, they could become hopelessly lost. They had enough batteries to last a long time, but they carried very little food and drink. And if their batteries did eventually run out, they would be plunged into absolute blackness, with no hope of ever finding an exit.

On the assumption that the gradient in this section of the drainage system ran down towards the river, Michael had established that following the culvert upwards should take them to a major tunnel leading due east. With any luck, that would take them through to al-Azbakiyya or Bab al-Sha'riyya.

They allowed themselves fifteen minutes' rest. Butrus was most in need of the respite. The descent had jarred his shoulder almost constantly, and he was in terrible pain. A'isha examined his wound anxiously, taking great care not to let it come in contact with any of the filth that surrounded them. The bullet-hole was badly inflamed, and the shoulder itself had swollen.

"I think his shoulder-bone may have been chipped or even broken," she said. "That would explain the severity of his pain. I think you should let him have some morphine."

"He has to stay awake. What if he'd lost consciousness on that ladder?"

"We're at the bottom now. A few grains will help without actually knocking him out."

Michael hesitated, then nodded. A'isha took a hypodermic from a bag she carried around her neck and administered a small dose to Butrus. It took effect rapidly, dulling, but by no means quelling, the pain.

"It's time to go," said Michael. He was anxious. The discovery of the half-eaten remains had filled him with a nagging disquiet.

Crouching low, they crept through the short passage into the wider tunnel. Here, the roof was higher, but still too low to let the adults walk through without bending. Only Fadwa experienced no difficulty. But now they were in the tunnels, the temporary confidence the little girl had found while helping Butrus make the descent had almost wholly vanished. With every step she cast nervous glances around her. And every time a rat slithered in or out of the water, she gave an involuntary jump.

They had come to a dark, desperate world, a world so far cut off from any other that it alone might have been the universe. In Michael's hand, the needle of the tiny compass bobbed and shifted, seeking its anchor always in the north. But in this dense darkness, its gyrations were meaningless, a fluttering dance that bore no relation to the winding or the weaving or the imperceptible shifting of the cramped tunnels. They felt the walls upon them, heavy and damp, generation upon generation of fashioned and fractured stone, and the terrible weight of the city pressing down, until they felt crushed and tiny and unable to breathe.

The tunnel through which they waded was egg-shaped, wider at the bottom than the top, and lined with ancient, crumbling bricks of Mamluk manufacture. Every few yards, holes in the walls marked the position of street drains entering the system. It was at these spots that the rats would be most active, coming and going without any apparent pattern to their movements. The water reached to just below their knees, rather higher on Fadwa. The light of the torches turned it a bright pea-soup color. A fetid, stagnant smell rose from it, forcing them to breathe through bits of cloth held against their mouths.

Normally conditions in the sewers below Bulaq would have been much worse, serving as they did one of the most densely populated sectors of one of the world's most populous cities. And even though Bulaq was now a cemetery, it was not possible to wipe out centuries of filth in a matter of weeks. The water ran thick with all the city did not want: dead rats, dead cats and dogs, dead leaves, wasted lives.

The tunnel seemed to stretch on forever. Without light

beyond that from their torches, they could form no proper sense of distance. From time to time they passed the gaping mouths of side tunnels, too low and narrow to offer passage. By now, they were heading south, and the main tunnel Michael had anticipated had still not come in sight.

They must have gone about half a mile when A'isha noticed for the first time that water was pouring into the culvert from a drainage channel at the side. A few yards further, a second pipe debouched into their tunnel, depositing a heavy flow of brown, muddy water. They halted, listening.

There was an unmistakable sound of rushing water that had not been there before. When they looked, it was obvious that the level of water in the culvert was rising.

"I think it's started raining outside," said Michael quietly to A'isha. "We'll have to hurry. We could be trapped if this channel fills."

If the rain began in earnest, he knew they might never make it out alive. Every drain and gully in the city would be pouring flood-water into the sewer system. The river would fill rapidly and start to back up at several points along both banks.

"It may not be too late to go back," said A'isha. "If the ladder holds . . ."

Michael shook his head.

"We can't get out that way," he said.

"Why not?"

"The little tunnel leading back from this culvert to the shaft has a much lower roof. It's designed to take outflow from the culvert once it gets above a certain level. By the time we get back there, enough water will have backed up into the tunnel and the shaft to make it impossible to get through. We'd never make it, certainly not Butrus. I'm sorry. We have no choice. We have to go on."

59

The water in the culvert was flowing faster now. Beneath their feet, the bottom was slippery with centuries of mud and slime. Twice, Fadwa slipped and fell into the stinking water. The dinghy would be no use to them in such a confined space: it would only swell to fit the sides of the culvert and trap them fast. Unless they reached deeper and wider water, they would have to walk or swim.

Michael gave Butrus the lifejacket to put on.

"Keep it inflated," he told him. "You'll need it if you lose your footing."

Fadwa was able to swim a little. As A'isha had nearly guessed, her brothers had taught her to swim in the Nile, whose waters flowed along the western border of Bulaq.

"Michael! I think we've reached the end of the culvert."

A'isha was walking ahead. Her torch had caught a break in the wall. Michael splashed towards her. She was right. A steep water-covered ramp led down to a much larger tunnel, exactly what they had been looking for. Water tumbled down the slope like a swollen stream pouring over a weir.

"I'll go down first," said A'isha.

"You'll need the rope. If you get swept into that current below, you'll never get out."

His fingers numb with cold, he tied the rope around her waist. In the wall ahead of him, he found a crevice into which he jammed the mooring pole in order to act as a brace. A'isha began to slide down the treacherous incline. Within seconds, her feet gave under her and she was swept bodily down into the lower tunnel.

The rope took the sudden strain as the current carried her around the corner. She was dashed under, then came up, torch in hand. Right beside her she could see a narrow ledge running the length of the tunnel. She tossed the torch onto it and rolled herself up.

The ledge was scarcely more than a foot wide and extremely slippery. There was a ring set in the wall a little higher up, one of several that had been placed at intervals along the tunnel. A'isha used it to pull herself upright. She flashed the torch up and down, revealing an old tunnel built from a dark, honeycombed brick that had crumbled entirely in places. It was wider and flatter than the one they had been in, and its roof was higher. Through the center ran a deep ditch through which a swollen body of water was running rapidly westward.

She untied the rope and shouted back to Michael that it was free. He reeled it in quickly, then tied it under Fadwa's shoulders. She was shaking with fright, but when Michael impressed on her that there was no other way, she nodded grimly and let herself be lowered down the ramp.

A'isha was waiting to grab her and pull her up onto the shelf. The rope was sent back again. This time, it was Butrus's turn.

"Let me do the work for you," Michael advised him. "A'isha and Fadwa will pull you in at the other end."

"What about you? How will you get down?"

"Let me worry about that."

"I've got the lifejacket."

"You need it. We don't have time to argue."

The next second, Butrus's legs were swept out from under him. He slipped over the crest of the ramp and was carried bodily down to the lower tunnel, dragging Michael off balance and pulling him down behind him.

They crashed into the ditch and were instantly prisoners of the current, tossed along in a maelstrom of foaming water. Butrus remained buoyant, but Michael was pulled under choking. As he rose to the surface, he knew he had seconds in which to act. He was still clutching the rope in one hand and the mooring pole in the other. Without stopping to think, he turned the pole horizontally against the sides of the ditch, wedging it at an angle, pressing with all his strength as he felt Butrus's weight tugging him forward.

"A'isha! . . . Quickly! . . ."

A rush of water snatched the words from him. Then she was there, reaching down for him.

"Get Butrus first! I can't . . . hold . . . him!"

A'isha scrambled along the ledge until she was within reach of Butrus. He was spinning helplessly on the rope, struggling to free himself with one hand. His left arm had been battered mercilessly against the sides.

Fadwa grabbed Michael, helping him take the strain on the rope. But he could feel the pole giving already. His throat and lungs were filled with water, he knew he was losing his hold.

The pull on the rope slackened. Fadwa held him tight to the side until A'isha was able to drag him onto the ledge. As he clambered up, he lost his grip on the pole. It went spinning off on a twisting of white water. He closed his eyes, fearing that, before the night was through, he would bitterly regret its loss.

They rested there as long as they dared, aware that, every moment they tarried, the water below them was rising another fraction of an inch. Butrus lay in agony. His left shoulder had taken a terrible battering during his fall and the twist that had hurled him around the bend. A'isha opened her bag to give him another shot of morphine, but the hypodermic had been smashed and the morphine powder turned to a watery slush. She took what she could of it and forced it between his lips.

She gave them ten minutes. Neither Michael nor Butrus was in good shape to move, but there was nothing else to do. If the rain continued to fall—worse still, if it grew heavier—they would be racing against time. She helped Michael to his feet. Together they raised Butrus.

Michael took the compass from his pocket and laid it flat on the ledge. The tunnel lay roughly on an east-west axis.

"The water's running west," he said. "Down to the river. We can't go that way. We have to head east."

"How do we get across the ramp?"

In entering the tunnel, they had of necessity been swept round to their left, following the current. To get to the section of ledge running east, they would have to cross the point where the tunnels joined. To make matters worse, Fadwa was the first on that side, and there was no room for anyone to cross.

"Can you lift her?" Michael asked.

"I'll try."

A'isha bent down slightly and told Fadwa to put her arms round her neck. Standing, she lifted her, swung her out over the rushing water, and turned at last back to the ledge. Michael took Fadwa's arm and held her steady. Carefully, A'isha stepped sideways to the edge.

"It's too far to jump. If the ledge was wider, there'd be no problem."

Michael thought quickly.

"Inflate the dinghy," he said.

She took the rubber raft from its bag and set it down on the ledge beside her. There was a yellow toggle which, when tugged, inflated it. A length of nylon rope was fastened to a ring beside it. Keeping firm hold of the rope, she pulled the toggle and hurriedly tossed the raft into the gap before it could swell and knock her off balance. In moments, it grew to full size.

She held it hard against the side. It almost filled the space between the two ledges. Handing the rope to Michael, she stepped carefully into the dinghy while he bent down to hold it against the side. It was like trying to stand on the back of a bucking horse. The raft was tossed and twisted this way and that by the current, rising, falling, and jerking unpredictably. On her knees, A'isha crept to the other side, then reached for the far ledge. Choosing her moment carefully, she got one leg onto it, then threw herself forwards and up. She hit the wall hard but kept her balance.

There was another ring in the wall near the corner. A'isha called out, asking Michael to throw the line across. Fadwa helped steady the raft, while he coiled the rope and tossed it over. Within moments A'isha had secured the raft to the ring by a short line.

Held now at both ends, the little craft was much steadier. Fadwa crossed without difficulty. Butrus followed, remaining in the raft while A'isha helped Michael across. They reorganized themselves on the ledge, with Michael in front, followed by Butrus, then A'isha, and finally Fadwa at the rear.

They released the dinghy and set off eastwards. Michael handed the rope of the raft to Fadwa. She trailed it behind her in the water like an over-eager dog on a leash. It was her new responsibility, Michael's latest ploy to keep her mind off other things. Such as creatures that slithered unsuspected through the tunnels.

The water was still rising. They walked as quickly as possible, without hurrying. The surface of the ledge was smooth and treacherous, and to fall from it would mean almost certain death. They held hands, shuffling like crabs, their backs tight against the wall. Only Michael carried a torch. A'isha held onto Fadwa by her upper arm. The little girl still carried the gun tightly in her hand.

No-one spoke. In their ears, the water sounded without

cessation. Away from the weir, it was less raucous, but it flowed through the ditch with undiminished force.

The roof and walls of the old tunnel were covered with moss and lichens, sickly green and yellow growths that shimmered uncannily in the light of Michael's torch. Toadstools grew everywhere, singly and in clumps, dark brown or ghostly white against the courses of damp brick.

"Stop!" Michael's voice sounded curiously hollow, as though he had suddenly been snatched far away. Through a haze of pain, Butrus felt Michael's hand tighten on his.

"I almost fell backwards," Michael said. "The wall gave way."

He let go of Butrus's hand in order to turn. Behind him, there was a gaping aperture where the wall had been. A large section had collapsed at some time in the past, years, possibly even centuries ago. On the other side lay a vast, hungry emptiness.

In the white beam of Michael's torch, a high chamber stood revealed, raked and fluted stone carved in gray segments from a solid block of darkness. A broad domed ceiling fluttered in the dancing light, intricate shadows woven with strands of pierced alabaster. Great stalactites of carved stone crowded the dome, their intricacies filled with spiders' webs and the wings of hanging bats.

The walls had once been white stucco, delicately carved with leaves and flowers and the wings of birds. Now only fragments remained to show what had been, like snatches of a tune that has long drifted into silence. Blue and crimson tiles still hung in little groups to the plaster, their patterns broken and incomplete. This had once been the central chamber of a large *hammam,* a public bath.

Where the floor had been was now a broad pool of stagnant water, choked with sewage and rubble. The water shone green where algae had formed across its surface. White froth lay in patches in the corners. Each time the tunnel overflowed, the pool would refill, then sink again. Michael could not guess how deep it might be.

They started to move on.

"Be very careful," Michael said. "There's only the ledge to balance on."

Slowly, they crossed the gap. They were almost at the other side when their blood was frozen by the sound of a low roaring, followed moments later by a high-pitched scream. A'isha felt Fadwa's arm plucked from hers, almost pulling her back into the opening.

Dropping Butrus's hand, she turned, fumbling for the torch she had stuck into a pocket of her overall. Fadwa had fallen through the hole. She was still screaming loudly. There was a terrible threshing sound. And from somewhere close by, another roar. A'isha's hand trembled as she switched on the torch.

Water, turbulent and covered in ripples. The deepest of darknesses. A child's screams. The sound of something heavy beating the water. The torch beam darting in and out of the darkness, finding nothing. The screaming suddenly cut off. A convulsion of water, like a cauldron boiling.

Then Fadwa's head suddenly appeared, her arms in the air, flailing helplessly, her body held fast in the jaws of her nightmare. A'isha screamed, feeling fear race through her like flames. At that moment it reappeared, the long head of a fully grown Nile crocodile, its jaws fastened round Fadwa's flanks, pulling her down into the water for the kill.

60

A'isha stood rooted, unable to move, unable to think. The crocodile was enormous: a fully grown adult, at least twenty feet long, its jaws crammed with vicious, jagged teeth. God alone knew how many years it had lurked down here: they could live to a hundred and more. The light danced briefly on its little, wicked eyes, on the bright, dilated pupils. For a second, it seemed as though it were staring directly at her in triumph.

Fadwa still struggled, silent now, choking on the stagnant water, weakening rapidly. The crocodile had her firmly in its grasp, it knew she could not break free. All it would take to finish her would be a rolling snap of its great head, tearing her in half. She fought gamely to keep her head above the water. Still clutched tightly in one hand, as though by a miracle, was Michael's gun, thrust into the air like a talisman that might bring her to safety.

A'isha did not stop to work things out. She jumped into the water, heading straight for the child. Two strokes, three strokes, and she was beside her. The torch had gone, she was in pitch darkness, guided only by the sound of churning water. She reached out and felt the wet roughness of the crocodile's back, the thick scales cold and unyielding to the touch. Why had she dropped the torch? She could do nothing without light. The crocodile shook itself, rolling away from her. She reached out, thrashing water, and dashed her empty hand against nothing.

Suddenly, a white beam cut through the darkness. Michael was kneeling at the opening.

"Get the gun, A'isha! Get the gun!"

She kicked out and threw herself across the crocodile's head, reaching for Fadwa. The reptile lifted itself and twisted away, throwing her to one side, back into the water. The light remained steady, confusing the crocodile. A'isha dived, kicking blindly underwater, resurfacing moments later just beyond the reptile, in reach of Fadwa. She grabbed the child's arm with one hand and, with the other, snatched the gun from her.

It was now or never, there would not be a second chance. Holding fast to Fadwa with her left arm, A'isha twisted, pressing the barrel of the gun into the huge open mouth of the crocodile. The weapon was wet, she was sure it would not fire. She pulled the trigger. Nothing happened. And again. Nothing. She closed her eyes, certain of death. The crocodile twisted, trying to jerk her off. She pulled again.

There was a huge bang. The crocodile reared up and back, throwing its mouth wide open to roar in pain. A'isha kept her grip on the child with both hands now, letting the gun fall to the bottom of the pool. All round them the water boiled and seethed as the wounded monster flailed in a mad passion with its tail.

"Swim for the opening! I'll take her now!" Michael was beside them in the water, A'isha had no idea how. When she looked up, she saw Butrus holding a torch in one hand, leaning for balance against the side, his teeth gritted in pain. She swam for the opening.

Butrus made way for her as she scrambled back onto the ledge. The shock of the attack had brought him to his senses. He placed the torch between his legs and reached out a hand to help A'isha steady herself. Moments later, Michael floundered to the side and lifted Fadwa to the ledge. Behind him, the crocodile still threshed the water.

"Hurry up!" Michael shouted. "There may be others. We have to move."

Fadwa was half conscious, frozen as much by fear as pain. She was bleeding badly around the waist and buttocks, where the sharp teeth had torn strips from her flesh. They managed to stand her on the ledge between them, forcing her head down in order to cough out as much water as possible.

"Let's get out of here," said Michael.

He looked round for the raft, hoping to use it as a sort of ambulance on which to carry Fadwa and possibly Butrus. But it had been swept away on the current the moment Fadwa had let go of the rope. It was not even in sight now. They had no choice but to maneuver the wounded child along the narrow pathway.

They began to shuffle along the ledge again, desperately trying to distance themselves from the aperture. Michael and A'isha held Fadwa steady between them, dragging her away from the nightmare. She was light, like a bundle of dried sticks. Until now, they had not realized how pitifully thin she was. From time to time they were forced to halt while she retched and shook convulsively, almost throwing herself into the water at her feet.

The rain had not stopped. If anything, it must have grown more furious. As more and more water thundered into the main tunnel, the stream rose until it was almost level with the ledge. In minutes their feet would be under water, their precarious footing impossible to hold.

Suddenly, Butrus called out, his voice weak above the piling stream.

"A ladder! There's a ladder on the other side!"

His torch had picked out the rungs of an access ladder set into a shallow niche in the opposite wall. There was a broad platform in front of it, protected from the ditch by a loosely slung chain.

Michael looked across. Only a few yards separated them from the ladder, but it might have been half a mile. With a sinking feeling, he realized that, had he not lost the mooring pole, he might have been able to stretch across and hook the chain. Without it, he would have to risk being swept away by the current.

"Butrus," he said. "Go up a few yards further. Take Fadwa if you can. We'll follow you."

He tied the rope round his waist again and gave the end to A'isha to hold. She was wet and bruised and stinking, but he wanted to kiss her and tell her he loved her. Instead, he touched her cheek lightly with his fingers, then turned and leaped into the freezing water.

The current pulled him under and swung him away from the opposite wall, but he had expected that. The rope took the strain, holding him level with the platform. Rising, he took a deep breath, then let himself drop again. One foot touched bottom. He bent his legs, gaining a fragile purchase, then kicked hard, rising.

His hand caught the edge of the platform and held. The current dragged hard at him, trying to pluck him away, but he was holding on with both hands now. Pulling himself up, he swung for the chain, missing it by inches. He could feel his fingers slipping on the wet stone. A second effort. This time he just made it, getting his frozen fingers round the rusted links. He rested briefly, then hauled himself up onto the platform.

Getting the others across took time, almost more than they could safely spare. While Michael held the rope, A'isha came over holding Fadwa, then Butrus. By the time they were all on the platform, water was lapping over it.

Fadwa had still not come around. A'isha examined her as best she could. Apart from the lacerations where the teeth had first taken hold of her, it looked as if the pressure of the huge jaws had cracked several of her ribs. She was breathing heavily, with a dark rasping sound that made A'isha's hair stand on end.

"We'll never get her up the ladder, Michael."

"There's no other way. She'll make it. She has to."

A'isha shook her head.

"I'm frightened, Michael. Her breathing's bad, I think a rib may have pierced one of her lungs. She's lost a lot of blood."

"If we don't get her out, she'll drown in here."

A'isha looked down at the drawn face of the little girl. As she did so, Fadwa's eyes fluttered open. She jerked her head back, trying to pull away, her throat stretched tight as though in a scream. A'isha reached out a hand to her.

"It's all right," she said. "You're safe. It's dead. It can't get you now."

But Fadwa was locked so deeply in her fear and pain that nothing reached her.

"Hurry, Michael. We've got to get her to someone who can help."

He looked back once, then started the ascent. The ladder was old, but its moorings were more secure than those of the one they had come down by. A quick glance had shown that it went straight upwards into the darkness. Michael prayed that it led to a way out.

He was thinking of nothing now but escape and fresh air. Nothing else mattered. Not Paul, not al-Qurtubi, not Father Gregory and his tales of mayhem. There was only this, the ladder and the sound of water rushing below, the darkness and the hope of light.

The ladder ended at a metal platform where a second began. Up here, the water was only a memory, a murmuring far away. He had to steel himself to think of A'isha, Butrus, and the little girl still waiting down there, watching the water rise. He started up the second ladder.

Forty feet higher it stopped at a tall metal grille. He switched on the torch. A small chamber with a manhole cover in its roof. He pushed the grille. Nothing happened.

He pushed again, harder this time. Still it refused to give. He shone the torch on it. There was no padlock, no obvious means of securing it. He put his shoulder against it and pushed with all his strength. It would not give. And then he looked more closely.

It had been welded shut.

61

Even as he climbed back down, he realized what had happened. The authorities had been one step ahead of them, blocking off all exists from Bulaq. Not them in particular, of course—there had been no time for that—but anyone seeking to escape the plague ghetto they had created. It was only as he reached the bottom of the ladder that it crossed his mind there must still be ways open. Apart from the dismembered body at the very beginning—which Michael now realized must have been the victim of another crocodile—they had stumbled across no human remains.

Of course, that might mean nothing: there could be dozens, even hundreds scattered through this warren, or they might all have been carried to the river by flooding. But he did not dwell on that. Better to think that some had escaped after all, that there might indeed be a way out, if only they could get to it in time.

The water was at the first rung of the bottom ladder. A'isha and her two companions sat in it without caring. As Michael stepped down, A'isha got to her feet wearily, getting ready for the last stage. He did not have to say a word. One look told her everything. The light went out of her eyes.

She looked down at Fadwa. The child was starting to come around. It might have been better to have left her to the crocodile.

"There must be more exits further on," Michael pleaded. "They won't have blocked them all. We can't give up now."

A'isha looked at him oddly. For the first time since they met, she despised him, felt revolted by him. What use was his English sang froid here? What was the point of making a good show of it? They would drown in a filthy ditch, with vermin and excrement and aborted fetuses. He and his kind had brought them to this, with their power games and their dreams of empire. Butrus had been right. They had all been pawns.

"I'm staying here," she said in a voice that had grown dull and resigned. "There's no point in going further, don't you see? Fadwa needs to rest. Butrus is almost done for. We'll die here anyway."

Michael sank down beside her.

"Is that what you want?" he asked. "Just to give in?"

"What do you care?" She was shivering. He tried to put his arm around her, but she pulled away.

"Don't you think Fadwa deserves just one more try?"

A'isha looked round involuntarily. The little girl was sitting with her back to the wall, staring at the light of Butrus's torch where it played on the moss-covered roof. Her skin was pale, her eyes sunken. She was deep in a nightmare no-one could unlock. The water all around her was stained pink with blood.

A'isha shook her head.

"It's too late, Michael. You go on alone if you like. But let us stay here."

He felt the strangest mixture of emotions fight within him. Grief, sadness, anger, disappointment, a bitter sense of injustice. To lie down and die went against everything he believed. And yet in such a place as this, it seemed to make perfect sense. He knelt down in front of her and took her face between his hands. There was so little light, he could scarcely discern her features.

"Look at me, A'isha." She looked into his eyes with a vacant expression.

"Coming down here was our decision," he said. "One we took together. Neither Butrus nor Fadwa had a hand in it or any real choice. Now, there's just a chance that a little further down this tunnel there's a way out. They can't get there by themselves, they can't even ask us to find it for them. That leaves it up to us again. We can lie here and keep them company while they drown. Maybe even make it easy for them, put them out of their misery quickly. Perhaps we should do that now, it wouldn't take us long. Or we can push on further and maybe—just maybe—get them out of here. And ourselves. What do you say?"

He couldn't do it without her, he knew he couldn't. Even had he known with complete certainty that there was a way out just around the next bend, he could not have gone there if A'isha had opted to stay here. His fate, all their fates, lay in her hands. It seemed a lifetime before she spoke.

"Very well," she said. Her voice was still dull, her eyes had not lost their vacant look. "One more try."

They roused the others and got them to their feet. Butrus's shoulder had swollen so badly it was almost the size of a small melon. Fadwa was only half aware of what was happening. She told A'isha that her sides were hurting badly and that she was finding it hard to breathe. A'isha reassured her as best she could, saying she had only a little way to go. She did not think Fadwa would see daylight again. She wished there were a God, but what God would reach as low as this?

The ledge on this side of the tunnel was slightly broader than the one they had been walking on before. But whatever they gained by that was canceled out by the fact that it now lay three or four inches under the surface of the water. Having widened out considerably beyond the limits of the ditch in which it had previously been confined, the current had slackened; but it still had sufficient force left to sweep them away if they slipped.

They had gone less than fifty yards when they saw it: a low tunnel below the level of the ledge. Only the upper section was still showing above the water-line. The tunnel itself was completely filled. If it was a discharge tunnel similar to the one that had taken them into the original culvert, it should lead into a shaft. A few seconds under water, then out again. But if it was not? If it went on for half a mile?

Michael thought it over quickly. There was no point in going further. Any minute now Butrus or Fadwa would be swept off their feet and snatched away by the stream. Now they had found a conduit, there was unlikely to be another for some distance. And if there was, it would probably be identical to this anyway. Identical and, perhaps, even further under water or invisible.

"I'll swim through," said Michael. "With luck, I'll come out on the other side in a few seconds. I'll take the rope. Once I'm through I'll pull on it three times if all looks well. Put the end around Fadwa's shoulders and tell her to hold her breath as hard as she can. I'll come back for Butrus, then you."

She took the torch from her pocket and shone it on his face. All the anger had gone, all the rancor. It all seemed so out of place here, so petty. She leaned forward and touched his lips with hers. It was not a kiss. But in that moment she thought she lived in her lips.

"I love you, Michael," she said.

He said nothing in reply, but he squeezed her hand and looked at her with a look of such regret and such longing that she had to turn her face away. Moments later, he was gone.

He had never known such perfect fear. Every moment, he thought the water must end, that he must break free into an exaltation of air. But there was no end to it, until he was certain it must continue forever. The tunnel was too narrow to swim in. He held his hands tight against his sides and kicked. Each time he pushed forward, his head would rise and touch the roof. There was no turning back. His lungs were bursting, in another second he would have to let go. And when he breathed in again, he would take in water and begin to drown. Another kick. Still the hard stone roof. A little breath escaped him, filling the water with bubbles. Kick. The roof again. His chest was on fire, his eyes were washed with red. Behind the red he could see the shape of a pyramid, a black pyramid shining like darkness become rock. Just one more kick. His head grazed stone. More bubbles. He was almost done. One more kick and then he would be free. He kicked.

This time his head kept on rising. He was still in water, but the tunnel had ended. He could not have risen for more than a second or two, but it seemed like hours. And then air, and his breath jerking out of him, and the first gulping snatch of oxygen, air so sweet it made him cry.

He took out his torch and switched it on. He was bobbing in about ten feet of water at the bottom of a tall shaft. A ladder rose into the darkness beside him. Several feet above his head, a metal grating provided a platform. There was no point in wasting time checking what lay at the top of the ladder.

Taking a deep breath, he climbed to the bottom of the shaft and pulled three times on the rope. There was an answering tug, then a pause while A'isha got Fadwa ready. Michael resurfaced, took another lungful of air, and went back down. A second tug. He drew Fadwa to him like a fisherman reeling in his catch. She came through without catching, her eyes closed fast, her cheeks distended, bubbles rising as the breath left her. Without pausing, he grabbed her, banging her legs on the roof of the tunnel, and lifted her above the water. She had swallowed several mouthfuls of water and was choking badly by the time he got her to the ladder.

He held her steady for a little while, then helped her climb to the platform.

"How do you feel?" he asked, but she did not answer.

There was no time to waste. He dived, bringing the rope with him, and squeezed into the tunnel. Once, for a terrible moment, his overall caught on a projection in the roof, holding him. Then the fabric tore and he was free again.

When he came out, the water in the main tunnel had risen further. Aisha was standing, holding Butrus. The surface of the water was already above their knees. Michael rested while A'isha busied herself with the rope, tying it to Butrus's waist.

"I'm worried, Michael," she whispered. "I don't know if he can hold his breath long enough. The morphine had a stronger effect than I thought."

"It won't be more than twenty seconds, twenty-five at the outside."

He turned to Butrus.

"Can you hold the rope with one hand while I pull you through?"

Butrus nodded, but Michael could see that he was not fully conscious.

"I'll go this time," A'isha said.

"I'm familiar with it now. I'll have to go back anyway."

She shook her head.

"You need time to catch your breath. As long as I know there's air at the other end, I'll be all right."

"You don't . . ."

"For God's sake, it's safer this way. Stay here."

Without waiting for further objections, she dived. Michael waited. Now the first euphoria had worn off, he realized that the air in the main tunnel was growing stale. He knew that sewers filled with noxious gases and that under certain conditions these could leak out. How ironic it would be if, after all they had gone through, the air itself were to turn against them.

He talked to Butrus, trying to keep him alert. The Copt had found places within his pain where he could rest, secluded corners where he could hide. Michael had to drag him out again, however much torment that caused.

He glanced at his watch. More than three minutes had passed. He fixed his eyes on the rope, willing it to move. Each time the current lifted it, he thought it was A'isha signaling she was ready. And each time it fell back limply again. Four minutes now. Something was wrong. He would give her another minute before starting down the tunnel.

The rope twitched. Once, twice, three times. Michael stood at the opening of the tunnel with Butrus, helping him get ready. The current snatched at them with the beginnings of a strong underflow. The rope moved again.

Butrus breathed in. Michael pushed him down into the opening. He had never felt so much like an executioner. The rope tautened and Butrus vanished.

Five minutes later, Michael made his third entry to the tunnel. The sense of constriction was worse than ever. It was as though he had always been there, pushing, kicking, struggling to be free.

He came up choking to find A'isha standing on the bottom rung, her hand held towards him, ready to pull him up.

"Are they all right?" he asked.

She nodded.

She went up first, as far as the little grating. Fadwa and Butrus were lying together. A'isha looked at them anxiously. Michael reached the platform behind her.

"I thought they would die," he whispered.

"There's still time for that," she said.

"Let's get this over with." Now the time had come, he thought it almost better not to know.

"I'll go," she said.

"Not this time. It was my decision to come here."

She laughed.

"You're very wet," she said. "I've never seen anybody so wet."

He smiled weakly.

"You haven't seen yourself."

Suddenly, she threw her arms round him, holding him as though she would never let go. They stood like that for a long time, wet and trembling, listening to the water rise. At last he broke away.

"We have to know," he said.

It was not far to the top. The ladder ended beneath a manhole cover. Michael braced himself and put his shoulders to it, then pushed up hard.

The cover lifted. Using his hands now, he pushed it further and slid it to one side. He felt his heart slither to a halt. "Dear God," he whispered, "don't let this be an entrance to another sewer."

He took two more steps up. It was still night. There were no stars. There was no moon. There were no streetlights. But it was raining. Heavy, heavy rain that he could have kissed.

62

London
Vauxhall House

The message reached London at 2243 hours and was taken immediately and by hand to Percy Haviland's office. Its arrival was not logged, nor was any copy kept by the operator who handled it: the identification code had alerted him at once to the need to follow special procedures. "Special procedures" was House slang for "treat as private communication for the DG's eyes only." Such private communications were technically illegal; but infringing Percy Haviland's God-given right to receive them would guarantee even the best-placed janissary a swift and permanent posting to a part of the Third World not even the aid agencies would touch. The message lay on Haviland's desk at 2247 hours precisely.

There was a little white telephone on Haviland's desk that he liked to play with now and then. It provided him with a secure line, a line that was as free of bugs as a surgeon's knife come newly from the sterilizer, a line that gave him immediate access to a dozen numbers, numbers so private that they were not merely unlisted: as far as the telephone service was aware, they did not exist at all.

He sat for a few golden moments glancing through the details of the message, as though to reassure himself that it was not, after all, some sort of hoax. With slim fingers, he lifted a piece of dark Valrhona chocolate to his lips and bit down hard. Seventy per cent, a mixture of the best cocoas. Chocolate always reassured him, its darkness and bitterness made him feel relaxed. His hand moved to the white telephone and he punched a single digit. There was no dialing tone, no sound of a number being encoded, no ring at the other end. Had he not known otherwise, he would have assumed the phone was dead. It was not. About five seconds passed, then a voice came on the line. Haviland spoke before the other man had finished.

"This is Haviland. I want to speak to Sir Lionel right away. No, it can't wait. And, yes, I know it's late. You know bloody well this is an emergency line."

A few moments of silence passed, then a second voice came on the line. A soft voice, the sort of voice that belonged on a line like this.

"Yes, Percy. What can I do for you?"

"Holly is through. He was spotted earlier today at a place about two hundred miles west of Cairo." He hesitated. "Unfortunately, our man lost track of him after that. He thinks Holly knew he was being watched and managed to give him the slip. However, that may not matter greatly. Not if he keeps his rendezvous with Hunt. Which I would expect him to do."

"What about Hunt? Will he be there?"

There was a pause.

"That's hard to say. He was almost captured last night at his radio operator's. It's very likely he never received the message we sent to fix up their meeting. But the Dutchman thinks the woman, Manfaluti, managed to reach him. She may have passed it on."

"Where is he now?"

"Hard to say. He seems to have got himself into some sort of no-go area. The Egyptians are being a bit tight-lipped about it."

"Will it make a difference?"

"No. We don't need them together, that's just for the sake of appearances."

"Well, then, everything seems to be going according to plan. Why on earth are you ringing at this hour just to tell me this? Couldn't it have waited until morning?"

Haviland paused.

"I thought . . . I thought you might like to know that al-Qurtubi was declared President of Egypt tonight."

"He was what?"

"He made a broadcast on state television at nine o'-clock. There was a simultaneous radio transmission. It was picked up in Caversham. Well, everywhere, actually. All the listening stations."

"That wasn't the plan."

"No, it wasn't. You're perfectly right, Lionel. But I don't see that it's going to do us any harm."

"It's too bloody risky. Too up front."

"He can give us what we need."

"Yes, but what's his price going to be now?"

A pause.

"That will remain to be negotiated, I expect. Or would you rather we pulled out?"

"Pull out? At this stage? We can't afford to do that. If necessary, we can eliminate al-Qurtubi. Pin it on Hunt and Holly. That would look well."

"With respect, Lionel, it might not. We'll have to have a word with al-Qurtubi and his Dutch friend. He may have other plans."

"I'm beginning to think so. I knew we should never have trusted a dirty little Arab like that."

"Well, he isn't exactly an Arab, Lionel."

"Whatever you want to call him, Percy, he's still a bloody barrow boy."

"Nevertheless, we're in too deep. He won't ditch us, not yet; not while we still have things to offer him."

"He may grow overconfident."

"That's possible, yes." Haviland pondered. "Perhaps

we should send someone in discreetly. Someone who can have a word in our friend's ear."

There was a long silence. For a moment, Haviland thought the line had gone dead. Then Sir Lionel's voice came on again.

"Do you know, Percy, I think that's an excellent idea." He paused. "And I think you're the right man for the job. He trusts you, or says he does. He knows you have influence in certain essential places. Yes, I think you should pack a bag tonight. I'm sure you have ways of getting into the place."

"But . . . but . . ." spluttered Haviland. "I'm not that easily dispensable. A younger man would fit the part far better. I . . ."

"No, Percy, no-one else. A younger man just won't do. I mean that. It may mean a little sweat. But for a man about to receive a knighthood, a man who has shown himself so dedicated to our cause . . . It would be a significant gesture, Percy. And, under the circumstances, rather a necessary one. You understand me?"

"Of course. It's just that . . ."

"Excellent. Just be sure there are no cock-ups, Percy. Not at this stage."

The line did not go dead. There was just a soft click and the voice was there no longer.

Haviland held the receiver in his hand a few moments longer, then returned it to its cradle. His hand shook as he did so. He stared around his comfortable office, at the paintings on the walls, the group of sculptures on a low table near the door. He had risen very near the top. In a matter of days, he might be there. Or he might tumble. It would not matter then if he had not reached the pinnacle he sought, the fall would be as swift and as fatal. And he knew that, if he fell, he would fall alone.

PART IX

"Who is like unto the beast? who is able to make war with him?"

REVELATION 13:4

63

Stealing cars was something they taught you on basic training. This one was easier than most. It was a dark green Renault 4, and most of it was hanging together with bits of string. Somebody's pride and joy, perhaps; but not tonight. Tonight, it was going to get them out of the rain and to a place of safety. If such a place existed.

It took several attempts to start the engine, and all the while Michael was looking up and down the alley in which the car had been parked, expecting to see the owner rushing out to tackle him or a wakeful neighbor raise the alarm. But the relentless rain and the lateness of the hour proved disincentives to curiosity or action.

At last the engine coughed into life. He drove back to the road and found the doorway in which the others sat huddled, half sheltered against the unending downpour.

Fadwa was critically ill. A'isha was certain she would not last the night unless she received treatment in a hospital. But all the hospitals were closed. Butrus lay insensible against the wall. If something was not done quickly, he would lose the arm, if it was not as good as lost already.

They bundled Fadwa into the back seat, with A'isha

beside her, holding her head on her lap. Butrus slumped in the front, mumbling words and phrases no-one could disentangle.

A'isha had recognized the street. The manhole had opened onto Najib al-Rihani, slightly west of the Victoria Hotel.

"Where to?" she asked.

"They'll still be watching our apartments," Michael answered. "If they know what they're doing. And Abu Musa knows what he's doing, believe me."

"You can't be sure that's who it is."

"Yes," he said. He let in the clutch and set off, heading east. He had only one place left to go. "I am sure. I know how badly he wants me."

"Why? It's an old feud, you said so yourself. This isn't a time for feuds."

Michael shook his head. They were crossing Clot Bey now, passing through Bab al-Sha'riyya, on their way to the city's eastern outskirts. The streets were empty, rain-washed, and preternaturally still. He prayed there were no police patrols.

"It's not that," he said. "Not just that. He knows I was in Alexandria, that I made certain discoveries there. But he doesn't know exactly what, and he has no way of finding out. Not without me."

"I don't understand. Abu Musa works for Egyptian intelligence. Surely he should be helping you."

Michael shook his head.

"I don't think it's that simple. He's playing some sort of game of his own. His name came up several times in Alexandria. I think your uncle was on to him as well, but had nothing to pin him down with. Now he's taken care of Ahmad, it's essential he finds me and kills me before I can talk."

"Who would you talk to?"

He pursed his lips, turning a corner. This all seemed so pointless. Beside him Butrus groaned.

"I don't know any longer. Everything's changed. My chief contacts in the *mukhabarat* have been taken out and shot or transferred to positions where they have no influence."

They drove on through the driving rain. There was no reason for them to be together, no common thread running through their lives. Their intimacy was part of the madness of the times, that was all.

He turned left into al-Husayniyya. The street was dark and full of the same uneasy silence he remembered from his first arrival there, three days ago. He cut the engine and let the car drift to a halt a few yards beyond the side-street in which the Vatican safe-house was situated. Silence washed over them like waves on an empty beach. Michael shivered and opened the door.

"Wait here," he said. "I want to be sure."

"Hurry up, Michael, please. She's dying. We have to get her dry and warm at least."

He nodded and walked off.

His neighbors were quiet tonight, both the living and the dead. He crept up the stairs to the flat on tip-toe. Above him, he could hear the steady rain hammering on a tin roof. A baby cried in a room on his left, then grew silent once more.

He slipped the key into the lock and pushed the door open. It led directly into the living room. He stepped inside and shut the door behind him before switching on the light. Someone was sitting in the only chair the room possessed, blinking in the sudden glare.

"Hello, Michael," he said. "I was growing worried."

"You," said Michael. "I thought you'd left the country. I thought Verhaeren took you with him."

"No," sighed Father Gregory. "I told him I wanted to stay." He stood and stepped across the room. "I knew I might still be needed. He gave me this address, and a key."

"You can explain later," said Michael. "First I need your help. I have a car outside with a little girl and a man in need of medical assistance. The little girl is going to die if we don't get her to a doctor soon."

"I understand." He took a deep breath. "Is anyone else with you?" he asked.

"A'isha. A'isha Manfaluti. I told you . . ."

Gregory raised his eyebrows.

"You found her? I'm pleased. You must be happy."

"Father—the child."

"Yes. Yes, of course. I'll come with you. Will there be room for another passenger?"

"You can squeeze in. But . . ."

"Don't ask questions. You'll find out."

The car shuddered as it skidded round a bend, then straightened itself. Michael strained to see the road through streaming rain. There were no streetlights; in the dark the streets all looked the same.

In the back of the car, Gregory sat in silence, praying inwardly. Fadwa lay stretched over his lap and A'isha's. She was shivering, still losing blood. The priest looked through the window at the blackness. He had never been so afraid. He had stayed to make an end of things, for a final stand at the end of days, and yet it all came down to this, a wet child shivering and bleeding to death on his lap.

From time to time, Gregory would lean forward to tap Michael gently on the shoulder and tell him to make a turn.

They stopped outside a nondescript Coptic church from which the cross and other ornamental features had recently been removed.

"The Church of Amir Tadrus," Gregory said. "It was one of the dozens that were built under Sadat. This was a Coptic area." He looked round at the dark street. "It's almost deserted now."

"Why have you brought us here?" asked Michael.

"You'll see." He turned to A'isha. "Bring the child. I'll help Michael with Butrus. Go to the side door."

The church seemed silent and deserted. No lights showed, however dimly, in any of its windows. The doors were shut fast. But when they reached the side entrance, Gregory knocked hard. Nothing happened. He knocked again, more forcibly this time, in a regular pattern: three knocks, then three, then three.

"The Trinity," he explained.

Footsteps sounded inside, faint and hollow. Moments later, the edge of the door was pulled back. A thin figure stood in the opening, holding an oil lamp above his head.

"My name is Father Gregory," the priest said. "Tell Anba Yu'annis I am here. Tell him I've brought two injured people. One is a child."

The stranger in the doorway shone his lamp in their faces, one at a time. The light flickered dully across Fadwa's features. She was sheathed in a sheen of blood, like copper.

"Come inside," he said. "Anba Yu'annis is down-stairs."

As they passed through the unlit church, Michael was reminded of the night he had entered St Savior's to find his brother nailed above the altar. He did not understand what Gregory was up to, bringing them here. They needed a doc-tor, not a priest. The air was full of incense, a dark, clumsy smell. And behind it something else, an antiseptic perfume, as though someone had disinfected the building.

The custodian led them to a low door in the north wall of the church, just below a small wooden iconostasis. As they passed it, the light cut through the dark, revealing blank patches where the icons had once blazed with red and gold.

The door led to a flight of stairs. They had no need of the lamp here, for the stairwell was properly lit by electric lights. Michael was puzzled at first, then he made out a steady humming sound which, he guessed, came from a small generator.

A'isha went first, carrying Fadwa. At the foot of the stairs, she was halted by a young man holding a sub-machine gun. He glanced at her and at Fadwa, then nodded and stepped aside.

There was a sharp corner, then an archway into a dimly lit room whose true dimensions could not be determined. A'isha stood in the entrance, on the verge of tears, despairing, not knowing what to do next. Then a figure came out of the shadows, a young man in jeans and a tee-shirt.

"My name is Anba Yu'annis," he whispered. Then he looked down at Fadwa. He turned and called gently into the darkness. A second man appeared, dressed in a white coat. Moments later, a woman dressed in a nurse's uniform materialized beside him.

A'isha felt someone lift Fadwa from her. A gurney was wheeled in from nowhere. There was a bustling of men and women in white clothes, lights flickering on in a side room, hushed voices, Butrus stumbling and being caught, an arm around her shoulder, a concerned voice whispering about a bath and dry clothes, and lights whirling, and voices echoing back and forth, the room lifting and spinning and turning dark, hands catching her as she fell and fell and fell.

64

They were in a dark room, Michael and the old priest, huddled together like birds fresh from a storm. A single, low-powered light cast a weak glow across bare walls and the arms of a small Coptic cross above the door. Michael had been given a change of clothing and a cup of hot *mahlab* to drink. A doctor had looked him over while a nurse dressed his wounds. He had received numerous cuts and bruises, and his forehead was gashed when he had been swept from the culvert into the main ditch of the sewer. A'isha had been put to bed in another side room. There was a bed for Michael when he wanted it.

"How did they do it?" he asked. "They've turned the church into a hospital. They even have an operating theater. I've never seen anything like it."

Gregory nodded. He felt splendidly elated, like an apprentice magician who has just pulled a rabbit out of his hat.

"It was Father Yu'annis who thought it all through. This is only one of several refuges he set up. When word was first leaked of plans to round up the city's doctors and paramedics, he realized what the consequences might be. He had started training as a doctor himself before his call to the priesthood. Many of his friends were doctors from the Coptic Hospital and the Kitchener Memorial in Shubra. He started out with Coptic doctors, people he knew he could trust, but before long he had a group almost equally made up of Copts and Muslims, as well as some non-Coptic Christians. I believe your friend Dr. Ibrahimian was one of them.

"They drew up contingency plans in case the decree went through. Equipment and medical supplies were slipped out of stores across the city. Churches and other buildings in non-Muslim neighborhoods were selected and turned into emergency centers. They knew from the start there was very little they could do, but they wanted to make a gesture. It was defiance as much as anything, a way of telling the regime they can't have it all their own way.

"The plan was to rescue the more seriously ill patients who had a good chance of survival. A lot of very hard decisions had to be made. People with poor prognoses or in need of specialized equipment or drugs had to be left behind. Patients who were suffering but not at immediate risk had to be sent home.

"The Muslim doctors proved the most enthusiastic. They felt particularly betrayed by the regime. Some of them had tried to argue the case for Western medicine as something that had grown out of the Islamic tradition. They had pointed out that caring for the sick is an Islamic duty, as important as prayer or fasting. And they'd been turned away or threatened with arrest."

There was a knock at the door. Michael opened it. Anba Yu'annis was standing in the doorway.

"Do you mind if I come in? Or would you rather I came back later in the morning? You must be very tired."

Michael shook his head.

"It's all right," he said. "We were talking."

The young priest came into the room, shutting the door behind him. He greeted Gregory and sat down on the end of Michael's bed. Now that he saw him more clearly, Michael noticed that Yu'annis seemed even more tired than himself.

There were heavy bags under his eyes, his skin was gray, he held himself stiffly, as though braced against an attack.

"How are you feeling now, Mr. Hunt?" he asked.

"Better," said Michael. "Thank you. This place is a sort of miracle."

A look of sorrow passed over the priest's face.

"A miracle?" He shook his head. "There are no miracles here, Mr. Hunt. I wish to God there were. The whole of Egypt needs a miracle. But as usual, God seems to have other things to do." He glanced at Gregory. "I'm sorry, Father. I hope I have not offended you."

Gregory shook his head.

"You are not the first to say or think such a thing. I have thought it often enough myself. But Mr. Hunt was right. You have performed a miracle. Perhaps God is not entirely preoccupied with other matters."

The Copt bowed his head. The God he had once believed in had deserted him. He was hoping that somewhere, in a small corner of his pain, he might find another, less presumptuous divinity. He looked up and turned to Michael.

"Mr. Hunt, can you tell me how your friend Butrus came by his bullet wound? It's extremely important. We have to take considerable care that we are not discovered by the authorities. A great many lives depend upon our secret remaining undiscovered."

Michael explained as best he could. The priest's face grew grave as he listened. When Michael finished, Yu'annis remained silent for a while. When he spoke, his voice betrayed the strain he was living under.

"I will let Butrus stay for a few days until his shoulder is less painful. Then he will have to leave. I cannot risk his bringing the *muhtasibin* to these doors. You and Mrs. Manfaluti will have to leave tomorrow evening, once it is dark. I'm sorry, but I have no choice. Apart from the danger, we cannot afford to feed you. There is already a shortage of food."

Michael nodded.

"It's all right," he said. "I understand. You saved two lives, we have much to be grateful to you for."

Yu'annis hesitated, then spoke quietly.

"I am not so sure about the child's life. I do not think you can speak of it as saved. I pray it will be the case, but it is still early."

"How badly injured is she?"

"Quite badly, I'm afraid. The crocodile tore a lot of flesh away. We have no facilities here for performing skin grafts. Four of her ribs are broken. Fortunately, none of her internal organs seems to have suffered damage, but we will only know for sure when we have X-rays. She has been given blood and sedatives, and her condition is stable for the moment. But we are ill-equipped, she could die as easily as live. I'm sorry, but I don't want to raise false hopes."

"Thank you anyway. Thank you for trying."

"It's not me you have to thank. They've done their best. If there's any chance at all, she'll live. I'm sure of it. Now, I think I'd better leave you. Father, are you coming?"

Gregory shook his head.

"There are still some matters Michael and I have to discuss. If you're not too tired, Michael?"

Michael shook his head.

"Very well, I'll leave you both." Yu'annis stood and walked to the door. As he reached it, the light fell on his back. Where the tee-shirt had rested against his skin, there were streaks of blood. Michael leaned forward.

"Father . . ."

Gregory grabbed Michael's arm, frowning and shaking his head. Yu'annis half turned.

"It's all right, Father," said Michael. "I just wanted to thank you again."

Yu'annis nodded.

"Tell me," he said, "if the child lives, what will happen to her?"

Michael pursed his lips.

"I don't know," he added. "Her family are all dead. She has no-one."

"Were they Copts or Muslims?"

"Muslims, I think. Does it make a difference?"

Yu'annis shook his head wearily.

"No," he said. "Not any longer."

When he had left, Michael turned to Gregory.

"I don't understand, Father. That blood . . ."

"The authorities had him in custody for a little while about two weeks ago. They beat him rather badly. The experience left more scars than the ones you saw. He doesn't like to be reminded."

Michael picked up the cup of *mahlab*. It had grown cold. He set it to one side. From somewhere outside came a hollow sound of coughing. Feet padded softly across a bare linoleum floor. The coughing subsided slowly. Silence draped itself in folds about the makeshift hospital.

"Michael," Gregory said hesitantly, leaning forward, "there's something I have to ask you."

"Yes?"

"Now . . . now that you've found this woman again, what do you plan to do?"

Michael did not reply at once.

"I don't have any plans," he said finally. "There hasn't been time to think that far ahead."

"Do you want to leave? Take her away from all this? The child too, if she lives?"

"I suppose so. Get out of Egypt, yes, there's no question about that. If I can manage it."

He told Gregory about Holly, how it might be possible for them to leave with him.

"You too, Father. We may be able to get you out. If you stay here, you'll be caught and killed. Or die of plague. There's not much choice."

The priest drew a deep breath. He could feel his small heart beating in the cavity of his chest. If he closed his eyes he could see the pyramid in the dream, the sphinxes lined up like funeral cars in the never-ending desert. He shook his head.

"I can't leave," he said. "Surely you understand that. I am still the guardian . . . of that place."

"Surely that's not important now."

The priest shook his head.

"Important? I don't know," he said. "But it was a responsibility given to me by God. I can no more relinquish it than I can relinquish my vows as a priest."

"Isn't there someone else? Someone younger, someone who could take it from you?"

Gregory was silent for a while. The long night continued to pass. It had too many sounds, too many silences. He fumbled beneath his soiled black robes, and finally drew out the heavy key on a thin chain around his neck. Hesitantly, he held it out to Michael.

"If I offered it to you," he said in a half-whisper, "would you take it?"

"You said it was your responsibility . . ."

"It has to be passed on . . ."

"But not to me. I'm not a priest. Not even a believer . . ."

Gregory shook his head.

"You would be my choice."

Michael frowned.

"Please," said Gregory. "Take it. If you do not keep it for yourself, pass it to someone else, someone you trust." He looked silently into Michael's eyes. "As I trust you." He held the key closer. Michael's fingers touched it. The key was cold, black with age, an intricate thing. It had not broken, not in centuries. Michael felt his fingers close round it.

"You know what he is," whispered Gregory. "You have seen the painting, and you understand."

He let the chain slip from his fingers. It was as though, relinquishing it, the old man stripped from himself a burden he had carried far too long. His face seemed to relax. His eyes filled with tears.

Michael pressed the key in his hand.

"I promise nothing," he said.

"There is no need," said Father Gregory. "You will know what to do when the time comes."

65

He watched the sun rise out of the desert like a ball of fire. An old desert, dark, treacherous, full of storms. There had been lightning on the previous night, the sky angry and full of quick, nervous coruscations. He had lain up in a hollow between ridges of rain-packed sand, full of silence, waiting for the night to pass. Somewhere below him lay Bahariyya Oasis and the last stage of his journey. The road to Cairo was clearly visible just beyond the village of al-Jadida. He was very tired.

Now that he was here and had time to think, he had begun to wonder whether he had been right to come after all. There were so many imponderables. Nothing quite added up. At times he thought he had taken leave of his senses and would have to spend the rest of his life picking up the pieces.

It would be hell for Linda and the children, but he had known that when he decided to leave. He wondered what they would have told her. That he was a traitor, had they told her that? That he had gone AWOL, betrayed his sacred trust? Would they try to embarrass her, make her feel contaminated, the wife of a man who had let the side down?

She'd tell them where to go, of course, tell them to their faces that they were silly boogers and did they even know what they were talking about. He could hear her saying it, every word, in those blunt Yorkshire tones. Silly boogers the lot of them.

But he knew too that they had their little ways, their tried-and-tested methods of wearing people down: wan smiles, caustic hints, artfully raised eyebrows, cudgels for someone vulnerable and open to suggestion. Which she would be, in spite of everything. Vulnerable, cast down, frightened, and alone.

Or perhaps they would plead with her to put their minds at rest, to give them reasons they could set against his departure, grounds for believing he had suffered what they would politely call a "breakdown," as though he were a Bugatti on the blink. It was far from uncommon in the trade, an occupational hazard, like alcoholism for doctors or broken bones for stunt-car drivers. Had she concocted for them a tale of loveless nights, of fraught sessions with their long-suffering bank manager, worries about the children, mother, the cat, the dripping tap? Or sent them off with a flea in each ear, hugging his sanity to herself like a five-year guarantee?

But Linda was not his greatest worry. When they had taken what they wanted from her, or told her what they had to tell her, they would leave her alone. She would be safe enough until he returned. She knew how to wait, like all Vauxhall wives. To wait, to be patient, to hide her tawdry fears and uncouth anxieties in little unswept corners deep inside herself. In one of those places the English never examine. On balance, he thought it might be better if they told her he was dead. Snuffed out.

In the meantime, he had other things to think about. Such as what Control was doing at this moment. Not this precise moment, of course: it was still dark in England, two hours before dawn. Haviland would be asleep. But what would he be dreaming of? His knighthood, long overdue?

His new mistress, reputed to be indecently young and demanding? Or the coming together of the brightest and fairest in his rose-pink dreamworld of a post-communist intelligence community?

Holly had a good idea how the old bugger envisaged it all. He had known the man long enough, been privy to his little cocktail fantasies. In the DG's dream, the Lords of Lothlorien would sit on thrones about a magic table in a sterile room, where white draperies fluttered in an air-conditioned breeze: Americans on one side, Russians on the other, and, right in the middle, Percy Haviland, smiling benignly on them all. The Elfin King come into his own at last, and about bloody time too.

Somewhere in that fantasy, Holly was not quite sure where, lurked the dwarves of Mirkwood, al-Qurtubi and his people. At this point, of course, it ceased to be good Sir Percy's fantasy and became his own—the blatant paranoia of an old Middle East hand who had internalized every hackneyed fear about a conspiracy to return the region to the Middle Ages and revive the days of holy war.

Except . . . Except that, all the same, something was going on. Something not remotely like fantasy. Before leaving, he had managed to blow the whistle, if only quietly. He had approached a friend in MI5, a man called Crawford, someone he could trust. Crawford had the ear of several people in Whitehall, could even get as far as the PM if he stuck his neck out far enough. But even Crawford was vulnerable. One wrong step and he would find himself working for a third-rate security firm in Huddersfield, alongside men with tattoos and beer bellies. Holly had no illusions about his chances.

Percy Haviland was owed too many favors, had smiled and ratted his way into too many lives. He stood at the door of his little café, beckoning passers-by inside. And upstairs he had his brothel chambers, his poker tables, his hashish dens; if you knew what was good for you, you kept your mouth tight shut and let him get on with the show downstairs. Otherwise the boys would shut your mouth for you. Permanently.

The best thing, the *only* thing under the circumstances, Holly had decided, was to leave the café, walk out of the street without looking back, clear out of town. So here he was, watching the sun rise behind a two-horse hole in the ground called al-Jadida.

He crawled out of his sleeping-bag, rubbing his eyes, and clambered out of the hollow to the top of a low ridge. From a leather pouch by his side he took out a pair of Zeiss binoculars, an ancient pair he had inherited from his father. Lying flat, he trained the glasses on the road. The car was still there. He would give it another half hour, then make his way down to it. He hoped the boy had put enough petrol in the tank: he had paid him enough after all.

It was a long shot, the longest shot he had ever played. There was nothing moving on or near the highway. He scanned the area all round the village. All quiet. Snow had started falling. Magnified in the lenses of his binoculars, the heavy white flakes came swooping through the air like birds. He lowered the glasses and slipped them back in the pouch. Everywhere he looked, the sky was filling with snow clouds. The sand was already turning white. Every moment, the flakes grew heavier and faster. It was time for a cold breakfast.

PART X

"How many a city have We destroyed in its wickedness"

QUR'AN 22:45

66

Butrus swam up from a deep sleep, stifling a cry of terror. He woke to find his shoulder securely bandaged and the agony that had been so much part of it no more than a dull ache. There was such solitude in the absence of pain. Until this moment, he had never in his life been so completely with himself, with his own body and thoughts. The pain had been so absolute, so all-consuming that his mind had taken flight. He could remember almost nothing of the past twenty-four hours, or, if he did remember, it was as a series of bewilderments, a chaos of sounds and sights and sensations with no particular order, all heard and seen and felt through the distorting medium of pain.

He took a deep breath. Somewhere, nestling deep inside him, the pain still lurked. He knew that it was only held at bay by drugs, that at any moment it might return to devour him. But they had removed the bullet and reset his shoulder, and he was no longer afraid he was going to die. It was just a matter of time now, and he had plenty of that. More time than there was in the world.

There was no clock. It might have been morning or night, he had no way of knowing. But something made him think it was early afternoon. There had been sounds of a trolley making its rounds, of plates and cups being served and collected again.

Someone had told him he was in a church, but that didn't make sense. This was a hospital, there were doctors and nurses in white uniforms, he had seen no-one resembling a priest. No, that wasn't quite right: there had been a priest last night, someone the Englishman had called "Father," a Coptic priest, an old man.

He remembered something of the sewers, but in the fashion that nightmares are remembered, spasmodically, without sequence or logic: water, the play of torchlight on mildewed walls, a thin ledge that ran on and on into the stench and shadow. He knew suddenly what he had to do. With his right hand he pulled himself upright in bed.

There had been a child. A little girl. Something had attacked her and gone away again. He wondered what would become of her. And A'isha had been there, with the Englishman who was her lover. Yes, he thought. He knew exactly what he had to do.

Getting out of bed was not too hard. He still felt stiff and very weak, and he was groggy from whatever anesthetic they had used. But the pain had gone and his will-power had returned. He could make himself do it, he knew he could. They had put him in a little alcove with a striped curtain across the opening. His clothes were draped across a chair, still wet and stinking with raw sewage. He stripped off the nightgown they had given him. Shivering in the cold, he forced himself to pull his trousers on. It was all he could manage with one arm in a sling. The little metal cross around his neck felt hard against his skin. He remembered that it had reassured the nurses the night before. They would not be watching him too closely.

He managed to slip one arm into the sleeve of his overcoat, then, drawing it over his left shoulder, he buttoned it up most of the way. He removed the laces from his shoes: he could not tie them, and if they were left to dangle, he could trip. He was glad there was no mirror in the little room for him to examine himself in.

With infinite caution, he crossed to the curtain and peered through the narrow slit into the room beyond. It took only moments to make sense of his surroundings. If this was indeed a church, then he must be in the crypt. The stairway opposite must lead up to the main body of the building.

People were moving about, but unlike a regular hospital, there was little sense of urgency or bustle. There were no emergencies, no new admissions, no visitors. The day had its allotted tasks and, except when this patient or that required urgent assistance, most things could be done without undue haste. He knew right away that he would have to create a diversion.

He waited until it was quiet outside. A group of doctors and nurses stood around one of the beds, all their attention focused on the patient. But they were between him and the stairs. Softly, he slipped out of his cubicle and parted the curtain of the alcove next to it.

Perfect. Someone was fast asleep or unconscious in bed. Various items of medical machinery surrounded them. Butrus slipped through the curtain and let it fall behind him. He had not yet thought what he was going to do, but he knew something would occur to him.

It did. The patient, a woman in her fifties by the look of her, was attached to various drips and pipes. On a console next to the bed, little green screens monitored her heartbeat and other vital functions. A wire ran from the console to the outside. He guessed that it must lead to an alarm.

On top of a trolley at the back of the cubicle lay a metal dish containing a variety of surgical tools, including two scalpels. Butrus took one out and wiped it on his coat. It was a moment's work to cut two of the leads connecting the woman to the machinery. The console went berserk at once. Lights started flashing. A pulsing tracer that might have been her heartbeat went into spasm briefly before flattening out. Somewhere, an alarm started buzzing. Butrus did not stop to think. He slipped the scalpel into his coat pocket and stepped back to the curtain.

He slipped back into his own cubicle without anyone seeing him. They had been too busy attending to the alarm and deciding which patient had set it off. Moments later, footsteps came pounding into the alcove where he had just been. Voices shouted. There was the sound of a trolley being wheeled quickly across the floor.

He let it settle. When all had gone quiet again, he peeked out. The way was clear. All the medical personnel on duty had crowded into the emergency cubicle, leaving only patients on the floor of the ward. It was now or never. He slipped through the curtain and walked quickly down the long room, not daring to look back. His heart was thumping. It seemed to miss every other beat, he felt giddy, he was sure he would not make it after all. The stairs seemed so far away. His head had started spinning and he had only got a few yards. Every moment he expected to hear the sound of feet in pursuit. He had not forgotten the chase through the alleyways, the firing of guns through the darkness.

He reached the stairs without being challenged. Once past the opening, he felt safe. He stood stock still, catching his breath, letting the giddiness subside. It was a long time since he had eaten. He felt both sick and hungry. Time to go.

He climbed the stairs slowly. So far, luck had been on his side. If only he could make it as far as the street. He would like to have seen A'isha one last time, but when he thought it over, perhaps it was just as well not. It would only confuse him. He was sure what he had to do. He gritted his teeth and climbed a few more steps. What if the painkiller started to wear off before he reached his destination? Well, no doubt someone would see him straight.

At the top of the stairs was a wooden door. Even here, he could smell the church, the sanctity of it, the stench of incense and wax. He opened the door a crack and looked out. The nave was empty. To the right, the sanctuary was still. Above it, set in a low dome, the figure of Christ Pantokrator looked down, while all about him golden seraphim wheeled through a painted sky.

Butrus crept out into the body of the church. There were so many shadows here. He remembered his childhood, the eloquent mystery of the liturgy, recited in a language no-one but the priests understood. The candles and the shadows of their light, the dim halos that fell on the faces of the congregation, on his own face, on his own cheeks. Briefly, he felt a stab of shame at what he was about to do.

He was half-way to the door when a voice stopped him. He turned and saw someone coming to him quickly from the direction of the sanctuary. A youngish man dressed in a tee-shirt and jeans. He did not have the strength to run away.

The man came right up to him. He looked at him strangely, then let out a long breath, as though in relief.

"I'm sorry," he said, "I thought . . . You're the man Mr. Hunt brought here last night, aren't you? What on earth are you doing? Surely Dr. Rashid hasn't let you leave in this condition? And in those clothes."

"Who are you?"

"I'm sorry, you weren't fully conscious when they brought you here last night. I'm Father Yu'annis. This is my church. Look, I really don't understand what's going on. They said you'd need at least a couple of days' rest in bed."

"I have to go. There are things . . . I have things to do."

"That may be so, but you're ill. That shoulder won't heal properly. If you leave here, we can't let you come back. Do you understand? There won't be anywhere else for you to go. You won't find painkillers or bandages or antibiotics anywhere else."

"It doesn't matter. We're all going to die anyway."

"That isn't true." The priest reached out for Butrus, slipped an arm round his left shoulder, where the coat was lifted by thick bandages. Butrus tried to pull away, but Yu'annis held him as firmly as he dared.

Unnoticed, Butrus slipped his right hand into his coat pocket. He found the handle of the scalpel.

"Come back with me. Once you're feeling a bit better, you can do whatever it is you have to."

Butrus felt tears start down his cheeks.

"It's all right," whispered Father Yu'annis. "You've been under a terrible strain. We can talk later, for as long as you need."

"I'm sorry, Father. I'm very sorry. She should have loved me."

The priest looked into his eyes. He could feel the pain in them like a blow.

"Forgive me, Father."

The blade was very sharp. It was like stroking a cat, just a gentle movement of the hand across the throat, and the blade took care of the rest.

67

It was a day like any other in the City of the Dead. As always, the sun laid slanting patterns of light and shadow across the tombs. As always, Cairo proper was nothing more than a shimmering and a murmur of traffic carried on the thin afternoon air. The dead were as dead as they had ever been, the living had to get on with things. Nobody stayed here who did not have to stay: the dead because they were dead, the poor because they were poor. Nothing ever changed.

Tom Holly had been here too many times in the past to find it strange or forbidding any longer. He walked along a side-street just north of the Khandaq Marwan. A couple of yards away, two thin dogs fought one another for a scrap of meat. From the doorway of an Ottoman tomb, a child stared at him with wide, entrancing eyes. A woman's voice came from the next street, high-pitched, a little out of tune, singing a melancholy song about the end of love. The snow was falling heavily now, without respite.

To the south and east of Cairo, two great cemetery complexes spread out between the city and the Muqattam Hills. Between them, they covered some two miles. The Qarafa al-Kubra was the larger of the two, stretching from a

point just south of the Citadel as far as the city's outer extremities. It was a small town like any other, with streets,
houses, shops, cafés, water, and a little electricity. The only
difference was that the dwellings had not been built to house
the living, but to entomb the dead.

It was not an altogether gloomy place, Tom thought.
Women had hung their washing out to dry on lines strung
between one mausoleum and the next. The clothes were
stiff with frost and snow, like cardboard cutouts. Playing children filled the long, regular streets with shouts and laughter,
men sat in the cafés sipping coffee and smoking. But it was
hard to shake off the knowledge that, behind this wall or
that, underneath this floor, on the other side of that door,
lay heaps of moldering bones. At night, shadows filled the
streets. Shadows and the thoughts of shadows.

The building Tom sought was a small *qubba,* a domed
tomb housing the remains of Sidi Idris al-Fasi, a Moroccan
holy man who had founded an order of Sufi mystics in Cairo
late in the eighteenth century. His descendant, Shaykh
Ibrahim ibn Fadl Allah, was the present head of the Idrisiyya
order. The brotherhood's main center was in al-Jamaliyya,
but the shaykh chose to live here, in the tomb of his ances-
tor, side by side with the remains of his father, grandfather,
and more distant forebears. Every Thursday night, a car
used to come to take him into town, where he led his disci-
ples in the *hadra* according to the rites laid down by Sidi
Idris. Once a year, dervishes from all over Egypt had assembled in the Qarafa to celebrate their *mulid,* the anniversary
of their founder's birth. Now, the orders were banned, their
ceremonies outlawed, their rites proscribed. Under the new
regime, only the most strictly orthodox forms of Islam were
permitted.

Tom found Shaykh Ibrahim seated in a tiny, white-
washed room, cross-legged on a small mat, reading a manual of Sufi instruction. He stood at the door for a long time,
waiting for the shaykh to notice him.

Shaykh Ibrahim looked up. His eyes met Tom's. He closed the little book.

"I have been expecting you," he said.

"I'm sorry," Tom said. "I had no choice. I had to come."

"Sit down. I'll ask Fu'ad to bring some coffee." The shaykh called out. Moments later, a young boy entered. He was about fourteen, soulful, with a smooth, unblemished face like a girl's. The shaykh told him to prepare coffee. He bowed and left the room, smiling at Tom as he went.

Tom sat with his back against one wall, facing Shaykh Ibrahim. The *murshid* remained in silence, his eyes on his visitor's face. He wore the plain clothes of a dervish, a woolen robe, a turban, a long rosary around his neck, another in his hand, the fingers moving the beads slowly. On the wall behind him, a giant rosary, as big as a man, was hanging between two steel hooks. Beside it hung framed religious texts, verses from the Qur'an skillfully arranged in the form of lions, trees, and mosques. There were several shallow niches in which books had been placed. A cloying odor of incense filled the air. Tom felt hemmed in, suffocated. A paraffin heater in one corner had made the little chamber unbearably close. An oil lamp filled the room more with shadows than with light.

"I came alone," Tom said.

"But for God. 'He is closer to you than your life vein.' "

Tom nodded. He remembered many such meetings. Once he had come here seeking wisdom. Today, he had come in search of something quite different. It was time enough, he thought, to leave wisdom to the wise.

"With God, then."

"I pray you will go with God."

The door opened and the boy returned, carrying a tray with two glasses and a brass coffee jug. He was dressed simply in a striped cotton *jalabiyya,* but his hair had been well cut and oiled. When he smiled, Tom noticed that he had perfect teeth, like little white pearls. His eyes were like olives, their lashes long and silken. When he had poured the first cups, the boy bowed and left. Tom watched the door close, then turned to the shaykh.

"Have you found anything?" he asked.

The shaykh nodded.

"I'm sorry," said Tom. "I didn't want to bring you into this."

"Why do you think you had anything to do with it?"

"I asked you to help. To ask questions. To discover what you could."

The shaykh shook his head.

"I was his teacher once. Just as I was your teacher for a time. Partly, I am responsible for what he is. If I had been a better guide, he might not have chosen the path he is on."

"Al-Qurtubi would have become what he is in spite of anything anybody could have done. It was written."

Shaykh Ibrahim frowned. Without answering, he picked up a cup of cardamom-flavored coffee. *"Bismi 'llah,"* he murmured before taking the first sip.

The shaykh scrutinized his guest, as though weighing him in invisible scales.

"What do you see?" he asked.

"I see you. I see this room."

The shaykh shook his head.

"That is incorrect," he said. "You see neither. You think you see them, but what you see is merely an illusion. Ibn al-'Arabi says: *'fa 'l-'alam mutawahham, ma lahu wujud haqiqi.* The world is nothing but illusion. It has no real existence. This is the meaning of "imagination." It merely seems to you that the world is separate from God, but in reality it is not so . . . You yourself are nothing but imagination. And all you perceive is imagination. All things are merely imagination within imagination.' "

Tom's theology was not up to this.

"Doesn't Ibn al-'Arabi also say that the world is God manifested? That it has its reality from His reality?"

"There is a Tradition," said the shaykh. " 'All men are

sleeping. Only when they die will they awaken.' '' He looked round at the shadowed room. "You said you could see this room? What would you see if you could look beyond it, beyond these walls?''

"The bones of your ancestors."

The shaykh smiled, as though at a private joke.

"That is also incorrect," he said. "What you see is a *silsila,* a chain of initiation that connects me to the Prophet. And the Prophet to the Holy Spirit. And the Holy Spirit to God. Now, what if I told you that, in spite of that, in spite of the power God has given me, I am still afraid of that man?''

"I would say I was surprised."

The shaykh frowned and put down his little cup. Gently, ever so gently on the rough stone floor.

"You would be surprised because you are sleeping, because everything you see and hear and feel is a dream. That is the purpose of our Path, to awaken men before they die. In spite of that, I am afraid." He paused. "You know what he is. Who he is."

Tom watched the shaykh's fingers turn the little beads, heard each in turn click against its neighbor.

Tom shook his head. It was hard to make sense. The warmth and the shadows and the smells of paraffin mixed with incense were fuddling his brain.

"What have you found for me?" he asked at last.

The shaykh sighed.

"He plans to start the terror campaign in Europe tomorrow. What happened before this was just preparation. Something to show people what he is capable of. His people are all in place. They have all the bombs and guns they need."

"Do you know the identity of any of the targets?"

Shaykh Ibrahim shook his head.

"Only that they include churches and synagogues."

Tom looked desperate.

"I need more information. We have to stop him."

The shaykh nodded.

"I agree. But my contact is already taking terrible risks."

"I know that. But hundreds of lives are at stake. We need to know more."

The shaykh hesitated. It was not that he was afraid to reveal what he knew. But he had spent his life pondering the consequences of knowledge and action.

"If I tell you what I know, it will commit you to a course of action you would rather have avoided."

"I can't help that. Things have gone too far."

"Yes," whispered the shaykh. "Much too far." He looked sadly at his old friend. "Very well. What do you know of the plan to hold an ecumenical conference in Jerusalem at the beginning of the year?"

Tom shrugged.

"What anybody knows. The Pope will be there. Other religious leaders."

"Quite correct. The heads of the Greek Orthodox and Coptic Churches. Syrian and Armenian Christian bishops. Muslims. Jews. Druze. There will be a conference, the delegates will make charming speeches about brotherhood and harmony, they will read passages from their respective holy books and recite prayers for universal peace. And when it is all over, they will go back to their churches and mosques and synagogues as if nothing had happened. It is entirely predictable."

He saw Tom raise his eyebrows.

"You think me cynical? Perhaps I am. But you will also see that I am right. True religious unity has never been in the interests of theologians or prelates, however much they may like to fool themselves. However, the conference is beside the point. It's nothing but a front. The Pope knows perfectly well that such gatherings are a waste of time; but he still has faith in the possibilities of political dialogue."

The shaykh halted. He was coming to the point now. In a moment, there would be no going back.

"After the interfaith conference, there is to be another

meeting. Not by any means so public. It's to be held in private, there will be no press, no television cameras, no hangers-on. The Pope has personally invited a selected group of politicians to take part. Goldberg, the Israeli president, will be there in person, along with his minister for home affairs."

"Rabinovitch? The hardliner?"

Shaykh Ibrahim nodded.

"He's one of the reasons for the secrecy. This will be the first time he's sat at a table with anyone from the other side. The new PLO chairman, Butrus al-Hammadi, will be there. Sayyid Husayn Adelshahi, the Iranian foreign minister. The Syrian ambassador to the UN. Robbins from the United States. A couple of others."

Tom whistled.

"You're sure this isn't just something your source dreamed up?"

The shaykh shook his head.

"I've known of it for some time. It's the result of diplomatic initiatives that started after the Middle East peace talks finally broke down in 1994. But I have only now discovered what al-Qurtubi is planning."

"Al-Qurtubi?"

Tom felt himself go cold.

"He intends to kidnap the Pope. I don't know how or where, nor exactly when. But he means to ensure that the Pope never gets to Jerusalem. Without him, the peace negotiations will founder. And in their place, al-Qurtubi's European terrorist campaign will begin."

He paused. The walls seemed to have narrowed around them.

"That's all I know," he said. "Except for one thing."

Reaching inside his robes, he drew out a folded sheet of paper and passed it to Tom. The Englishman unfolded it and read it through slowly. It was a list of names. The names of the men who had attended the meeting at Sir Lionel Bailey's home. And the names of others who had stayed in

Europe that day. Men who had attended briefings in Alexandria. When Tom looked up at last, it was with astonishment in his face.

"How on earth did you get this?" he asked. He had recognized over half the names, knew at once the value of the document he held. The value and the danger.

"Your friend Mr. Hunt asked a lot of questions in Alexandria. He stirred things up a little. This list had been obtained by al-Qurtubi and kept as a kind of insurance, in case he ever needed to get any of his own people out of prison in Europe. He wanted to keep it safe, out of Hunt's hands. My contact got to hear of it. He found it and took it. You may be able to use it as evidence."

"Yes," said Tom. He understood why. He had recognized the handwriting: it belonged to Percy Haviland. "If I can get it back to England."

"Will it make a difference if you do?"

"A difference?"

"To the world. To man's suffering."

"Yes," said Tom. "I think so. It may save lives."

"Then, like me, you think nothing is written?"

"Nothing we can't erase."

"I hope so," whispered the shaykh. "I hope you are right."

Outside, in the hush of falling snow, in the gray, driven blizzard, the sound of a *mu'adhdhin*'s voice sang out like glass ringing among the tombs.

68

"Good to see you, Percy."

"Thank you, Prime Minister. Good to see you looking so well."

"Please, take a seat."

The politeness of princes, the soft thrill of being in their presence. Both overrated. Percy Haviland glanced at the Prime Minister and decided, not for the first time, that the man was not in the prince league. Not even minor aristocrat or jumped-up mandarin class. Just a horrible little prick who had worked his way up assiduously to where he was now, mainly by the licking of that part of the collective anatomy other tongues would not have dreamt of reaching.

The little prick had some money and a gaggle of pushy friends and a certain hectoring manner that went down well on the back benches when the county set were in town and howling for blood. He ran a circus, not a parliament. How Haviland despised him: his ill-cut mustache, his hard-earned lower second, his not-quite-plebeian, not-quite-pukka parentage, his evangelical-wing-of-the-Church-of-England niceness, his liking for Puccini, his taste for milk chocolate, his gangling innocence, his little sulks, his pats on the back. "Thank you, Percy. Well done, Percy. Good show, Percy."

"Thank you, PM," Percy grimaced, seating himself with the languid grace he had so often been assured he possessed. They were in the PM's private office, out of the reach of secretaries, under-secretaries, and odious little men bearing cups of well-brewed tea. Recently, they had started offering people coffee in the afternoons; Percy wondered where it would end.

"Did you get that chocolate I sent you, PM?"

"Chocolate? Oh, that. Yes, indeed. Got it last week. Thanks very much. What a lovely bow it had. Super."

"The thing is, did you enjoy it? I can have some more sent around. You just have to say the word. Our man in Brussels goes to the shop regularly. Sends me some every week."

"Ah, well, to be perfectly honest, Percy, I found it a trifle bitter for my taste. A bit French, if you know what I mean."

"It was Belgian, Prime Minister."

"Yes, of course. You did mention Brussels. Same thing, Percy; same thing. It may be plebeian of me, but I do prefer the real thing. Milk Tray, Galaxy, that sort of thing. More to my palate. Each to his own, eh, Percy."

"Yes, Prime Minister. Quite. Each to his own."

There was a knock on the door. A man in pinstriped trousers entered obsequiously.

"Pardon me, sir. Would Mr. Haviland like tea or coffee this morning?"

"Prime Minister, I thought we weren't going to be disturbed."

"Quite right, Percy, quite right. Hawkins, could you pop in a little later? I'm sure Mr. Haviland would like a drop of coffee after our little chat." He looked meaningfully at the clock. "If there's time."

"Very good, sir." Hawkins departed, not without a resentful glance in Haviland's direction.

"Now, Percy, you'd better fill me in on things."

"Of course, Prime Minister. That's what I'm here for."

He lifted his briefcase, a rather smart Bruno Magli item his wife had bought for him three Christmases ago, and took out a handful of papers. Most of them were marked Top Secret, but Haviland could happily have left them all on top of a Number 45 bus and gone home whistling. He had put the stamps on himself before coming out, just to impress little Johnny here. Damned if he was going to bring any genuinely confidential material to Number 10.

"I understand from the FO that there have been a few changes since we last spoke."

"That's right, Prime Minister. You'll be aware of course that a new man has taken power in Egypt."

"Yes, news reached me last night. Know anything about him?"

Haviland shook his head.

"Very little as yet, sir. Bit of a dark horse. Came out of the woodwork, or whatever it is they've got out there. But, then, it is all a bit of a mess there at the moment. This plague business seems to have got out of hand."

"Yes. A terrible thing. Is there any chance this new man will make some concessions, let the World Health people into the country? MPs are already getting sackfuls of letters asking why the government isn't doing anything."

Haviland shrugged.

"As I said, sir, this Qurtubi's a dark horse. From the sound of it, he's a hardliner. Which could mean that things will get worse before they get better. On the other hand, I have already had an indication that he may want to deal with the West."

"Really? Is that so?" The PM's brows shot up. He seemed almost animated.

Haviland brought a folded paper from his inside jacket pocket. He had arranged for its despatch the night before, after speaking with Sir Lionel.

"This came through earlier this morning, sir. Via a European terrorist connection. Best if I don't say anything more specific in your presence, sir. Prudence, you know."

"What is it?"

"Well, it seems that it's by way of being a consultation document, sir." Haviland passed it across the broad desk.

The Prime Minister glanced through it quickly, then looked up at Haviland.

"Percy, what do you make of this?"

"Well, some of it's quite clear, sir. He wants to take as many European Muslims off our hands as we'll give him. That bit's quite straightforward."

"In return for rather a lot of money, Percy."

"Yes, it isn't quite an altruistic gesture, I will admit. However, he will need that kind of funding in order to house them, set up jobs, schools, hospitals, and so on."

"We don't have that sort of money, Percy. The Treasury wouldn't give this a second glance."

"Well, sir, I rather think we may have some of it."

"Really? Where on earth from?"

"Well, if you think back to—when was it?—back to 1991, when we shut down that Arab bank, BCCI, you may remember that some of our banking fraternity got a good deal out of it. There was a lot of loose money knocking about; loose credit, loose influence. I think there could be a lot available for this sort of scheme, sir. If we tied it in to broader trade agreements. Not just with the Egyptians, but with other Arab countries. They're bound to go for it. It would take some of the burden off their shoulders."

"Burden?"

"Naturally, he's bound to go to them in the end. The oil states anyway."

"I'm not sure you should be telling me this, Percy."

"Quite right, Prime Minister, I shouldn't. But I know I can rely on you. Implicitly. A fellow-chocolate-lover."

Haviland smiled at his own joke.

The PM tweaked at his mustache. Sometimes Haviland thought it was a fake, a stage prop glued on every morning. Something in him longed to reach out and rip it off. Or cause, at the very least, pain to that weak upper lip, that upper lip whose ineffectuality it was the purpose of the little tuft to conceal.

"Do we want to get rid of our Muslims, though, Percy? That's the thing. I know some of them can be an infernal nuisance, with their *fatwas* and whatnot; but most of them are very solid British citizens. I'm not sure we could legislate to have them forcibly removed. A lot of people wouldn't like that."

"Fewer than you imagine, sir. Ask your policy people. Public opinion has been swinging against immigrants for some time now. The right sort of legislation could win a lot of votes. Strict but laced with compassion. It would be just like the Jews going to Israel. Starting a new life. Making the desert bloom. People would applaud you."

"But why should he want to do this, Percy? There must be more to it than the money."

"I really don't know, sir. But I'd advise you to look it over carefully. If nothing else, it's a starting point. I've no doubt there are similar documents being studied in all the European capitals this very moment."

"No doubt you're right, Percy, but all the same . . ."

"He wants me to go out there to start negotiations."

The PM's eyes opened wide.

"What? You can't be serious. Does he know who you are?"

"I don't imagine he knows my real function. But he seems to have met me somewhere, on one of my diplomatic postings. Thinks he can trust me."

"Do you think it's wise, Percy? Under present conditions."

"I think I can do some good, sir. We still have people out there we'd like to see released. I've been promised diplomatic immunity."

"Well, all the same, it does sound chancy. When are you supposed to go?"

"Today, sir. I've already got a flight arranged."

"I can order you not to go, you know."

"I'd rather you didn't, sir. To be honest, I think I may be able to achieve something. Get some of those concessions you were talking about."

"Even though he's a hardliner?"

"That's just it, sir. I may be able to use that fact in our favor. Make him offers that suit his policy. Turn a blind eye to the more Islamic side of things."

"Well, in that case . . . Be careful, Percy. Insist on having the embassy reopened."

"I've already done that. It seemed the right thing to do whatever happened."

"Very good. Well, that's settled."

The Prime Minister nodded and slipped the paper into a drawer. He sat for a few moments, contemplating his Head of Intelligence, rather like a diver preparing to plunge into icy water. Reaching for a file in the tray to his left, he drew out a slim document and slid it across the desk to Haviland.

"Have you seen this yet, Percy?"

Haviland glanced at it. It was a report from the Joint School of Photographic Interpretation at RAF Wyton. It did not look familiar. On top, it bore yesterday's date and a red stamp declaring it Top Secret. Haviland shook his head.

"I don't believe so, sir."

"I didn't think so. Acheson's been a bit cagey about this. Kept it to his own boys until yesterday, then sent it straight to me. As if I'd know what to do with it."

"I don't understand, sir. What is it?"

The Prime Minister took a wad of photographs from the file and pushed them at Haviland. The DG began to leaf through them one by one. The Prime Minister continued speaking while he scanned them.

"They were taken by the Israeli Mogen satellite and passed to Acheson's lot for help in identification. You'll see that the first ones are dated June second. Almost seven months ago."

"Yes, sir. I know."

"Five months before the Egyptian revolution. Now, if you look closely, you'll see that they show a site roughly seven hundred feet square. It's located about fifty miles west of the Dakhla oasis, not far from the great Sand Sea. Close to the Libyan border."

"I know where the great Sand Sea is, sir."

"Really? Had to look it up in an atlas myself."

Percy Haviland said nothing. But he was listening attentively. There had been rumors, but surely . . .

"I don't expect you to make any more sense of the pictures than I did, Percy. But the report doesn't leave much doubt. The earliest shots show nothing but a camp. That's what attracted MOSSAD's attention in the first place. There isn't really any reason for a military installation out that far. The nearest place of any importance on the Libyan side is Khufra. It hardly seemed worth anybody's effort."

He paused. Haviland noted inwardly—and not for the first time—that the PM could be disgustingly well briefed.

"Then some sort of excavations were started. It looked like an archaeological dig, but on a very grand scale. Equipment was flown in by helicopter. The Israelis made discreet enquiries at archaeology departments around the world. No digs were scheduled for that area or anywhere remotely near it. So our friends kept on taking snapshots every time the Mogen passed over. The pace of work actually increased after the revolution. You can see the results for yourself."

Percy looked more carefully at the photographs. They showed something emerging slowly from the sand. Something very large, yet unclear, hazy, like a black square set against the desert sand.

"This was taken two days ago," the Prime Minister said. "The Israelis sent in a fighter equipped with cameras. What they got was perfectly clear. The thing is, Percy— what the hell does it mean?"

Percy looked down. The photograph was in color, and what it showed was unmistakable: a pyramid of black, polished stone, as wide and as high as the tallest of the three main pyramids that had stood at Giza.

When Haviland had gone, the Prime Minister sat immobile for a moment. Then he lifted one of the phones on his desk.

"Hawkins, will you come in, please?"

Moments later, the PM's private secretary appeared in the doorway.

"Hawkins, will you please see to it that I am not disturbed for the next half hour? You're not to allow anyone in, not even the Queen."

"Very good, sir."

No sooner had the man closed the heavy oak door behind him than the Prime Minister lifted a second telephone and tapped a short number.

"Simpson, is that tail on Percy Haviland still in place? Good. See it stays there. And while we're speaking, could you ask one of your boys to get me a direct line to that number in Cairo I used last week?"

69

A'isha woke out of the deepest sleep she had ever known. There had been dreams, dreadful dreams. She could remember little of them now, but the traces they left in her thoughts were harrowing and ugly.

She dressed and parted the curtain of the cubicle in which she had been sleeping. The little hospital was quiet. She had a faint memory of some disturbance an hour or two earlier, but there was no sign now of anything untoward.

On her left was the cubicle into which she had seen Fadwa wheeled the night before. Surely no-one would mind if she looked in on the child. She parted the curtain and glanced inside.

A low light burned by the bed. Under it, a nurse in a white uniform sat reading. She looked up as the curtain rattled, and smiled when she saw A'isha.

"May I come in?" A'isha asked in a whisper.

"Of course." The nurse put down her book. "You needn't whisper—she can't hear you. She won't be coming around for a little while yet."

A'isha stepped inside and drew the curtain behind her. The little room was crammed with bits and pieces of equipment. There seemed to be pipes and wires and leads everywhere. From a metal pole, a drip ran down to Fadwa's arm.

The little girl lay beneath stark white sheets, her head cradled on high, starched pillows. Her face was shockingly pale. Her eyes were closed. All around them, the skin was dark blue, as though from bruising. Her breathing was shallow and uneven. On a tiny green screen, a moving blip registered the fragile murmur of her heartbeat.

"How is she?" A'isha asked. She felt bad, having spent so long asleep, leaving Fadwa on her own. She had promised not to leave her alone again.

The nurse shook her head.

"Not good," she said. "She lost a lot of blood and there were internal injuries. With proper facilities . . ." She shrugged. "But I think she may pull through. There's reason to be hopeful. It will take time. Is she strong? In herself, I mean."

"I don't know," said A'isha. "But I think so."

The nurse looked surprised.

"I thought she was your daughter."

A'isha shook her head.

"No. She has no parents. I don't think she has anyone." She explained as best she could.

The nurse looked around at the sleeping child. A'isha saw that her hand was clenched tightly. She was in her early twenties, still vulnerable, still naive enough to care.

"Poor thing," she whispered.

"What about my friend Butrus?" A'isha asked.

"I'm not sure. I've been here most of the day. You'd better ask Dr. Fishawi, I think he was in charge of his case." She glanced at her watch. "He should be on duty now. You'll find him in the staff room at the rear of the ward."

"Thank you."

A'isha stepped to the side of the bed. She bent down and kissed Fadwa softly on the forehead. The child stirred at the touch. Her lips parted as though to speak, then closed again. A'isha looked thoughtfully at her. If only they could get out of here, take Fadwa and themselves somewhere sane. She sighed. Before this, she had never wanted a child; now it looked as though she had acquired one.

She moved quietly away from the bed, thanked the nurse, and stepped into the ward. Michael was waiting for her.

"The nurse thinks Fadwa may pull through," she said. "If she's strong enough. Do you think . . ." She hesitated. "If we get out of this, Michael, I'd like . . . I think I'd like to adopt her. Only . . ."

"Only you can't do it on your own."

"Not in Egypt, no. But we've got to get out of Egypt anyway. In England . . ."

"It's not easy to get in there now," he reminded her. "For refugees. They've pulled up the portcullis."

"Michael, I . . ."

"You want me to marry you?" He sighed. "You know about Carol, about . . ."

"You only have one life, Michael. I only have one. Fadwa only has one." She stopped. "I'm sorry, this is no time . . ."

He took her hand.

"No," he whispered. "You're quite right. If we don't talk about this now, we'll never do it. Carol seems quite far away now. Maybe she never existed. She wants a divorce, so why should I stand in her way?"

"We don't have to get married, Michael. Just . . . I just want to be with you when all this is over."

"And Fadwa?"

She nodded.

He kissed her gently, knowing it was madness, knowing that hopes meant nothing here.

"It's snowing outside," he said. "Very heavily."

"Have you been out?"

"Only briefly. I went to look for Butrus."

"Butrus?"

"He's gone. Earlier this morning." Michael paused.

"The staff think he may have killed one of the other patients in order to escape."

"But . . . he wasn't a prisoner."

"No, but he knew they would have tried to stop him leaving. Because he's ill. And because they can't risk anyone leading the authorities here, however inadvertently. I said I'd do my best to find him, if only to be sure he's all right. Do you have any idea where he might have gone?"

She shook her head.

"He'd run out of places to hide. We both had. But he was worried about his parents. He may have gone there to see if they've returned."

She told him the address.

"It's a long shot," he said, "but I'll try. After that, I'll have to go to the Sukaria to meet Tom. If he's there. Will you wait for me here?"

"Where else?"

She smiled and kissed him lightly on the lips.

"I'll be back," he said. "You can count on it."

70

A'isha went back to bed. She needed a little more sleep, more time to herself, some distance from the rapidity of events. The dreams returned, more insistent than before. She woke suddenly, startled, to see the figure of a man standing over her.

"It's all right, Mrs. Manfaluti. Nothing's wrong. But Dr. Fishawi has just finished his operations and says he'd like a word with you. Just a few minutes. He's in the staff room. I'll show you the way."

Dr. Fishawi looked up anxiously as A'isha came in.

"Mrs. Manfaluti. How are you feeling now?"

"Much better, thank you. I just needed to sleep. I've been visiting Fadwa. She seems peaceful."

"Excellent. We have hopes that she will recover. Mrs. Manfaluti, I've been meaning to speak with you. Perhaps Mr. Hunt has already told you. It's about your friend Butrus. He's disappeared. We think he may have engineered an alarm by attacking and killing one of our patients, so he could slip out when no-one was looking. His trousers and overcoat are missing."

"I still don't understand why Butrus would do something so foolish. He wasn't in any fit state to leave."

"But the fact remains that he has gone. It's snowing heavily outside, he may not get very far. What's possibly more disturbing is that no-one can find Father Yu'annis anywhere."

"Father Yu'annis? Oh, yes—the priest who was here last night. Perhaps they went somewhere together."

"We're working on that assumption. All the same, it's not in Yu'annis's character to leave the church without telling anyone. The guard on the door didn't see either of them leave."

The doctor paused, as though about to tell a patient unpleasant news.

"Mrs. Manfaluti," he continued, "I have to know what's going on. Yuannis told me a little, but that's not enough. I can't allow you or your friends to put the security of this hospital at risk. There are lives at stake. Including your own and that of the little girl you brought here. If you can tell me anything that may help, please don't hold back."

She shook her head.

"Doctor, I'm as much in the dark as you are. Butrus is a Copt. He and I have been hiding from the authorities for a few weeks now. He certainly has no reason to tell them about this place. I don't think you've any need to worry on that score."

"No doubt you're right. But he must be in great pain by now. He'll have expected as much when he left. I can only assume he had a very strong reason for leaving."

"Could he be delirious? Is that possible?"

Fishawi shook his head. A'isha noticed how tired he seemed. His face seemed young, but his hair was streaked with gray.

"Could somebody here have spoken to him?" she asked. "About a friend or relative perhaps. There may have been someone who knew either him or his family. I know there are people he's worried about. His parents were taken by the *muhtasibin*. He's desperate to find them."

Fishawi shook his head.

"I doubt it. He'll have been under fairly heavy sedation and probably didn't come around till a little before the time he disappeared. Nobody will have had a chance to speak with him. Whatever made him desperate to leave was something he brought here with him."

At that moment, the door of the staff room opened and another doctor entered. He was a young man with a thick mustache. He looked panic-stricken.

"Dr. Fishawi, you'll have to come. It's . . ."

He glanced at A'isha, registering her presence for the first time.

"I'm sorry, miss, I didn't see you there." Turning back to Fishawi, he hurried on. "Nagib wants you upstairs right away. They've found Yu'annis."

His throat had been cut cleanly from side to side and the body thrust into the large font in the baptistry. Someone had noticed the pool of water that had spilled over onto the floor and gone to investigate. The priest had been lifted out and laid carefully on the flags of the north aisle. Someone had already turned on several lights around him.

"I can't believe Butrus was responsible for this," said A'isha. "He's a gentle man."

"There can't be any other explanation." Fishawi covered the body with his white coat. "No-one else can have got in. Just one entrance is in use. The only other door that's open now was locked on the inside when the guard checked it this morning. We think that's how Butrus got out."

"But he . . ."

Somewhere, faint as rain, came a sound of breaking glass. A'isha stopped speaking and looked around. It had seemed as though it came from the street.

"Mrs. Manfaluti," Fishawi went on, "your friend was brought here last night with a bullet-wound. Father Yu'annis told me a little of what your friend Mr. Hunt said to him last night. You are not involved in harmless activities. If you know anything about this, then for God's sake tell me."

Another sound outside. Someone had switched off an engine. There was something about the silence that followed, something that tugged at A'isha's memory.

A small crowd had begun to gather. Two nurses, another doctor, all horror-struck. The wound in Father Yu'annis's throat gaped desperately, like a fish's mouth. The water had washed it clean of blood. Someone brought a sheet and covered him.

The door opened. The young man who had been on guard duty stood framed in the opening, his gun cradled in his hands.

"The street's gone very quiet," he said. "I don't like it. I think something's up."

All at once A'isha remembered. There had been a deep silence all around the bookshop before the raid. The same sort of silence as this, strained, punctured by tiny sounds. She took a step towards the guard.

"Don't waste any time," she began. "There may be . . ."

The man's chest opened in front of her eyes. A gaping hole appeared in its center as though someone had punched a fist through him. His eyes froze in an expression of mild surprise. There had not been time for more. His legs scissored and gave way. He fell like an ox in a slaughter-house.

No-one had time to move. A *muhtasib* appeared in the doorway and stepped lightly over the body. His feet slithered on the widening pool of blood all round it. He carried a large pistol. After him came a second man with a sub-machine gun. Behind them, all awry, snow was driving across the street, a vast, moving whiteness that had no form and no dimension.

71

Time stood still as the little group round Father Yu'annis straightened or turned towards the door. A'isha felt the breath leave her body. It was an effort to bring it back again, an effort to keep from throwing up. She looked at Fishawi, then back at the doorway. All about her the church shook. There were sounds of heavy vehicles and running feet. She could hear someone beside her reciting a prayer. One of the nurses was sobbing.

The doorway was empty. On either side of it, the two *muhtasibin* stood guard, apparently oblivious of the blood trickling by their feet. An age seemed to pass. And then a figure appeared. He was tall and handsome and dressed perfectly, like a prophet, and she knew instantly who he was. The blond beard, the blue eyes, the arrogant, unsmiling lips.

There was nothing in his face. Just a terrible blankness, the whiteness of faith that has bypassed emotion or murdered it. He could kill for his God as easily as weep. His hands were soft, the fingers manicured; he was neat and clean, strict in his ablutions, lesser and greater, he was observant in everything but compassion. The heaven for which he strove was a white place, white like the storm outside, a place quite dreadful to all but the exact, full of open spaces where God's face stared unblinking at eternity.

For a very long time he stood in the opening, not hesitating, but bringing his presence to bear on them like a judgment. A'isha felt unclean, she felt a ball of guilt clotted inside her, age-old guilt that he had come to burn in his fire. Her eyes were locked on his eyes, she could feel his gaze scouring her like a wind as he looked from one to the other.

The Dutchman snapped an order at one of the two *muhtasibin*. The man saluted and stepped outside. A moment later, Butrus came to the doorway. He looked wretched, aching, but not in pain. There had been morphine for his pain. He was not a prisoner, at least not their prisoner. He had gone to the Dutchman of his own free will, had thrown himself on his mercy—if that is what it was— had been received with open arms. If all went well, his mother and father would be free tonight. And the Englishman would be dead. Even now he was unsure which had been more important to him, freeing his parents or securing Hunt's death.

Butrus pointed at A'isha. The Dutchman nodded and took two steps into the church. His eyes were on her now. Butrus trailed behind him like a pet dog. They had given him fresh clothes, he no longer stank or shivered. He could hear his mother's voice whispering to him, teaching him his prayers. Once, he tried to look at A'isha, but he found he could not. He would have betrayed God Himself for her.

"Round these people up," ordered the Dutchman. "Take them downstairs."

More *muhtasibin* appeared now, all heavily armed. They swarmed through the church, taking hold of anyone they could find.

Dr. Fishawi stepped forward. A'isha could see that he was trembling with indignation.

"You have no right to do this," he protested. "This is a Christian church. A sanctuary. These people are *ahl al-*

dhimma, they are guaranteed the protection of the Muslim state."

The Dutchman said nothing. Fishawi pressed closer.

"Didn't you hear me?" he insisted. "The law is clear about the treatment of Christians and Christian churches. The Caliph 'Umar would not pray in the Church of the Holy Sepulchre for fear it be turned into a mosque."

"This is not a church," said the Dutchman. "You have transformed it illegally into a hospital, you and your People of the Book. You will have to bear the consequences." He held out his hand.

"Hospitals are sacred places too," the doctor protested. "There are sick people here. Dying people."

"Dead people," whispered the Dutchman. A *muhtasib* approached him and placed a pistol in his hand. He raised it, aimed at Fishawi, and shot him in the face.

One of the nurses screamed. The other fainted away. The Dutchman handed the pistol back to the *muhtasib* and nodded. The *muhtasib* stepped up to the two women and shot them at point-blank range. They died instantly. Butrus turned away and threw up in a corner.

"You," said the Dutchman to A'isha, "stay with me. Stay very close."

Butrus, wiping vomit from his mouth, came to A'isha's side, but she ignored him.

The *muhtasibin* had found the entrance to the stairs and were pouring down them into the hospital. When the last one had disappeared into the opening, the Dutchman took A'isha's arm and pulled her with him to the stairway.

"This way," he said.

The crypt was filled with *muhtasibin.* Most of the staff had already been lined up against one wall. Others were being hauled roughly out of their beds in the cubicles.

The Dutchman beckoned to the *muhtasib* who seemed to be in charge of the exercise.

"The others as well," he said, indicating the patients.

"No exceptions. Then bring petrol. Burn everything. The entire building."

"Some of them are too ill to stand," the man pointed out.

"I said 'No exceptions.' "

The man swallowed hard, turned, and ordered his men to start clearing the beds.

"There's a child," began A'isha. "A little girl. She's done nothing wrong. Please don't harm her."

"You heard what I just told my lieutenant."

"Yes, but that's impossible. Sick people . . . A little girl . . ."

He turned and stared at her. His eyes were hard and unyielding, like stone.

"Which is worse?" he asked. "Physical sickness or spiritual? These people have been infected. If they are allowed to roam free, they will infect others in their turn."

"You know nothing about them. They're just sick people. It's not their fault they're here."

"Fault? Who's talking about fault? The angels won't ask about your faults when they interrogate you in the grave. They'll ask 'did you obey the law? Did you pray when it was time to pray? Did you fast? Did you perform the pilgrimage?' Fault is a Western concept. What arrogance."

A'isha watched as the *muhtasibin* started hauling patients from their beds. Most were too ill to stand. They were dragged bodily across the floor and heaped against the wall. Father Gregory was brought out and lined up with the staff. A'isha looked around as one man came out of a cubicle carrying Fadwa. She was wide awake and crying with fear. A'isha made to run to her, but the Dutchman grabbed her arm, holding her fast.

"For God's sake," she cried. "She isn't a murderer or an adulterer. She's barely nine years old. The religious law doesn't even apply to her yet. She can't be held responsible for her actions."

"Come with me," said the Dutchman. Keeping a firm

grip on her arm, he brought her across the ward to a tall cupboard.

"Open it," he said.

It was packed with medical supplies: dressings, syringes, drugs. The Dutchman scanned the shelves and finally lifted down a bottle of surgical spirit. From another shelf he took a flask of purified water. He found a measuring glass and poured in water almost to the top.

"This is pure water," he said. "Quite untainted. Quite unlike the water everyone else has to drink in this city." He unscrewed the bottle of spirit and carefully tipped a single drop into the glass of water.

"Sip it," he said.

A'isha did not move.

"I said drink."

She lifted the glass and took a tiny sip.

"Did you taste anything?" he asked.

"No, of course not. Only water." Her heart was beating quickly. She could think of nothing but Fadwa. What was this madman up to?

He poured a second drop into the glass.

"Again."

She took another sip.

"Still no taste?"

She shook her head.

"The water is lawful," he said. "The spirit is alcohol and unlawful. Of course, no-one would drink it in this form, I understand that. This is merely a demonstration. Now, a single drop of alcohol did not render the water illegal. It would not intoxicate, which is considered the reason for the prohibition. Two drops in the glass will not intoxicate. So why not four? Why not eight? Why not one hundred drops? I am sure a hundred drops will not intoxicate. When, precisely, do you stop? When, precisely, does the water become an unlawful substance? Once you have begun to compromise, it is always easy to add another drop. And another. Until the alcohol predominates. If I touch you, it is wrong, but it is not unlawful. If I kiss you, it is reprehensible, but it is not adultery. Where would we stop? Why should we stop?"

He fell silent. One hand reached out and stroked her cheek. It was monstrous to be touched by him. She recoiled, but he turned his hand and ran its back along her skin. The Dutchman did not smile.

"Tell me something," he said, "and I may let you go. Where can I find Tom Holly? Is he here? Has he made contact with your friend Michael Hunt yet?"

A'isha said nothing.

"You understand that I will find him anyway. He was seen this morning on his way to Cairo. It would make things easier for you if you told me when and where they are to meet."

Still she did not reply.

"Very well. Perhaps I can provide more direct encouragement."

He turned his back on her and stalked across the room to where the staff and patients were lined against the wall.

"That one," he said, pointing to Fadwa. A *muhtasib* brought her forward. She was bleeding again. Her eyes were tightly closed in pain.

The Dutchman laid one hand against Fadwa's neck.

"She would be the first drop," he said, turning to A'isha. Butrus held her now.

The Dutchman's hand was massive. It encircled the child's frail neck easily. There was a murmur in the crowd. An old man pushed his way past the *muhtasibin* and crossed the floor to where the Dutchman was standing. It was Father Gregory.

"Leave the child alone," he said. "You can have me in her place."

The Dutchman relaxed his grip on the child's neck. He looked at the priest for a long time, as though weighing him against the little girl.

"I know you," he said finally. "Your name is Gregory."

He pushed Fadwa away from him, into the hands of a *muhtasib,* and stepped up to the priest.

"Are you so eager to be with your God?"

Gregory said nothing.

"Your life for hers. Is that what you want?"

The old man nodded.

"Very well."

The Dutchman held out his hand again for the pistol. The *muhtasib* handed it to him and he ordered Gregory to kneel. The old man did so with all the dignity he could muster, in spite of the pain in his back and legs. What did pain matter now? The Dutchman pressed the barrel against the priest's forehead. As he did so, Gregory lifted his head and looked directly into his eyes. He whispered something very softly, so softly that only the Dutchman heard him. A'isha saw the blood drain from the Dutchman's cheeks, saw a terrible rage flicker across his face, saw him pull the trigger, throwing the old man backwards like a discarded rag doll, his white hair suddenly spattered with blood.

The Dutchman seemed to make an extraordinary effort to regain control of himself. His hand was shaking, his cheeks and lips were white, his eyes were unfocused. He stood over the priest's body in the long hush that followed the gunshot, as though expecting the old man to move. But Father Gregory lay perfectly still while a ring of blood formed around his head.

Abruptly, the Dutchman swiveled, reaching out for Fadwa. The anger had left him and been replaced by redoubled coldness. He swept the crypt with his eyes, as though challenging those present to defy him.

A'isha cried out, but he ignored her. The child was limp and unable to stand on her feet. The Dutchman brought the gun quickly to her temple. His hand no longer shook. He looked at A'isha again.

"The first drop," he repeated, then pulled the trigger.

A'isha tore herself from Butrus's grasp. In a blind, unreasoning fury, she threw herself at the Dutchman, but he was prepared for her and knocked her down with a single blow. She fell to the floor, dazing herself. The Dutchman raised his gun again, but even as he did so, Butrus ran at him out of nowhere, knocking his arm back and holding it fixed.

"I remember," he shouted. "I remember now. They talked about a message. A message from London. She put it in her pocket, I can remember seeing her. They thought I was sleeping, but the pain kept me awake. I could hear everything."

Leaving the Dutchman, he crossed to A'isha. He dared not look her in the eyes. Awkwardly, he reached for her jacket and plunged his hand into one pocket, then another. He drew it out finally, clutching a tiny wad of paper, still damp. Carefully, he laid it on the floor and bent to unfold it. It broke up a little, but the sentence they needed was almost intact: *Santa Claus will be at the Sugar Palace between 1500 hours and 2200 hours nightly 31st and 1st.*

She looked at the Dutchman in horror. He was smiling bleakly at her.

"What is the Sugar Palace?" he asked in a low voice. "Where is it?"

She could remember her own voice in the silence of Bulaq, asking the same question. The answer was very simple. She shook her head.

"I don't know," she lied.

Butrus glanced down at the scrap of paper on the floor. It made sense now. He remembered the snatches of conversation he had overheard that night, their voices in the darkness, the quick movements of a torch, the pain in his shoulder, the pangs of jealousy. Such terrible jealousy.

"The Sukaria café," he whispered. "They're meeting in the Sukaria."

He turned to A'isha.

"Forgive me, A'isha," he said. "I had to do it. For your sake."

But she was not even listening.

72

He was in a teeming city full of frightened people, shouting madly for silence. And no-one could hear him or wanted to hear him above the incessant racket of their fear. All he wanted was silence, a little respite in which to think over everything that had happened. Instead, the voices and the tambourines only redoubled their shouting and their banging, leaving him deaf and punch-drunk on a street full of jostling people.

Walking to the café, he tried to blend in with the crowds and found he could not achieve it with the ease to which he had been accustomed. The streets around the Azhar were full of snow. Every inch thronged with petitioners and litigants seeking *fatwas* or deeds of redress for judgments that had gone unfairly against them. All legal and spiritual matters were being directed here, and day and night the shaykhs were in session, handing down rulings, calling witnesses, signing judgments, consulting the books of law, bleeding the Qur'an dry for legal analogies.

Michael brushed past them in the streets, wide-eyed folk scurrying by in a delirium of anxiety, their heads bent down against the snow, their lips moving restlessly with prayers and invocations and talismanic formulae. Their heads were covered with little knitted skull-caps or woven shawls or the high hoods of *galabiyyas,* their feet were shod in an assortment of ancient and modern shoes and sandals, or they went bare-footed through the cold alleyways. At the street corners and by the fountains of Mamluk squares, they stood or squatted in anxious, squabbling groups, their eyes darting to left and right, this one seeking from that a direction to the best shaykh for contracts, the right *mufti* for land tenure. And over everything, over each transaction and each judgment, unspeakable, unnamed, lay a single fear like a shadow. No-one talked about the plague, no-one mentioned death. No-one had to.

From the outside, the café seemed quiet. It was familiar, so familiar that Michael could have sketched it without opening his eyes. He and Tom Holly had spent a lot of time together here at one time, putting the world and its citizens to rights. And all the while Michael's own life had been disintegrating messily like a skein of wool one hand has let fall. Back then, he had envied Tom the solidity of his marriage, the unswerving loyalty he and Linda had to one another. There had been Carol then, and the beginnings of emptiness. And now he had A'isha, but the world was no longer capable of being put to rights. Not by him or Tom Holly or all the King's men.

He watched the café entrance carefully for a long time, shuffling at a discreet distance like a man with nowhere to go. Only a few customers went in or came out, all men, all shabbily dressed. Standards had dropped since he had last been here. The shops on either side of the street were almost deserted. Trade was slack, customers were afraid to spend what little money they had salvaged from the banks. But the owners still sat on their stone benches smoking or reading the Qur'an or telling beads, while the light of fluorescent lamps flickered over their faces. Michael scrutinized them carefully, peering for a sign of too much watchfulness, a hint of edginess.

Coming here was a calculated risk, one he had no choice but to take. If Qasim Rif'at had been forced to talk, Abu Musa would know that a meeting had been arranged between Holly and himself. He would know the days and the times. All he would not know would be the meaning of the phrase. "The Sugar Palace." Would he guess? Did he have a file somewhere that mentioned the Sukaria as their regular meeting-place? He prayed not. And what about the Dutch-man? How much did he know? Would he have been able to follow him here? If Tom had made it, he would be in there waiting. Only when he had been watching for an hour did he decide to take the plunge.

Santa Claus was waiting at their old table at the back. He gave no sign of recognition, but Michael knew he had seen him. It had always been a knack of Holly's to look authentically Circassian rather than European. He dressed for the part, he spoke Arabic with a broad Syrian accent that might have passed muster in Damascus, he blended into the crowd. Nobody seemed to be paying him undue attention.

Michael ignored him and went to the counter, where he ordered a cup of weak coffee and a stale pastry. He took the third table from Holly and sat with his back to him. Sipping his coffee, he took a copy of *al-Jumhuriyya* from his pocket and spread it on the table. It amazed him that any papers were still being published. And yet, in spite of everything, there was an air of determined normality about the city. Everything had changed, yet no-one admitted it. The paper still carried radio and television listings, the programs heav-ily weighted to religion and Islamic culture. There were no sports pages, no photographs of women, no advertisements for films or alcoholic beverages. But there were news items, articles, even a women's page with recipes and hints on how to dress in the prescribed fashion.

He finished his pastry and ordered a second cup of coffee. A little spilled on the paper; he wiped it off with his handkerchief. He glanced up and saw in a mirror Holly watching him cautiously. Casually, he folded the paper and pushed it to one side.

There was a tap on his shoulder.

"Min fadlak. Have you finished with your paper?"

He turned. Holly was standing beside him. He resisted the urge to embrace his friend.

"Itfaddal," he said, handing it to Holly.

Holly thanked him and turned to go. Just then, he turned back and exclaimed, *"Wa'llah al-'azim!* It's . . . Good God, I'll be forgetting my own name next."

"Osman Fahmi. And it's Mahmud Rayhan, isn't it?" Michael knew he was free to give his friend any name he pleased. Holly would not have needed to invent an alias yet.

"That's right. Good God, it's been years. May I sit down?"

He sat and they kept up the pretense for several more minutes, subsiding gradually into casual conversation as people at the other tables lost interest in their reunion. It had all been very low key, no-one had done more than glance up in mild curiosity.

"I think we're all right," said Michael at last. He stuck to Arabic.

Holly nodded.

"I've been checking the place out since I got here. It's as clean as a whistle, I'd stake my life on it."

"You may have to." Michael paused. He looked Holly over. His friend was strung out. He had the smell of the desert on him, his eyes had not yet readjusted to the human distances and confined vistas of the city. On his head he wore an old Afghan cap acquired at fourth or fifth hand in a little *suq* in Damascus or Amman, Michael could not remember which. It had been a constant companion, a badge, a landmark. It made Michael feel at home. He reached across the table and squeezed Holly's hand. Tom looked wretchedly embarrassed.

"Watch out, old man. They'll think we're a couple of queers."

"No fear of that. The queers are all dead. So the good old Daily Bugle says, and it should know. And please don't be rude about queers. Not at the moment."

"Oh?"

"Qasim's dead. Qasim Rif'at."

"Never met him."

"Yes, you did once. He was my radio operator."

"Ah, yes. I remember him now. Ran a bookshop. You say he's dead?"

Michael explained as well as he could.

"Do you think he talked?"

Michael shook his head.

"They'd have been here if he had."

"Maybe." Holly looked round. "Maybe." He paused. "Have you noticed anything?" he said.

Michael glanced around the long room.

"It's not as full as it was. Nothing strange in that. A lot of people think there's still a curfew."

"Several customers have left, Michael, but no-one's come in here for about half an hour."

Michael looked around again. Two men got up and walked through the door. It closed softly behind them. Michael and Holly were almost the last people in the café.

"Is there a back way?" Michael asked.

"I wondered when you were going to ask. The window of the toilet gives onto a little alleyway. We might make it. But if they know what they're doing, they'll have someone there. Bound to."

Tom took out a gun and laid it on the table. Michael shook his head.

"There's no point," he said.

"It's for you," said Tom. Outside, there was a sound like wind in branches. "Take it. Quickly."

Michael did as he was told. He slipped the gun into his pocket.

"Michael, there's something you have to know."

He told him all that Shaykh Ibrahim had said. About

al-Qurtubi, the conference in Jerusalem, the plan to kidnap the Pope.

"Why?" asked Michael. "What's the point? What does he gain?"

Tom shook his head.

"I don't know, Michael. He doesn't think like us, he has his own motives for everything he does."

"Can he be stopped?"

Tom shrugged.

"Stopped? I doubt it."

"But you want us to try."

"I want *you* to try. I won't be coming with you."

Michael opened his mouth to protest, but before he could utter a word, Tom held up a hand decisively.

"There isn't time to argue about this, Michael. It's imperative that you get out. I have something I want you to take back to England."

He passed across the table the list of names he had been given by Shaykh Ibrahim.

"It's a membership list of a rightwing coalition al-Qurtubi has been working with. It has branches throughout Europe, including a British organization called Stalwart. One of Stalwart's top people is Percy Haviland. Percy was our mole all the time. This membership list is in his handwriting. I want you to get it back and put it in the right hands."

"How the hell am I supposed to get to England?"

Tom shook his head.

"I don't know, Michael. But someone has to take this out. Otherwise this will all have been the most Godawful waste of time."

Another customer left. Then the door opened. A man in a green *galabiyya* came in and went up to the counter. He talked in hushed tones with the owner for a few minutes, then left. The owner came around the counter, went over to the last three customers—but not to Tom and Michael—and spoke discreetly to them. They all got up and left. The two

Englishmen were the last ones left. The owner did not even cast a glance in their direction. He turned off the burner beneath his coffee machine, took off his grubby apron, and went out. He left the lights on.

A minute or two passed, full of silence. The cups of coffee in front of them were cold. On the floor, sawdust lay like snow. Michael thought he would choke on the silence.

"You can get out with me," he protested. "There's still a chance."

Tom shook his head.

"They'll have the place surrounded. One of us stands a chance if the other makes a diversion."

"Then let me make the diversion."

"I need you back in England with everything you know about Alexandria and al-Qurtubi."

Before Michael could do anything, Tom stood, took a last look at his friend, and headed for the front door. Michael took a deep breath. He was helpless. He stood and went through the curtain that hung over the entrance to the kitchen. Someone had left a *galabiyya* hanging on a hook near the door. Michael threw it over his head and pulled up the hood. He heard the door being opened, loud voices, then a burst of pistol-fire. He opened the back door in time to catch sight of a *muhtasib* running along the alley, heading for the front of the café. It was still snowing. A sub-machine gun fired. When the sound died away, you could hear the snowflakes landing on the shadowed ground.

Michael ran back to the end of the alley. He knew he had only moments in which to make his escape. The side-street into which the alley led was deserted: all attention had been diverted to the area around the café entrance. Softly, Michael stepped out onto the snow-covered pavement.

He scarcely heard the click. When he looked round, he saw nothing but shadows. Then there was a movement. The Dutchman stepped into the light. Michael raised his gun, then lowered it again. The Dutchman was holding A'isha firmly by her wrist and had a gun pressed hard against her temple. Michael tossed his gun to the ground without a word. The snow kept falling.

73

Cairo
1530 hours

Percy Haviland had been flown directly from London to the British airbase at Akrotiri in Cyprus, where they had fixed him up with a Cessna and a pilot to take him to Egypt. He was desperately annoyed. Annoyed with Lionel Bailey for forcing him to fly to this Godforsaken place, annoyed with this *prima donna* al-Qurtubi for getting ideas into his wooly Spanish head, annoyed that he would miss the long-planned celebrations for his knighthood tomorrow. There had better be some substantial reward for all this, or he would see to it that someone regretted treating him so shabbily.

Being the plane's only passenger made the whole journey seem more tedious somehow. The RAF was not exactly generous or imaginative with its on-board rations. He had managed to slip a small bottle of gin and some tonic on board, though he supposed he would have to give them up on arrival. On the other hand, he mused that he was hardly likely to be subjected to the indignities of a customs examination, even for form's sake. He was traveling as a diplomat, after all. If he had brought a big enough bag, he could have brought in crates of gin. Not that he expected or wanted to stay long enough to drink even a full bottle.

The landing had been cleared by the president's own

office. Even so, they were shadowed over Egyptian airspace by a couple of fighters. He could see one through the window now, almost close enough to make out the pilot in his cockpit. If al-Qurtubi wanted any more of these toys, he'd better start thinking up some good explanations. Everything was set to go tomorrow; they could not afford any slip-ups on account of al-Qurtubi's political ambitions. On the other hand, Percy thought, if al-Qurtubi really was in control and could hold on to his position, perhaps it would all turn out for the best. A lot of money *would* be passing hands in a month or two, and he was in a position to make sure that a sizeable chunk of it came his way.

The pilot announced that he was about to make a descent to Cairo airport. Haviland leaned back and checked the clasp on his seatbelt. He had kept it fastened all the way. With the snowstorm outside, it had been a bumpy trip. The little plane banked and started to drop at a speed no civilian pilot could have got away with.

He had expected something different. Sun and sand and camels. Instead, there was driving snow. A runway had been cleared for the landing, but once down they had to taxi across packed snow. Haviland glanced out the window. For some reason they were heading away from the main terminal buildings. They drew up near a large hangar. There was a pause, then the engines were cut. Moments later, the pilot pulled aside the curtain that separated the cockpit from the rest of the plane.

"Mr. Haviland. I'm afraid they want you to disembark out here, sir. For reasons of security, it appears."

"That isn't really very convenient. Apart from anything else, it's snowing heavily. Can't you just ignore them like a good chap and leave me off somewhere more civilized?"

The pilot shook his head.

"Sorry, sir, but I think they'd cut up rough. They don't sound like people who are willing to put up with things. If you get my meaning, sir."

"Yes, I get your bloody meaning. Very well, then. How do I get out of this contraption?"

"I'll have the door open in a jiffy, sir. You'll just have to wait till I can put down some steps."

Another few minutes passed, then the pilot indicated that everything was ready. Haviland stood, put on his overcoat and scarf, snatched up his briefcase, and took a deep breath. Best get it over with, he thought.

He descended the narrow steps gingerly. There was no-one on the tarmac, no welcoming committee, not even a steward of any description. This was no way to treat a guest of his standing. These Arabs had a few things to learn. Thank God this alliance with al-Qurtubi was only temporary. He hated to think what it would be like keeping this up on a permanent basis.

As he reached the tarmac, he almost lost his footing on the slippery snow. It was extremely cold. He shivered and drew his scarf more tightly around his neck. Everywhere he looked, the airport was deserted. What was the point of bringing him out here?

He heard feet on the steps behind him. The pilot was coming to join him.

"I'm very sorry about this, Mr. Haviland. Truly I am. But orders are orders."

Haviland had half turned to say something scathing when the bullet struck him in the temple. He jerked once, then his feet slithered out from under him. Even before he reached the ground he was dead. Bright red blood poured onto the snow and froze.

The pilot replaced the pistol in its holster, checked that Haviland was indeed lifeless, and climbed slowly back into the plane. He would be back in Akrotiri well in time for the start of the squadron's New Year party.

PART XI

"*And the beast was taken, and with him the false prophet that wrought miracles before him, with which he deceived them that had received the mark of the beast, and them that worshipped his image*"
REVELATION 19:20

74

The Pope's private aircraft
1920 hours

The papal jet had left Rome's Fiumicino airport exactly fifty minutes earlier and was now over the Ionian Sea, about one hundred miles past the Italian mainland, heading southeast. It was a chartered Alitalia 737, specially converted and refitted for the present flight. For security purposes, it carried no papal insignia, and the flight number it had been assigned was one of several regularly available for Alitalia charters.

The flight-path had been carefully calculated and passed to the air traffic controllers only minutes before take-off. Ordinary airline priorities had been changed without warning, giving the Pope's aircraft a straight run to Tel Aviv. There was no escort, nothing to draw attention to the plane.

Up front, a section had been curtained off. Here, the Pope's private secretaries, officials from the Secretariat of State, and a handful of deputies from other Vatican departments were still working frantically to get the final details right for tomorrow's conference.

A private room had been constructed for the Pope at the rear of the jet. He had gone there immediately on boarding the aircraft. There was a small bed, but he had no intention of resting. Seated at a little table of polished walnut, he frowned repeatedly as he worked at his declaration. He would not be speaking *ex cathedra,* invested with the infallibility of his office, but as a man to other men, a leader to other leaders. For all that, he knew his words would be weighed and sifted, their every nuance picked over by statesmen and journalists in the first instance, by theologians in years to come, all seeking meanings in them that he had never intended.

Hence his overwhelming need to make himself crystal clear, to eradicate from every sentence and every phrase the slightest hint of ambiguity. The main translations—Arabic, Hebrew, French, German, and Spanish—would be made that evening and overnight, and he owed it to his hard-pressed staff to provide them with a final text as soon as possible.

There was a soft knock on the door. Father Patrick Nualan, his chief secretary, entered the little chamber. For a moment, there was a hum of voices and machinery, then silence settled once more as the door closed.

"I'm very sorry to disturb you, Your Holiness, but you said you wanted to see anything that came through about the Egyptian situation."

He handed a sheet of pale blue paper to the Pope.

"This just arrived from our intelligence directorate. They've intercepted a US satellite report that shows the withdrawal of Egyptian troops from the Israeli border. It looks like good news. Apparently that's how they're interpreting it in Langley. Our people say they should have confirmation in ten or fifteen minutes."

The Pope took off his glasses and rubbed his eyes hard.

"That's very good news, Patrick." He looked quickly over the report. "Yes, excellent news. It does look like a genuine pull-back. What do you think was responsible?"

"I'm not sure, Your Holiness. We're still unable to get any direct information out of the country."

"What about Verhaeren? Is there still no word of him?"

Nualan shook his head. He had close-cropped, jet-black hair and a physique that had done damage in its day in games of hurley at Maynooth; but in the Pope's presence he seemed the meekest and the rawest of men. No defenses, no hard places, no misplaced strength. Devotion had riddled him with mildness and strength of a different order.

"He never made it to the boat, that's been confirmed. And the airplane that went in from Cyprus failed to make the rendezvous. But we can still hope."

"Yes," the Pope said, shifting his eyes away. "We can hope. And we can pray."

Thinking of Verhaeren had drawn his thoughts reluctantly to other matters, matters that unsettled him deeply and made him afraid for the future. There was still a long time to go, a full year perhaps, before they might consider the threat of al-Qurtubi past. He had had the dream the night before, and he had not slept a wink afterwards. It had not proceeded to its normal climax. He shuddered even now to think of it.

"Are you all right, Your Holiness?"

The Pope pulled himself together with an effort.

"Yes," he said. "Yes, I'm all right."

There was a second knock on the door.

"Come in."

The door opened and a nun stepped into the room. She was younger and prettier than strict Vatican convention allowed. She had also been the top Yale graduate of her year, held a Ph.D., and was a leading authority on Middle East politics. That too was more than convention thought permissible, but the Pope had made a point of including her on this mission. There were, in any case, few things he found more hateful than old, desiccated nuns. Ugliness and desiccation were not, he thought, the aim of the religious life, however hard some people might strive to make them so.

"Sister Frances. What can I do for you?"

"I really do apologize for disturbing you like this, Your Holiness. I know you're busy. But . . ."

She held out a sheet of fax paper.

"This just came through," she said. "It was transmitted from an unidentified source. Not the Vatican. Not any source known to us. I think it is important enough for you to see it immediately."

The Pope stretched out his hand. A dark sense of premonition washed over him. As a young priest, he had struggled to keep his vocation intact. In Belfast, the struggle had been for his life. But since becoming Pope, he had battled every day for his soul. Was he about to lose that battle now?

He read the fax. It was not long. It took him only seconds to read. But the color drained from his face as he reached the end. He let the sheet of flimsy paper flutter to the floor. For a long time he said nothing. The plane dipped once, passing through pockets of troubled air. A low shudder, then buoyancy again. The Pope turned to his right and raised the blind over the side window. It was pitch dark outside. He could see his face reflected in the glass, the pallor, the impatient, harrowed eyes. In a matter of hours a new century and a new millennium would begin. But whose century? Whose millennium?

He pulled down the blind and turned to Sister Frances.

"Sister, I would like you to return to your station. Please inform Father Menichini that he is to shut down all systems immediately. There are to be no more transmissions from this aircraft. There must be no reception of messages from the Vatican. Menichini is to leave open the radio channel specified in the message you brought."

The nun stood in the doorway, stunned, unable to comprehend.

"But, Your Holiness, surely you aren't going to give in to . . ."

"Please, Sister, do as I ask."

"Yes, Your Holiness."

When she had gone, the Pope turned to Father Nualan.

"Father, please instruct the pilot to alter course. He is to head directly for Cairo airport. A flight path has been cleared for us. He is not to communicate with ground control or with any other aircraft. Do you understand?"

Nualan bent and picked up the dropped fax. He read it quickly, then looked at the Pope.

"My God, surely this is a bluff."

The Pope shook his head.

"No, Patrick, it is no bluff. He is entirely serious. He will do what he says if I do not cooperate."

"But, I don't understand. You appear to know who this is."

The Pope nodded.

"Yes, Patrick. I know very well who he is. Now, please carry out my instructions. We have only a few more minutes in which to change course. After that I shall speak to all of you together."

Nualan left. The Pope remained seated, staring at the wall in front of him. The helplessness of his shattered legs flooded through him like a tide. Minutes passed and he did not move. Then, slowly, the right wing of the aircraft dipped and they began to turn. Outside, a break in the clouds allowed the moon to shine through briefly. The white light fell on a thick cloud layer, turning it into a troubled vision of heaven. But there were no angels. There were no angels anywhere.

75

Cairo
2018 hours

The papal jet landed behind schedule. The airport was deserted and silent—hardly an airport at all. The runways were thick with snow now, except for runway 2, which had been cleared for the Pope's landing. Percy Haviland's body, discovered so mysteriously near a hangar on the outskirts of the airfield, had long been removed and taken to a city mortuary. No-one was quite sure what to do with him. The RAF plane had taken off again without obstruction.

All Egyptair planes had been grounded, ordered into hangars or shunted unceremoniously to a lonely corner of the field. The only aircraft in sight were green-painted military models, mainly fighters and attack helicopters. All along the illuminated periphery of the airfield, a line of 235 M1AZ battle tanks kept at bay whatever unknown threat lurked beyond the high electrified fence.

The plane taxied to a halt outside Gate Six. The silence deepened as the last engine was switched off. All round the airplane, Jeeps belonging to the *muhtasibin* waited like jackals about a dying lion. Men with rifles stood guard. Harsh lights flared across the stretch of ground that separated the aircraft from the nearest building.

A small lift was wheeled across the tarmac and set

against the fuselage. Moments later, the side door opened. A steward stood framed in the opening momentarily, then ducked inside again. The Pope appeared, dressed in white, seated in his wheelchair. He was wheeled onto the platform by Father Nualan. Someone pressed a button, and they sank slowly to the ground, the priest upright, his hand on the back of the chair, the Pope preserving what dignity was possible to him, his hands folded in his lap, his face without expression.

The lift came to a halt. A *muhtasib* unfastened the bar and Nualan pushed the chair forward onto the tarmac. Moments later, a tall man in perfectly pressed robes stepped towards them. They halted, facing him.

"Welcome to Egypt, Your Holiness," he said in flawless English. His voice held not a hint of irony. The Pope could see at a glance that he was not Egyptian.

"You do not choose your words with sufficient care," he replied. "You have brought me here under duress, as a hostage, not as a guest. Please do not pretend to treat me otherwise. I have put myself in your hands. I am your prisoner. So I insist that you behave towards me accordingly."

The Dutchman frowned and glanced awkwardly away, barely concealing his tension. He was having difficulty controlling his emotions. Inside him, the Catholic child, the first communicant, the would-be priest squirmed with embarrassment and awe. On them he had for so long imposed the tyrant of his new faith, the circumcised and bearded grown-up with his Arabic prayers and constant ablutions, that he had almost forgotten his long vigils at another altar, the nights he had spent on his knees, long ago, before a different shrine.

"You are to follow me," he snapped, crushing the child in him without remorse.

"I go nowhere without assurances," declared the Pope.

"You are scarcely in a position . . ."

"First. My secretarial staff and the aircrew on board my

jet are to be permitted to leave Egypt as soon as the aircraft has been refueled and prepared for take-off.''

''I cannot . . .''

''Second. My presence here in Egypt is to be announced to the world's press this evening. You may say, if you wish, that I came here of my own accord and that I mean to leave again with the same freedom.''

''That is out of the question. You were told . . .''

''Third. All foreign Christians currently held on Egyptian soil are to be released from custody immediately and allowed to return to their homes. The exact nature of the arrangements I leave to your discretion. But they are not to be harmed in any way.''

''That is acceptable. However, there are some Copts with dual nationality, mainly American. I regret that they . . .''

''They are to be allowed to leave. Those are my terms. I may have more later. I shall let you know.''

''I do not think you understand.'' The Dutchman was growing angry now. He had to show the pontiff just how much power he possessed. ''You are not in a position to lay down terms. The message you received was quite explicit. If you do not reach your destination by midnight, the first Copts will begin to die. You have my word on that. My deputies have already received their orders.''

The Pope stiffened visibly. Nualan, who had known him for many years, could only guess what was going through his mind. There was something troubling the Holy Father, something above and beyond the immediate situation, something that had been there long before they left the Vatican. The Pope seemed afraid, and at the same time filled with a deep, unappeasable rage.

''When do I meet President al-Qurtubi?''

''He will be waiting at your destination. I am to tell you that he looks forward to your reunion with the keenest interest.''

. . .

They drove past the city to the north, heading west. They had been taken to a large black car and bundled inside. The Dutchman sat in front. On the rear seat were the Pope and Father Nualan. Facing them, on jumpseats, were Michael and A'isha, their wrists tightly fastened by handcuffs. On one side sat an armed *muhtasib* watching them carefully. The Pope sat on the left side of the car, gazing out into the darkness, at the electric lights of roads and buildings in the distance, the city piling up in the south, Babylon the Harlot, Babel, the Great City, Sodom and Egypt, the city of towers, city of monsters, blasphemies, deformities, Cairo the Victorious. He could not understand why the sky was so bright, why a red glow suffused the horizon. The sun had set long ago, the brightness was in the south, not the west.

"What is that light? Over there, in the sky."

The Dutchman barely turned his head. He knew the answer without having to look.

"Cairo is burning," he said. He spoke without inflection, without emotion, as though he was an old and jaded guide, a bored drago-man reeling off for the thousandth time an event in the long life of the metropolis, some minor conflagration under the Fatimids or the Mamluks, the burning of a palace, the laying waste of a street or a quarter, nothing more.

The Pope looked again. This time he saw that he had been mistaken, that the redness he had taken for illumination in the sky itself was, in reality, cast against low clouds by a battery of flames that rose up from a point not far distant. Had it been daylight, he would have seen a pall of black smoke choking the skyline. It seemed to stretch for miles.

"Cairo? The entire city? Surely you can't mean that."

"It began a few hours ago. A preacher started it in a mosque in Sayyida Zaynab. He said the city was damned, like the Cities of the Plain. God had set His mark on it. He would not lift His hand until the believers put the city to the torch. Only thus would the plague be burned out—out of Cairo, out of Egypt, out of our souls."

"Isn't anything being done?" asked Michael.

The Dutchman shrugged.

"Done? What can be done? Why should anything be done? It is God's will. What would we want to do?"

"But there are millions of people living there," protested the Pope. "There'll be enormous loss of life. The government has to do something. You have to save as many as possible."

The Dutchman turned and looked at his prisoner. Their relationship was growing clear now. All ambiguity had vanished.

"What do you suggest we do, Holy Father? There are mobs in there, roaming from place to place, carrying torches, setting fire to buildings, watching the flames burn the plague away, watching God's purification do its work. Who can tell? Perhaps they're right. All the victims of the plague now in the city will perish. There's bound to be less contagion once it's over."

"And afterwards? When the survivors are left without food or water or sanitation? Won't it all begin again, worse than ever?"

"There will be very few survivors," said the Dutchman.

A'isha leaned forward.

"You started the fire yourselves, didn't you?" she said. "You wanted this to happen."

The Dutchman looked out of the window.

"It is God's will," he whispered to the night.

And on the horizon, God's will burned and burned and burned, a burning bright enough to be seen from space, if anyone had been there to watch.

76

Cairo fell away behind them, like a beacon at sea, drifting into darkness. To the north, the sky above the city was lit up wonderfully. Even at a distance of several miles, the conflagration dominated the horizon like a bonfire on a high hill. Michael wondered if it would end here, or whether Egypt was a necklace of burning towns and blazing villages strung along the Nile and clustered through the fields of the Delta. For a long time, pieces of hot ash fell all about them like a shower of black snow. They drifted through the beam of their headlights: ashes of wood, ashes of silk, ashes of velvet, ashes of flesh. For miles, the flat white bed of snow across which they drove was pocked and blackened by burnt fragments fallen from the sky.

A few miles further and the sky cleared, and with it the ground, as though purified by a sudden wind. The heavens were crystal clear, moon-cold, crammed with stars, utterly soundless, echoless. They stretched forever. On either side of them, the world was a perfect layering of white, as though tens of thousands of linen shrouds had fallen on it in a dream.

The desert lay cold and open all about the car, a sterile

darkness fissured by bright stars. The snow had stopped falling an hour ago, and now pale moonlight bounced off a vast expanse of white. Above, the stars seemed endless, they stretched the fabric of the universe further than was allowed. If there was a God, He was not there, hiding in the dust of galaxies; He was down here, dead and buried beneath the rubble of centuries, choked by sand, His bones crushed and broken, His spirit lost and wandering among the rocks and pebbles.

The Pope slumped in his seat, fighting a wave of depression that had settled in him about half an hour after leaving Cairo. He felt no personal fear, no anguish for himself: he had gone through the worst of that in Belfast. Nor did he feel anything more than a normal concern for the Copts whose lives hung so delicately in the balance: it is impossible to feel deeply for those you do not know personally, to experience universal terror. He had no shame about his lack of feeling for them. What he did experience was an overwhelming sense of religious fear, an almost superstitious dread that his God was truly dead, that the Beast had outsmarted him, that the Enemy was on the verge of eternal victory, and that from tonight nothing would be the same. And for this failure he felt the keenest sense of personal guilt, a guilt that had neither measure nor reckoning. He had ignored Paul Hunt's warnings, he had trusted in his inviolability, in the sanctity of his office. In a moment of pride, he had put his faith in his own artifice. And now it was all driving to a bitter end in the loneliest and bleakest of places, in a darkness where there was no God, not even a God of pretense.

There was no sound out here, except for the rushing of the heavy military car, its wheels singing against the snow as the driver struggled to keep to the road. No-one had spoken since Cairo. The Dutchman sat as still as a statue, his gaze fixed firmly ahead. Father Nualan was praying. He had been mouthing silent prayers since they started, as though for him God were still a possibility or salvation merely a matter of so many miles, so many minutes, so many Hail Marys.

They crested little heights and sank down into deep hollows, as though trying to escape the narrow scrutiny of the stars. But always the car rose again, flinging a momentary light at the sky, grazing the edges of the waning moon where it hung, tenuous, uncared for, like a tattered rag above a low horizon.

There was a sudden alteration in the sound outside as the wheels tore into the sand and gravel that lay just beneath the snow. They had turned off the long highway that connects Cairo with the oases and headed out into the trackless wilderness. It was not apparent how the driver steered, or what landmark he had taken for his cue to leave the paved road behind. Surely there were no longer any landmarks in this white emptiness. The car lurched and pitched violently on a bed of coarse rock and scrub, throwing its passengers about. The Pope gritted his teeth and hung on tightly.

At one point they came down into the mouth of a steep defile, a washed-out gully whose sides towered as high as cathedral walls. The driver pulled to a halt and turned off the engine. Silence sang in the ravine as though a tight string had been plucked and left to die away. The Dutchman turned in his seat.

"It is not possible to go any further by car. But there will be alternative transportation."

The driver flashed his lights three times. Seconds later, an answering flash stabbed through the darkness. Several minutes passed, then a dim figure appeared in the beam of the headlights, followed moments later by others. They were all dressed in thick winter *galabiyyas,* the hoods pulled down over their heads, their faces shadowed. Each man rode a mule and was leading another at the end of a thin bridle.

Father Nualan leaned forward, putting a hand on the Dutchman's shoulder.

"For heaven's sake," he said, "surely you don't expect

the Holy Father to ride on one of those. Not over ground like this. He's an invalid, man, he can't . . .''

The Pope rested a hand gently on his secretary's arm and shook his head. But the Dutchman had already turned and fixed his eyes on the priest. In the little light that bounced back from the headlights, the Dutchman's face was barely visible. His voice was low, almost inaudible.

"Father," he said, "let me make clear to you the nature of your position here. This is not the Vatican. This is not a Christian country. You have been permitted to accompany this man so far because he is, as you have just explained, an invalid, and in need of a companion. But your presence will not be necessary beyond this point. These men will take you back to Cairo. You can wait at the airport for your master."

"That's absurd. You can't take him any further on his own. I have to be with him."

The Dutchman scarcely raised his voice.

"I told you your presence was no longer needed. If necessary, I will have you shot. It's all the same to me. Do I make myself understood?"

The Pope reached out his hand and placed it on Nualan's arm.

"Go back with them, Patrick. I'll be all right. If you want to help me, pray for me. And be sure to get yourself out in one piece. There'll be a need for someone who can tell about this when the time comes."

The priest made to protest, but the Pope tightened his grip.

There were four mule drivers in all; each led one beast alongside the one he rode. The leader opened a saddlebag that was slung over the back of his mule and lifted out four heavy *galabiyyas*. The Dutchman took one and passed the others into the rear. With the door open, a biting, ruinous cold took hold of them. Nualan helped slip a *galabiyya* over the Pope's head.

"I wish you would force him to let me come with you," he whispered.

The Pope shook his head.

"It's no good, Patrick. He'd as soon kill you. Better you go back. Tell the others I'm all right."

They embraced briefly. As they did so, Nualan whispered into the Pope's ear.

"Father, have you guessed who the other prisoner is? The man."

"No."

"It's Michael Hunt. Paul's brother. He may be able to get you out of this."

"I want no violence."

"You may have no choice. When the time comes."

The Dutchman came and separated them. He held the door open and ordered the Pope to step outside. Michael and A'isha followed. The *muhtasib* took a key from his pocket and removed their handcuffs. The muleteers helped maneuver the pontiff from the car onto the largest of the animals, a white mule with a polished bridle and a brushed cloth that had been prepared especially for him. The men were gentle, lifting the Pope with care, helping him find his balance on the back of the patient beast. If they sensed any irony in the situation, they did not remark on it. Michael and A'isha were directed to their own mounts.

Apart from a brief, whispered conversation between the Dutchman and the leader of the guides, no-one said a word. The small caravan set off down the defile at a steady pace, its passage marked only by the clinking of the mules' feet as they picked their way over the loose rocks and gravel of the ravine floor.

The defile seemed to stretch away forever, twisting and bending ever more deeply into the solitary heart of the desert. Below them, they could feel the ground sloping gently downwards. They were well below sea level here, yet with each mile that passed the walls of the great canyon seemed to rise up still further, almost blotting out the tiny points of the stars.

What little light managed to filter down to them from

above glistened and shivered on sheets of frost that lay like silver on the rocky ground. The cold was bright, shimmering, and intense, a cold of galaxies, an unearthly thing that had never known a moment's warmth, that had no conception of what warmth might be. In spite of the heavy *galabiyyas,* they suffered badly, shivering as they rode. The Pope realized that, if they did not find shelter soon, he could die out here from exposure. He rode a few paces behind the Dutchman, keeping a close watch on his huddled and hooded figure. Michael and A'isha rode behind silently. They both knew there could be no escape, not from this emptiness. Unless death itself was an escape.

77

Paris
2230 hours

To the north of the Rue de Rivoli in Paris's St-Gervais quarter, a small Jewish district nestles among the decayed *hôtels* of the Marais. In the Rue des Écouffes, between a kosher butcher's and a baker selling *challah* loaves stood a small Orthodox synagogue. The street was deserted: everyone was indoors for Shabbat. No-one noticed the young man in dark clothes as he picked the lock of the synagogue and let himself in to the building. He was carrying a small bag over one shoulder.

The only light came from the *ner tamid,* a small oil lamp burning in front of the ark, where the Torah scrolls were kept. The intruder turned on a small flashlight and made his way without hesitation to the *bimah,* a high, raised platform in the center of the room. Everything had been planned well in advance.

Bending, he took a small packet from his bag. Setting the bomb on the flat surface of the *bimah,* he made several adjustments to the timing mechanism. Then, very carefully, he placed the bomb under the reading table, where it was concealed by a thick cloth embroidered with the Star of David. Everything was quiet. There was nobody to challenge him. A final flick of a switch and the bomb was primed. It would explode in twelve hours' time, during the morning service.

The bomber zipped up his bag and left as he had come, unseen, unsuspected.

Two doors away, in a third-floor apartment, Chaim Hersch was going through a Torah reading with his son. Tomorrow was the boy's *bar mitzvah,* when he would be called for the first time to read from the Torah in the synagogue as an adult.

"I think you're ready now," said Hersch. He was proud of his son, of the ease with which he read the Hebrew words without prompting. The whole family would be there to watch, and afterwards there would be a celebration.

The boy nodded.

"Were you nervous before your *bar mitzvah,* Father?" he asked.

Hersch nodded.

"Of course," he said. "It's a big moment. But you'll do well. You don't have to feel worried. Everybody there will be on your side."

The boy smiled.

"Time for bed, I think," his father said. "You don't want to be late in the morning."

PART XII

"The beast that was, and is not, and yet is"

REVELATION 17:8

78

Dawn forced its way through cracks in a rough and blackened sky. Smoke from the burning of Cairo had drifted west and south during the night, flattening into a high, noxious cloud that darkened the land. Michael struggled out of a troubled half-sleep, shivering. Ahead of him, he could see the figures of the Pope and the Dutchman growing solid in the gray light.

They trudged on in silence, eight mules in a sea of white. They had stopped for only a few hours during the night, to eat and sleep. On the surface of the snow, a thin crust of frost sparkled like broken glass. In the east, the sun came angrily into the sky.

And then, straight ahead of them, at the bottom of a long slope, a mile or so away, he saw it. What he had taken for a smudge of darkness traversing the long horizon he now saw to be a vast, uncomplicated wall of stone that seemed almost to circle the earth. As the sun rose and the light grew in strength, the wall appeared to carve itself out of the darkness in which it had been hidden, mile upon mile of brick and mortared stone, stark against the dazzling whiteness of the snow, a towering thing made of shadows and fears. Fear of the plague, fear of God, fear of an outside world grown complex and unstable.

Hard against its flanks, it was possible to believe the world ended here, that there was nothing beyond this but emptiness and madness. And when the time eventually came for people to overcome their fears, when the unknown ceased to be threatening and grew enticing once more, then how simple it would be to put up lights and wires and gun emplacements, how easy to turn the face of the wall inwards.

And yet, for all its brooding magnitude, it was not the wall that held his attention. For the wall itself was overshadowed here by something greater, darker, and more ancient: a pyramid, black and shining like the one in his dreams, yet taller and more sinister. But he was not sleeping now, and he was not dreaming. What he saw before him was stone.

They all caught sight of it at almost the same moment. Michael noticed the Pope sit up on the saddle as though to brace himself. He saw him raise an arm, like someone warding off a blow. And he saw the arm fall a moment later in a gesture of defeat. Earlier, in the car, he had noticed how very tired the pontiff seemed, how bereft.

The pyramid slipped inexorably towards them from a high bank of mist, like a ship in the depths of the ocean rising without warning out of a white fog. A black ship, a plague ship, a ghost ship loosed from the past and set adrift on steep unsalted waters.

They rode down a low defile cut through the sand. On either side, they could make out the half-buried forms of basalt sphinxes, two long rows that led to a tall door in the pyramid's side. From beneath a veil of frosted sand two lines of brutal faces watched them pass.

All signs of excavation had been removed. There were no lorries or diggers, no gangs of laborers straining past with heavy baskets on their shoulders. High up on the eastern flank of the pyramid, a tarpaulin left behind by a workman snapped loudly in the early morning wind. Polished and slippery with frost, the taut, smooth surface of the giant construction moved beneath the sun. It was like a lake of black oil stretched upwards into the sky, held there by nothing but surface tension. At any moment, or so it seemed, it would come crashing down on them, oil or glass or stone, it scarcely mattered, falling on their heads pitilessly, driving them down into the cold sand.

There was a light in the doorway, a cold white light that only served to enhance the blackness in which it was set. The opening stood at the top of a flight of stone steps, like the door of a spaceship in some old B movie. Michael expected a figure to appear in it, tall and helmeted, etched against the light. But it remained empty.

The muleteers dismounted at the foot of the pyramid and helped the Pope gently down from his mule. One man stayed to look after the animals, one kept a close eye on Michael and A'isha, and the others, one on either side, began to help the pontiff climb the steep, ice-marbled steps. As the old man climbed, the Dutchman stood gazing upwards, as though fearful lest, having come this far, his charge might stumble and hurt himself. Ten minutes passed before the Pope reached the top. When he was at last safely inside the doorway, the Dutchman turned.

"Follow me."

It was all he said. Turning his back on them, he led the way up the steps. The muleteer who had been watching Michael and A'isha now waved a gun at them, indicating that they should precede him. Hand in hand, they started to climb.

Entering the pyramid was the hardest thing Michael had ever done. No amount of rationalization could dispel the primitive, unconscious fear that filled his mind.

"What is this place?" he whispered.

"I don't know," A'isha answered. "There's no record of a pyramid ever having been built this far out."

"Can he have built it? Al-Qurtubi."

She shook her head.

"Look at it, Michael. A thing like this would take years to build, even using modern methods. We'd have heard of it long ago. He must have excavated it. And quite recently too."

"Have you any idea how old it is?"

She hesitated.

"In this form, it wouldn't be older than the fourth dynasty. No earlier than 2500 B.C. The last real pyramids we know of would have been built in the twelfth dynasty. Say 1600 B.C. I really can't say more than that without a much closer look. There may be an inscription. If the inside is as well preserved as the exterior, it shouldn't be too hard."

They were at the doorway. Evidently, it had originally been bricked up. The blocks used to seal the entrance lay at the top of the stairs and just inside the opening. And beyond the opening a dark passage stretched away at an angle, lit by a string of bare electric bulbs.

"They must have a generator somewhere," said Michael.

The Dutchman was waiting for them at the top of the steps. Once they were inside, he led the way along the passage. The walls were made from massive blocks of undressed limestone on which occasional marks in red ochre could be made out.

"Those are quarry marks," whispered A'isha, pointing. "If I could get a close look, it might tell us something about this place. I'd guess the blocks themselves were carted here all the way from Gebelein, near Thebes. They'd have come via the Kharqa and Dakhla oases."

"You think the same as I do, then?"

"What's that?"

"That we're west of Dakhla."

She nodded.

"More or less."

The corridor continued to climb at an angle of about twenty degrees. The floor was ridged every couple of feet, making the ascent easier. The lights revealed a low ceiling that forced the Dutchman to stoop. Suddenly, the passage stopped rising, and they found themselves entering a horizontal corridor that was both wider and higher. The walls here were faced with polished granite blocks on which the tall figures of gods had been incised in lines of perfect purity.

At the end of the corridor, a wooden ladder led up into a dark opening. Two thick ropes hung on either side of it, placed there, presumably, to assist the Pope. Passing through the opening, they found themselves in a large burial chamber filled with coffins and the unsepulchred bodies of innumerable mummies. There was no telling how many there were. The light did not shed enough illumination for them to see the walls. There might have been thousands of bodies there. It was as though they had set foot in a mass grave.

A path had been cleared through the brightly painted coffins. The Dutchman led them to a low doorway and, beyond it, into a narrow shaft that angled gently upwards. At its end, a distance of some fifty or sixty yards, a stooping, almost crawling journey, they came to a much higher cross-corridor. The Dutchman turned left, and they had no choice but to follow.

Ten yards later, the corridor ended abruptly at a wooden door. The original door, heavy, fashioned from planks of sandalwood and hung from copper pivots. A modern hasp and lock had been fitted to it. The Dutchman opened the door and motioned for them to step inside.

The room they entered was small and dark. Hanging from a nail near the door was a small brass lamp holding a candle. The Dutchman took a box of matches from his pocket and lit it.

"You're to stay here for the moment," he said. "Mas'ud will be outside to make sure you stay put."

"Why did you bring us here?" asked Michael.

"I brought Dr. Manfaluti for what she is. You, for what you know. I shall speak with you both later. When there is time to spare, you will be given something to eat and drink."

Without another word, he turned and left. They saw him stand for a moment in the passage, a pale creature sliced out of shadows by the yellow light. Then the door was closed and the lock fastened.

It was another burial chamber, packed from wall to wall with the mummified remains of children. Many of the wrappings had crumbled away, revealing dried flesh or white bone.

They sat down in the center of the room, back to back, resting at last. There was very little horror here for either of them. The darkness was an old friend, bones were merely bones, the rustling of spiders was a sign of life.

"What if we fall asleep?" asked A'isha. "Fall asleep and never wake again?"

"Would you like that?"

"Perhaps. We might dream forever."

"Dream? I'm tired of dreams," he said.

Thinking of where they were, of the dried things with whom they shared the room, he remembered two lines from a play by Yeats, *The Dreaming of the Bones*. Softly, he whispered them under his breath:

"Dry bones that dream are bitter
They dream and darken our sun."

"What was that?" A'isha asked.

"A poem," he said. "Just an old poem."

And those other lines, he thought, those other lines he dared not whisper:

"Night by night she dreams herself awake
And gathers to her breast a dreaming man."

She turned to face him. In the semi-darkness, they could see almost nothing of one another. She touched his lips with her fingers, brushed his cheek with her lips.

"I'm not a dream," she said. "Our bodies are not dreams."

He stroked her cheek, ran a hand through her dry hair. She would overpower him with her reality. Reality lay beneath the flesh, beneath skin and muscle, reality lay all around them whispering in the dark, yellow bones dreaming of flesh, empty sockets dreaming of eyes, dryness dreaming of moisture.

. . . and the tomb-nested owl
At the foot's level beats with a vague wing.

"I love you," he said. "Even if this is all there is."

They sat together for a long time, in perfect silence. Once, they heard Mas'ud, their guard, cough outside the door, then the silence returned. Michael wondered what was happening, where the Dutchman had taken the Pope.

"Michael."

"Yes? What is it?"

"On the wall over there. I can make out an inscription."

A'isha stood and took the lamp from its nail. Crossing to the side wall, she raised the light. It revealed part of a large funerary painting incorporating the figure of a pharaoh making an offering to Anubis. By the king's head a long inscription had been painted in black. Stretching up, she brushed it with her hand. It was quite legible. Slowly, she began to read.

" '*Hia't-sep medju, 'abd medju, 'akht su 21, kher hem en netjer nefer neb ta'wy nasut-bity . . .*' " She paused. " 'Year 2, first month of Inundation, day 21, under the Majesty of the good god, lord of the two lands, the King of Upper and Lower Egypt, Senwosret, son of Re', Kha'-kaure', granted life eternally and forever, Re' Harakhti . . .' "

She paused again.

"Did you follow that?"

"Perfectly."

"Kha'kaure' is the first cartouche name for the pharaoh Senwosret III. He was the fifth king of the twelfth dynasty." She thought briefly. "I can't be sure, but that would put him somewhere in the first part of the nineteenth century B.C. Shall I go on?"

He nodded.

" 'Ptah South-of-His-Wall, Lord of Onkhtowe, Mut

Lady of Ishru and Khuns-Neferhotpe, being arisen upon the
Horus-throne of the Living like his father Harakhti, eternally
and evermore.' I'm afraid they took a long time getting to
the point in those days. 'On this day has been completed the
pyramid which is the Great God Re' on the Horizon of
Atum.' "

"I'm sorry, I don't understand. They thought the pyramid was a god?"

She shook her head.

"No. Every pyramid has its own name. 'The Pyramid
which is Beautiful of Places,' or 'The Pyramid of the Ba
Spirit.' This one reads *A Re' em akht Atum.*"

Suddenly, she stopped. It was as though, in the midst of
speech, she had been struck dumb.

"A'isha? A'isha, what is it?"

She looked at him helplessly. Her eyes were wide open
and filled with dread.

"Oh, God, Michael. I know what this place is."

He felt a shiver pass through him.

"It's mentioned in a papyrus from the Ptolemaic period. As the origin of a Greek word. Ancient Egyptian writing doesn't include vowels. So the Greeks just made them
up."

She looked at him pleadingly, as though his solid English common sense could take away what she knew.

"Armageddon," she said, almost inaudibly. *'A Re' em
akht Atum* was mangled into *Armageddon*. That's where
we are, Michael. That's what this place is."

79

He had been prepared for many things, but not this. His captors had brought him, gently yet quite insistently, through the long corridors and shafts of the pyramid until they came to a tall door, a door of ebony inlaid with hieroglyphs of ivory, words he could not read. It was bitterly cold inside the great tomb—for so he thought of it—and he thought he would never see the sun again. The little yellow bulbs struggled unsuccessfully against the darkness beneath the stone.

They made him wait. He was not insulted by their curtness or their lack of respect for his office. On a street in Belfast, he had lost whatever *amour propre* he might once have had, and not even the papal throne had reinfected him. But the threat of force, the barely concealed willingness, eagerness even, to resort to violence filled him as always with sickness and loathing.

The Dutchman arrived, unhurried, unsmiling, seemingly untouched by the cold or the darkness.

"It is time," he said.

One of the muleteers opened the door while the other slipped the Pope's arm over his shoulder and helped him inside.

It was not at first clear what sort of room they had brought him to. At first, it seemed horribly dark. Then he saw that it was lit, not by electricity, but by candles, hundreds of them, flickering fitfully in the heavy drugged air. The air was thick with incense, a rich, indefinable aroma of exotic and dangerous flowers that had been laid over the fundamental ancient smell of the place, the crushing intolerance of the stone itself.

His first impression, that he had walked into a church, was reinforced immediately. The lights made bird-wing patterns against high, painted walls on which the figures of the old gods stood out in bold relief, half men, half animals. But at the far end someone had erected a high altar and hung above it a great golden cross.

They brought him to the center of the room, where a low chair was waiting for him. He sat at once, grateful for the respite, but feeling dirty, unshaven, and in need of a toilet. He knew he had to remain calm, but he felt a ball of fear growing inside his stomach with every moment that passed.

Looking round him, he saw that the cross was not the only Christian image to have been brought into the pyramid. On either side of the altar, plaster statues of saints had been arranged on makeshift plinths. The altar itself was covered in an elaborately ornamented white cloth embroidered with golden thread, and on top of it rested six golden candlesticks and a tall cross.

Moments after he was seated, he noticed a movement in the shadows at the top of the room. At the same instant, his flesh crept at the sound of voices chanting in Latin. Out of the darkness, a group of men dressed in the robes of Catholic priests appeared and lined themselves before the altar. He wanted to stand, to shout out, to end the mockery. But he had no strength left for gestures.

He guessed who the priest in the center was, the one officiating at the mass. It was almost a disappointment. In his unconscious, he had expected something else. But what, in truth, had that been? What had his dreams suggested to him? A man certainly. A beast, perhaps? Or half a man and half a beast, like those figures out of the past?

The mass continued after the old fashion, the intoned liturgy echoing against the bare walls. The priest did not falter or stumble once. It was as if he had been doing this every day of his life. There was no hint of mockery in his voice, no suggestion of the blasphemy he was committing.

And then, as he ended, he turned. An ordinary face, but eyes that could see forever, in the silence, in the cave. He turned and raised his arms, stretching them out on either side, the palms facing forward. His eyes held the Pope's like a lover holding his beloved.

"It is finished," he said in a loud voice.

The Pope closed his eyes and looked away. When he opened them again, al-Qurtubi was standing next to him, looking down silently.

"It has been a long time, Martin," he said at last. He spoke in English with a strong Spanish accent. His voice was rich and sad. "Over thirty years."

The Pope said nothing. He was still searching in the face of the man in front of him for the features of the friend he had known and lost so very long ago. They had studied together at the Pontifical Academy in Rome, had shared a room, had become closer than brothers. He had thought he had known Leopoldo Alarcón y Mendoza as well almost as himself. And then there had been that dreadful day when Leopoldo had disappeared, and that other day, a few months later, when word had come of his friend's conversion to Islam. The Academy authorities had questioned him for days on end, then priests from the Congregation for the Doctrine of Faith, until he had grown sick of their questions. He had been able to tell them nothing, because he knew nothing.

"What's wrong, Martin? Are you afraid of me? Do you think I'm a ghost?" Al-Qurtubi paused. "I'm real, very real—you may be assured of that."

"They asked me why," the Pope said. "And I couldn't tell them. You'd kept it all from me, every real thought, every real temptation."

"You wouldn't have understood. You wouldn't understand now."

"All the same, I have a right to know why. It has brought us to this, after all."

Al-Qurtubi bent his head momentarily, then looked up and directly into the Pope's eyes.

"Do you remember that I went home in the autumn of 1968? When I was there, I visited the Great Mosque in Cordova. It was the first time I had ever set foot inside it. I was all alone, I lost my way among pillars and arches, like someone walking through a great forest. There were no tourists that day, the weather was bad, I had the mosque to myself, I could listen to the stone, I could forget who I was, what I was. I felt quite naked, as though everything had been stripped away from me but what I was in my heart. And what I saw I loathed.

"They had built a cathedral in the middle of the mosque, a horrendous thing, a Baroque monstrosity. It had been built to signal the triumph of the Christian faith, but what it achieved was the opposite. It was dwarfed by the simplicity of the earlier building in which it stood. It proclaimed greed and arrogance and power. And when I saw it I realized that everything I had ever believed in was dust. Just that."

He paused.

"You see," he said. "You do not understand."

"On the contrary," said the Pope, "I can understand your conversion. What is beyond me is why you distorted something so simple into such a monstrous thing."

"Monstrous?"

"It is monstrous to kill."

"On the contrary, it is monstrous to acquiesce in injustice."

"You can speak of justice? You force me here against my will . . ."

"No-one has forced you here. You are free to go at any time."

"I received a threat."

"No-one has threatened you."

"You said that . . ."

"I said that, if you did not come, I would have to take measures against the Copts. That is quite correct. I threatened their lives in order to bring you here. I never threatened yours. You were free to ignore my message, to continue on your journey."

"That is splitting hairs. You gave me no choice."

"I have to contradict you. I left the matter entirely in your own hands. You chose to come here. You chose to be with me. Today of all days. It was your destiny."

"What do you want with me?"

"Don't you know?" he asked. "Can't you guess?"

The Pope said nothing.

"We are both actors, Martin. Troubadours. Mummers. We've made a stage for ourselves out of other men's faith. We put on masks and perform our rituals for their entertainment. And they believe us when we say they will go to heaven if they applaud loudly and long enough. Look around you, at the masks the old gods wore. It's been a game, it's always been a game. The Theater of Divinity.

"I was a priest and now I am the Antichrist. Tomorrow, I may be something else again."

"You were excommunicated."

"Do you think that makes the slightest difference? I am writing the script now. I've brought you on to play your part, I can send you back just as easily."

He paused.

"Martin, I would like to talk. A lot happens in thirty years: we would have a lot to say to one another. But there isn't time. This pyramid is the last pagan structure left in Egypt. With its destruction, a new age will begin. I have had it mined from top to bottom with high explosives. In . . ."—he glanced at a watch on his wrist—"just over an hour, it will be just rubble. Shortly after that, I shall send the signal to authorize the Fath al-Andalus in Europe. The West is about to pay the price for its pride and aggression.

"When the first wave of terror has passed, I shall make my demands. I expect each of them to be met. The governments of all the European states will be given twenty-four hours in which to respond with firm guarantees. If they do not, the terror will recommence. And I will then make my demands again."

The Pope interrupted.

"They'll go to war before they capitulate to tactics like those."

"No, they will not, because you will be with me. You will be my hostage."

The Pope did not move. He kept his eyes on al-Qurtubi, wondering how the universe could produce such a thing. A man who wanted desolation, death, a destiny that called for so much blood. It was cold, so cold.

"You had better kill me now," said the Pope. "I want no part of your triumph. I will not be your hostage. It is you who are nothing. All that emptiness outside, that wall, that desert—that is what you are, Leopoldo. Why don't you kill me now, why don't you finish it? Then the killing can start in earnest."

Al-Qurtubi said nothing. He stared at the man on the chair in front of him. An old, old friend, someone he might, at another time, in a different place, have pitied or exonerated. But the friend was almost unrecognizable beneath the robes and the soiled white skullcap.

"That suits me equally well," he said brusquely. "Your body will serve as a message of our intent. It will show that we are prepared to stop at nothing."

He looked up and motioned to the Dutchman.

"Take care of it," he said.

80

―――――

"What will happen to us?" A'isha asked.

"Happen?" Michael shrugged. "I don't know. If it was just the Dutchman, I'd think the obvious. But al-Qurtubi is unpredictable. He may have uses for us."

"You think he's here?"

"I'm sure of it."

There was a short pause.

"Michael, I think we should try to get out of here. Take the Pope with us if we can."

"Where could we go?"

"If we can make it as far as Dakhla, we should be able to get back to Cairo."

"Cairo's finished. You saw that for yourself."

"Alexandria, then. Michael, while we're talking in here anything could be happening. We have to do something."

"Such as?"

"You're the expert. You think of something."

She was right, they had to act before it was too late. Michael stood and looked round the room.

"All right," he said. "Get behind the door. On that side. When I grab the guard, go for his gun. Make sure you get it: he won't give you a second chance."

When she was in position, Michael rummaged among the mummies, tearing off strips of cloth at random. Carrying an armful of the dried bandages, he spread them out near the door.

"Are you ready?"

A'isha nodded.

Michael lifted down the lamp and touched the flame gently to the heap of rags. They caught fire almost instantly, and within seconds heavy smoke was billowing into the room. Michael fanned the little blaze until it was spreading securely, then began to shout.

"Help! There's a fire in here! Let us out for God's sake."

On the other side of the door, the guard turned to see smoke creeping through the bottom and sides. Suddenly, a flame appeared at the foot. The wood had started to catch. Someone was banging on the door and shouting. He fumbled with the makeshift lock, managed to get it open, and pulled the door wide. There was smoke everywhere. He panicked, knowing how much importance the Dutchman placed on his two prisoners.

The guard ran inside and was immediately engulfed by a cloud of acrid, choking smoke. The next instant, he felt himself pulled backwards as Michael caught him by the neck.

A'isha moved in rapidly, grabbing the man's weapon and tearing it from his surprised grip. Michael pulled the struggling *muhtasib* aside and struck him heavily on the side of the neck. The guard crumpled and dropped to the floor against a heap of bodies.

It took them over a minute to get the fire under control.

"Are you all right?" asked Michael.

"Just about. Here, you'd better take this. I've never really used one." She passed the weapon, a Beretta MP 12, to Michael. He took it, then turned back to the unconscious guard. Removing his uniform, *galabiyya* and *thawb,* he slipped them on. The *muhtasib* had been wearing a holster round his waist.

"Here," he said, holding up a pistol. "This is lighter. Even if you just wave it, it should help."

"Thank you," she said. "I can use a handgun. Rashid taught me how."

"Good. That's even better. Use it if you have to."

Outside, the passage was deserted. The banging and shouting had not drawn the attention of anyone else. Michael locked the door behind him and put the key in his pocket. If he was determined, the guard could break the door down easily enough, but Michael did not think he was likely to come round for a couple of hours.

There was only one way to go, if they were not to retrace their own steps. Michael went in front, holding the Beretta at the ready. The gallery went on for about one hundred yards before turning abruptly at right angles. They stopped at the corner. Michael held A'isha in front of him, as though escorting her. They stepped round the corner.

There was a short passage and, at its end, an ebony door. Outside it, a single *muhtasib* kept watch. He was careless, protected as he was by the walls of the pyramid and hundreds of miles of desert. An attack on this place was inconceivable.

They got within a few feet before the man realized anything was the matter. By the time his first suspicions surfaced, Michael's gun was pressed against his temple.

"Just let your gun fall slowly to the floor. Take your time and don't get ideas about a martyr's crown."

The man obeyed sullenly.

"How many are inside?"

The *muhtasib* said nothing.

Michael hit him very hard in the face, breaking his nose. He cried out in pain.

"I need to know how many."

The man still refused to answer. Michael drew back his fist.

"The *shaykh*. The Dutchman. The old man. A few priests. That's all. I swear."

Michael struck him hard on the temple with the butt of the gun. Too many lives were at stake to be over-scrupulous.

A'isha opened the door and Michael moved smoothly into the opening, covering the room with the Beretta while his eyes swept it.

The Pope was on a chair. A man whom Michael took to be al-Qurtubi stood near him. The Dutchman was standing behind the Pope, holding a pistol at the nape of his neck. As Michael entered, he swung round.

"I advise you against firing, Mr. Hunt," he said. "I may shoot him first, you never know."

Michael hesitated.

"It will be the last thing you ever do."

"Nevertheless."

There was a long silence. Michael could not risk shooting. Even a reflex action would send a bullet into the Pope's brain.

"Now," said the Dutchman. "Throw down your weapon. You know me well enough by now, I think. I won't hesitate to shoot him. His life depends on you."

Michael threw down the gun.

"I'm glad to see you still have some intelligence, Mr. Hunt." The Dutchman turned his gun on Michael. "Step this way."

Michael took several steps forward. He felt keyed up, all his anger and frustration focusing itself in this one man. All the hatreds of his life concentrated their force in the Dutchman, and yet there was nothing he could do.

"Kneel down."

Reluctantly, Michael knelt. He remembered how the Dutchman had cut a man's throat in a café full of silence. And he heard from A'isha about his summary executions of Gregory and Fadwa.

"It was never your destiny to kill me, Mr. Hunt. God

needs me. He has chosen me as His sword. Anything and anyone that stands in my way will be swept aside."

He lowered the gun until it touched the nape of Michael's neck. It meant nothing to him, he had done it before, he would do it again. As he prepared to fire, he heard a sharp click. He looked up.

The woman, Manfaluti, was pointing a gun at him. He had forgotten her. He had taught himself for so many years now to regard women as nothing that they had truly become invisible to him. A terrible anger rushed through him. No woman had the right to lift her hand against him. The anger seethed in him, burning him. He lifted his hand.

She fired. The shot echoed twice. The bullet hit the Dutchman in the chest, sending him back, staggering, appalled.

"No!" he shouted. "You have no right!"

She fired again. Again, he was hit.

"God has . . . chosen me!"

His hand shook, but he pointed his gun and fired. The shot went wide. A'isha fired again, hitting him in the shoulder. He reeled backwards, stumbled, and fell to his knees.

"Do you remember a little girl?" she asked. "She was the first drop, you told me. You were right."

She fired again, three times in quick succession. The gun fell from his fingers. He looked at her. Almost, she thought he pleaded with her. Almost, she thought he wanted mercy. She shook her head. God was all-merciful. Let God sort it out for once. She shot him for the last time.

81

Al-Qurtubi was unarmed. The Dutchman had been his shield, and now he was gone. For a moment, he was about to spring on Michael, but he thought better of it. The priests who had taken part in his masquerade were gone: they had scampered away through the narrow opening near the altar, through which they had all made their entry earlier. Perhaps they would bring help. They were all former priests like himself, whom he had persuaded to take part in his game.

"Are you all right, Your Holiness?" Michael slipped to the Pope's side while A'isha kept al-Qurtubi covered.

"Yes, Mr. Hunt. I'm very well. A little tired, but otherwise quite all right. Thank you. Thank you for coming to me."

"It's not going to be easy getting you out of here. One of us has to keep an eye on our prisoner, and there's every likelihood he has more guards in here."

The Pope shook his head.

"I won't be leaving here," he said.

"I don't understand."

"You and your friend have to get out as quickly as you can. He's mined the entire pyramid with explosives. It goes up in less than an hour. I'd never make it, even if you were completely free to help me. There are too many stairs, too many shafts."

"We can't just leave you here."

"I won't be alone." He nodded at al-Qurtubi. "He will be with me. We have a lot to talk about. The time will pass quickly."

"But he has to be taken back."

The Pope looked impatiently at al-Qurtubi, then back at Michael.

"What for? To face justice? What human justice could deal with a creature like this? He's President of Egypt now. That alone will guarantee him sanctuary. It will be in someone's interest to see he stays unharmed. Listen, if he stays here he will be unable to give the go-ahead for his terrorist campaign. You, on the other hand, can tell the world what happened here. I know who you are, I can guess what you may be able to do. I was very fond of your brother. He thought very highly of you. Please go, Michael. Before it's too late."

"But I . . ."

"I am the Pope, Michael. I must be granted authority over my own life and death. Now, don't waste time arguing. Let me have the Dutchman's pistol. I'll need it to keep Leopoldo quiet."

They both realized there was nothing they could do. The Pope was right. If they tried to carry him out, they would all be killed. Michael retrieved the Dutchman's pistol and passed it to the Pope.

"Come and sit on the floor beside me, Leopoldo. Our friends have other things on their mind."

His hand did not waver as he pointed the pistol at al-Qurtubi. The Spaniard seemed about to refuse, then he sat down facing his old friend.

"Goodbye, Michael. I'm glad to have met you. Please pray for me."

Michael stepped forward and kissed the old man's hand. A'isha did the same.

As they turned to leave, al-Qurtubi spoke for the first time.

"He's bluffing, you know. There are no explosives."

"Good," said Michael. "You'll be quite safe, then."

No-one tried to stop them. Word of the Dutchman's death and the impending explosion had spread, and the guards had decided to save their own skins. Their worst fear was that they might lose their way in the tangle of shafts and tunnels that had been built into the pyramid or cut through it after its completion. A'isha went ahead, trusting her sense of familiarity with ancient structures to help her find the way out. The worst moment came somewhere around the half-way point, when they were faced with two seemingly identical galleries radiating from the shaft in which they stood. The wrong decision would cost them their lives.

"I don't remember seeing this on the way in."

Michael shook his head.

"We had our backs to it. And we were scarcely in a position to take notes."

"The right-hand gallery is more in line with the shaft. If we have to gamble, it's as good a bet as any."

"You're the boss."

They set off again. Over twenty minutes had gone by. They had to get out of the pyramid and well away before the first explosions. The gallery went on, straight as a die, plunging through the vast edifice without twist or bend.

That was when the lights went out. They flickered for a few moments, then went dead. It was unimaginably dark. Like being buried alive.

Michael still had the flashlight he had used in the sewers. The batteries had run down badly, and it gave out a very weak beam, but it was enough to enable them to keep moving. He prayed it would not give out before they reached the exit. If there was an exit.

They were reckless now, no longer walking, but running through the dark tunnel, the little light bobbing up and down a couple of feet in front of them. If they had not been so anxious, they would have seen the vertical shaft.

A'isha had passed Michael and was running three or four feet ahead of him when she suddenly screamed and disappeared from view. Instinctively, he stopped. Inches in front of him, the floor opened in a broad pit. There was a terrible silence.

Michael crept to the edge and shone the torch into the hole. It was useless. The beam reached down a couple of feet and gave out. He could see nothing but blackness beyond. He slumped back in despair. To have come this far only to be defeated by a moment's carelessness.

Suddenly, he heard a sound. Then A'isha's voice from below.

"Michael . . . Can you . . . hear me?"

He leaned over the edge again. He could not believe it. She was still alive.

"I can hear you. How far have you fallen?"

"Not far . . . I . . . I think I've landed on a ledge. There's . . . no way of telling how deep the shaft is. I can see your light just above me. Can . . . you reach down? I'll try to get your hand."

He leaned over as far as he dared, swinging his hand down into the darkness. For a long moment, there was no contact. She was out of reach. And time was slipping past. He tried again, lunging downwards, swinging his arm from left to right. And there it was, the grazing touch of her fingers passing his.

"Can you stand any higher?"

"I'm on tiptoe. Michael, I'm going to try jumping. Just keep your hand where it was."

She jumped, stretching for his fingers, but missed and fell back to the ledge. She did not know what it was made of or how strong it was, whether it would bear repeated shocks.

"Again," she called.

This time their hands touched, but before Michael could grab her, she had dropped back. This time she felt the ledge shake. There was a sound of crumbling rock falling. It went on falling for a long time.

She closed her eyes.

"Are you ready, Michael?"

"Yes."

"When I say 'go.' "

There was a moment's pause.

"Go!"

She jumped and he leaned in with all his strength. His fingers circled her wrist. This time he did not let go. But he thought his shoulder was about to be wrenched out of its socket. Bracing himself, he began to pull her up. She scrabbled for footholds as best she could. One foot, two feet, her arms and knees grazing against the rock, three feet, then her arms were over the side. He had her with both hands now, he was pulling her towards him, and all at once she was lying spreadeagled on the firm ground, panting and crying with relief.

He did not let her rest.

"We've got to get moving," he said. "This place is going up in about fifteen minutes."

"We'll have to go back to that fork."

"There's no time. We just have to jump this pit."

He shone the flashlight across the opening, but the other side was out of reach of the beam.

"How broad could it be?" he asked.

"Not broad. Four, maybe five feet."

"I'll go first. If I make it, I can catch you."

She began to protest, but it was too late. He had left the flashlight by the edge and was already running. She saw him jump, then lost sight of him as his figure vanished into the shadows. Moments later, she heard the crash as he landed on the other side. There was silence, then his voice, breathless.

"More like six. Can you jump it?"

"I don't have any choice. What about the flashlight?"

"You'll have to leave it. You can't risk jumping without it."

She went back as far as she could, took a deep breath, and ran. Moments later, she had launched herself into the darkness. Her feet touched the other side, then Michael was there, pulling her to safety.

"Let's go," was all he said.

The passage began to descend at a steep angle. About one hundred yards later, it turned abruptly. Ahead of them, they could see a light. In less than a minute, they had arrived at the opening through which they had originally entered the pyramid. Outside, the open desert lay white and sparkling like a polar landscape set down in Africa by a genie summoned by a mad Sultan eager to see snow and ice.

They hurried along the avenue of sphinxes. The guard had taken most of the animals and ridden off in haste. But three mules had been left behind. They mounted hurriedly and started off, following the tracks left by the *muhtasibin*. It was then that they heard the first explosion, a muffled rumbling that seemed to come from deep beneath the ground. It was followed by another, then a series of louder bangs.

They looked round. High up on the west face of the pyramid, a huge crack had appeared. There was another explosion, and the crack became a gaping hole. Suddenly, a massive chain of blasts ricocheted through the fabric of the pyramid, breaching the superstructure in several places at once. Smoke appeared, black and ugly against the clear air. The entire edifice began to shake and to collapse in on itself. More explosions followed, these lower down and apparently deeper inside the structure.

It took perhaps half an hour. They watched the whole time, unable to tear themselves away. When it was finished, nothing remained of the black pyramid except an enormous heap of rubble. Smoke continued to plume into the sky. It would be visible for miles. They turned their mules and started the long journey to Dakhla.

They rode slowly, unable to force their mounts beyond a sullen walking pace. Even here, still many miles east of the great Sand Sea, small sand-dunes ran across their path, everywhere lying from north to south. Further west, the dunes rose to well over a thousand feet. Their eastern flanks were thick with snow, but on the west they were still a dull reddish brown. From time to time, a gust of dry wind would skim across their summits, sending tall plumes of sand into the air, like smoke blown from the peaks of white and black pyramids.

By noon, a soft mist had come up out of nowhere, blurring the already featureless landscape. They passed in and out of swirling banks of white. The mist was cold and damp, and it seemed to seep through their skin down to their bones. They were tired and cold and hungry, and Michael had begun to wonder whether there was any point to what had happened. It all seemed so senseless.

Sometimes, the mist would roll aside as if by magic, and they would see, hazy in the distance, fields of tall, frosted dunes; the rays of the sun would slant across them, hitting their flat western edges crookedly, and they would seem to rise into the melting air like the sails of great ships on a northern sea, endless against a blurred horizon. They passed the bleached bones of camels and from time to time the scattered trunks of petrified trees, frosted remains of an ancient forest that had grown here before the sun and the wind had together turned everything to sand. Then the mist would crowd in on them again, folding itself around them and their beasts in soft white banners that flapped and rippled as they passed.

A'isha shivered and brought her mule close to Michael's. It was as if they had come to a bewitched country without birds or music, as though they had sailed across high seas for years and landed in the end of things upon a shore so far from all others that it might have belonged to a different world entirely.

"Did I say I loved you?" Michael asked, conscious of the mist pressing in.

"Yes," she said. "But say it again."

He said it. Without sin, without remorse, without thought of past or future, priest or penance or punishment. She reached across the little gap and touched his arm with her fingers, gently, as though he might break or vanish like the mist.

"My brother was wrong," he said, stroking her hand.

"Wrong?"

"To fear this. To find sin in this. In you."

"I love you too," she whispered.

Behind them, the mist parted momentarily. A plume of black smoke rose into the air. Then the mist returned and blotted it from sight.

82

"We knew about Percy Haviland, of course."

The Prime Minister sat back in his chair, quite content. With al-Qurtubi out of the way, Percy Haviland reduced to ashes, and the Pope and his damned conferences things of the past, everything seemed to be turning out better than he might have hoped. He had been listening patiently while Michael Hunt gave him a full account of what had gone on. He supposed Hunt would want a medal or something. Well, he would see what he could do. The man had obviously been through something of an ordeal.

Michael and A'isha had made it to Dakhla. It had taken them two days, and they had almost died. By the time they got there, things had started to fall apart in Egypt. News of al-Qurtubi's death, carried to the authorities by the men who had escaped the pyramid, had thrown the regime into a panic. Michael had discovered in his wallet the telephone number given him by Yusuf al-Haydari after the massacre on the train. It had been a gamble to make contact with him, but by then neither he nor A'isha could think of any other option.

Al-Haydari was by that stage as desperate to leave Egypt as they were. In return for Michael's assistance in entering the United Kingdom, he had smuggled them to Alexandria and onto a boat that took them to Cyprus. From there, the RAF had flown them to London. Tom Holly had set up the escape route before leaving England. It had taken another four days to fix up the meeting with the Prime Minister.

"I suppose," the PM said, "that now al-Qurtubi and this Dutchman are dead, the People of Silence or whatever they're called will fade away. It's the general way of things out there, isn't it? Take away the charismatic leader and what have you left?"

"I'm sorry, sir. I don't agree. I don't think the threat is over yet."

"Really. That's most disappointing. People are terribly anxious after this business with the Pope. It would be nice to be able to tell them we've dealt with the people behind it all."

"I don't think we've quite done that, sir. I . . . Tom Holly gave me something before he died. A list."

Michael reached into his pocket and brought out the sheet of paper Tom had given him. He thought of Tom now, all he had gone through just for this. Michael still had to face visiting Linda, telling her what he knew.

The Prime Minister glanced at the list and laid it down on his desk.

"I don't understand," he said. "What exactly is this?"

Michael told him. A look of horror crossed the politician's face.

"You aren't seriously suggesting that . . . some of these people have been involved in this conspiracy? These are very important names. We can't just . . ."

"The list is in Percy Haviland's hand. You can have that checked, I expect. I think you'll find that, if you go through Percy's private files, you'll get most of the evidence you need. MI5 or Special Branch should have no difficulty tying up loose ends. And the Europeans can be dealt with by their individual agencies."

There was a long silence.

"Is this . . .? Are there any other copies of this list?"

Michael shook his head.

"No, sir. That is the original."

"I see. Thank you for bringing it to me. I assume I may keep it?"

"Yes. It's out of my hands now."

"Quite. You've done more than enough. But I don't need to tell you what a shock this is. I know several of these men personally, some of them very well."

"I'm sure you won't allow that to influence you, sir."

"What? No, of course not. Certainly not. However, you will appreciate that this is . . . a most delicate matter. Your training will have taught you that. We can't just . . . make this sort of thing public. It will have to be handled discreetly. It may take a little time. To do properly."

"But not too long, sir. The terror campaign may begin at any time."

"Yes, I fully appreciate that. There is a need for haste. I'll see the right people get working on this straight away. Thank you, Mr. Hunt. I'm very grateful to you. And I assure you, your services will not go unrecognized." He glanced at his watch. "Goodness me, is that the time? You'll have to excuse me, but I have an important appointment with the Syrian ambassador in a few minutes."

The Prime Minister rose and stretched out his hand. Michael smiled and shook it. The door opened and the PM's private secretary was waiting to show him out.

"Thank you for seeing me, Prime Minister. I'll leave everything in your hands."

"Yes, indeed. It will all be taken care of, I assure you. Thank you again. And good luck."

When Michael had gone, the Prime Minister instructed his secretary to see he was not disturbed. He read through the list Michael had given him, taking note of each of the names. Finally, he wrote down three of them on a separate piece of paper. Having done that, he tore the original sheet into shreds and tossed it into his wastepaper basket. It was all very well, he thought, for people like Michael Hunt to pontificate and draw up lists. But it wouldn't do. You could not go around arresting men like Sir Lionel Bailey without causing a great deal of bad feeling. There was enough discontent in the country without fueling it with rumors and scandals. The three hangers-on on his revised list would be enough for form's sake. He would have a quiet word with Lionel at the weekend. Lionel had common sense. A little friendly advice would go a long way. All anyone needed was a modicum of discretion, after all.

CODA

83

Oxford
August 2000

They walked away from the grave into the brightness of the afternoon. He had seen some people whispering during the service, pointing A'isha out as "that woman." His sister had not spoken to him. Carol had stayed away. It had been a phantom pregnancy after all, but she had found someone else to marry, a television producer who had once achieved a passing notoriety for a fruit gum commercial. He hoped she would be happy. It was strange, but he really did.

His mother had become ill soon after news of Paul's death reached her. Her whole Egyptian family had been wiped out in the fire-storm that had destroyed Cairo. She had never recovered. She had not wanted to. Michael hoped there might be some sort of afterlife for her to be happy too.

When the last mourners had gone, he went out to the summer house at the bottom of the garden. She left him alone for an hour or more, then joined him.

"I'm going back to London this evening," she said.

"That's a pity. Do you have to go?"

She nodded.

"There's a meeting of the committee," she said. "I have to be there."

Since coming to England, A'isha had become a leading figure in the liberal opposition movement working to overthrow the new regime in Egypt. The British government tolerated their activities while keeping a close eye on them. There was talk of CIA funding, which A'isha denied. Egypt was still an Islamic republic. Both the plague and the great fire had convinced the population that all the evils visited on them had been the work of outside agencies. Even now, they would not allow relief agencies into the country.

"How long will you be gone?" he asked.

"A couple of days. You could come with me. You don't have to stay here."

He shook his head.

"I have work to do," he said.

He had secured a post at Oxford University, in St Anthony's College. The pay was poor, but his teaching load would be light. He planned to write a book, a study of fundamentalism.

"On the book?"

He shook his head.

"No," he said. "I think it's time."

"Time for what?"

"Come inside. Let me show you something."

He went up to his bedroom, the one he had slept in as a child, and brought down a box file.

Out of it he took a letter embossed with the papal coat of arms. Underneath was a small box containing a papal decoration. He set them aside. In a bag of plain linen he kept a large key. One day, he would return to the ashes of Babylon in order to open the crypt of Abu Sarga and destroy the painting.

From beneath the key he took a thick file. The first sheet in it was a photocopy of the list he had given to the Prime Minister. He had lied when he had said there were no other copies. Even if this one were destroyed, he had others. Clipped to Percy Haviland's list was a longer list, the same names together with addresses, photographs, and full personal details. He had not been idle since his return.

Michael knew there was no point in going back to Downing Street. After reading a report in the news that Sir Lionel Bailey had been appointed British ambassador to France, he had tried to contact the Prime Minister. The PM had thanked him for all his help, but regretted that his busy schedule did not allow him to see Michael at present. Michael had noticed the Special Branch men watching him from a distance. He wondered if they knew he had seen them. It made no difference.

The Fath al-Andalus had started, a couple of months behind schedule, in early March. There had been atrocities almost every week since then. Over three thousand people had died. There had been only five arrests. A rumor had started in Egypt that Abu 'Abd Allah al-Qurtubi was still alive and awaiting the right moment for his reappearance. One of Michael's sources had reported that there was a son living in Tanta, a man in his mid-thirties by the name of Hasan. It was said that elements of the Ahl al-Samt were already regrouping around him.

He took out a heavy automatic pistol and a box of ammunition.

"How far do you think you'll get?" A'isha asked.

He shrugged.

"Far enough. I don't have to get them all. Just break up the network, let a little panic set in."

"Michael, why does it have to be you? You have contacts. Surely someone else . . ."

He shook his head. Taking the key from its pouch, he laid it on the table.

"This was given to me," he said. "I didn't want it then. I don't want it now. But it's mine. Somebody has to do this, A'isha. Somebody has to see this thing through to the end."

"And then?"

"Nothing then," he said. "There'll *be* an end."

She shook her head.

"No," she said. "Nothing like this ever ends, ever really ends. For every one you kill, there will be others. Your bullets won't change anything. You can't kill the fear, the prejudice, any of that. And unless you do, there'll always be an excuse for men like these."

"Then why do you waste your time with politics? You can't destroy fanaticism overnight."

"I do it because I have to, Michael."

"It's the same thing, then."

She shook her head.

"No, love, it's not the same at all."

"You think I should leave it, then? Let them go?"

She thought for a moment, then shook her head slowly.

"No. No, I don't think that. They're responsible for the deaths of hundreds of innocent people. They can't go unpunished. Just as long as you understand this won't finish anything."

He stood and went to the window. The room overlooked the garden. The lawn needed cutting, the roses had not been pruned since his father died. He wanted to come back here to live. He and A'isha could have children.

"I still have that dream," he said.

"The pyramid? You didn't tell me."

"About once a week. I can't shake it off."

"Maybe you should see someone about it. A doctor . . ."

He shook his head.

"No, that wouldn't help. They don't have pills for something like this."

She came to him and held him; tightly, very tightly. Outside, the sun was shining. It was a glorious day, a rare day, a day without clouds or the threat of rain.

"It will be autumn soon," he said.

She nodded.

"Yes," she said. "Then winter."

⬛ HarperPaperbacks *By Mail*

READ THE BESTSELLERS EVERYONE'S TALKING ABOUT

COLONY
Anne Rivers Siddons
When Maude Chambliss first arrives at Retreat, the seasonal Maine home of her husband's aristocratic family, she is an outsider — a nineteen-year-old bride fresh from South Carolina's low country. But over the many summers and generations, Maude becomes the matriarch who will ultimately determine the colony's future.
"An outstanding multigenerational novel." — *The New York Times*

SANTA FE RULES
Stuart Woods
When successful Hollywood producer Wolf Willett reads in the *New York Times* that a brutal triple murder has taken place in his Santa Fe home, he knows that he will be the principal suspect. With the help of a hot-shot attorney, Wolf races to clear his own name — and dodge the real killer.
"A roller-coaster ride of breathtaking speed." — *L.A. Life*

FATHERLAND
Robert Harris
Twenty years after winning the war, all of Germany is gearing up to celebrate Adolf Hitler's seventy-fifth birthday in 1964. But amid the preparations, disillusioned detective Xavier March stumbles across a conspiracy that threatens the very underpinnings of the Nazi empire.
"A dazzler." — *Detroit Free Press*

THE THIEF OF ALWAYS
Clive Barker
Mr. Hood's Holiday House has stood for a thousand years, welcoming countless children into its embrace. It is a place of miracles, a blissful round of treats and seasons, where every childhood whim may be satisfied. But there is a price to be paid, as young Harvey Swick is about to find out.
"Both cute and horrifying." — *Publishers Weekly*

LOST BOYS
Orson Scott Card
Step and DeAnne Fletcher and their kids move to Steuben, North Carolina thinking they've found paradise, but their eight-year-old son, Stevie, feels an omnipresent evil there. The Fletchers' concern turns to terror when they learn that many boys in the community have mysteriously disappeared — and Stevie's next on the list.
"An overlayer of rising suspense." — *Publishers Weekly*

MORE THAN FRIENDS
Barbara Delinsky
The Maxwells and the Popes are two families whose lives are interwoven like the threads of a beautiful, yet ultimately delicate, tapestry. When their idyllic lives are unexpectedly shattered by one event, their faith in each other — and in themselves — is put to the supreme test.

"Intriguing women's fiction." — *Publishers Weekly*

CITY OF GOLD
Len Deighton
Amid the turmoil of World War II, Rommel's forces in Egypt relentlessly advance across the Sahara aided by ready access to Allied intelligence. Sent to Cairo on special assignment, Captain Bert Cutler's mission is formidable: whatever the risk, whatever the cost, he must catch Rommel's spy.

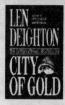

"Wonderful." — *Seattle Times/Post-Intelligencer*

DEATH PENALTY
William J. Coughlin
Former hot-shot attorney Charley Sloan gets a chance to resurrect his career with the case of a lifetime — an extortion scam that implicates his life-long mentor, a respected judge. Battling against inner demons and corrupt associates, Sloan's quest for the truth climaxes in one dramatic showdown of justice.

"Superb!"
— *The Detroit News*

A MATTER OF HONOR

When Adam Scott opens the yellowed envelope bequeathed to him in his father's will, he triggers an incredible drama that sends him on a tailspin flight across Europe. For the terrible secret that shadowed his father's military career is now a ticking time bomb of intrigue, passions, and greed—one that could forever change the balance of global power. "Sizzles along at a pace that would peel the paint off a spaceship." —*The New York Times Book Review*

A TWIST IN THE TALE

A philandering husband and a very dead mistress...A game of strip chess with a sexy stranger...A wine expert put to the acid test. Jeffrey Archer now unveils a richly woven tapestry of fateful encounters. With deft, urbane style and witty sophistication, this dazzling collection suitably crowns his brilliant reputation as a master storyteller. "Cunning plots....Silken style." —*The New York Times Book Review*

AS THE CROW FLIES

When Charlie Trumper inherits his grandfather's vegetable cart, he also inherits his enterprising spirit. But before Charlie can realize his greatest success, he must embark on an epic journey that carries him across three continents and through the triumphs and disasters of the twentieth century. "Archer is a master entertainer." —*Time* magazine